INFINITY BEACH

INFINITY BEACH

JACK McDEVITT

HarperPrism

The underwater sequence in chapter XIV is loosely adapted from "In the Tower," *Universe 17*, Doubleday (1987).

The epigraph for chapter XVI is from "The Ballad of Kansas McGriff," © 1997 by Bud Webster, and first appeared in *The Hobo Times*, Fall 1997. Used by permission of the author.

This is a work of fiction. The characters, incidents, and dialogues are products of the author's imagination and are not to be construed as real. Any resemblance to actual events or persons, living or dead, is entirely coincidental.

FIRST EDITION

Designed by Helene Wald Berinsky

ISBN 0–06–105123–3

For the Brunswick Five:

> *Ted Barton,*
> *John Goff,*
> *Jack Kraus,*
> *Ron Peiffer, and*
> *George Tindle*

They haven't quite worked out the secret of life,
but they know it has something to do with lunch.

Acknowledgments

The author appreciates the advice and assistance of Jeffrey Hall of the Lowell Observatory; of Jimmy Durden, the Glynn County, Georgia, coroner; of my agent and friend, Ralph Vicinanza; of my son Chris McDevitt for devising FAULS; of writers Walt Cuirle and Brian A. Hopkins for their advice on early versions of the manuscript. Thanks also to Will Jenkins/Murray Leinster, for "First Contact," and for his other magnificent forays into the imagination. To Caitlin Blasdell, my editor at HarperPrism. To Rebecca Springer. And of course to Maureen.

We have always stood along a beach opening onto an infinite sea. That sea beckons us, but for ages we were limited to looking across its expanse with our telescopes and our imaginations. In time, we learned to build outriggers and we got to a few of the barrier islands. Today we have finally in our hands a true four-master, a ship that will take us beyond whatever horizons may exist.

—KHALID ALNIRI, The "Infinity Beach"
Speech at Wesleyan

■   ■   ■

We've known for a long time that contact might eventually happen, maybe would have to happen, and that when it did it would change everything, our technology, our sense of who we are, our notions of what the universe is. We've seen this particular lightning strike coming and we've played with the idea of what it might mean for eleven hundred years. We've imagined that other intelligences exist, we've imagined them as fearsome or gentle, as impossibly strange or remarkably familiar, as godlike, as remote, as indifferent. Well, I wonder whether the bolt is about to arrive. With you and me at the impact point.

—SOLLY HOBBS to KIM BRANDYWINE,
On the occasion of their visit to Alnitak

Dates, unless otherwise indicated, are given in the Greenway calendar, whose Year 1 coincides with the first landing on that world in 2411 of the common era. The Greenway and terrestrial year are almost identical in duration, which is one of the reasons that world was selected for terraforming.

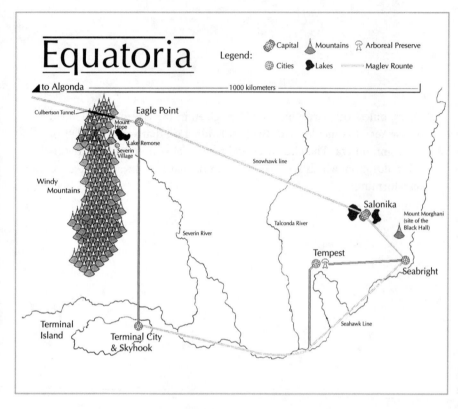

Equatoria

Legend:
- Capital
- Cities
- Mountains
- Lakes
- Arboreal Preserve
- Maglev Rounte

to Algonda — 1000 kilometers —

Culbertson Tunnel
Eagle Point
Mount Hope
Lake Remorse
Severin Village
Windy Mountains
Severin River
Snowhawk line
Talconda River
Salonika
Mount Morghani (site of the Black Hall)
Tempest
Seabright
Terminal Island
Terminal City & Skyhook
Seahawk Line

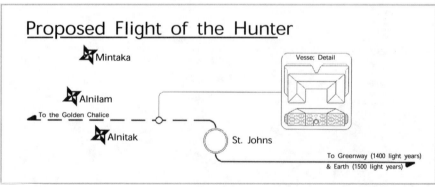

Proposed Flight of the Hunter

Mintaka

Alnilam

To the Golden Chalice

Alnitak

St. Johns

Vesse; Detail

To Greenway (1400 light years)
& Earth (1500 light years)

Illustrations by James P. Beery

APRIL 3, 573

"Don't do it." Kane, covered in blood, stood framed in the doorway.

"—no choice—" Tripley called as the flyer lifted off the pad. "Do what you can for her."

As he'd feared, the bastards did not show up on his screen. But he could *see* their eerie companion, the spectral thing that floated through the moonlight. It was tracking northwest, toward Mount Hope. He had to assume it was escorting them. Riding shotgun.

The village fell away, and he was out over the lake. He switched to manual, climbed to fifteen hundred meters, and gave it everything it had, which wasn't much. The flyer rattled and creaked but got up to two hundred fifty klicks. To his surprise he saw that he *was* gaining ground.

Was that possible? Or had the *thing* slowed down, to lure him on?

Three of Greenway's moons, in their first quarter, floated in a cloudless sky, illuminating the distant peaks, the cool, dark lake, the dam, the fleeing cloud.

What was it anyhow?

It had drawn itself almost into a sphere, trailing long, hazy tendrils. Like a comet, he thought; unlike any other that had sailed past the world. Lethal and efficient and starkly graceful, framed against the snowcapped mountains.

But the sensor return was getting louder. He *was* gaining.

In these first quiet moments since everything had come undone, he listened to the wind and the burble of his electronics, and he wished desperately he could go back and change everything.

Ahead, the comet-shape was moving ever slower. And beginning to dissolve.

Tripley braked.

He knew that the ship would be continuing straight on. He laughed, thinking of it in those terms. A *ship* that no one could see, that didn't show up on the screens, that could lose itself out there without any fear of being found.

And there lay the problem. He could not follow without the telltale cloud to lead him. And he would have to kill the cloud to survive himself. How in hell had things gotten so desperately out of hand?

Kill the cloud.

Was the damned thing even alive?

They'd passed over the northwest shore. Dark forest lay below, the Gray Mountains rose ahead.

It turned to confront him.

He watched it spread across the night, opening for him, expanding into a kind of *blossom*, waiting to receive him. It had filaments, backlit by the moons, through which something, a nutrient, a life force, pulsed steadily.

He hesitated briefly, suddenly fearful, and then accelerated again to full throttle. He would kill the bastard or die himself.

Close the vents. Check windows and doors. He didn't want any part of it getting into the cabin.

The night was full of regrets. He'd made the wrong call at every turn, had gotten people killed, and God knew what he'd unleashed on the world. But maybe he could start making amends now.

The wind roared across his stubby wings, and the creature floated in the moonlight, waiting. He could see the constellations in its veils.

It was unspeakably lovely, a mixture of mist and starlight, moving easily with the wind. He aimed directly at the center of the thing. He'd plow through and come around and rip into it again and *keep* slicing it apart until it was scattered across the sky.

And when that was done, he'd get back on the base course of the fleeing ship. There *had* to be a way to run it to ground. But one thing at a time.

The comm buzzer alerted him that someone was trying to reach him. *Kane.*

The apparition began to move, tried to draw aside. Tripley felt a surge of joy. It was afraid of him. *No, you son of a bitch.* He adjusted course to keep it in his mental crosshairs.

The buzzer sounded again.

He knew what Kane would say. *She's dead.* And: *Let it go.* But it was too late now for common sense. Wasn't that what Kane had been saying from the beginning: Use common sense? But it had been hard to sort out, to know what to do—

Tripley braced himself, not knowing what to expect. The cloud was growing thinner as he approached, but that might have been an illusion, the way mist seems to dissipate when one plunges into it.

"I'm sorry," he said, not sure to whom he was speaking.

And then he ripped into the cloud. Through it. Came out into clear starlight.

He looked back and saw that he'd blown a hole through its center. Parts of it were drifting away.

He went hard right, circling around for a second pass. He was confident now that it couldn't hurt him. Its suppleness appeared to be gone. It was struggling.

He raced through it again from a different angle, hurling its fragments into the night, exhilarated by the taste of vengeance.

That was for Yoshi.

And this—

Everything failed. The soft murmur of the magnetics changed to a whine and died.

The instrument panel lights blinked out. And suddenly the only sound was the whisper of the wind.

The flyer fell through the night.

He fought the controls, trying frantically to restart as the trees rushed up. Above him, silhouetted against Glory, the largest moon, the cloud was trying to re-form. And in those last moments, riven with fear and despair, a brilliant white light erupted on the slopes of Mount Hope. A second sun. He watched it expand, watched it engulf the world.

And he felt a final rush of satisfaction. It *had* to be the ship. The thing's masters, at least, were dead.

And then it ceased to matter.

▤ NEW YEAR'S EVE, 599

It seems safe now to assume that the terrestrial origin of life was a unique event. Some will quibble that we have, after all, seen only a few thousand of the billions of worlds drifting through the gently curving corridors we once called biozones. But we have stood on too many warm beaches and looked across seas over which no gulls hover, that throw forth neither shells, nor strands of weed, nor algae. They are peaceful seas, bounded by rock and sand.

The universe has come to resemble a magnificent but sterile wilderness, an ocean which boasts no friendly coast, no sails, no sign that any have passed this way before. And we cannot help but tremble in the gray light of these vast distances. Maybe that is why we are converting the great interstellar liners into museums, or selling them for parts. Why we have begun to retreat, why the Nine Worlds are now really six, why the frontier is collapsing, why we are going home to our island.

We are coming back at last to Earth. To the forests of our innocence. To the shores of night. Where we need not listen to the seaborne wind.

Farewell, Centaurus. Farewell to all we might have been.

　　　　　　—ELIO KARDI, "The Shores of Night," *Voyagers,* 571

"Nova goes in three minutes."

Dr. Kimberly Brandywine looked out across the dozen or so faces in the briefing room. In back, lenses were pointed at her, sending the event out across the nets. Behind, her projections read HELLO TO THE UNIVERSE and KNOCK and IS ANYBODY OUT THERE?

Several flatscreens were positioned around the walls, showing technicians bent over terminals in the *Trent*. These were the teams that would ignite the nova, but the images were fourteen hours old, the time required for the hypercomm transmissions to arrive.

Everyone present was attractive and youthful, except sometimes for their eyes. However vital and agile people were, their true age tended to reveal itself in their gaze. There was a hardness that came with advancing years, eyes that somehow lost their depth and their animation. Kim was in her midthirties, with exquisite features and hair the color of a raven's wing. In an earlier era, they would have launched ships for her. In her own age, she was just part of the crowd.

"If we haven't found anybody after all this time," the representative from Seabright Communications was saying, "it can only be because there's nobody to find. Or, if there is, they're so far away it doesn't matter."

She delivered her standard reply, discounting the great silence, pointing out that even after eight centuries humans had still inspected only a few thousand star systems. "But you may be right," she admitted. "Maybe we *are* alone. But the fact is that we really don't know. So we'll keep trying."

Kim had long since concluded that Seabright was right. They hadn't found so much as an amoeba out there. Briefly, at the beginning of the Space Age, there'd been speculation that life might exist in Europa's seas. Or in Jupiter's clouds. There'd even been a piece of meteoric rock thought to contain evidence of Martian bacteria. It was as close to extraterrestrial life as we'd ever come.

Hands were still waving.

"One more question," she said.

She gave it to Canon Woodbridge, a science advisor for the Grand Council of the Republic. He was tall, dark, bearded, almost satanic in appearance, yet a congenial fiend, one who meant no harm. "Kim," he said, "why do you think we're so afraid of being alone? Why do we want so much to find our own reflections out there?" He glanced in the direction of the screens, where the technicians continued their almost-ceremonial activities.

How on earth would she know? "I have no idea, Canon," she said.

"But you're deeply involved in the Beacon Project. And your sister devoted her life to the same goal."

"Maybe it's in the wiring." Emily, her clone actually, had vanished when Kim was seven. She paused momentarily and tried to deliver a thoughtful response, something about the human need to communicate and to explore. "I suspect," she said, "if there's really nothing out there, if the universe is *really* empty, or at least *this* part of it is, then maybe a lot of us would feel there's no point to the trip." There was more to it than that, she knew. Some primal urge not to be *alone*. But when she tried to put it into words she floundered around, gave up, and glanced at the clock.

One minute to midnight, New Year's Eve, in the two hundred eleventh year of the Republic and the six hundredth year since Marquand's landing. One minute to detonation.

"How are we doing on time?" asked one of the journalists. "Are they on schedule?"

"Yes," Kim said. "As of ten A.M. this morning." The hypercomm signal from the *Trent* required fourteen hours and some odd minutes to travel the 580 light-years from the scene of detonation. "I think we're safe to assume that the nova is imminent."

She activated an overhead screen, which picked up an image of the target star. Alpha Maxim was a bright AO-class. Hydrogen lines prominent. Surface temperature 11,000° C. Luminosity sixty times that of Helios. Five planets. All barren. Like every other known world, save the few that had been terraformed.

It would be the first of six novas. All would occur within a volume of space which measured approximately five hundred cubic light-years. And they would be triggered at sixty-day intervals. It would be a demonstration that could not help but draw the attention of anyone who might be watching. The ultimate message to the stars: *We are here.*

But she believed, as almost everyone else did, that the great silence would continue to roll back.

> We live along the shores of night,
> At the edge of the eternal sea.

The effort was called the Beacon Project. Its sponsor was Kim's employer, the Seabright Institute. But even there, among those who had pushed the project, who had worked for years to bring it to fruition, there was a deep, pervading pessimism. Maybe it resulted from the knowledge that they'd all be dead before any possible answer could come back. Or maybe, as she wholeheartedly believed, it grew from a sense that this was a final gesture, more farewell than serious attempt at communication.

Emily, who had given her life to the great quest, would have been ashamed of her. It just demonstrated, Kim thought, how little the DNA really counted.

The *Trent* lay at a distance of five AUs from its target. The ship was an ancient cargo vessel refitted specifically for Beacon. Immediately after detonation, its crew and technicians would transfer to another vessel, which would transit into hyperspace, out of harm's way. The *Trent* would be left to probe and measure the nova until the blast silenced it.

Kim threw a switch, and a computer-generated image of the LK6, a modified antique transport, formed in the center of the room. The LK6 was loaded with antimatter, contained within a magnetic bubble. It was traveling in hyperspace and, within a few seconds, would emerge in the solar core. If all went well, the resulting explosion would destabilize the star and, according to theory, ignite the first artificial nova.

A clock in the lower right-hand corner indicated the time of the image, and a counter ticked off the last seconds, simultaneously the last of the century and the last before the LK6 entry.

Kim watched the numbers go to zeroes. The year rolled over to 600 and 580 light-years away the missile inserted itself and its payload into the heart of the star.

Outside, the Institute people applauded. In the briefing room, the mood was strange, almost somber. Maxim was older than Helios, and there was a general sense that ending its existence was somehow *wrong*.

"Ladies and gentlemen," said Kim, "the pictures will be in tomorrow, and we'll have them for you at the news conference." She thanked them and stepped away from the lectern, and they began to file out of the room.

Woodbridge lingered, looking out the window at the Institute's grounds. They were covered with a thin layer of snow. He waited for Kim to join him. "I wonder," he said, "whether it's a good idea to advertise our presence until we know who the neighbors are." He wore a dark brown robe belted with a silver sash, and his sea green eyes were thoughtful.

"It's a valid question, Canon," she said, "but surely anyone intelligent enough to develop interstellar travel would be above shooting up strangers."

"Hard to say." He shrugged. "If we guess wrong, we could pay a substantial price." He looked up at the clear, bright sky. "It's obvious that Whoever designed the cosmos wanted to put distance between His creatures."

They pulled on their jackets and walked out onto a terrace. The night was cold.

Seabright was only a few hundred kilometers north of the equator, but Greenway, despite its name, was not a particularly warm world. The bulk of its population was concentrated in equatorial latitudes.

An array of telescopes had been set up at the north end of the terrace, away from the buildings. A technician stood beside one, talking with a girl. The telescope was pointed toward the southeast, where Alpha Maxim was just one more pinpoint of light.

The girl's name was Lyra. She was the technician's daughter, probably ten years old, and could reasonably expect to live two centuries.

"I wonder if she thinks she'll be able to see the nova," said Woodbridge.

Kim stepped to one side. "Ask her."

He did, and Lyra smiled one of those vaguely contemptuous smiles that children use when they think adults are being condescending. "No, Canon," she said, while her mother looked pleased. "It will not change in my lifetime."

Nor of her kids, thought Kim. Light was so *slow*.

Woodbridge turned back to her. "Kim," he said, "may I ask you a personal question?"

"Of course."

"Do you have *any* idea what happened to Emily?"

It was a strange question, coming apparently from nowhere. But maybe not, now that she thought about it. Emily would have wanted to be here tonight. Woodbridge had known her, and he understood that about her. "No," Kim said. "She got in that taxi and never showed up at the hotel. That's all I know." She looked past the telescopes. Lyra's mother had decided it was too cold to stay out any longer, and she was ushering the child inside. "We never heard a word."

Woodbridge nodded. "It's hard to understand how something like that could happen." They lived in a society in which crime was almost unknown.

"I know. It was hard on the family." She pulled her collar higher to ward off the night air. "She'd have supported Beacon, but she would have been impatient with it."

"Why?"

"Takes too long. We're trying to say hello in a scientific way, but nobody expects a reply for millennia. At best. She'd have wanted results tonight."

"What about you?"

"What about what?"

"How do you feel about all this? I can't believe you're satisfied with Beacon either."

She looked at the sky. *Utterly empty, as far as the eye can see.* "Canon," she said, "I'd like to know the truth. But it isn't something that drives my life." *I am not my sister.*

"I feel much the same way. But I must admit I'd prefer it if we're alone. Much safer that way."

Kim nodded. "Why did you ask?" she said. "About my sister?"

"No reason, really. You look so much alike. And you're both so caught up in the same issue. In there tonight, listening to you, I almost felt she were back."

Kim called a cab and went up to the roof. While she waited she checked her mail and found a message from Solly: *Don't forget tomorrow.*

Solly was one of the Institute's pilots and a fellow diving enthusiast. They'd made plans several days ago to go down to the wreck of the *Caledonian*. That would be in the late afternoon, after the transmissions had come in from the *Trent*, and everyone had celebrated properly, and the media people had gone off to put together their stories.

Kim had visited the wreck before. The *Caledonian* was a fishing yacht, lying in twenty fathoms, on the seaward side of Capelo Island. She liked the sense of timelessness the sunken ship evoked, the feeling that she was living simultaneously in different eras. The excursion would also provide a break from the long hours and extended effort of the last few weeks.

The cab landed and she climbed in, touched her bracelet to the dex, and told it to take her home. It lifted, arced around toward the east, and accelerated. She heard the *blatt* of a horn as she left, a final farewell from someone celebrating either the blast or New Year's. Then she was sailing over forest and parkland. Seabright's towers in the north glittered with lights. The parks fell away into sandy beach and the cab arced out over the sea.

Greenway was predominantly a water world. Its single continent was Equatoria, and Seabright lay on its eastern coast. At its widest, it was just over seven hundred kilometers across. The globe-spanning ocean had no name.

The cab skimmed low over the water, crossed Bagby Inlet and the hotball courts on Branch Island. It sailed out beyond the channel, passed a couple of yachts, and began its approach to Korbee Island, a two-kilometer-long strip of land so narrow that many of its houses had ocean views front and back.

Kim's home, like most of the others in the area, was a modest two-story with a wraparound lower deck. It was rounded at the corners to counter the force of the winds that blew almost constantly off the ocean.

The cab descended onto her landing pad, which was located behind the house on a platform elevated over the incoming tide. She climbed down and stood wearily for a moment, listening to the sea. The rest of the island seemed dark and silent except for the Dickensons, who were still celebrating the new year. Out on the beach, she could see a campfire. Kids.

It had been a long day and she was tired and glad to be home. But she suspected her weariness was not a result of the sixteen or so hours that had passed since she'd left home this morning; rather it had risen from her knowledge that she'd come to the end of something important. Beacon had been launched, and the public relations aspect of it would be given over to someone else. She would go back to her regular fundraising duties. Damned poor career for an astrophysicist. The reality was that she didn't sparkle at her specialty, but she *did* have a talent for talking people into giving substantial contributions.

Damn.

She started toward the house and the taxi lifted off. Lights came on. The door opened for her. *"Good evening, Kim,"* said Shepard. *"I see the program went well."* Shepard was the household AI.

"Yes, it did, Shep. As far as we know, everything's on schedule." Like all AIs, Shepard was theoretically not self-aware. Everything was simulation. True artificial intelligence remained beyond the reach of science, and the common wisdom now held that it was impossible. But one was never sure where simulation ended. "Of course we won't really know for another twelve hours."

"You had several calls," he said. *"Mostly congratulatory."* He ticked off a list of names, friends and professional colleagues, and a few relatives.

"And at least one," she said, "that *wasn't* congratulatory?"

"Well, this one too commended you. But that wasn't the reason he called. It was from Sheyel Tolliver."

Sheyel? That was a name out of the past. Sheyel had been a professor of history at the university during her undergraduate years. He'd been a superb instructor, and he'd taken an interest in her despite the fact that she was a physics major. She was somewhat adrift then. Her parents had died in a flyer accident, the first one recorded in Seabright in five years. It had happened during her second year, and Sheyel had gone out of his way for her, had made himself available when she wanted to talk, had encouraged her, reassured her, and in the end got her to believe in herself. But that was fifteen years ago. "Did he say what he wanted?"

"Only that he wishes to speak with you. I don't think he's well."

"Where is he?"

"In Tempest." Three hundred kilometers away.

She was pleased that he'd remembered her. But she couldn't imagine why he was contacting her after so many years. "That's really strange," she said.

"He asked that you call him directly when you returned home."

She glanced at her link. It was past 1:00 A.M. "I'll call him in the morning."

"Kim, he was quite specific."

"It'll have to wait. I'm sure he didn't expect me to get him up in the middle of the night." She went into the kitchen and made a cup of coffee, talked idly with the AI for twenty minutes, and decided to call it a night.

She showered, turned out the lights, and stood at her window looking at the breakers. The section of the sky which held Alpha Maxim had rotated up over the roof where she couldn't see it. The fire on the beach had apparently been abandoned but had not quite gone out. She watched sparks rising into the night.

"It is beautiful," said Shepard.

Something ached within her, but she couldn't have said what it was. The tide was out and had not yet turned, so the sea was silent. She could almost have believed the ocean wasn't there tonight, gone into the dark with Emily.

It was hard, on this special night, to put her sister out of her mind. Their last day together had included a frolic in the surf. They'd had a rubber sea horse from which Kim kept deliberately sliding off. *Help,*

Emily. And the beautiful woman whose image she knew she'd one day inherit had pretended endlessly to be startled anew and would splash to her rescue. That Kim would one day *be* Emily had made her impossibly happy. There'd been pictures of Emily at seven, and Mom had always shaken her head over them. "Why, isn't that Kim?" she would say, knowing quite well who was in the picture.

At the end of that afternoon, Emily had told her she was going away for fifteen months. An eternity to a child. Kim had been angry, had refused to speak as they rode home in a taxi.

It was the last time she saw her sister. And there had rarely been a day in all the years since that she had not wished she could get that taxi ride back.

A few months later she'd been leaving for school and her mother had sat her down and told her something had happened, they weren't sure what, but—

Nobody could find her. Emily was supposed to have come home, and had come back to Greenway ahead of schedule. She'd come down from Sky Harbor into Terminal City and gotten into a cab with another woman to go to their hotel. But she never got there. And nobody knew what had happened.

Someone was walking on the beach. A woman with a dog. Despite the cold. Kim watched until they disappeared around the bend at the shoal and the beach was empty again. "Yes, it is beautiful, Shep," she said.

She pulled on a fresh pair of pajamas, which were of course connected to Shepard's systems and capable of producing a wide range of sensations. The curtains rustled in a sudden breeze and she climbed into bed. Shepard turned out the lights. *"Program tonight, Kim?"* he asked.

"Please."

"You wish me to choose?" She usually left it to him. It was more exciting that way.

"Yes."

"Goodnight, Kim," he said.

Cyrus was apologetic. *"Kim,"* he said, *"the insertion won't work. That means the programming is useless."* He looked impossibly handsome in the subdued light of the operations center.

"Which means you can't detonate the payload."

"That's right."

She glanced up at Alpha Maxim on the screens. *"We don't have time to rewrite the code."*

He nodded. *"Mission's blown."*

"Maybe not," she said. *"We can try to do it by the seat of our pants."*

"Kim, we both know that's not possible." His eyes widened. *"I say we concede the effort and make the most of the moment—"*

"Cyrus—"

"I love you, Kim. What do we care whether the star goes up or not?"

Shepard woke her at seven. Orange juice and toast were waiting. *"You know,"* he observed, *"he's not a responsible commander."*

"I know," she said.

"Do you want me—?"

The juice was delicious. "Keep the program the way it is," she said.

"As you wish, Kim." He was laughing at her. *"And you have an incoming call. From Professor Tolliver."*

At seven o'clock? "Put him through," she said.

Sheyel Tolliver had aged. The energy seemed to have drained away. His face had grown sallow. His beard, black in the old days, had gone to gray. But he smiled when he saw her. "Kim," he said, "I apologize for calling you so early. I wanted to get you before you left for work."

"It's good to hear from you, Professor. It's been a long time."

"Yes, it has." He sat propped against a couple of cushions in an exquisitely carved chair with dragon's-claw arms. "I saw you last night. You're very good." Kim had been on most of the newscasts. "I should congratulate you, by the way. You've done well for yourself."

She let him see she did not like the job. "It's not the field I'd have chosen."

"Yes." He looked uncomfortable. "One never knows how things will turn out, I suppose. You had planned to be an astronomer, as I recall."

"An astrophysicist."

"But you're quite good behind a lectern. And I thought you'd have made a decent historian."

"Thanks. I appreciate that."

His mood darkened, became somber. "I'd like to talk to you about something quite serious, and I want you to hear me out."

"Why would I not do that?"

"Save the question for a few minutes, Kim. Let me ask you first about the Beacon Project. Have you any influence over it?"

"None whatever," she said. "I just do their PR."

He nodded. "Pity."

"Why is that?"

He thought very carefully about his reply. "I'd like to see it stopped."

She stared at him. "Why?" There'd been some protest groups who thought triggering stars was immoral, even though no ecosystem was involved. But she couldn't believe that her tough-minded old teacher could be involved with *that* crowd.

He rearranged his cushions. "Kim, I don't think it's prudent to advertise our presence when we don't know what's out there."

Her respect for him dropped several levels on the spot. That was the kind of sentiment she could accept from someone like Woodbridge, who never thought about the sciences other than as a route to better engineering. But Sheyel was another matter altogether.

"I really think any concerns along those lines are groundless, Professor."

He pressed an index finger against his jaw. "We have a connection you probably don't know about, Kim. Yoshi was my great granddaughter."

"Yoshi—?"

"—Amara."

Kim caught her breath. Yoshi Amara had been the other woman in Emily's cab. She'd also been one of her sister's colleagues on the *Hunter*, on its last mission.

Both women had returned with the *Hunter* after another fruitless search for extraterrestrial life, this one cut short by an equipment malfunction. They'd gone down in the elevator to Terminal City, where they were booked at the Royal Palms Hotel. They'd taken the cab and ridden right off the planet.

"You're right," Kim said. "I didn't know."

He reached beside him, picked up a cup, and sipped from it. A wisp of steam rose into the air. "I recall thinking when I first saw you," he said, "how closely you resembled Emily. But you were young then. Now you're identical. Are you a clone, if you don't mind my asking?"

"Yes," said Kim. "There are several of us spread across four generations." Save for nuances of expression and their hair styles, they were impossible to tell apart. "You knew Emily, then?"

"I only met her once. At the farewell party before the mission left. Yoshi invited me. Your sister was a brilliant woman. A bit *driven*, I thought. But then, so was Yoshi."

"I think we all are, Professor," Kim said. "At least everybody worth knowing."

"Yes, I quite agree." He studied her for a long moment. "How much do you know about the last voyage? On the *Hunter*?"

Actually, not much. Kim wasn't aware there was anything to know. Emily wanted to find extraterrestrial life. Preferably *intelligent* extraterrestrial life. And she'd cared about little else, except Kim. Emily had gone through two marriages with men who simply did not want to deal with an absentee wife. She'd shipped out on the *Hunter* any number of times, often on voyages of more than a year's duration. They'd found nothing, and she had come back on each occasion certain that next time would be different. "They didn't get far. They had engine trouble, and they came home." She felt puzzled. What did he expect her to say?

His smile left her feeling as if she were once again an undergraduate. Was it really that long ago he had led them in work songs from the era then under study, the terraforming years on Greenway? His classroom had rocked with "Granite John" and "Lay My Bones in the Deep Blue Sea."

"I think there was a little more to it," he said. "I think they found something."

"*Something*? What kind of *something*?"

"What they were looking for."

Had it been anyone else, she would have simply found a way to terminate the conversation. "Professor Tolliver, if they did, they forgot to mention it when they got back."

"I know," he said. "They kept it quiet."

"Why would they do that?" She adopted her best let's-be-reasonable tone.

"I don't know. Maybe they were frightened by what they'd found."

Frightened? The ship's captain was Markis Kane. A war hero who had a wing of the Mighty Third Memorial Museum all to himself. He'd been killed a few years ago while attempting to rescue children during a forest fire in North America. "That's hard to believe," she said.

"Nevertheless, I think it's what happened."

There'd been only four people on the *Hunter*. Kane, Emily, Yoshi. And Kile Tripley, head of the Tripley Foundation, which had sponsored the missions. He too had vanished, and that was an odd business. Tripley and Kane had both lived in the Severin Valley in the western mountain region of Equatoria. Three days after the *Hunter* had returned from its mission, after the women had disappeared, a still-unexplained explosion had ripped apart the eastern face of Mount Hope, had leveled Severin Village and killed three hundred people. Tripley had never been found after the event and was presumed buried somewhere in the rubble.

Most of the experts at the Institute thought it had been a meteor, but no trace of the object had ever been found. The force of the explosion had been estimated at roughly equivalent to a small nuclear bomb.

"It's all connected," Tolliver said. "The *Hunter* mission, the disappearances, the explosion."

There'd been stories to that effect for years. It was a favorite subject of the conspiracy theorists. And maybe there was something to it. But there was no evidence, and she hated sitting here with Sheyel Tolliver talking about Mount Hope. It saddened her to see her old teacher reduced to a believer in cover-ups and visitors from other worlds.

There were all sorts of lunatic theories about the incident. Some said that a micro black hole had come to ground. They'd searched the logs of ships and aircraft on the other side of Greenway looking for an indication that the hole had emerged from the ocean. Much as researchers had a thousand years before, after the Tunguska event. As it turned out, there *had* been a spout under a heavy sky, so the story had gained credence. Even though everyone knew there could be no such thing as a micro black hole.

Others were convinced a government experiment had gone wrong. The experiment was said by one group to have involved time-travel research; by another, mass transference. Still others thought an antimatter alien ship had exploded while trying to land.

"Kim," he said, "how much do you know about Kile Tripley?"

"I know he was a wealthy freelance enthusiast who wanted to make a name for himself." Tripley had been the CEO of Interstellar, Inc., which specialized in restoring and maintaining jump engines, which moved starships into and out of hyperspace.

"He was a tough-minded man, had to be in that business," Tolliver said. "Have you by any chance read Korkel's biography?"

She hadn't.

"He made it quite clear that Tripley wasn't going to be satisfied just bagging a bacterium somewhere. He wanted to find a thinking creature.

A *civilization*. It was the whole purpose of the Foundation—the whole purpose of his existence."

Like Emily.

One of the saddest places anywhere in the Nine Worlds was the abandoned radio telescope array on the far side of Earth's moon, designed explicitly to search for artificial radio signals. Far more versatile than anything that had gone before, it had closed down its SETI function after something over a century and a half of futility, and was eventually diverted to other uses. By now, it was obsolete, standing only as a monument to a lost dream. *We're alone.*

There's never been a signal. Never a sign of a supercivilization building Dyson spheres. Never a visitor. There was really only one conclusion to draw.

She spread her hands helplessly, wondering how to break off the conversation. "Professor—"

"My name is *Sheyel*, Kim."

"Sheyel. I'm inclined to accept whatever you say simply because it comes from you. But I'm reminded of—"

"—The danger of assigning too much credence to the source when weighing the validity of an argument. Of course, after this you may categorize me as an unreliable source."

"I'm thinking about it," she admitted. "You must know something you haven't told me."

"I do." He rearranged the cushions. "The *Hunter* left St. Johns February twelfth, 573." St. Johns was an outpost in the Cynex system, last water hole before leaping into the unknown. "They were bound for the Golden Chalice in the Drum Nebula. Lots of old, yellow suns. First stop was to be—" he looked down at something she couldn't see, "—QCY449187, a class G. But of course they never got that far."

"They had a problem with the jump engines," said Kim.

"According to the record, yes. They came out of hyperspace in the middle of nowhere, made temporary repairs, and turned back.

"But they didn't return to St. Johns. Kane decided St. Johns couldn't manage the problem. So they came all the way home to Sky Harbor, arriving March thirtieth. It was ironic, of course, that the *Hunter*, whose owner had made a fortune repairing and maintaining jump engines, should suffer such a breakdown. But nevertheless—"

There it was.

"Okay," said Kim, in a tone that suggested she saw nothing out of the way in any of this.

He produced another picture. Yoshi, Tripley, and Emily in Foundation jumpsuits. Yoshi had chiseled cheekbones and riveting dark eyes. A white scarf highlighted her youth. Kim saw a monogram on the scarf and asked about it.

"It's a crescent," he explained. His gaze turned inward. "She liked crescents. Collected them. Wore them as jewelry and monograms.

"Anyway, an hour or so after they docked at Sky Harbor, Yoshi *called* me."

That got Kim's attention. "What did she say?"

"'Granpop, we struck gold.'"

"Gold?"

"That's right. She said that she'd be in touch, but she couldn't say anything more for the moment. Asked me to say nothing."

"Sheyel—"

"It can only have one meaning."

Kim tried to hide her frustration. "She might have been talking about a romance."

"She said 'we.'"

"Did you talk to Kane?"

"Of course. He maintained that nothing unusual happened. He told me he was sorry about the others, all three missing within a few days of the return, but he had no idea what had happened to them."

She sat watching him a long time. "Sheyel," she said at last, "I don't know what you want me to do about any of this."

"Okay." His expression revealed nothing. "I understand."

"To be honest, I haven't heard anything that persuades me they made contact. That *is* what you're implying, isn't it?"

"I appreciate your time, Kim." He moved to cut her off.

"Wait," she said. "We've both suffered losses in this incident. That's painful. Especially since we don't know what happened. My mother was haunted by it until the day she died." She took a deep breath, knowing this would be a good time to break away. "Is there anything you're not telling me?"

He watched her for a long moment. "You mentioned contact. I think they brought something back with them."

The conversation had already been too exotic for anything to surprise her now. But that statement came close. "What kind of *something*?"

"I don't know." His eyes flickered and seemed to lose focus. "Read the accounts about the aftermath in the Severin Valley. For years after the explosion, people have claimed they've seen things in the woods. Lights, apparitions. There were reports of horses and dogs showing signs of restlessness."

Kim felt embarrassed for him, and he saw it.

"They abandoned the *town*," he persisted. "They *left*."

"They abandoned it because the explosion weakened a dam. The dam was too expensive to repair so the authorities just encouraged everyone to move out. Anyway people had bad memories."

"They took down the dam," said Sheyel, "because everyone was leaving. Kim, I've been there. There *is* something loose up there."

She listened to the air currents circulating through the room. "Did you ever *see* anything, Sheyel?"

"I've *felt* it. Go look for yourself. After dark. Do *that* much. It's all I ask."

"Sheyel—"

"But don't go alone."

2

We may never know what really happened at Mount Hope. Those who maintain that a secret government project hidden on the slopes went terribly awry on that April night have to explain how a government notoriously unable to keep any kind of secret could have kept this one for so many years. The theory that the area was struck by a micro black hole seems equally indefensible until someone proves that such an exotic object can even exist. As to the antimatter explanation, the board, after exhaustive investigation, can find no conceivable source. For now, at least, the cause of the Mount Hope event cannot be satisfactorily explained.

—Report of the Conciliar Commission, March 3, 584

In effect, Kim and her charges, a combination of commentators, contributors, and political heavyweights, were afloat in the void at relatively close range to Alpha Maxim. They were seated in four rows of armchairs, some sipping coffee or fruit juice, one or two pushed back as if it might be possible to fall. The sun's glare was muted. Its apparent size was about twice that of Helios at noon.

Two clocks, positioned among the stars, counted down to ignition.

Kim, in the rear, was doing a play-by-play. "The LK6 is now two minutes from making its jump into the solar core. When it does, it will try to materialize in an area already densely packed with matter." Canon Woodbridge, seated up front, was talking on a phone while he watched.

"This alone would be enough to create a massive explosion. But the LK6 is loaded with a cargo of antimatter. The reaction will be enough to destabilize the star."

Beside her, a technician signaled that the operation was still on schedule.

"We have a report from the *McCollum* that the last crewmembers have left the *Trent*, and that they have begun to pull away."

One of the observers wanted to know about safety margins. How long would it take before the shock wave hit the *Trent*?

"There's no danger to any of the personnel. They'll be gone long before the first effects of the nova reach their former location. Incidentally, the *Trent* won't be destroyed by the shock wave. The light will get there first, and that'll be quite enough."

Could she explain?

"A nova puts out a lot of photons. Think of a near-solid wall moving at lightspeed."

The clock produced a string of zeroes.

"Insertion is complete," she said.

"Kim." It was the representative of a corporation that almost routinely underwrote Institute activities. "How long will it be before we start to see the first effects?"

"That's a gray area, Ann. To be honest, we have no idea."

There were skeptics among the witnesses, some who believed that the Institute had overreached, that blowing up a star was simply beyond human capability. Several, she knew, would have been pleased to see the effort fail. Some did not like the Institute; some did not like its director. Others were simply uncomfortable at the prospect of human beings wielding that kind of power. Woodbridge was among these. Despite his remarks the previous evening, Kim knew that his real misgivings flowed from a basic distrust of human nature.

Minutes passed and nothing happened. She heard something fall and strike the invisible floor. They grew restless. In their experience, explosions were supposed to happen when they were triggered.

The first signs of stress showed up at zero plus eighteen minutes and change. Bright lines appeared around Alpha Maxim's belt. The chromosphere became visibly turbulent. Fountains of light erupted off the solar surface.

At zero plus twenty-two minutes the sun began to visibly expand. The process was slow: it might have been a balloon filling gradually with water. Enormous tidal forces started to overwhelm the spherical shape, flattening it, disrupting it, inducing monumental quakes.

At twenty-six minutes, eleven seconds, it exploded.

■　　■　　■

It was often possible to make a reasonable guess at a person's age from the physical characteristics his or her parents had selected. Different eras favored different skin tones, body types, hair colors. Concepts of beauty changed: women from one age tended to be well developed, their centers of gravity, as Solly Hobbs had once remarked, several centimeters in front of them; another era favored willowy, boyish women. Men's physiques ranged from heroic to slim. The current fashion was to consider bulk as somehow in poor taste. Males born during the next few years were going to resemble a generation of ballet dancers.

During the eighties, parents of both sexes had opted for classic features, the long jawline, eyes wide apart, straight nose. Teenage girls now looked by and large as if they'd stepped down from pedestals in the Acropolis. Kim had come from an earlier time when the pixie look was in vogue. She tried to compensate by maintaining a straightforward nononsense attitude, and by avoiding a programmed tendency to cant her head and smile sweetly. She also adapted her hair style to cover her somewhat elvin ears.

Solomon Hobbs was from an age that had favored biceps and shoulders, although he had allowed things to deteriorate somewhat. Solly was one of the Institute's four starship pilots. Kim had come to know him, however, not through an official connection, but because of their mutual interest in diving. Solly had been a member of the Sea Knights when Kim joined.

He had clear blue eyes, brown hair that was always in disarray, and a careless joviality that contrasted with a culture that thought of having fun as serious business, something one did to maintain a proper psychological balance.

After the lights came on and her guests had drifted away, Kim caught a cab which deposited her at the foot of Solly's pier. The dive on the *Caledonian* was to be their way of welcoming the new year. They'd been looking forward to it for weeks, but as they rounded Capelo Island, riding a cold wind, Kim began to describe her conversation with Sheyel. It wasn't a story she enjoyed telling, because it cast her former teacher as a crank. Yet she felt driven to talk about it. When she finished, he asked gently how much confidence she had in Tolliver.

"If you'd asked me two days ago—" she said.

"People lose touch as they get older." Solly squinted at the sun. The sloop rose and fell. "It happens."

They listened to the sea.

"I almost feel," said Kim, "as if I owe it to Emily to do *something*."

"Emily would tell you to forget it."

Kim laughed. That *was* funny. Emily was by no means a mark for every weird idea, but there had been something in her that wanted to get beyond the merely physical universe. Given a choice between daylight and darkness, she'd have opted for the night every time. "No," she said. "Emily would have wanted me to do *something*. Not just let it go."

"Like run up to Severin?"

She made a face. "I know. It's dumb even to think about it."

Solly shrugged. "Turn it into a vacation."

"I'm going to have to get back to him. To Sheyel. I don't like the way we left things."

"And you don't want to call him and tell him—"

"—Right. That I didn't bother to check out the woods."

They both laughed. The wind brought some spray inboard.

"Solly, I'll just say I didn't have time to go. That I'll get around to it when I can."

"Didn't you tell me this guy was a good teacher?"

"Yeah. He was good."

"And you're going to tell him you didn't have time to check something out for him? That you were too busy? Even though your sister was involved?"

"Solly, I don't really want to get caught up in this."

"Then don't." His sensors picked up the wreck, and he tacked a few points to port. "Moving up on it," he said.

"I mean, what happens to my reputation if it gets around I've gone ghost hunting?"

"Kim, why don't you take him at his word? We both know you're not going to sleep until you do. Look, it's only a few hours to Severin. Do it. What did he say was out there? A spook?"

"He didn't exactly say. 'Something's loose.'"

"Well, that could be pretty much anything."

"I think he was suggesting I'd know it when I saw it."

"Give it a chance. When nothing happens you can tell him you tried."

He dropped anchor and they changed into their wet suits. Kim folded her clothes carefully on the cabin bunk, then removed her silver earrings and laid them on top of her blouse. They were dolphins, given to her years ago by an otherwise forgettable amour. Then they sat down on the deck and resumed the conversation while they pulled on flippers and adjusted thermostats. Kim knew that the dive could not be made until the Tolliver issue was settled.

"You think I owe him that," she said.

"I think you owe it to yourself." He put his mask on, adjusted it, attached the converter, and took a deep breath. "I'll go with you, if you want."

"You really would?"

"I'm on an off-rotation for a couple of weeks. Plenty of time available if you'd like to do it."

Actually, she did. "Okay," she said. "I'm supposed to talk to the Germane Society the day after tomorrow. Wednesday. And I've got a fund-raiser at Sky Harbor next Saturday."

"What's next Saturday?"

"The *Star Queen* christening. Maybe this weekend would be a good time."

"I don't think I want to ask you what the Germane Society is."

"They are *relevant*."

Solly grinned. "Is it a luncheon?"

"Yes."

"Why wait till the weekend? Eagle Point's a tourist spot. Cheaper to hit it now. Why don't we leave Wednesday afternoon? After the Relevant Society—?"

"—Germane—"

"Whatever."

"You sound terribly interested all of a sudden."

"A night in the Severin Valley with a beautiful woman? Why wouldn't I be interested?"

Her relationship with Solly was purely platonic. He'd been married when they first met, so they became friends before they could have become lovers. She'd liked him from the first. When Solly became eligible after he and his wife had failed to renew the marriage, she had considered signaling a romantic interest. But he'd seemed reluctant. Best way he knew of, he said, to put a rift between them. She'd wondered whether there was a secret agenda somewhere, perhaps another woman. Or whether he meant what he said. Eventually the arrangement came to seem quite natural.

"I used the VR this morning," she said, "after I got off the circuit with Sheyel." She pulled the converter on over her shoulders and connected it. "I spent an hour looking at the Severin woods. They're just woods."

"It's not quite the same as *being* there," said Solly.

A wave passed under the boat and set it rocking. He dipped his mask in the water and put it on. "What about Kane? What happened to him?"

"He retired after the *Hunter* incident. Went into seclusion, I guess. I haven't done much research on him yet."

"*Aha.*"

"What *aha*? What are you trying to say?"

"Research? So we *are* interested in this, are we?"

She rolled her eyes. "Just curiosity. He stayed in Severin Village until they evacuated. When they took down the dam. He moved to Terminal City after that, and then he headed out. Eventually landed on Earth. Canada. Lived on his retirement income, I guess."

"Is he still alive?"

"He died a few years ago trying to rescue some kids. In a forest fire."

Solly pulled on his flippers. "And he always told the same story?"

"The conspiracy freaks were constantly after him. That appears to be the reason he left Greenway. But yes: He maintains that nothing unusual happened on the *Hunter* mission. They went out. They had an engine problem. They came back. Doesn't know what happened to the women. Thinks Tripley died in the blast."

"Mount Hope."

"Yes."

He lowered himself into the water, and his voice came in over her 'phones. "There *is* someone you might try talking to."

She watched him start down, and then followed him in. "Who's that?"

"Benton Tripley. Kile's son. His office is at Sky Harbor. When you go there next weekend, why don't you stop by and see him? He might be able to tell you something."

"I don't know." She slipped beneath the surface and filled her lungs several times to assure herself the converter was working properly. The air was sweet and cool. When she was satisfied, she started down. "I think I'll settle for just looking at the woods and let it go at that."

Bars of sunlight faded quickly. A long rainbow-colored fish darted past. The oceans of Greenway had filled rapidly with lobsters and tarpon and whales and algae and seaweed.

She dropped through alternating warm and cold currents. Solly, now trailing behind her, switched on his wristlamp.

The *Caledonian* had been running among the islands on its way out to the banks with nineteen passengers and a three-person crew when a freak storm blew up. It became a legendary event because there'd been some famous people on board, and because there'd been only two survivors. One had been the unfortunate captain, later held negligent by a board of inquiry, charging failure to train his crew, poor ship handling, failure to develop emergency procedures. His situation was exacerbated by the suspicion that on the night of the accident he'd been frolicking in his quarters with a married passenger.

The ship's wheel was on display at the Marine Museum in Seabright. Other divers had gone over the wreck and taken whatever they could. Even Kim, who was usually inclined to respect such things, had removed a latch from a cabin door. The latch was now inside a block of crystal, which she kept hidden in her bedroom because visitors had made a point of showing their disapproval. Moves were currently afoot to declare the area a seapark, install monitoring equipment, and thereby protect it from future looters. Kim, with the quiet hypocrisy that seems wired into the human soul, favored the measure. She soothed her conscience by promising herself she'd donate the latch to the museum. When the time came.

She left her own lamp off, savoring the dark and the solitude and the moving water. The bottom came into view. A school of fish, drawn by Solly's light, hurried past.

Ahead she could make out the wreck. It lay on its starboard side in the mud, half buried. Its rudder was gone, the spars were gone, planking was gone. Anything that could be carried off had been taken. Still it retained a kind of pathetic dignity.

The seabottoms of Greenway, unlike those of Earth, were not littered with the wrecks of thousands of years of seafaring and warmaking. It was in fact possible to count the number of sinkings along the eastern coast, during five centuries, on two hands. Only one, the *Caledonian*, had been a ship in the true sense of the word. The others had all been skimmers. The loss of a vessel was so rare an event that anything that went down became immediately a subject of folklore.

They were approaching bow-on. Kim switched on her light. "Spooky as ever," said Solly.

It wasn't the adjective Kim would have used. *Forlorn*, perhaps. *Abandoned*.

Yet maybe he was right.

They drifted down toward the foredeck.

The other survivor had testified that the ship's captain had done what he could.

The unfortunate skipper's name was Jon Halvert. He'd used a lantern to signal passengers to the lifeboats, and renderings of the incident invariably showed him holding the lantern high, helping men and women off the stricken ship. But it had all come too late and the *Caledonian* had turned over within seconds and plunged to the bottom. Historians believed that, the view of the board of inquiry notwithstanding, nothing the captain could have done would have made any significant difference. But there had been, as always, the need to establish responsibility. To lay blame.

Kim felt a special affection for him. Halvert seemed to represent the human condition: struggling under impossible circumstances, answerable for lack of perfection, holding the lantern nonetheless. But in the end it makes no difference.

Within a year of the event he died, and it became a popular legend that his spirit hovered in the vicinity of the wreck.

Divers only visit the Caledonian *when the weather is good. But when the wind is stirring and rain is on the horizon, you can sail out to the spot and look down through the water, and you'll see the glow of the captain's lantern moving along the decks and ladders while he urges his passengers toward the boats.*

Kim had read that in *True Equatorian Specters.* One version of the story had it that he was damned to continue the search until the last victim had been rescued.

Solly must have known what she was thinking. "There he is," he said, directing her attention toward a luminous jellyfish over the port quarter.

They swam down to the pilothouse and passed before the empty frames. There was nothing left inside. Even the wheel mount was missing. But it was easy to conjure up the voyagers that night, lounging about the decks, looking forward to a week at sea, suddenly aware of a threatening sky.

They emerged on the starboard side and moved aft. Kim used her wristlamp to illuminate the interior. The cabins were, of course, stark and empty.

Forty minutes later they surfaced, climbed aboard the sloop, and changed. Then they broke out dinner: turkey and salad and cold beer. It was beginning to get dark. The sky was cloudless, the sea a sheet of glass.

"This place is a good example of what stage management does," said

Solly. "It *feels* as if the supernatural can happen down there. The stories are pure fantasy, but when I'm near the wreck I'm not so sure. That's the way the Severin Woods will be."

"Different sets of rules," she agreed. "Take away the light, and were-wolves are possible." She touched a presspad and soft music came out of the speakers.

They sat in the cabin, the food spread out on a table. A couple of islands lay on the horizon. In the distance another sailboat was moving across their line of vision. Solly made a sandwich and took a bite. "Kim," he said when he'd gotten enough down that he could talk again, "do you believe ghosts are possible?"

She studied him, and decided he was quite serious. "Running into a real ghost would change everything we believe about the way the universe works."

"I'm not so sure about it," he said.

"Why?"

"I once served aboard the *Persepholis.* It had a haunted stateroom."

"Haunted how?"

"Strange noises. Voices no one could account for. Cold spots."

"You ever see any of this?"

He considered the question. "Yeah. I can remember walking past it on watch, hearing voices inside."

"Might have been the passengers."

"This was after they stopped using it for passengers, Kim. It became a storage area."

"Did you look inside?"

"First couple of times, yes. Didn't see anything. After that I just let it go."

"Not that I doubt you," she said, "but I'd have to see it for myself."

They ate quietly. Solly looked out toward the mainland, just visible in the east. "Plato believed in ghosts," he said.

"Plato?" Kim was skeptical.

"He thought ghosts came from drinking too much wine." He laughed at her reaction. "It's true. He says somewhere that when people get too attracted to their earthly lives, too many good times, too much sex, that when they die their souls get tangled up with the flesh and can't get free. He thinks that's why spirits hang around cemeteries. They're sort of pinned to their bodies."

Kim finished the sandwich, scooped up some cranberry sauce, and washed everything down with the beer. "You're really caught up on this Severin business, aren't you, Solly?"

He was refilling their glasses. "No. Not really. But when the sun goes down, it becomes a different kind of world."

"Hell of an attitude for a starship pilot."

He let her see how much he was enjoying the beer. "Maybe I've been out in the dark too many times," he said.

Alpha Maxim had erupted in an explosion that would be visible for a billion light-years. Of course, if a response had to come from that kind of distance nothing human would be here to receive it. The species would long since have evolved into something else.

The news accounts were filled with Beacon stories, including excerpts from religious and conservation figures, who'd entered into an unusual alliance, declaring the detonations either acts against God or against the environment.

Kim understood people's objection to blowing up suns, even suns with planetary systems which would never be home to anything except iron and methane. The worlds that had been engulfed yesterday had been orbiting Maxim for time out of mind, and it seemed indecent to disturb them.

She shook off the misapprehension and her thoughts drifted to Sheyel Tolliver. She'd been tempted to call him after she got back from the *Caledonian* dive, talk to him casually as though last night's conversation had not been at all unusual, to assure herself that he was okay, that he had taken no offense. But she decided it was better left alone.

She spent much of the following day in a conference with Matt Flexner, trying to draw up a strategy for squeezing additional funds from the central government. Elections were imminent and the Premier knew that either of his prospective opponents would turn money for the Institute into another example of government waste.

The problem, as Kim saw it, was to demonstrate why the Institute was valuable to the taxpayers, who tended to see it as a way to create jobs for overeducated people with nowhere to go. Kim hated to admit it, but she wasn't sure the taxpayers were altogether wrong. She did not, of course, share that opinion with Matt. Only Solly knew how she felt.

Matt Flexner had literally been around the Seabright Institute for a century. At thirty, he'd been one of its showpieces, a world-class physicist, doing breakthrough work in transdimensional structure. But the extension of life had underscored quite clearly what scientists had always known: that truly creative work must be done during the early years, or it will not be done at all. Genius fades quickly, like the rose in midsummer. And all the genetic enhancement known to science had not been able to change that melancholy reality.

Matt had adjusted, passed his work unfinished to younger hands, and gone into less demanding fields. Public relations, Kim thought sadly, recognizing that *her* genius had never got off the train. If Matt had come up short, at least he'd been in the game. People would remember him.

He still looked thirty, of course. He had a broad forehead and a whimsical smile and a long nose. His hair and beard were black, and he was an extraordinarily gifted tennis player.

Kim was his chief lieutenant.

She told him that she'd be gone for a couple of days. Her schedule was her own. Nobody cared how she came and went as long as she got the job done. And the immediate job was to persuade the members of the Germane Society that the Institute was a worthy recipient for donations.

It would, she thought, be rather nice if she could find a supernatural being in the Severin Woods. It would open a whole new field of scientific inquiry.

She went home early, slept for an hour, then made some hot chocolate and carried it into the living room. "Shep," she said, "see what you can find out about Markis Kane after 573."

"*Searching,*" he said.

The sky was gray and cold. A stiff wind beat against the house.

"*Not much here. He was an artist of some note.*"

"Artist? You sure it's the same guy?"

"*Oh yes. It's the same person. Apparently his work has a modest reputation.*"

"Okay. What else?"

"*He left Greenway in June 579, on a flight to Earth. Worked several years there in Canada as a consultant for flight-deck design. Retired from that in 591. Moved to Old Wisconsin. Died in 596.*"

"He never served as a ship's captain again? After the *Hunter* mission?"

"*Not that I can find.*"

It *was* odd. Three people disappear. And the fourth gives up his career.

Nothing remained of Severin Village except a few buildings jutting out of the lake that had formed when they took down the dam. The lake itself, appropriately named Remorse, was quite large, more than twenty kilometers across at its widest point, and lined with forest. In some places there were piles of uprooted trees.

"Shepard," she said, "take me there."

The living room dissolved to lakeshore.

"Weather conditions?"

"Springlike. April. Maybe throw in a shower."

Kim's chair was at the water's edge. The wind rose and a small boat with two fishermen was making for land. A sheet of rain was moving across the lake, coming her way. Near shore, brick walls and chimneys broke the surface.

She sat for a long time at the water's edge. Since she was not dressed for stimulation, the storm would have no effect on her and the illusion would be ruined. So Shepard kept the rain out to the north.

There were no artificial lights anywhere, save for a lantern in the fishing boat. "Nearest town, Shep?" she asked.

"Eagle Point. Population about seventeen thousand. Approximate distance thirty-three kilometers."

Eagle Point. They had some of Kane's sketches there, at the Gould Art Gallery.

She hesitated. Then: "Shep, let me talk to Emily."

The AI's electronics murmured. *"Kim, are you sure?"* It had been years.

"Do it, Shep."

Lights brightened and dimmed again. Kim was still on the beach at Remorse. But she was no longer alone.

"Hello, Kimberly." Emily wore the same leisure outfit, loose white top and baggy pants, that Kim was wearing. Both were barefoot. It had never been quite like this before when Kim had called up her lost sister. Then she'd been an adolescent talking with a grown woman. Now they were on equal terms.

"Hello, Emily. It's good to see you again." The years had not assuaged the grief of loss. Maybe it had to do with the fact that there'd never been a body. Kim had never really given up hope that her sister, *her other self,* would come back.

"You see me in every mirror. How've you been doing?"

"Pretty good. I'm working at the Seabright Institute."

"Wonderful. What do you do?"

"Public relations. Fund-raising."

"I beg your pardon?"

"It's not exactly what I wanted. But I'm good at it. And the pay's not bad."

"I'm glad to hear it." She lowered herself onto a log. *"I'm surprised to be here. Has something happened?"*

"No. Yes. Do you remember Yoshi Amara?"

"Of course. She was the fourth crewmember on the last flight."

"An old teacher of mine called me. It turns out he was related to Yoshi."

"Really? What did he want?"

"He wants me to look into her disappearance."

"Oh."

"What happened to you, Emily? Where on earth did you go that night?"

"I wish I knew. I really do." She used her heel to draw a line through the sand. *"What does he think you can do that hasn't already been done?"*

"You know the stories about Mount Hope."

"I know that Markis would never try to steal a fuel cell. Or at least I know that if he did, he'd succeed and wouldn't blow everybody up."

Kim leaned forward in her chair. She would have liked to embrace Emily, to hold onto her, to prevent her inevitable retreat into the shades. "Sheyel says there's something strange about the valley. He's implying you brought something back with you. And it got loose."

She sighed. *"What can I say to that? Your former teacher shouldn't be allowed out by himself."*

Kim looked past her, out onto the lake. "Emily, did you ever have any reason to distrust either of them? Kane or Tripley?"

"No," she said. *"Kile was a little erratic. But I'd have trusted him with my life. In a heartbeat."*

"And Kane?"

"Markis was a man you meet once in a lifetime. I hope one day you're as fortunate, Kim."

"How about Yoshi?"

"Yoshi. I can't really answer that because I barely knew her prior to the last mission. She seemed okay. A little shallow. But she was very young."

They had talked about the disappearance before, years ago. And it was unlikely that Shep could have fed her fresh information. Yet framing questions for Emily helped her think.

"I've agreed to go up to the Severin Valley with Solly."

"Why?"

"To look for whatever you brought back from wherever you were."

"Well, I hope Solly's good company. Because other than that, you'll be in for a long trip." She tilted her head. *"It's cool out here."*

Kim felt only the warmth of the living room. "I miss you, Emily. I wish you'd come back."

"I know—I'm sorry. I wish there were a way to do it all again. And have it come out differently."

3

When I, sitting, heard the astronomer, where he lectured
        with such applause in the lecture room,
How soon, unaccountable, I became tired and sick;
Till rising and gliding out, I wander'd off by myself,
In the mystical moist night-air, and from time to time,
Look'd up in perfect silence at the stars.
                                        —WALT WHITMAN, *Leaves of Grass,* 1865, C.E.

The Germane Society held its monthly luncheon on the first Saturday of the month, at the Pioneer Hotel in downtown Seabright. They sponsored exceptional students for extended education grants, provided emotional support for those who had begun their final decline, and underwrote the Midwinter Carnival. They also tried, each month, to reward someone for outstanding service.

On the day that Kim attended, the award was presented to a nineteen-year-old woman who'd rescued her mountain climber buddy from falling to his death. Watching the presentation, Kim was impressed by the woman's exploit, which had required her to hold on to him for almost ten minutes while he dangled from the lip of a deep gorge.

The thought of cliff-hanging heroics chilled Kim, who doubted she could imitate the feat. Still, the young woman was nervous in front of the audience. She hung her head and mumbled her acceptance, and Kim took a degree of perverse satisfaction in that. *We all have our demons.*

They read the minutes from the last meeting, took some motions, heard the results of the annual midwinter tree sale. And then it was her turn.

The emcee read her bio from the printed card she'd given him. It identified her as an astrophysicist with a specialty in galactic evolution. During the business portion of the luncheon someone had argued that they needed to think *big* about a proposal to expand membership, and the emcee couldn't resist inserting a lame joke that someone who thought about galaxy construction was just the person they needed. She rose to polite applause.

They were a good audience. She had an advantage at these affairs because everybody expected to be bored silly by an astrophysicist. She'd learned long ago that the correct way to begin with a group was to violate the old adage about starting with a gag. Her aim was to win them over and she always did that by recognizing the work performed by her listeners and glamorizing it where she could. When she spoke to librarians she described them as the guardians of civilization. Teachers were the first line of defense. For service groups, like the Germane Society, she offered a similar tack.

She started by congratulating the young mountain climber on her courage. "People these days are inclined to tell us we're all going downhill," she said. "But I have to tell you, as long as we have people like Amy here, we'll be all right." The woman blushed prettily. "If I could be certain that, in a hundred years, the Germane Society will still be here, still recognizing the heroes among us, and still providing help where needed, then I'd have no qualms about the future of the Republic."

Now of course she had them.

She compared their goals with those of the Institute, stretching the facts a little, because the Institute didn't go out of its way to help anybody, not directly at least. But that was okay. People did profit in the long run from scientific advance. And if the forward movement was slower than it used to be, that was all right too. Her listeners were concerned about where the nation was going. They were interested in the Beacon Project, and anxious to show they weren't among those who thought stars were sacred.

"If eventually," she concluded, "the program gets a response, and someone shows up to see what we're really like, I believe I'd try to bring them over here to sit down with you folks and have lunch. I know that would get everything off to a good start. Thank you very much." She stepped away from the lectern as her audience broke into enthusiastic applause, and sat down. Overall time consumed was roughly thirteen minutes.

Solly, waiting just outside the entrance to the dining room, had caught most of it. "You have no shame at all," he said, when they were alone.

She grinned. "To be honest, if I could arrange to have our first visitors eat with the Germane Society, instead of with the Council, I'd do it in a minute."

Solly had rented a lime-colored, twin-mag Starlight for the flight to the Severin Valley. They went up to the roof and climbed in.

"I expected to go by train," she said.

"We always take trains," he replied. "I thought it would be nice to fly for a change."

"Okay. How about we make for Eagle Point? Get settled in there first."

He turned on the magnetics and they lifted off the pad and headed west.

Kim had spent much of the previous evening researching Severin legends and folklore. There were indeed tales of apparitions, of strange lights, of voices in the forest. There had been for years, long before the Mount Hope incident. But there did seem to have been an acceleration, although much of that might be attributed to efforts by residents of nearby Eagle Point to drum up the tourist trade.

Severin's prime claim to fame, at the time of the incident, was that it had been the home of Markis Kane. Artist. War hero. Starship captain. The lone survivor of the *Hunter*.

And fan of Eve Colon's classic detective, Veronica King. Kane had served a term as president of the Scarlet Sleeve Society, a group dedicated to the sleuth and named for one of her more celebrated exploits.

During Greenway's war with Pacifica, the sole interworld conflict in history, he'd been captain of the famed *376*, and was probably best known for the attack on the *Hammurabi*, the only capital ship ever put out of action by a single escort vessel.

When peace came, Kane left the fleet and spent half a century piloting vessels around the Nine Worlds and their outposts. He compiled an exemplary record, engendered no complaint by any employer, no problem of any kind. His crews were unfailingly loyal, and no one seemed to have a bad word to say about him.

Kim used the Starlight's AI to bring up photos: Kane at flight school on Earth's moon, Kane as a young lieutenant in Greenway's self-defense force, Kane running a tug, Kane in full-dress uniform. She found six wedding pictures, and six brides; a certificate of appreciation from the Severin Valley Art Society; a graduation picture, Kane at eighteen, wearing a smirk that bordered on the mischievous. She found several commendations, Kane retaining control of a cargo ship after its main engines had started an explosive decompression, Kane rescuing a lost child during a Severin flood, Kane talking a suicide down from a window.

He favored decorated shirts and loose trousers tucked into ankle boots. And flashy tunics and wide sashes. In later pictures, after his time with the Tripley Foundation, he'd grown a black beard and let his hair grow to shoulder length. Something about the man in those later years had darkened, intensified. The older Markis Kane gazed out of his photos with equal parts disdain and resignation.

And there was Kane the artist. His posted work consisted primarily of portraits, landscapes, and a few experimental paintings. Most of the portraits were of women. One, dated 575, two years after the *Hunter*, shocked her.

"That's *you*," said Solly.

"My God." It was Emily.

"He was using your sister for a model?"

She looked at the date again. "More or less. He must have used a virtual. This was done two years after she disappeared."

Emily was posed near a window through which one could see a late summer forest, heaped leaves, and, rising over the trees, a ringed world. Her jacket was draped carelessly over her shoulders, leaving one breast exposed, yet there was no hint of erotic intent. Indeed Emily was simultaneously lovely and forlorn. The work was titled *Autumn*.

"You're a little out in the open there," Solly said.

Autumn, as well as several other pieces, was housed in a gallery at Eagle Point. It might be worth taking a look at them. "Why was he still using Emily?" she wondered.

Solly's face was green in the glow of the instrument panel. "I wouldn't expect him to do that unless—"

"What?"

"I'd guess he was in love with her."

"Or she was still alive."

"Or both," he said. "It's a possibility."

A story dated 576, three years after the disaster, described how Kane had paid his debts, closed out his accounts, said goodbye to his few friends, and watched the waters of the Severin close over his villa. That was when they took down the dam. He moved to Terminal City.

The flyer crossed the Takonda River, which more or less marked the middle of Equatoria. They ran into a rain storm at about the same time, and the afternoon turned cold. Solly was in a talkative mood, going on about Mount Hope, and how he hoped there would really turn out to be something there. She had mixed feelings, would have liked to solve the old mystery, would have done anything to find out what had happened to Emily. But on the other hand she knew she didn't want to run into whatever had unnerved Sheyel.

They flew into the twilight. The countryside became progressively rougher. Mountains rose around them. The storm got worse and high winds began to buffet the aircraft. Solly went higher until they could look down on the turbulence.

Eventually the landscape opened out into cultivated areas and farm buildings, silos and lakes. They watched a train moving smoothly across the treetops through the approaching twilight. Then woodland again, broken by a lone house or, enigmatically, a tennis court or swimming pool. There were no roads, of course.

Over 75 percent of Greenway's population was concentrated in its towns, which were scattered across her thousands of islands, or buried in Equatorian forests. The half-dozen or so major cities of the Republic were now the province of those who pursued active careers, or those who were looking for mates. The rest of the world was satisfied to live near trees and cardinals, watch the train come in once a day, and spend their afternoons fishing.

Eagle Point was by local standards a small metropolis. It straddled both banks of the Severin, thirty-three kilometers north of Mount Hope. Its two sections were connected by a pair of exquisitely designed bridges, which, according to the townspeople, visitors came to see from all over Greenway. Eagle Point also featured skiing on several world-class slopes, natural hot springs, a magnificent walkway seven hundred meters over Dead Man's Gorge, seven major casinos, and the Cartoonists' Hall of Fame.

They arrived in the gathering twilight, landed atop the Gateway Inn, checked in, and got directions to the Gould Art Gallery, which was located at ground level a block from the hotel. A man in a heavy black sweater was just finishing with a customer when they arrived. Although he bore no physical indication of advancing age, he moved with a deliberation that suggested he was well along in his second century. "Are you Mr. Gould?" Kim asked.

The man brightened and bowed slightly. "Yes," he said. "Please call me Jorge. Would you like something hot to drink?"

They accepted some cider and Kim introduced herself and Solly. Gould had a print of Lisa Barton's *Evening on Lyra* on display. It was an example of the empyrean school, those works which embodied off-world themes to achieve their effects. The Barton was a self-portrait, depicting the artist in an armchair on a clearly hostile moonscape, contemplating a globular cluster floating over a nearby ridge. Kim had read that the globular cluster in the painting was the one in Serpens, twenty-seven thousand light-years away, vastly outside the human bubble. The painting radiated nobility, solitude, and grandeur, of both the nebula and the woman.

The proprietor noted her interest. "There are only one hundred prints," he said. "Signed by the artist herself. I can let you have this one at a very reasonable price."

"Thank you, no," she said. "But I *am* interested in Markis Kane. You have his *Autumn*, I understand?"

"Oh yes. One of his best." He gazed at Kim, frowned, and sucked in his breath. "That's remarkable," he whispered. "Is it really *you*?" His voice trembled.

Kim had never seen the man before and she was momentarily at a loss to understand his reaction. "Emily," he said. Solly moved closer to her.

The model for *Autumn*.

Kim smiled. "No," she said. "It's not me."

Gould stood back to get a better view. He pressed his lips together and nodded. "Yes," he said. "I'd thought the model had died. Before he did the painting." He shook his head. "Nevertheless, you are a close match. Are you connected in some way?"

"I'm her sister."

He pulled his sweater tightly around him, as if to protect from a sudden chill. "I'm sorry. It *was* thoughtless of me."

"It's quite all right, Mr. Gould. It's been a long time."

"Yes. Of course." He studied her. "You're as lovely as she."

"Thank you. You're very kind."

He paused and collected himself. "As I say, I *do* have the *Autumn*. But it's not for sale."

Solly glanced at her. *He expects to hit us pretty hard.*

"It's for display only," the proprietor continued. "It's really quite valuable."

"May we see it?" asked Kim.

"Of course." He still did not move, still gazed at Kim's features.

She wanted to break the paralysis. "Tell me about Markis Kane," she said.

"We have five originals by him. Other than the *Autumn*. One of them, *Glory*, also uses Emily as the model." He led the way through a door at the rear of the building and turned on the lights. *Autumn* was set in an exquisite, hand-carved wooden frame, mounted on an easel. More lights blinked on, designed to show the work to maximum effect.

Kim studied it. The woman in the window. The line of frost. The leaf-covered lawn. The ringed world just touching the tops of the trees. The planet was setting. There was no conscious way to make that determination, but she knew it to be true. A couple of crescent moons that she didn't recall from the online image drifted through the gathering night.

Autumn radiated *loss*. The trees writhed in a dark wind, the giant planet was painted in October colors, and even its rings suggested dissolution.

Emily looked both beautiful and melancholy.

"He's pretty good," Solly commented, "for a pilot."

"He's one of the best we've had," said Gould. "The world is just beginning to recognize it."

Glory was named for the largest of Greenway's satellites. Emily was posed dreamily against a track of moonlit water. Shoulders bare, one hand laid along her cheek, eyes luminous and thoughtful. It was dated three years *before* the flight.

Tora was a portrait of Kane's daughter at about ten. In *River Voyage*, a handful of rafters try to hang on in rock-strewn white water. *Night Passage* depicted an interstellar liner passing a cobalt-blue gas giant.

Kim asked for the dates. All four preceded the *Hunter* incident. "Is it my imagination," she asked Gould, "or is there a change in tone between his earlier and later work?"

"Oh," he said, "there very certainly is." He touched a keyboard. A screen lit up and they were looking at *Bringing the Mail*, a painting of a freighter crossing a nebula. The freighter was squat and gray, bleak, its running lights casting eerie shadows across the superstructure. The nebula silhouetted the starship, emitting a twilight glow. "This is his last known work."

"Everything after Mount Hope seems kind of downbeat," said Solly.

"Oh yes. Beginning with this one." He brought up a landscape. "His work entered a dark period from which it never really emerged. This is *Storm Warning*, from 574." They were looking at distorted trees, ruins in the distance silhouetted against summer lightning, churning clouds. "When he becomes recognized as a major figure, people will recognize this as the first major work of his gothic phase."

"Did you know him?" asked Kim. "Personally?"

"I knew him quite well. When he lived in the area."

"Do you have a print of this one? Of *Storm Warning*?"

Gould consulted a catalog. "Yes," he said. "I have two left. But they're not signed."

"It's okay," said Kim, grateful that the price would be diminished by that much. "How much is it?"

"Two hundred."

"Not cheap," said Solly.

"I'll take it," said Kim.

"It's a limited edition," Gould purred soothingly. "You can be sure it'll hold its value." He excused himself and disappeared up a narrow staircase.

"That costs an arm and a leg," Solly complained.

"I know. But we want to keep him talking to us. We *should* buy something."

He indicated a dancing nude.

"Right," she said.

Gould returned with her print and held it up for her to see. "This is quite lovely," he said. "You'll find it's an excellent investment. Would you like me to have it framed for you?"

"No, thank you," she said. "I'll take it as is." She was wondering where she'd put it and began to wish she'd gone for something out of Kane's early years. They made appreciative sounds over the print for a minute, and then Gould rolled it up and put it into a tube.

"Did he become depressed after the Mount Hope event?" asked Solly casually.

Gould pressed his fingertips against his temples as if the memory were painful. "Oh yes. He was never the same after that."

"In what way?"

"It's hard to explain. He'd always been friendly, outgoing, easy to talk to. Well, maybe that's an exaggeration. But he wasn't a difficult man, in the way that talents frequently are. But all that went away. He became exceedingly withdrawn. About that time, I was going to Severin Village most nights. My wife lived there then. We weren't married yet, you understand. And I used to make it a point to go by his place, Kane's place, to see how he was doing. He wasn't known then the way he is now. But I knew, I *always* knew, he was going to be great one day.

"He sold his work through me. He wasn't getting much for it in those days, nothing like what it would command now. But he didn't need the money. The paintings were just something he did. You know what I mean?"

She nodded.

"Did I tell you I was there when it happened? When the mountain blew up?

"It was terrible. The town was kind of down low and sheltered so it didn't get hit directly or we'd've all been dead. But pieces of rock and whole trees fell out of the sky. We didn't know what hit us. Then there was the dust. People choking and dying—" His eyes had gone distant. "Sasha and I did what we could, but—" He held out his hands. "But you don't want to hear this."

Kim and Solly stood quietly, waiting.

"By then I was trying to hold onto his work. Buying his paintings myself because I knew they were undervalued. I brought them back here and just waited for the price to go up. Now they're worth thirty, forty times what they were. And it's still a seller's market." He turned back toward the *Autumn*. "Look at that; you ever see *anyone* with that kind of range? Maybe Crabbe. Maybe Hoskin. No, *not* Hoskin." He shook his head vehemently, dismissing Hoskin.

"Did you by any chance know Kile Tripley?" asked Kim.

"Tripley? No. Tripley lived in a villa well away from everybody else. He was above spending time with the common people."

"Would you say he and Kane were friends?"

"Not particularly. No."

"He was Kane's employer," said Kim.

"That's not the same thing as being a friend."

Kim was having a hard time keeping her eyes off the *Autumn*. "One more thing, Mr. Gould," she said. "I'm interested in what caused his dark period. Did you sense there was anything other than the explosion that might have influenced his later work? A lost woman, perhaps?"

"I know he was affected by what happened to *her*." He looked meaningfully at Emily's image.

"Did he *say* that?"

"You can see it in his work. But he never outright said it, no."

"Anything else?"

"Not other than what I've told you. He just more or less went into a shell. Rattled around inside that big house. Sealed off the den, even."

"Sealed off the den? How do you mean?"

"It had been, I'd stop by, we'd go into the den, have a few drinks. He'd tell me about his latest project. The living room was a formal, stiff place where he didn't like to go. Then suddenly we were always in the living room and I never saw the den again. I don't suppose it meant anything, but it was strange. As if he were hiding a woman in there."

They had dinner at a place called The Rucksack. Snow was beginning to fall and a crisp wind had blown up. Solly plowed steadily through the meat and greens. "As soon as we're finished here," he said, "I think we ought to get going."

"Yeah. Before the weather gets any *worse*." The predictions called for the snow to stop around midnight, and for colder temperatures to set in.

"I'm surprised at your choice of artwork," said Solly.

"Why? It's quite attractive."

"I'd have thought you'd have wanted one with Emily. The *Autumn*. You seemed taken by that."

She lifted a wine glass and watched it sparkle in the light from the fireplace. "I don't think so," she said. "I wanted something I could hang on the wall."

Solly looked at her. "Is it still that painful?"

She shrugged. "That. And the nudity."

"I didn't think you were a prude."

"I am," she said, "when the model looks too much like me."

Solly had been a friend for a long time. Kim felt especially drawn to him that night, perhaps because he'd come with her even though, despite what he said, he thought she was pursuing an illusion. Well, they *both* thought that.

That night, standing beside him on the walkway overlooking Eagle Point, with the snow blowing and the Severin Woods just downriver a few kilometers, she nearly suggested that they spend the night together. Forget the ghost. But when Solly mentioned that it was late and they should get going, she put the thought aside, and fastened her jacket.

4

. . . The most famous of the apparitions is undoubtedly the Severin Phantom, which haunts the ruined village whose name it bears. There have been more than two hundred confirmed sightings over the last quarter century. Several deaths have been attributed to it. Today, few persons are foolish enough to venture into the valley after dark.
—TERI KAPER, *Legends of the Northwest*, 597

It was after eleven-thirty when they lifted off the Gateway's roof and turned south.

Snow was falling steadily. The lights of the casinos and clubs were smeared by the storm, and they faded quickly as the Starlight gained altitude. The screen showed almost no air traffic.

"Do you feel as dumb as I do?" she asked Solly.

He was relaxed, sipping coffee, letting the AI fly the aircraft. "It was an excuse to come," he said. "Think how warm your bed'll feel tonight when you get to it."

The sensors picked out the river, running between wide, forest-laden banks. She looked out into the snowswept darkness and saw another set of lights coming from the west. Probably a train, although it was difficult to be sure.

She took out the town map she'd printed earlier and studied it. "When we get to Severin," she said, "I think we should do more than just land and hang around for a bit."

"In this blizzard? What did you have in mind, Kim?"

"Take advantage of the opportunity to look at Tripley's villa."

"Why?" asked Solly.

"Who knows what we might find?"

"After twenty-seven years?"

"Nothing to lose by looking."

"Okay," he said. "Whatever you say. But if there's anything there to connect him with the explosion or the missing women, I'd think the police would have found it a long time ago."

"As far as I can tell from the accounts, the police never looked."

"They didn't? Why not?"

"Nobody raised the question. My guess is that there was no substantive reason to think Tripley had anything to do with either incident, and the family had a lot of influence. There was already enough grief. He was presumed lost in the general disaster. What was to be gained by an investigation? Under the circumstances, maybe nobody wanted to irritate the family."

"Okay," Solly said. "If you want. Do we know where to find it?"

"As it happens," she grinned, "I have it marked here." She tapped her pen on the map.

"Why stop with Tripley? Why not take a look at Kane's place while we're at it?"

The Starlight was picking up a heavy headwind. "Kane's place is underwater." She showed him.

"I wasn't serious," he said.

"When are you? Serious?"

"Never on ghost hunts." It was cold in the cabin. Solly pulled his jacket tighter, and she raised the temperature.

"If I'd known we were going on an expedition," he said, "I'd have suggested doing it by daylight."

Kim was thinking of what she'd say to Sheyel. We went out to the valley. We spent time in the woods. And we even looked in Tripley's house. There's *nothing*.

But she wanted to get it done now. Didn't want to make a second trip in the morning.

Another aircraft, a patrol flyer, appeared on the edge of the short-range scan, headed in the opposite direction. It passed within two hundred meters, but they never did actually *see* it.

Eagle Point had receded into the darkness, and there were now no lights visible anywhere. The AI followed the Severin River south, displaying its winding image on the sensor screen. It narrowed and entered the first of a series of gorges which would take it down to the dam.

Her preoccupation with the legends increased as they flew deeper into the night. Even Solly seemed affected. They spoke with lowered voices, the way people do in empty churches, and Kim found herself sinking down inside her jacket even though the temperature in the cabin had now reached a comfortable level. The conversation consisted mostly of bravado. Remarks like how no self-respecting spook would be abroad in weather like this. Or how Solly thought he saw something moving out there. Ha-ha.

Solly's story of the haunted stateroom came back to trouble her now. At the moment, in the snow, in the glow of the instrument panel, such things seemed possible.

They were only a few hundred meters off the ground when they broke out of the storm. The remains of the Severin Dam loomed just ahead.

The structure had not actually been removed. Weakened sections had been taken down and the rest simply left standing. Now, the river roared around piles of rubble and concrete slabs. The slabs seemed to be moving, an effect created by the flyer's lights reflected off the water. The aircraft dropped lower and a last few flakes whirled up.

They passed over the ruins. On the south side, the river ran through a narrow corridor and emptied into Lake Remorse. The sky was still heavily overcast and the lake remained shrouded until they were out over it.

Solly directed the AI to turn on the aircraft's spotlights. It complied, and twin beams swept the darkness, but they could see nothing other than water.

"It's almost an inland sea," said Kim, recalling that at its widest it was more than twenty kilometers across.

They rode through the night, beneath heavy skies, not saying much. Eventually a coastline appeared onscreen. Forest, mostly. Some hills, some open spaces. And then she saw a few stone walls and broken houses jutting out of the shallows.

The village had occupied the south shore of the original lake, then also called Severin. But after the dam had been taken down, the lake had expanded, swallowing most of the town.

Kim looked down at a world covered by snow.

"I'm surprised no one's claimed the area," said Solly. "It wouldn't take much to rebuild here now."

They circled, trying to locate Tripley's villa. The map placed it atop a low rise just outside the town line, about a hundred meters north of the

Scott Randal Stables, which had been a well-known producer of race-horses at the time of the event. They found the stables, now just a few crumbling buildings and a couple of fences. The rest was easy.

"Problem is," said Solly, "there's no open ground here anywhere."

"There." A strip of beach.

Solly looked at it reluctantly. "It'll be a long walk," he said. But it was all they had, and the AI took them down.

They settled into the snow. Kim pulled her hood up and adjusted the foul-weather mask while Solly changed into boots. The lake surface was rough in the lights, and when she opened the door the wind tried to tear it out of her hand.

They couldn't see much of the village, just one or two houses in the water. An old lifeguard tower stood near the tree line. And a white building stenciled SNACK SHED was sinking into the sand. "This is Cabry's Beach," said Kim, reading the name off the map.

Solly climbed down and looked around. The wind blew his hair into his eyes.

"Didn't you bring anything to wear on your head?" she asked.

"No," he said. "I didn't know we were going for a walk."

"You'll freeze." She looked into the backseat. "I've got a mountain hat back here somewhere."

"It's okay, Kim. I'll be fine."

She found it and held it out for him. But he looked stubbornly back at her. She shrugged and switched on her wristlamp. "Maybe you should wait here."

"Let's go," he grumbled, pulling up his jacket collar and stuffing his hands into his pockets.

She turned up the heat in her jacket, and they started for the trees. Their boots crunched in the snow. The wind blew in steadily off the lake and they walked with their backs to it. Neither tried to talk until they'd made it to the shelter of the forest.

"You okay?" he asked when they were in the trees. His hair was already covered with blown snow.

"I'm fine." It was a deep hood and she felt as if she were looking out of a tunnel.

He pointed the way and took the lead. Overhead, something shook snow out of the branches.

Kim looked up, and wondered about the wildlife. "Solly," she whispered, "are there, do you suppose, any animals here we need to worry about? Cougars, maybe? Or bears?" The terraformers in their wisdom had neglected nothing. Greenway even had mosquitoes.

"I never thought of it. I don't know."

"Are you by any chance carrying a weapon?"

"No," he said. "If we run into something, we'll beat it off with a stick."

"Good," she grinned. "Nothing like being prepared."

They pushed through thick brambles and shrubbery, crossed glades, and eventually found a trail that seemed to be going in their direction.

They passed a collapsed house, entangled in new-growth trees, almost invisible until they were within a couple of meters. And a bench, incongruously set off to one side of the trail. "This was probably the way to the beach at one time," Solly said.

She looked at her map. "Yes. Here it is."

"How're we doing?"

"Headed in the right direction. It's not much farther."

"You don't think we ought to come back and do this in the morning?"

"We're here now, Solly. Let's just take a quick look, so I can say I've been here, and then we can head out."

After Tripley's disappearance, the villa and its furnishings had been willed to Sara Baines, his mother. According to the reports, Sara had closed up the house, but had been unable to sell it. The town was emptying out; people had too many bad memories, there were doubts whether the rest of the mountain might come down, the dam could go at any time.

So nobody had really lived in the house since Tripley came back from that last flight.

They left the trail at a glade with a tumbled shed, clumped through a stream, skidded down a slope, and got confused about directions because nobody had thought to bring a compass. "Don't blame me," said Solly. "I thought we were going to sit in the flyer and look at the lake."

Kim was now in the lead. The trees closed in again. In some places the snow was too deep for her hiking shoes. It got down her ankles, and her feet got cold.

It was hard to keep a sense of direction. On one occasion they came out in a swampy area along the lake shore. They turned back, retraced their steps for about a hundred paces, and struck off in a new direction. Kim had never been a hiking enthusiast, and she was beginning to have second thoughts when the ground started to rise.

"This might be it," she said. "The place was on the brow of a low hill." It was a slippery climb. They took turns falling down and suddenly they were tumbling in the snow and Solly, who probably would have preferred to look irritable, couldn't resist laughing.

But they got to the summit, and there it stood!

Whatever lawn might have once existed behind a peeling wooden fence had been swallowed by bushes, weeds, and shrubbery. The villa itself lay in a tangle of spruce and oak trees. Vines had grown over it and the wind had taken the roof off. The front door was missing.

She played her lantern across it and compared it with pictures she'd brought. "Yes," she said. "This is it. No question."

They circled around to the rear. A side wall had collapsed. Windows were broken, frames shattered. An oak was threatening to push over the east wing.

It was made mostly of brick. Two stories, glass dome, oval windows, rotunda, turret. None of that cheap mass-produced stuff for Kile Tripley. Kim stood in the snow, transfixed by the ruin.

"What are you thinking?"

"About transience, I guess. I was wondering if Emily was ever here."

Followed by Solly, she stepped over the threshold into the rotunda. It was good to get out of the wind. She flashed her beam around the interior, which the elements had destroyed. Overhead, two stories up, the dome was covered with dirt and vegetation. During Tripley's time it would have revealed the stars.

The walls were mottled and crumbling. A sagging staircase arced up to the second floor where it became a circular balcony. There were several doorways on both levels, and a fireplace on the lower.

One door hung out of its frame. Others were missing altogether. A central corridor opened off the rear of the rotunda directly in front of her and ran to the back of the house. Solly pointed his lamp into it, and they saw at the far end a flight of stairs leading down.

The floor creaked. "Careful where you put your weight," he said.

Everything was covered with leaves and dirt. The ground-level rooms looked empty. Kim swung her lamp beam up, trying to see through the second-floor doorways. Shadows moved around the walls.

"I don't think we'll find much here," Solly said.

Claws scrabbled across a hard surface. An animal retreated from the light, but she couldn't see what it was.

"Probably a squirrel," said Solly.

"Or a rat."

The wind howled around the house. Branches creaked.

Had she been alone, she would have called it off at that point and gone back to the flyer. She had met, and exceeded, her obligation to Sheyel. To Emily.

But they'd come all this way and Solly would expect her at least to look in the rooms.

Stairs first. Go up and confront the rat. Solly took the lead, testing each step as they went. The entire structure swayed and sank under their weight. Near the top a board gave way underfoot. He lost his balance and grabbed the banister, which sagged outward. Solly would have gone down the quick way had Kim not grabbed him and hauled him back. She took a moment to compare herself favorably with the young woman at the Germane Society.

"This might not be a really good idea," he said, shaken. They went cautiously the rest of the way to the top and peeked quickly through each doorway. In some, ceilings had given way. The rooms were filled with dirt and dry leaves. Carpets had turned to mold.

They found a broken bed frame and a bureau with no drawers, a smashed table, a couple of chairs. The *smell* of the place was strong.

Pipes stuck out from broken walls. Basins, tubs, and showers were filled with the detritus of decades.

They went back downstairs.

The rooms at ground level were not quite so ill-used because they were slightly less open to the elements. But here again no usable furniture was left. Cables hung out of ceilings, the floors were in a state of decay, and they found a dead, half-eaten squirrel in a corner behind a collapsed table whose top, when she cleared it off, had a chessboard design. Kim had read somewhere that Kane enjoyed the game and wondered whether he and Tripley had ever played here. And if so, who had won.

She crossed to the kitchen and dining areas, found a broken chair and shattered pottery. Weeds pushed up through the floor.

Solly was standing in the middle of the rotunda, idly shining his lamp around, bored, shivering, ready to go.

Kim walked back to the down-stairway at the rear of the house. "Let's take a quick look," she said, testing the handrail.

"Careful," he cautioned.

The stairs sank under her weight. "Maybe *you* should stay here," she said. "I'm not sure it'll support you."

He thought about it, looked at the stairway, pushed at the rail and watched the structure sway. Then he pointed his light down into the room below. It looked harmless enough, with a long table, a couple of chairs, and several trash bags stacked against a wall.

"I think we ought to just pass," he said.

"Only take a minute." She went down, testing each step, and was glad to get off at the bottom. The basement was less cold and damp than the rest of the house.

There were three rooms and a bath. She found a broken sofa decaying in one, and some carpets stacked up in another.

The table had data feeds, housings, and connections for electronic equipment. A mount hung from the ceiling. Probably for a VR unit.

"See anything?" asked Solly. The beam from his lamp illuminated the stairway.

"It was a workroom or lab at one time. I'll be up in a minute."

The walls were cedar-paneled, and they'd held up fairly well. The floor was artificial brick. There were magnets where pictures or plaques had once hung.

"Well," she said, "*that's* interesting."

"What is?" called Solly.

The stairway started to swing. "Don't try to come down," she said. "It's a trash can." With the imprint EIV 4471886. She checked her notes: It was *Hunter's* designator.

It was half-filled with metal parts and crumpled paper and rags. There were expended cartridges of compressed air and cleaning fluid canisters and an empty wine bottle. She found food wrappers and packing for computer disks and reams of printed pages.

They consisted of lists of names, possibly donors for the Foundation; financial statements; purchase records; test results for various engine configurations; and all kinds of other data whose purpose she couldn't make out. But all had dates, and the most recent she could find was January 8, 573. Before Tripley had left on the last *Hunter* voyage.

Several of the trash bags had been ripped open, probably by animals. She turned them over one by one and spilled their contents, finding corroded cables and hardened towels and dust cloths and battered monitor housings and interfaces and juice cartons.

Someone more thorough than she was might have been willing to take the time to go methodically through the trash. Who knew what might be there? But it was getting colder. And it seemed pointless.

The wind moved through the house like something alive. There were noises in the walls and tree limbs brushed windows upstairs. She turned the beam around the room, watching the darkness retreat and close in again.

"I don't think there's anything here," she told Solly. "I'll be up in a minute." She hoisted herself onto the table, took off her shoes and socks, and rubbed her feet, which had lost all feeling. When she got the circulation going she turned the socks inside out. It didn't help much because they were stiff and cold, but it was something.

When she was finished she dropped back onto the floor. Amid the debris, she saw a woman's shoe. It was impossible to know what color it had originally been, but it had a curious kind of fibrous sole, unlike any she'd seen before.

What was it?

She put it into her utility bag.

"Kim." Solly's voice betrayed impatience. "Are we ready yet?"

"Coming up," she said.

He provided light, angling his lamp so it wouldn't be in her eyes, told her to be careful, and appeared to be holding his breath, waiting for the staircase to collapse. She was about halfway up when a support broke and the whole structure dropped a few centimeters. She grabbed for the rail. He leaned forward as if to come to her aid but instantly thought better of adding his weight to hers. In that moment her own lamp silhouetted him, and she saw something draw back into the darkness.

She froze, the swaying staircase forgotten.

"Take your time," said Solly.

She was *sure* she had seen it.

A piece of the darkness that infested the house. A piece that had broken off and withdrawn.

When she got to the top she swung her beam around the kitchen, looked into the doorways, and stepped out into the middle of the rotunda to survey the upper level.

"What's wrong?" asked Solly.

There were shadows everywhere. "Nothing," she said.

He knew better, but he didn't pursue the issue, other than to follow her eyes. "I don't guess you found anything?"

She held out the shoe. "Ever see one like this?"

He played his light over it. "Sure," he said. "It's a grip shoe."

"A *what*?"

"A *grip shoe.*" He took it from her and pushed it against a wall. It stuck momentarily, and then fell. "Well," he said, "it's kind of beat up, but they're used on starships in zero-gravity situations."

"—Used on starships." She held it against her own foot. Too small. It couldn't have been Emily's.

"What are you thinking, Kim?"

"Just wondering who it belonged to."

The wind had died down and some of the clouds had blown off. Out over the lake, one of the moons had broken through.

They retraced their steps back down the hill and into the trees. They found the place where they'd doubled back and turned away from the river. Their prints were still deep and clean and they followed them back toward the flyer, moving deliberately, driven by the knowledge that it would be warm and dry in the aircraft.

But suddenly the prints stopped. In the middle of the trail, they were there, and beyond a certain point, between one step and another, they were *not.*

"The wind must have covered them over," said Solly.

They were quite clear here, his large prints, her small; and they were simply missing *there.* They turned on their lamps. Incredibly, it was as if the two of them, earlier in the evening, had simply materialized out of the air. Materialized with his left footprint, her right, behind which there was only virgin snow.

She looked behind them, playing her light against the trees and along the trail. Nothing moved. "Yes," she said. "Must have been the wind."

They hurried forward, expecting the tracks to show up again momentarily. The lamp beams bobbed in front of them. Neither spoke now, and Solly picked up Kim's habit of looking behind at regular intervals.

"I remember this oak," she said. "We came right past here. I *know* we did." But the snow was deep and apparently undisturbed.

Eventually the path divided and they hesitated.

"Which way?" she asked.

"The lake's on the left," whispered Solly. "Stay close to the lake." Solly seemed unsettled and that positively *terrified* her.

They got lost, as was inevitable under the circumstances. At one point Kim caught her jacket on a dog-rose bush and tore it.

They broke finally into the glade with the tumbled shed and the footprints began again. She should have been glad to see them, but they were simply *there*, appearing in the middle of the glade, nothing on this side of them except unbroken snow, as if their earlier selves had stepped off the world. The sight chilled her.

"Keep going," said Solly.

That part of the mind which withdraws from fear and watches emotional eruptions with dispatch now suggested she was in a VR scenario, that what she was experiencing could not happen in the real world.

Or that Sheyel had been right.

They came out of the tree line and saw the lake and the flyer. Kim fought down an urge to run for it. They walked deliberately across the beach, moving with comic swiftness.

Behind them, the forest remained dark and quiet. Far off to the east, a string of lights moved against the sky. The train from Terminal Island bound for Eagle Point. Solly keyed the remote and the flyer's lights came on. The hatch opened and the ladder dropped.

Out on the water something glimmered. A reflection. A lamp. *Something.*

Kim paused long enough to make sure the backseat was empty, and climbed in. Solly followed her and shut the hatch. Ordinarily her first thought would have been to get out of her wet shoes and socks. Instead she sat still while Solly inserted the key card into the dex and punched the GO button.

"*Solomon,*" the AI said. "*What is our destination?*"

"Up," Solly said. "*Up.*"

Those who rise to the top of organizations, who live to direct others, to wield power, are inevitably afflicted by weak egos, by a need to prove themselves. This explains why they are so easily frightened and so easily manipulated. And why they are so dangerous.

—SHEYEL TOLLIVER, *Notebooks*, 482

"You really weren't rattled?"

Solly's eyes closed and he shook his head sadly, as in the presence of unlimited ignorance. "No, I *really* wasn't rattled. I was *cold.*"

They were seated over coffee, salad, and fresh fruit in the hotel restaurant, Dean's Top of the World. The mountains were crisp and clear in the morning sun, and the skyways were already crowded with vacationers. A train had just rounded Mount White and was gliding in over the treetops.

"Okay," she said. "Me too."

In the daylight, it was hard to believe she'd been so fearful. She'd learned something about herself that she didn't know, didn't *want* to know: She was a coward.

"It was odd about the tracks, though," he said.

"Yes, it was."

He frowned and waved it away. "Where are you going to hang the Kane print?"

"I don't know. It's a little somber for my tastes."

"Then why didn't you get something else?"

"I should have," she agreed.

They took almost an hour to finish eating. Kim's thoughts wandered while they admired the mountains and gorges visible through the window. She felt relieved to be rid of her obligation to Sheyel. We went out and inspected the woods, she would tell him with a clear conscience, and nothing untoward happened. Absolutely nothing. He'd be disappointed, of course. But maybe a dose of reality was what he needed.

Solly was saying how he'd never learned to ski and was asking whether she knew her way around a pair of poles. She didn't, and was surprised when he suggested they should come back when their schedules permitted and learn. "There's a school out on the slopes where they give lessons," he added.

She thought she was too old to pick up skiing. But— "I'd be willing to try if you are."

He rewarded her with a smile.

Back at the hotel room, Solly packed while Kim decided to get the call over with. She punched in Sheyel's code and sat down on the sofa. The AI answered, asked who she was, and put her through immediately.

"Kim." He sounded pleased to hear her voice. "It's good to hear from you so quickly." He left it on audio only.

"I'm at Eagle Point," she said.

"You're going into the valley?" he asked.

"I was there last night."

"Wonderful. Oh, by the way, please forgive me. No picture; I'm not dressed."

"It's okay, Sheyel."

"Did you see anything?"

"Like what?"

"*Anything.* Anything unusual."

Suddenly she couldn't bring herself to lie to him. "I'm not sure," she said, throwing her planned response overboard. She described the missing footprints. And she almost told him about the moving shadows she'd seen behind Solly, but that sounded downright paranoid so she let it go.

"Yes," he said. "That is precisely the sort of thing that seems to happen regularly out there. Or used to, when there were people in the area." He recommended a couple of books on the subject and finished by asking if she was still convinced there was nothing strange going on.

"I think the wind did it, Sheyel."

"You really think that's possible? Well, never mind. What are you going to do next?"

"What's to do?" She listened for his answer, but only heard the silence draw out. "Maybe *you* can do something for *me*."

"If I can."

"Do you think you could find out Yoshi's shoe size?"

She listened to him thinking about it. "Not easily," he said at last. "She's been gone a long time. I doubt any of her shoes were kept."

"Was she a clone?"

"Yes. Oh yes, I see what you mean. Of course."

"When you find out, leave the information with Shep."

"Very good. I'll do it today." Solly came back into the room, ready to go. "May I ask why?"

"I'll tell you if it amounts to anything."

Kim couldn't resist suggesting they fly back over the Severin valley. Solly complied and they followed the river south again, this time in broad daylight. It was a bright, cloudless morning, already unseasonably warm. They watched a train come out of the Culbertson Tunnel, southwest of the city. At twenty-six kilometers, the Culbertson was the longest maglev tunnel in the world.

They stayed low so they could observe the countryside, gliding over canyons and through rifts. The previous night's snow had coated everything. Just before passing the dam, they saw a pair of deer strolling casually through a glade. At Kim's insistence, Solly took the Starlight around, but they were gone.

They came down low over the lake. Just offshore from Cabry's Beach, they saw a raft, left from the days when Severin was alive with swimmers. It was bobbing gently, as if waiting for someone to return.

They zeroed in on Tripley's villa and spent several minutes inspecting it from the air. It looked even more bleak by day.

The surrounding area was lonely and beautiful, adorned with its fresh coat of snow, its spruce and oak trees, its towering peaks. The surface of Lake Remorse gleamed in the sun. The skeletal houses provided a grotesque mixture of transience and majesty. Kim wondered what it was about desolation that inevitably seemed so compelling.

"Seen enough?" asked Solly, for whom flying in circles held no charms.

She nodded and he directed the AI to take them back to Seabright.

They rode in silence for the first several minutes. Then Solly reached behind him for the coffee, poured two cups, and handed her one. "How did we get the spot with the *Star Queen*?" he asked.

Her mind was picking again at the missing footprints, trying to construct an explanation, anything that was *possible*. Channeled wind. Local hoaxers. Solly's question consequently didn't immediately register and she had to replay it. "Matt has friends everywhere," she said. "There'll be a lot of VIPs on hand, and he thought it would be a good PR spot for us." The old liner was being converted into a hotel. The grand opening was Saturday.

"Have you reconsidered my suggestion?"

Lake Remorse drifted off the scopes. "What suggestion is that?"

"Talk to Benton Tripley. Since you're going to Sky Harbor anyhow, it should be no trouble. And he might be able to tell you something about his father and about the *Hunter*."

"You think he'd consent to talk to *me*?"

"Sure. Why not? He has a reputation for being pretty open to people."

"Yeah," she said. "What's to lose? I'd have to leave a day early, but I'll try it." She looked up the number for Interstellar executive offices and punched it into the commlink.

A male voice answered: "Interstellar. General Administration."

"Hello," she said. "My name's Dr. Kim Brandywine. I'm with the Seabright Institute. I'm going to be at Sky Harbor next Friday. Would it be possible to speak with Mr. Tripley? If he has some free time."

Solly rolled his eyes.

"And what would that concern, Dr. Brandywine?"

"I'd like to talk with him about the Mount Hope incident."

"I see. And you say Friday?"

"Yes."

After a pause: "I'm sorry. That really won't be possible. His schedule is booked for quite a while in advance. I can pencil you in for August eleventh."

"August?"

"Yes. That's really the best I can do."

"Let it go." She disconnected, turned and glared at Solly. "What?"

He shrugged.

"No," she continued. "You have something to say, say it."

"Kim, he *is* a CEO. You have to do better than suggest that *maybe* if he's free, you'd like to see him. If possible."

"What would you suggest?"

"Be a little less tentative. And have a better story than Mount Hope. You're writing a book and you need his input."

She pointed at the link. "Talk's cheap. You want to try your luck? See if you can get me in?"

"It's too late," he said. "You've blown it. You're going to have to take another tack."

She looked at him, waiting.

"Give him an award," Solly said.

"What?"

"*Give* him an award. Think public relations. Look at this as just another piece of public relations. Does Interstellar do anything for the Institute?"

"Yes," she said. "They're a major contributor. Not through generosity, of course. It's a good tax write-off for them. And they get a lot of favorable publicity."

"All right. Arrange for formal recognition. A plaque with his name on it. Take it up and present it to him."

"The Solomon J. Hobbs Award," she said.

"That would be good."

"For service above and beyond."

"My thought exactly."

Actually it wasn't a bad idea. It wouldn't cost anything. Just a trophy. All she'd have to do would be run it by Matt. He'd go for it in a minute. "You think Tripley'd be amenable? On such short notice?"

"Are you serious? These guys at the top of major organizations— You can't go wrong playing to their egos."

She resisted the idea because she should have taken this route from the start. But Solly was right, of course. She wrote out several versions of the inscription for the award, decided what they should call it, and put together a submission letter.

Then, because time was short, she called Matt and laid it all out. He listened, liked the idea as she knew he would, informed her she was to speak to the Civic Welfare Society in a few days, and told her he'd get back to her. Twenty minutes later he was on the circuit. "It's all set," he told her. "You've an appointment at the Interstellar executive suites Friday at two P.M."

"Very good," she said. The link was only audio, so a triumphant smile was safe.

"You're really getting into this," said Solly.

They flew through a cloudless sky. Kim saw another aircraft in the distance, headed north.

She connected with Shepard.

"*Hello, Kim,*" said her house AI. "*Can I be of assistance?*"

"Yes. Have you heard anything this morning from Sheyel Tolliver?"

"*No. Do you want me to alert you if something comes in?*"

"Yes," she said. "Please do."

"*Anything else?*"

"What can you tell me about the *Hunter*? The Tripley Foundation starship? What do we have on it?"

There was a brief pause. "*The Kile Tripley Foundation no longer exists. It was terminated thirteen years ago by Benton Tripley, and replaced with—*"

"Never mind that," said Kim. "Tell me about the ship."

"*The* Hunter," Shepard said, "*went into service for the Foundation Midwinter 3, 544.*" Midwinter was Greenway's thirteenth month, added after December to make the calendar come out right. Midwinter usually consisted of twenty-two days, but it occasionally dropped a day, much as February sometimes gained one on the home world, in order to keep the celestial and terrestrial calendars in sync. "*It was used primarily to make long-range exploratory voyages into previously unknown areas. It was sold by the Foundation to Alway Research in 578.*"

"Where is it now?"

"*It is currently the property of Worldwide Interior. It's docked at their Sky Harbor facility.*"

"Aren't you the lucky one?" said Solly.

She activated an auxiliary screen. "Can we have a look at it, Shep? As it was in 573?"

An index appeared on the monitor. She flipped through a series of diagrams. It was small as interstellars went, a rich man's yacht, designed by Tripley himself. It had been built as a duplicate of his home on Cedar Island. Main floor on the second level, centered on a gallery with staircases on both sides. Palomar carpeting, game room, study, main floor flight deck, upper floor mission control. External design had turrets and balconies. There were numerous viewing panels throughout, creating the standard illusion of windows inside and wraparounds on the external decks. One could sit on a porch, in effect, and look out at the cosmos as it would actually appear if the panels were made of glass.

Jump and main engines were located in the rear. Cargo, storage, and launch bay were on the bottom level.

She rotated the vessel and took the top off.

"You're pretty good at that," Solly said.

"At—?"

"Collecting and displaying data."

"It's the way I make my living. You don't think we just pick potential donors out of a hat, do you?"

"You actually do research on those guys?"

"Sure. Solly, it costs a lot of money to fund the Institute. We just don't have time to play hit-or-miss."

"But there are privacy laws."

"They're pretty loose. Most of what you've done is out there somewhere if you just know where to look. You want me to show you some samples from your own life?"

"Let it go," he said.

She smiled, brought the forward section of the *Hunter* in close, and examined the interior. Lush decor. Leather appointments. Plants. Wall hangings. Your classic executive mansion away from home.

Kim had been on an interstellar liner only once: when she was about twelve the family had gone to Minagwa, where her mother had relatives. It was an eleven-day voyage one way. If her memory was accurate, the rooms were small, the bulkheads dingy gray, and she'd thought the flight would never end. It had been exciting when they'd jumped out near that world's brilliant gold sun. And Minagwa itself was a lovely place, twin worlds, both inhabited, both with oceans. But it hadn't been worth the privations. When two months later she got back to Greenway she'd promised herself that was it. No more long-range travel bottled up in a glorified canister. And she kept her promise. She'd never done it again. Although she would have been willing to reconsider if someone had offered a flight on the *Hunter*.

The sale in 574 had been to a distillery executive. It changed hands several times over the next six years before Worldwide finally picked it up in a bankruptcy transaction. They were using it primarily to move executives and occasionally to chauffeur political figures.

She looked through the specifications, examining the details of the propulsion and navigation systems, life support, the onboard AI, and anything else that might eventually help. She was surprised to discover that the ship's radio was omnidirectional, with enhancements.

That seemed odd until she recalled *Hunter*'s mission and the expectations of its passengers. They were not looking simply for *life*, but for *intelligence*. For them, success would come in one of two ways: the discovery of a city, or an encounter with another ship. If they found a city, they'd need general, rather than directed, broadcast capabilities. Hello to everybody. Kim was impressed: these people didn't think small.

"Shepard," she said, "connect me with Worldwide."

The AI complied and a Worldwide graphic appeared onscreen, an animated starship smiling as it approached the corporation's orbiting facility. A bay opened and light blazed out. A human hand wrote the Worldwide motto in gold script: STYLE AND SUBSTANCE. Then Kim was looking at a young woman, tall, blond, reserved.

"Good evening, Dr. Brandywine," the woman said, reading Kim's name off her monitor. "My name is Melissa. May I be of assistance?"

"Hello, Melissa. I'm a researcher for the Seabright Institute. I'd like very much to get a look at the *Hunter*. In person."

She smiled and consulted something out of the picture. "Of course, Doctor. I can't see that there'd be any difficulty. When did you wish to come by?"

"Friday?"

"That'll be fine. Would late afternoon, say four P.M., be convenient?"

"Yes," said Kim. "Thank you. Oh, and one more thing? I'm especially interested in the ship's history."

"Ah yes." A smile appeared at the corners of Melissa's lips. "The Mount Hope business."

"That too," she said. "Can you tell me whether it's possible to see the logs for the last Tripley Foundation flight?"

"Oh, I'm afraid not, Dr. Brandywine. We really don't have anything to do with that. I mean, the logs were never here."

"Oh? Do you know who *would* have them?"

"I'm sure they'd have been turned over to the Archives when the ship first changed hands. That's required by law."

"Thank you, Melissa." She signed off and summoned Shepard again. "I want to send a hypercomm message."

"To?"

"I'm not sure. Operations at St. Johns. Check their administrative structure and *you* figure out where it should go."

"Very good. Text?"

"Request the flight plan for the *Hunter*, last mission for the Tripley

Foundation, Greenway year 573. Look up the date, whatever else it needs, and plug it in."

"You want it transmitted immediately?"

"As soon as it's ready."

"Transmission time both ways will be about four days, Kim. Plus whatever time it takes them to put the response together."

"Okay. And now you can get me the Archives, please."

The circular seal of the Republic appeared: a white star on a field of green. GRAND REPUBLIC OF EQUATORIA was engraved along the upper rim, and its motto, PEACE, JUSTICE, FREEDOM, along the lower. Beneath the star she read NATIONAL ARCHIVES. Then the seal vanished and a young man gazed at her from behind a desk. He looked quite interested in what she had to say, suggesting he was a virtual secretary.

"Good evening, Dr. Brandywine," he said. "I'm Harvey Stratton. How may I assist you?"

"Mr. Stratton, is it true the Archives stores the logs for interstellar flights?"

"And for interplanetary ones as well, Doctor."

"Would it be possible to see the logs from a voyage that was completed in 573?"

"Oh." His face clouded. "That comes under various privacy provisions. You'll need a court order, I'm afraid."

"A court order?"

"Oh yes. All ships' logs are covered by the privacy statutes. Are you a law enforcement official?"

"No," she said. "I was doing some research."

Solly looked vastly amused.

"There is a provisionary public domain statute, however," he said.

"Then they might be available after all?"

He consulted a screen. "For interstellar vessels, privately owned . . ." He hesitated, found what he wanted. "Looks like forty-five years from date of acquisition."

"So—?"

"They'll be available in eighteen years." He smiled. "I guess that's not much help."

He ran down the various grounds which might persuade a court. Mostly they had to do with legal actions or engineering issues. Nothing sounded close to idle curiosity. She signed off.

"What now?" asked Shep.

"What would *you* recommend?"

"It seems to me that none of this is a fruitful line of endeavor. Little green men. Ghosts. Surely there's a more advantageous way to spend your time, Kim."

Solly's eyes grew luminous. "Do you always get lectured by your AI?"

She ignored him. "What happened at Mount Hope, Shep?"

"I don't know. But I can speculate."

"Please do."

"I think it not unreasonable that someone was careless with a small quantity of antimatter. It is otherwise very hard to account for the estimated energy yield and the absence of meteoric residue."

"What would anyone have been doing with antimatter on the east slope of the mountain?"

"Perhaps trying to escape a pursuer. The explosion occurred three days after Kane and Tripley returned home from the Hunter. *Both lived in the area. One vanished. I think it not unlikely that we are looking at the result of a theft gone wrong."*

"You're suggesting Tripley stole his own fuel? Why?"

"It's possible Kane took it, Tripley recovered it, and was unable to contain it. This is, of course, speculation based on no evidence."

"What can you tell me about Benton Tripley?" she asked.

Shepard put everything on the screen. Benton was a clone of his father. In fact, more than half the population of Greenway during that period were clones. He was in his late thirties, had not married, but had a reputation as a womanizer. He was a board member for half a dozen influential organizations, a close personal friend of the Premier, the recipient of a dozen major philanthropic awards, the CEO of Interstellar, Inc., and the chairman of Lost Cause, which was the successor to the Tripley Foundation. Lost Cause devoted itself to raising money for various worthy enterprises. There were no poor anymore, but there were always children unexpectedly orphaned or cast aside, people who needed advanced educational opportunities, research possibilities, and so on. Lost Cause remained in the forefront of such efforts.

In fact, Lost Cause had stepped in to help Kim, providing scholarship funds after the deaths of her parents. But she'd never known much about the organization. There'd been a counselor who came around periodically to assure herself that Kim was all right, and the money transfers, which had arrived promptly every month. She'd eventually returned the money, but she'd always been grateful that Lost Cause was there when she needed them.

Benton Tripley looked precisely like his father, save that he was clean-shaven. He was tall, tanned, with brown, wavy hair brushed back, and a congenial smile that she didn't believe for a minute. And there, she concluded, was another difference: Kile looked honest. There was something in Benton's expression that she didn't trust.

Shepard put up a series of pictures. She saw him shaking hands with other industrialists and with political figures, saw him surrounded by women in various vacation spots, saw him defending himself against charges of unfair practices in court. He seemed to be everywhere. TRIPLEY WELCOMES BARRINGER ISLAND DELEGATION. TRIPLEY CONSULTS WITH NEW YORK COUNTERPART KIP ESTERHAUS. TRIPLEY SHOWS HIGH SCHOOL GROUP AROUND SKY HARBOR.

But there *was* something she could use: Kim saw three starship models in his office. *Three.*

And that gave her exactly the wedge she needed.

Shepard got back to her as the flyer approached Korbee Island. *"Message from Sheyel Tolliver,"* he said.

"Run it."

Sheyel's voice came on and gave the shoe size. *"Anything else, Kim?"* Shep asked.

She glanced at Solly, telling him silently that the size matched the shoe they'd found. "Yes. Put coffee on."

"It's a little less than definitive," Solly said. "How many women would you say wear that size?"

"Quite a few," she admitted. "How many of them do you think hang around starships?"

6

We are not alone.

Somewhere, in places remote beyond imagining, cities light the dark, and towers rise over broken shorelines. Who inhabits these distant cities, who looks out from these far towers, we do not at present know, and cannot guess. But one day we will arrive in their skies, and we will embrace our brothers and sisters.

—SHIM PADWA, *The Far Towers*, 321

"We should do more of this," Matt said. "Get ahead of the curve. Hand out prizes. It's an easy way to make friends for the Institute."

Well-heeled friends. Management had directed it be called the Morton Cable Award, after the man who'd done the breakthrough work for the development of transdimensional flight. Happily, Cable also had connections with the Institute.

Kim readily agreed—"great idea, Matt"—and suggested that, in view of Tripley's affinity for decorative starships, they put the award in that form, rather than using a standard plaque. Matt approved and left the details to her judgment.

The cab picked her up early Friday morning. The ocean was still misty as the flyer rose into a crystal sky and arced toward the mainland. There were relatively few private vehicles on Greenway because taxis were cheap, well maintained, and readily available. She saw no seagoing traffic, save for a westbound yacht. A couple of other cabs were in the air, circling aimlessly over the islands, waiting for calls.

Matt had arranged that Averill Hopkin would make the presentation to Tripley. Hopkin was a prizewinning authority in hyperspace propulsion techniques. He was already at Sky Harbor, doing consulting work for Interstellar. So it was all very convenient. Hopkin was dark skinned, dark eyed, a man without substance, Kim thought. His life seemed to be completely entwined in physics. She doubted that he had any idea how to enjoy himself.

The cab dropped her at the terminal. Fifteen minutes later she was on the Seahawk, a maglev gliding south over Seabright's parklands. The Institute passed on her right, and the beaches on her left. Once outside the city it accelerated smoothly to six hundred kilometers per hour, occasionally tracking over open water, leaving a roiling wake in its passage.

The view from her window became a blur of seacoast, forest, and rivers. Passengers drew their shades and settled in with their links or a book. Some slept, some put on a helmet and watched a selection from the train library.

Kim brought up the *Autumn* on the screen mounted in front of her seat and looked for a long time at her own image. It chilled her, yet produced a curious sense of her own beauty and power. Markis's affection for his subject was quite obvious.

Another passenger, a woman, paused in the aisle behind her. She self-consciously wiped the screen.

During the early days after Emily's disappearance, Kim had occasionally sat with her mother while she conducted conversations with a simulation of the lost daughter. Her father had objected. Emily was *his* daughter too, he'd said. And it was best for all of them to let her rest. He'd been right: it had been a chilling business, and Kim had sworn she'd never do anything like it herself. When someone is gone, she'd decided, she's *gone.* Using technology to pretend otherwise is *sick.* It had turned out to be easier to make the pledge than to keep it, though. Kim had spoken regularly with Emily during her adolescence, and with her lost parents in the years immediately following the accident. In character, her father had abjured her during these sessions to let go. *You have your own life to live, Kimberly,* he'd said, frowning. *You can manage on your own.*

The encounters had always left her hurting. Achieving maturity had been largely a matter of leaving phantasms behind. But she found that to do it, she had to confront the reality, to admit to herself that they were all really gone. To a degree, she understood that she'd been damaged by those conversations, especially those with Emily, because the woman who had vanished from her life when she was barely old enough to remember had lingered for another dozen years. By then, when Kim finally broke away, she had come to understand fully the depth of her loss.

She found a picture of Emily, Yoshi, and Tripley, taken during a farewell luncheon shortly before the departure of the *Hunter*. Emily was immaculately tailored in dark green slacks, light green blouse, off-white jacket. The ensemble emphasized the effect of her gold-flecked dark eyes.

Emily had had a reputation as an effective junior executive for a communications firm before joining the Tripley Foundation. Kim took a few minutes to listen to an address at a country club during which she described the purposes of the Foundation, what they had accomplished, and what they still hoped to achieve. *"There's life out there somewhere,"* she'd said. *"And with your help we mean to find it."*

Emily was passionate, with a comedic sense of timing. She had all the qualities of a good speaker: she knew where she was headed, she told jokes on herself, and she knew how to deliver a one-liner. The applause at the end of her speech was loud and enthusiastic, and it was obvious that Emily could have recruited the whole bunch had she desired.

She'd married twice, but was unattached at the time of her disappearance. There had been no children.

Terminal City was located on an equatorial island two kilometers offshore. The Seahawk left the mainland at Mikai, passed over a series of rocky headlands and began to slow down as it approached the Chibatsu Tunnel. The lights in the car brightened, and they saw a few gulls. Birds had learned to keep their distance from the trains, save at those sections along the route where they cut back to a safe velocity. From this point the train would be moving across the barrier islands, alternately accelerating and decelerating in rhythm with the tunnels. They were on the equator now, westbound.

Kim had begun reading Markis Kane's favorite detective, Veronica King. She'd finished four of the books during the week since returning from the Severin Valley, and made several efforts during the ride to start another, but it was hard to keep her mind on it. She was thinking ahead to her interview with Benton Tripley, sculpting the questions she would ask.

They stopped at Cleavis Island. The train almost emptied out, but more people swarmed aboard. After they'd gotten moving again, Kim wandered down to the dining car and had lunch.

As she finished up a meal of greens and chicken, the train cleared its last tunnel, leaped Morgantown Bay, and ran into a heavy rainstorm. Along this section of coastline, the mountains came directly down to the sea. The Seahawk plunged into a canyon, and crossed the Edmonton Defile, which was really a series of ridges and channels.

They were twenty meters over the ocean, running along the side of a cliff, when Kim returned her attention to Veronica King and "The Demon Lamp." The gimmick in the stories was that critical information was inevitably hidden in plain sight. "The Demon Lamp" was set at an archeological dig several layers deep on the large desert island Kawahl. Two people have been murdered, and the motive is said to be concealed in a tower. But there *is* no tower anywhere on that baking landscape. Except, of course, that there is: the dig site is the tower, now buried after several hundred years and a climate shift.

Kim finished the story as the Seahawk dropped gradually to sea level and the mountains fell away. She was on the wrong side of the train to see it, but she knew that the skyhook was now visible.

There were always a few gasps from travelers who were looking at it for the first time. Skyhooks were, if not the most incredible of human engineering marvels, then certainly the most spectacular. Five of the nine worlds had them, and one was under construction on Tigris. Greenway's skyhook, which was connected to Terminal City, was now about twelve kilometers away. Its enormous bulk rose out of the downtown area and soared into the clouds.

People were out of their seats, crowding to the right side of the car. Kim caught a glimpse of it, watched the sunlight strike its weathered sides. It always made her proud in some indefinable way.

Minutes later the train pulled into the terminal building and stopped. Passengers filed out into a vast agglomeration of shops and concourses, waiting areas and restaurants. Kim took a minute to locate herself, and then moved off at a leisurely pace toward the lift. There were people distributing religious literature, others soliciting signatures for political and social campaigns. Some wanted the board chairman of one of the train lines removed, others hoped to get support for a drive demanding research on increasing longevity.

Kim had some spare time, so she stopped on the main promenade for a glass of fruit juice. It occurred to her she'd put herself in Sheyel's position: unless she was careful, Benton Tripley was going to conclude she was a lunatic.

■   ■   ■

The lift went up every other hour. The vehicle was divided into a lounge area, a VR facility, a souvenir shop specializing in Sky Harbor mugs and T-shirts, a coffee shop, and the Four Moons, a private club where members could relax around a leather-lined bar, shoot billiards, take over a VR booth, or nap.

The coffee shop was Nik's. It was overpriced and the sandwiches tasted like plastic, but the coffee was good. The walls were covered with autographed pictures of celebrities who had passed through. Once on board, Kim headed directly for Nik's and found a corner table.

The lift's capacity was listed at 120 people. On this day it was carrying half that number. Kim ordered coffee and cantaloupe, looked out her window at the vast interior of the mall, and heard the announcement that they would be departing in a moment. The gates closed with a click.

The floor trembled and unseen engines engaged. The concourse, with its crowds and brightly decorated shops, began to fall away. Then Kim was passing through a tangle of struts and cables.

It was all she'd be able to see for about ten minutes. The lift would rise on the inside of the central support until it cleared the lower atmosphere. Then, when it was beyond potential wear and tear from weather conditions, it would emerge into the sunlight.

Several of her fellow travelers were VIPs also headed for the *Star Queen*. She finished her snack, leaving most of the cantaloupe, and wandered through Nik's, saying hello, renewing acquaintances. McWilliam was there from Extron Industries, and Larry Dixon from the National Philanthropic Society, and Jazz White, the counterball player who was featured in the *Star Queen*'s promotional campaign.

The lift came out of its protective sheath and the coffee shop filled with sunlight.

She strolled into the lounge and found a cushioned bench. Some of the passengers were buying souvenirs, and most of the kids were in the VR rec center. Others stood near the windows looking out at the view.

Like the "windows" on the *Hunter*, these were really screens, which displayed views from external imagers. Transparent panels were a hazard, the weakest point in an airtight environment, so they had long since been phased out. But only a close examination could reveal the difference.

Matt had wrangled the invitation to the *Star Queen* ceremonies by pointing out that the designer of her engines had been Max Esterly, onetime Institute director, and that an Institute presence on the day the great liner was converted into a hotel was only appropriate. In fact, a plaque of Esterly had been mounted in the vessel's main lounge. Matt's real purpose, of course, was to remind the assorted decision-makers of the joys of technology, and that nothing worthwhile came free. It was *Kim*'s job to make them believers.

He'd given her a set of points to be driven home: If society does not move forward, it will decline. It *is* declining. We need to make some changes in the way we do things. The primary force in modern scientific research is the Institute. That was probably something of an exaggeration, but they said it at every opportunity so it had acquired the ring of truth.

She didn't entirely agree with Matt's approach. The belief that society was in decline was a permanent characteristic of every era. People always believed they lived in a crumbling world. *They* themselves were of course okay, but everybody around them was headed downhill. It was a tired drumbeat and she didn't think bringing it up during the launch of the *Star Queen* Hotel would help generate anything except boredom.

Nevertheless she wondered whether something really *was* wrong. More than the end of scientific investigation. More than a society that sought its own pleasures to the exclusion of everything else. Some doomsayers were suggesting that the human race had simply grown old, exhausted itself in some metaphysical way. That it needed a challenge. Perhaps it needed to find others like itself, among the stars, with whom it could cooperate and compete. And trade war stories. That as things were, the species was just sitting on the back porch, waiting for God.

Much of the pessimism seemed to be coming from Earth, where it was almost the end of the third millennium, standard calendar. Historically such times had always generated cries that midnight had come for the race.

Whatever the truth might be, Kim thought that cutting the ribbon on the *Star Queen* Hotel was hardly an appropriate moment to throw a dead cat up the aisle.

Although the advent of artificial gravity had obviated the need for wheel-shaped space stations, the traditional configuration had remained in use everywhere except for the newest unit going up at Tigris. At one time there'd appeared to be a possibility for antigravity as well, but that breakthrough had proved elusive and was now thought to be impossible. Too bad: it was just the sort of goal the Institute needed to enlist the enthusiasm of the *Star Queen* crowd.

She was looking down on cloud banks and the curve of the world as the lift began to slow. People wandered about, collecting bags, making last-minute purchases, getting jackets onto their kids. It was a persistent belief among parents that Sky Harbor was drafty. The engines whined, the lift stopped, and the doors opened. Passengers filed out into the lobby of the Starview Hotel. Most inserted their cards into the registration dexes. Kim picked up the package she'd sent ahead, went to her room, showered, and worked on her remarks for the dedication. Through her window she could see Sky Harbor's tail, the enormous counterweight to the lift, snaking out toward Lark, the innermost moon.

First up on her schedule was the award for Benton Tripley.

She had just time for a quick nap. Then she dressed and checked herself in the mirror. Satisfied that she looked pretty good, she took the elevator down to C deck, where most of the corporate suites were located.

It was a luxurious section, well away from the tourist and operational areas, featuring dark-stained paneling, potted plants, and thick carpets. The walls were hung with landscapes. Soft music whispered out of unseen speakers. The lighting was restrained, lending an aspect of quiet significance to the digitals marking the individual offices.

Interstellar, Inc., was located behind a pair of frosted-glass double doors. A young dark-skinned woman looked up from a desk as she entered. "Good afternoon, Dr. Brandywine," she said. "They're waiting for you. Please follow me."

She showed Kim into a compact conference room. A recording crew was already at work, setting up for pictures. Averill Hopkin arrived on her heels, looking frazzled. After a minute's conversation Kim realized he didn't like making presentations. He was nervous and irritated, and not at all anxious to participate in a public forum. But there'd been no easy way out for him, and so here he was, his gaze running between Kim, the lectern, and the time. "I hate these things," he told her.

"It's the price of being celebrated," she said, keeping her amusement out of her voice. She thought briefly about advising him that 90 percent of everything is public relations, but prudently let it pass.

"I've just got more important things to do, Kim," he said. She put a hand on his arm. It was rigid. "I'm not good at this sort of thing," he persisted.

"Relax, Avy." She gave him an encouraging smile. One of her best. "You've nothing to prove. All they want is for you to be here. You could fall over a chair, and they'd think that's just the way genius behaves."

He nodded solemnly, accepting the accolade without a flicker of humility.

The lectern was set on a low platform at the front of the conference room, flanked by four chairs and a side table. Behind it, the company shield hung proudly on the wall, framed by blue and white bunting, Interstellar's colors. Kim had kept the award in its container, which she now placed on the side table after showing it to Hopkin.

Corporate employees were beginning to come in. She knew a couple of the executives, and she introduced the physicist to them. They fawned over him, and she was pleased to see him calm down somewhat.

A tall, blond woman entered and everyone snapped to attention. This, Kim knew, was Magda Kenneal, Triplet's chief administrative assistant. Magda took over, introduced herself to Hopkin, said hello distractedly to Kim, and began giving directions. There were now about twenty people in the room. After she'd gotten everyone satisfactorily seated, Magda apparently got a signal from somewhere. She nodded, stepped behind the lectern and the conversation stopped. "Ladies and gentlemen," she said, "I'd like to welcome you here this morning. As you may be aware, Mr. Tripley has long been a staunch supporter of the Seabright Institute—"

She continued in that vein for a few minutes, extolling her boss's efforts on behalf of a world of worthy causes. Then she stood aside. A door to her right opened, and Benton Tripley himself came in.

The audience applauded enthusiastically. There was no question here who signed the paychecks.

Tripley, dressed formally in white for the occasion, sat down on Kim's left. He smiled graciously at her, and she returned the gesture. Kim had never met him. Magda had always represented Lost Cause at Institute events.

Up close, she sensed that Benton was a more electric personality than his father. Everything she'd seen about Kile suggested a serious, somber man, with an intellectual side, and a tendency toward abruptness. But one did not get the feeling of unseen depths. The current Tripley, on the other hand, looked far more congenial, if she disregarded his eyes, which revealed a flatness that left her cold.

He was not a man she'd have over for dinner. Yet the charm was undeniably there, and it washed over her when he favored her with a broad smile. It made her want to be wrong about disliking him.

Magda identified Kim and then introduced Hopkin, who looked intimidated. The physicist shambled clumsily to the lectern, plopped his notes down, and began. He talked about the Beacon Project, and described a few other current initiatives. He explained why private help was needed to carry on scientific work in an age of belt-tightening. And he was starting in on some efforts he wanted especially to recommend to his audience when Kim succeeded in catching his eye and signaling that he should cut it short. Hopkin got the message and broke off in midsentence. "But that's of no real concern today," he finished lamely. "We're here this afternoon to present the Morton Cable Award to Mr. Tripley in appreciation of his exemplary contributions to the cause of science."

Tripley got up and joined him at the lectern.

Kim retrieved the container, unlatched it, and passed it to Hopkin. He opened it and brought out the model of the *Hunter*, circa 573. Its aluminum turrets and propulsion tubes gleamed in the lights. He held it up so everyone could see it. They got more applause. Then he read the inscription:

> The Morton Cable Award
> Benton Tripley
> For Extraordinary Effort in Support of the Pursuit of Science
> Recognized by the Seabright Institute
> January 12, 600

He handed it to Tripley, shook his hand, and sat down.

Tripley leaned into the mike. "It's beautiful," he said graciously. "My father would have been proud." He added a few remarks suitable for the occasion, that Interstellar would continue to support scientific research, and that he was pleased to be able to make a positive contribution to a good cause. He thanked everyone for coming, delivered a few more generalities, and gave the lectern back to Magda amid sustained applause.

After the ceremony, he invited Hopkin and Kim into his office and showed them where he planned to put his newest award: beside the

Regal, Admiral ben-Hadden's flagship which had led Greenway's fleet in the Pacifica War.

But he looked tired. It might have been a lassitude born of too many ceremonies that day, too many meetings with functionaries like Kim. She sensed that he was on automatic. It was hard not to conclude that, when he wasn't on stage, a different personality took over. Nonetheless, she could see that the *Hunter* trophy was a hit. Kim hadn't been certain he would recognize it.

The office was large for Sky Harbor, tastefully but not extravagantly furnished. Plaques and framed certificates and pictures of Tripley with various VIPs hung everywhere. A wall-length window looked out on the long planetary arc. Most of the visible land was white.

A portrait of a young girl playing with a dog stood prominently on his desk. His daughter, Choela, he explained. A virtual fire burned cheerfully in a grate. Bookshelves lined two walls. There were about eighty volumes, leather-bound antiques. And she saw, besides the *Hunter* and the *Regal*, three other starships.

"You did your homework," he said, indicating the *Hunter*. "Can I offer you some coffee?"

"Yes, please," she said. "Black."

Hopkin passed.

"I'm glad you like it," she said.

Tripley leaned toward a link, relayed her wish to someone on the other end. "It'll fit very nicely with the fleet." His features brightened and his eyes came alive. Whatever else he might be, she decided, he was an overgrown adolescent.

The *Regal* occupied a shelf of its own. A second model was encased on a table apparently designed specifically for the purpose. The two remaining ships were on opposite sides of the office, one on a side table near a chair, the other on a wall mount.

"They look realistic," said Hopkin, strolling from one to another. Kim suspected he could not have been less interested but was using the decorations to cover his social disorientation.

"Thank you."

The coffee arrived. Hopkin watched while his companions sampled the brew and commented on it. Then he continued, using a tone that signified he was now proceeding to serious matters. "You've an efficient operation here, Benton," he said. "But I wonder if I might suggest something—?"

"Of course."

"The engine designs—" Hopkin flashed disapproval. "You could do much better."

"They're standard," said Tripley, puzzled.

Hopkin had an idea to improve energy output. Kim lost track of it early, during his description of intensification of the magnetic fields at the moment of hyperspace penetration. Her physics was too weak to follow the logic, but Tripley listened closely, jotted some of it down, interrupted occasionally with a technical question, and finally nodded his head. "Put it on paper," he said. "Let me see a proposal."

She noticed that he never asked about cost.

The basic problem with flight through hyperspace was that the upper limits of velocity seemed to be fixed at a realspace equivalent of 38.1 light-years per standard day. The Karis Limit. It was fast enough for travel among the Nine Worlds and their outlying regions, but there were other places researchers would like to go. Like the center of the galaxy, to which a round-trip would require four and a half years. Would Hopkin's idea, she asked, push vehicles beyond the Karis Limit?

"No," he said. "I don't think there's any way to do that. But we *will* be able to save a considerable amount of fuel, and thereby significantly increase range."

She was eager to talk about Mount Hope. "It sounds," she said, "like the kind of drive the *Hunter* could have used."

Hopkin blinked, not sure of the reference. "Benton," he said, "I hate to cut this short, but I really do have to be going." He got up and smiled benevolently. "It was good to see you again, Kim." He bent to kiss her cheek, shook hands with Tripley, and disappeared out the door.

"It would be helpful," said Tripley, "if he could really do what he says." His gaze drifted from his notes to the model *Hunter*. "I take it the choice of trophy design was yours?"

"We thought it seemed appropriate. Most famous of the Foundation's vessels."

A cheese tray showed up. Kim sampled a piece. "I was impressed that you knew about the models," Tripley said.

"They provide a distinctive decor, Mr. Tripley. Do they represent actual vessels?"

"My name's Ben, Doctor. May I call you Kim?"

"Of course, Ben," she said.

His brow furrowed and his eyes caressed the *Regal*. It was long and sleek, its lines curving in unexpected directions, designed to resist enemy sensors. A beautiful ship. She wondered why warships, of whatever nature, were always so compelling. Was it their utilitarian nature, that they were designed for a single purpose? It suggested Eisenstadt's misdirected definition of a beautiful woman, but it seemed applicable in this case.

"My grandfather served on it," said Tripley.

"During the war?" asked Kim.

"He was ben-Hadden's helmsman." The pride in Tripley's voice was evident. He sat back quietly to allow her a moment of appreciation.

The other models were quite striking.

One was saucer-shaped. "This is the *Choela*," he said, glancing at the little girl with the dog. "It's corporate. We have two of them in service, actually."

And a liner. "The *Buckman*. Gave out years ago, I'm afraid. But it was Interstellar's first contract. In my father's time. Launched us, you might say."

The final vehicle was a flared teardrop mounted on an elliptical platform. Kim saw no propulsion tubes. It looked somewhat like a turtle. "It belonged to my father," he said. "It's purely fictitious. As you can see."

"No propulsion tubes," she ventured.

He nodded. "It's not a very thoughtful design, but it's what got me interested in the business."

"A boyhood toy?" asked Kim.

"Yes."

"What is its name?"

He actually managed to look sheepish. "I called it the *Valiant*."

"That sounds like a warship. It doesn't look like one." Toy warships usually came bristling with weapons.

"To a kid, *everything's* a warship."

Of the five models it was the most intricately detailed, with realistic antennas and sensor dishes and hatches. Its dark shell was tooled to catch the light. In the flickering glow cast by the fire it was sometimes black and sometimes purple. She touched it. Her fingertips tingled with the kind of sensation one gets from hewn marble. "I think *Valiant* is the right name," she said.

"In its day," he smiled, "it's gone out against all sorts of pirates and monsters." He took it down from its shelf and held it in both hands, as if weighing his childhood. "My grandmother passed it on to me."

"But," she said, "you discovered there were no pirates."

"Alas, no. At least not in starships." His fingers lingered against its burnished hull. "What's the old saying? The stuff of dreams."

The books on the shelves included Harcourt's *Principles of Galactic Formation*, Al Kafir's *Alone in the Universe*, McAdam's *The Shores of Night*, Magruder's *Far As the Eye Can See*, Ravakam's *The Limits of Knowledge*.

Not at all the sort of reading she'd have expected from a man whose primary concern was running a major corporation. One never knew.

The fireplace crackled and a log broke. Sparks rose into the room.

"The *Hunter* is a lovely ship," she said, to steer the conversation back toward Kile Tripley.

"Yes, it is. I was on it several times when I was a boy. But never in flight, I'm sorry to say."

"It was a Tripley Foundation vehicle for forty-some years, wasn't it?"

"Precisely thirty-three years, seven months," he said.

"They sold it after your father's death?" She deliberately misstated the facts, not wanting to seem too knowledgeable about the details.

"His disappearance," he said. "His body was never found. But yes, they sold it a few years after. There was no longer any point in keeping it. No one else was interested in deep-space research. At least, nobody who mattered. You know, of course, that's what they used it for."

"Yes," she said. "I know." Tripley, she was aware, had been eleven years old when he lost his father. He'd been living with his mother at the time, and apparently had seen little of the star-hopping Kile. "Do you share your father's interest in exploration?" she asked.

He shrugged. "Not especially. He wanted to find life somewhere. And sure, if it's out there, I wouldn't mind being the one who bags it. But no, I can't say I'm prepared to devote time and money to it. Too much else to do. And the odds are too long." He glanced at his commlink, checking the time. Signaling her that the meeting was drawing to a close.

"Ben," she said, "do you think the *Hunter* was in any way connected with the Mount Hope explosion?"

His face might have hardened. She couldn't be sure. But his voice cooled. "I've no idea. But I'm not sure I see how it could have been."

"There was a lot of talk about antimatter at the time," she said.

Suspicion clouded his face. "I'm sure you have the details tucked away where you can find them, if necessary, Kim. Look: I've heard the speculation too. God knows I grew up with it. But I honestly can't imagine why either Markis or my father would have removed any of the fuel from the *Hunter*, taken it to the village, and used it to blow up a mountain. Or for that matter, *how* they could have done it. Remove a cell from its magnetic container, and it explodes on the spot." He transfixed her with a stare that was not angry, but wary. And perhaps disappointed. "What do *you* think happened, Kim?"

She let her eyes lose focus. "I don't know what to think. The explosion does have an antimatter signature—"

"There's no evidence to support that."

"The yield suggests it."

He shook his head and let her see he'd lost confidence in her common sense. She had intended to say that the only people in the neighborhood who had a connection with antimatter were Kane and his father. But she was needlessly antagonizing him. And she didn't know for a fact there was no one else anyhow.

"Let me get this straight," Tripley said. "You think my father and Kane were conducting an experiment of some kind. And the experiment went wrong. Or that they were involved in a theft."

"I didn't say that."

"The implication is clear enough." He stared at her. "It didn't happen. My father wasn't an experimental physicist. He was an engineer. He wouldn't have been involved in anything like that. *Couldn't* have been."

"What about Markis?"

"Kane was a *starship captain*." He had settled back into his chair. "No. You can forget all that. Look, I don't know what happened in Severin any more than anyone else does. But I know damned well it wasn't my father playing around with a fuel cell. Chances are, it was a meteor. Plain and simple."

"Ben," she said, "do you have any idea whether Yoshi Amara might have been at your father's villa around the time of the explosion?"

His gaze sharpened. "What makes you think *that*? I've never heard *that* charge made before."

She'd gone too far. What was she going to tell him? That she'd found a *shoe* that was her size? "There's some indication," she said, plunging ahead.

Tripley looked like a man dealing with gnats. "May I ask what sort of indication?"

"Clothing. It's probably hers. No way to be sure."

"I see." He glanced over at the *Hunter.* "Sounds weak to me. Kim, I hope you aren't going to drag it all out again. Whatever might have happened, the principals are dead."

She nodded. "Not all the principals. Some of them are still wondering what happened to their relatives."

He clapped his hands together. "Of course," he said. "That's why you look so much like Emily."

"Yes."

"Her sister? daughter?"

"Sister."

"I'm sorry," he said. "I truly am. Then you must know how I feel. But I think it's a mutual loss that we simply have to accept." He'd come around the desk and was escorting her to the door. "Let it go, Kim. I don't know what happened to them any more than you do, but I've long since come to terms with it. I suggest you do the same."

Worldwide Interior specialized in custom decor for executive and personal yachts and the entire range of corporate vehicles. They were fond of saying that after Interstellar put in the electronics, Worldwide added the ambiance and made every vessel into a home.

Kim was given the tour by Jacob Isaacs, the public information officer. Isaacs was in his fourth quarter, as the saying went, in excess of a hundred fifty years old. He'd begun to gray, and he walked without energy. "They think I provide dignity," he confided to her with a smile. In fact, in a society in which almost everyone looked young, persons who'd begun to show their age were at a premium and were often given what some thought was an unfair preference in hiring and promotion.

They walked together around a virtual *Hunter,* while Jacob described the ship's features. Not her sensing capabilities or her propulsion systems, but the more cosmetic qualities. Hull design and esthetic considerations. Note the balance between architrave and portico. Observe the second-floor terraces. This was a ship that could have been placed on manorial grounds in the most sedate part of Marathon and it would not have been out of place. Except, of course, for the propulsion tubes extending from the rear.

And the lander, which was connected to the ship's underside.

She'd explained that she was working on a history of the corporate fleet during the past half century, and to this end she'd become interested in Worldwide. How had they gotten started refurbishing spacecraft interiors?

"The founder, Ester DelSol, started in food distribution. DelSol and Winnett." Isaacs looked at Kim as if she should have recognized the firm. She nodded as though she did. "The story is that she took a flight to Earth to visit her family and noticed how bad the onboard food was. And she saw her chance. She took over the franchise and provided the carriers first-class cuisine at reasonable prices. One thing led to another. There were plenty of corporations around to service engines and handle electronics, but the carriers themselves had to take care of the cosmetic stuff. It was expensive but necessary and it was done on a hit-or-miss basis."

"And now you're into all kinds of shipboard furnishings."

"And exteriors. The cosmetics, that is. We don't do food anymore, by the way. That was sold off years ago. But we handle pretty much everything else."

He took her down to operations to see the ship itself. It floated just off the wheel, connected by a support structure. A couple of technicians were replacing an antenna. "Is it going somewhere?" asked Kim.

"Tomorrow. It's bound for Pacifica."

They strolled over to the entry tube. "Did you want to look inside?"

"Please."

They went through the air lock and emerged on the main floor, in a gallery lined by a dozen doors. A foldback staircase mounted to the upper level. Another, directly opposite, descended to the lower.

The interior was elegant. Carpeting and furniture were of the highest order. Fixtures had the feel of silver. Windows were curtained, appointments polished, walls decorated with photos from the *Hunter*'s recent past. She found nothing related to the ship's days with the Tripley Foundation. And it was impossible not to contrast the *Hunter* with the drab, spartan vehicles that the Institute used to transport its technicians around the stellar neighborhood.

The mission control center took up much of the main floor. They inspected it, looked into the dining room and the rec area.

The pilot's room was upstairs. They went up and she stood before it, feeling the tug of history. Markis Kane's last mission as a starship captain. Inside, a pair of leather chairs faced a control panel and a set of screens. She went in and sat down in the left-hand chair, the pilot's position.

The rest of the upper floor was dedicated to living quarters. She wondered which cabin had belonged to Emily.

The utility area, which housed cargo, storage, and life support, was located on the bottom floor. It was spacious, considering the modest dimensions of the vehicle, and divided into five airtight compartments and a central corridor running the spine of the ship. "Kile Tripley knew from the beginning that he wanted the capacity to make long flights," said Isaacs. "So the *Hunter* has lots of storage capacity, as you can see. It's also got a water refiltering system that, when it was built, was far ahead of its time."

There was a cargo hold on either side of the passageway. Each had its own loading door, its own crane, its own sorter, and movable decks. Jacob showed her the refrigeration compartment. "We don't use much of this space anymore," he said. "Don't really need it on commuter flights."

The portside loading door was as broad as the compartment into which it opened. "Tripley always believed he'd find a ruin out there somewhere, some kind of place not built by us. By *people*. And he wanted to be able to bring back pieces of it and not be hindered by the size of his doors."

"A *ruin*?"

"Oh yes. He was convinced that other civilizations *had* developed, but he expected they'd all be dead. Thought there wasn't much chance of finding a living one. He certainly knew our own was in a state of decay." They were standing just outside the lander launch bay. The vessel's cockpit rose through the floor into its housing. "And of course he was right."

That startled her. "Right? In what way?"

"Well." Now it was his turn to look surprised. "Dr. Brandywine, we're going to hell in a handbasket. You know that. Everybody's out for himself now. Not like the old days."

"Oh," she said.

They strolled aft, talking idly, Kim agreeing, although she didn't really believe it, that times had been changing for the worse. The corridor ended outside the entrance to the power plant. "Jacob," she said, "I wonder if I could look at the maintenance records." Solly had assured her that, unlike the logs, a complete maintenance record was stored onboard for the life of the ship.

"If you want," he said. "I don't see any harm to it." He punched the control panel mounted beside the door. It opened, they went inside, and he sat down at a console. "But it strikes me," he said, "that maintenance makes for dull reading."

"My problem is that I don't know enough about these things. The maintenance records'll give me a feel for what it takes to keep a ship like this in operation."

"Do you want me to get our maintenance chief? He could probably answer whatever questions you might have."

"No, no," she said. "That's okay. No need to bother anybody."

Isaacs shrugged and brought up a menu. He had a little trouble finding what he wanted. He was, after all, a public information officer. But after a few anxious minutes she watched an engineering history of the Equatorian Interstellar Vehicle (EIV) 4471886 begin to scroll across the screen. Jacob got up and gave her the seat.

Kim paged through as casually as she was able, commenting innocuously on grades of lubrication and periods between engine inspections, trying the whole time to sound as if she were only interested in generalities.

She took it back to the beginning. The *Hunter* went into service Midwinter 3, 544. "It takes a lot of work to keep one of these things operating," she said innocently.

Isaacs agreed. She scrolled forward, locating and then familiarizing herself with the system which revealed the type of maintenance or repair and the signature of the technician. She noted the extensive maintenance performed toward the end of 572, prior to departure for St. Johns. Weeks later, a final inspection was completed at that distant outpost before the *Hunter* left for the Golden Pitcher.

On March 30 it was back at Sky Harbor, and another general inspection was done. She ran quickly through the items, and found that an airlock door had been replaced in the port cargo hold, and the jump engines had required repairs. She wondered what the problem had been with the door, but the record didn't say. As to the engines, she wasn't skilled enough to understand the significance of the damages. She saw only that numbered parts were installed and the engine pronounced okay.

The name of the technician was Gaerhard. She couldn't make out the first name. But it shouldn't matter.

She passed on through a few more pages, thanked Jacob, and left.

7

Where is it now, the glory and the dream?
—WILLIAM WORDSWORTH, *Intimations of Immortality*, 1807 C.E.

The following evening, Kim caught a shuttle to the *Star Queen* Hotel. The onetime liner was brilliantly illuminated, and pictures from groundside showed that, at least for this one night, there was a new star in the heavens.

No two interstellar liners look completely alike. Even those sharing the same basic design are painted and outfitted so there can be no question of their uniqueness. Some have a kind of rococo appearance, like a vast manor house brought in from the last century; others resemble malls, complete with walkways and parks; and still others have the brisk efficiency of a modern hotel complex. Starships, of course, have few limitations with regard to design, the prime specification being simply that they not disintegrate during acceleration or course change.

The *Star Queen* looked like a small city on a dish. The approach tube was designed to provide maximum view. Kim had seen virtuals of the *Queen*, but the real thing, up close, took her breath away.

The new owners had worked hard to create the impression of a living vessel that might leave at any time for Sirius or Sol. An enormous digital banner amidships displayed her name in proud black letters.

There were about a dozen people in the shuttle. Most, she judged, were upper-level employees of various Sky Harbor corporations, coming over for the party. One of the men tried to engage her in conversation, but she squirmed and looked uncomfortable and he got the message. She was not necessarily averse to adventures on the road, but at the moment she was too deeply caught up in her own thoughts to spoil the occasion fencing with a prowling male.

There was music at the dock, and automated porters, and hotel representatives anxious to assist. A news team stood off to one side interviewing someone Kim couldn't see.

She'd been on the *Queen* once before, when she was fresh out of college, as an Institute intern. She wandered now among its display rooms to refresh her memories of that earlier trip. Here was a memorial to Max Esterly, portraying him poised in thought over a computer console, presumably designing the engines which had made the *Queen* class of liners possible. And there was the presidential suite in which Jennifer Granville had drawn up the Articles. On the glass deck, so-called because of the view it provided, an assassin had brought down Pius XIX, last of the officially recognized popes. A plaque marked the spot off the main dining room where a team of rangers had started their assault against the Minagwan terrorists who had seized and held the ship for seventeen excruciating days in an act that had been a prelude to war.

Ali Bakai and Narimoto the Good had met secretly on the *Star Queen* to make the Peace of Ahriman, which neither of their constituencies wanted. The fabled Yakima Tai performed his last concert in the ballroom before ending his life and that of his wife. The Mid-Deck Bar had a plaque marking the fictional spot in which Veronica King met her long-time associate, bodyguard, and biographer, Archimedes Smith. Another plaque commemorated the stateroom in which Del Dellasandro wrote *Hypochondriacs Get Sick Too.* And in the main lobby an oil painting commemorated the *Star Queen*'s proudest moment: the attack on her by Pandik II's warships at Pacifica, while she was carrying supplies, technicians, and spare parts to the rebels.

Kim checked the monitor for her room number. A bouquet of orchids was waiting when she arrived, compliments of Cole Mendelson, coordinator of the evening's activities. The room was small, as one would expect on an interstellar. It was also luxurious, in a busy sort of way. The decor, drapes, bedcovers, furniture, everything seemed just short of garish.

Ordinarily she'd have headed immediately for the shower, but this time she plunked down on the bed and kicked off her shoes. She linked into the terminal and entered Gaerhard's name with a search command for TECHNICIAN, JUMP ENGINES.

The hit came right back. There was a Walt Gaerhard who fit the parameters working for Interstellar at Sky Harbor.

She called their operations and got a Melissa clone. "I'm trying to locate Walter Gaerhard," she said.

The Melissa clone glanced at her monitor, acquiring Kim's ID. "I'm sorry, Dr. Brandywine," she said. "He's not on duty at the moment."

"Could you possibly connect me with his quarters?"

"It's not our policy to do that. Is this an emergency?"

"No. No, it isn't. Can you tell me when I might be able to see him?"

"One moment please." She touched her keyboard, looked at the screen again, and pursed her lips. "He has the day shift tomorrow. Would you like me to leave a message?"

"No, that's fine. Thank you." Better to just show up. If anything out of the ordinary had occurred, it was best not to alert anyone.

The event was being conducted in the main dining room. A raised table stood at the front for speakers and special guests. Bunting and flags were strewn around the walls. Flowers and ribbons were everywhere.

Kim wore a burgundy evening gown with an orchid from Cole's bouquet. The neckline was modest but the gown was clingy, a characteristic that, she saw immediately, would be underscored by the shaded lighting at the lectern. Experience had taught her that the movers and shakers at these events tended to think of the Institute as tiresome, living in the past, hidebound. Consequently she was careful, save with specialized audiences, to demolish that notion. She'd found that female charm could not hurt the cause, and could generally be relied on to ignite the generosity of the donors.

Cole looked up from a conversation, saw her, waved, and came in her direction. He was redheaded, of indefinable age, with long fragile hands and the congenial but mildly vacuous expression that seems to be part of the uniform worn by public relations consultants. Kim returned the smile, knowing that Cole was thinking the same thing about her.

"Good to see you again, Kimberly," he said. They embraced, and she kissed his cheek and thanked him for the flowers.

They'd met on the luncheon circuit, which Cole had been traveling for the last year, making connections, pushing the advantages of using the *Star Queen*'s facilities for corporate conferences, reassuring all for whom off-world travel, even in an elevator, was unsettling. He was a good salesman, which was to say he could look people directly in the eye while making the most preposterous claims. But he did it cheerfully, with a wink, so to speak, as if to say, you and I know I'm a little over the top about this, but that's okay, if it's not quite at that level, it's still pretty good and you'll get your money's worth.

He introduced her around, and she paid close attention, making sure she got names and faces down. It would help tonight and possibly for years to come. It's not easy to turn your back on someone who knows your first name.

"I have someone special for you to meet," he said, steering her across the room. Toward Ben Tripley. He saw them coming and excused himself from his companions and turned toward her. Then he was breaking in on her, somehow fragmented, as if there were too much of him to take in at a single glance. His gaze swept across her bare shoulders, rose to her eyes, and signaled that he had concluded she was a lesser creature and nothing here could change his mind, but he wouldn't hold it against her.

"Nice to see you again, Kim," he said smoothly.

She returned the compliment and Cole seemed pleased to observe that they knew each other.

"Old friends," smiled Tripley. Without actually physically touching her he seemed to take possession. It was a momentary thing, like filing a claim. "I couldn't resist coming when I heard you'd be speaking," he said. There was an additional exchange at that level and then he was gone, having seen someone he needed to confer with, and she found it easier to breathe.

By the time they were ready to start, there were about four hundred people in the dining room. It was of course a well-off crowd, handsomely attired in satins and silks. Men wore the white or gold neckerchiefs and sashes popular at the time, and the women displayed formfitting gowns which in some cases left remarkably little to the imagination.

The waiters brought an array of meats, greens, and fruit. A bottle of wine showed up in front of Kim, but she passed on it, intending to wait until after she'd spoken. She was seated near the lectern, immediately to the right of the hotel's CEO, Talika McKay. McKay was a petite brown-haired woman, with angelic eyes, a benign smile, an effervescent manner, and the compassion of a shark. Kim had twice seen her in action when publicity efforts had gone awry.

Tripley was in the middle of the room, in earnest conversation with the other diners at his table, but his eyes occasionally found her. When they did there was an intensification of force, and the dining room tended to recede while Tripley came sharply into focus. *I know your secret,* he seemed to be telling her, *you are a woman who chases phantoms. You come here and pretend to be a person of scientific achievement, but you are really quite attractive and very little else.*

The head table was given over to McKay and Kim, to the president of the Greenway Travel Association, and to Abel Donner, who had supervised the conversion of starship into hotel. McKay functioned as master of ceremonies.

When the diners had finished, McKay stood up at the lectern, welcoming everyone to the grand opening of the *Star Queen* Hotel, giving mild emphasis to the last word. It would, she said, carry on in the grand tradition of the celebrated liner. She briefly outlined the capabilities of the *Star Queen*, recommended its facilities for executive training, and introduced the president and the chairman of the board, each of whom briefly gushed over his pleasure at being present.

She described some of the vacation packages that would be available, pointed out that a special connection had always existed between the *Star Queen* and the Seabright Institute, and turned to Kim, who wondered what the special connection was.

"Our principal speaker this evening—" she began.

Kim understood that politics had brought her to this event. Somebody at the *Star Queen* had owed somebody at the Institute a favor. They needed a representative, the Institute needed exposure, and voilà, Brandywine arrives at the lectern. They understood she'd make her pitch for the Institute, but she was also expected to say nice things about the new hotel.

Lecterns had survived the advance of technology that rendered them obsolete because they served to provide a barrier behind which a speaker could hide. Kim disliked them for that reason: they blocked her off from her audience. Had she been able, she would have pushed it aside.

"Thank you, Dr. McKay," she said. She went through the customary greetings, told a couple of jokes on herself, and described the one other time in her life she'd been aboard the *Star Queen*. "I was an intern with the Institute and we were scheduled to take a flight out to the physics lab on Lark. It happened that the *Queen* had just docked. It was in from Caribee. Just a detail, but I never forgot it. How far's Caribee? Eighty-some light-years? They were letting visitors on board, and we had a little time, so we came in through that entrance over there. By the ferns. And into this hall. The captain and a couple of his officers were shaking hands with passengers, saying goodbye, and I tried to imagine how far they had come, how big the void was between Greenway and Caribee.

"We all know there was a time when people thought such a voyage could never happen. Not ever. The travel that we take for granted was once somebody's dream.

"We launched an automated probe from Earth toward Alpha Centauri nine hundred years ago. Alpha Centauri, as I'm sure you know, is only four light-years from Sol. *Four*. But that probe is *still* en route. It's not quite halfway there. And we ask ourselves, why did they bother? They were all going to be dead by the time the probe arrived. Dead for two thousand years. Why do we do these things?

"Why did we just explode Alpha Maxim? We too will be gone for thousands of years before any results can possibly come in." She paused to sip from her glass of water. "I'll tell you why. We launched the long probe to Alpha Centauri for the same reason we built the jump engines that powered the *Queen*: We don't like horizons. We don't like limits. We always want to see beyond them. We don't stop at the water's edge, do we? What is a beach to us but a place from which to launch ourselves at the future?"

Tripley seemed distracted. His eyes locked on a point somewhere up near the ceiling lights.

"We're here this evening to celebrate the retirement of one of the symbols of that dream. The *Queen* has been carrying people and cargo among the Nine Worlds for a century and a half. She's earned a rest. And it's nice to know she'll get that rest in a place where future generations can *touch* her. Can know at least a little of what she was about."

She connected the *Star Queen* to the research ships operated by the Institute, mentioned Max Esterly's contribution to jump engine technology, and ended with the assertion that the ships would continue to push the frontier outward. "Some of us wonder why the cosmos is so large, so inconceivably *huge* that we can never even *see* more than a fraction of it. No matter how powerful the telescope, there's a universe of light out there that simply hasn't had time to reach us. Fifteen billion years, and it still hasn't gotten here. Well, maybe things are this way to reassure us, to let us know that no matter how far we go, there'll always be a horizon to challenge. There'll always be another bend in the river."

Tripley returned from wherever he'd been, caught her watching him, and tried to adopt a look of congenial interest.

A number of people came up afterward to ask about current Institute projects, always a sign that a presentation had gone well. They talked about Beacon, and the president of the Greenway Travel Association, a lovely blond in green and white, wondered whether it wasn't possible to do something similar in hyperspace, an all-points signal that would draw attention to itself, but which wouldn't require two million years to get a response.

"The problem's directional," said Kim. "You can't send a transmission that simply spreads out in all directions. Hyperspace communications have to be aimed. So, yes, if we knew where the celestials were, we could say hello." When the last of them had wandered off, Cole and McKay shook her hand, and Tripley approached.

"That was pretty good, Kim," he said when they were alone. "But I know you don't really believe it."

"*What* don't I believe?" she asked coolly.

"That we won't stop at the water's edge? That we don't like limits." His voice suggested it was a naive notion.

Kim was by no means above stretching the truth in a fund-raiser. But she truly believed that curiosity and the pursuit of knowledge were basic to the human character. "Do you?" she asked.

"Do I *what*?"

"Accept limitations?"

"It's a different matter."

"Why?"

"That's *me*. You were talking about the species."

"We're all wired pretty much the same, Ben. When *you're* willing to lock in the status quo and kick back on your front porch, let me know. I'd like to be there."

"That's a debater's trick, turning the question back on me. But it's time to face the truth, Kim. We're past our peak. This business here," he glanced around, taking in the entire banquet room, "is sad. The interstellars are coming home. I don't like it; it's not good for business. But it's the reality. We're retreating to the Nine Worlds and the big ships are going into mothballs. I wouldn't say this anywhere else, and if you repeat it I'll deny it, but the dream you're talking about was dead before you were born. It's just that the corpse is still warm."

"If you're right," said Kim, "we have no future. But I'm not ready to fold my cards yet."

"Good for you." There was a chill in his voice. "But you're refusing to look at the facts. Greenway and the other worlds are settling in for the long haul. Nobody's really going anywhere anymore. Life's too good for most people. Stay home and party. Let the machines run everything. I'll tell you what I think about Beacon: Somebody could answer tomorrow, and unless they threatened us, nobody would give a damn."

She was drinking a strawberry miconda. It was simultaneously cold and heat-producing. Good stuff. "You think it's a straight downhill run."

"Last days of the Empire," he said. "It's a good time to be alive, except at the very end. If you're a hedonist. As all men are."

"Are *you*, Ben?"

He considered the question. "Not exclusively," he said at last. His gaze bored into her. "No. You wouldn't want to mistake me for a hedonist."

During the course of the evening, she mingled with as many of the guests as she could. She invited everyone to come by the Institute, assured them of private tours, and promised to introduce them to the team that had put Beacon together. By two A.M., when she returned to her apartment weary and more than a little light-headed, she was satisfied that she'd done well by her employer.

But she'd spent six hours on arduous duty and wasn't quite ready to sleep.

She got a cup of hot chocolate from the dispenser, changed into pajamas, looked through the library, and picked out *The Queen Under Fire*, an account of the liner's service during the war against Pacifica. She read for about a half hour and then directed the room to turn out the lights.

They dimmed and went off. A female voice asked whether she wanted anything else.

Kim thought it over and gave her instructions.

She lay back, stared into the darkness, and thought about what Tripley had said. *End of the Empire.* Truth was, people had probably always been saying things like that. *People always believe they live in a crumbling world.*

The *Star Queen*'s flight deck materialized around her.

"Captain, we have company." Cyrus Klein's voice was steady.

The situation flashed onscreen. Eight blips moving toward them, intercept course, off the port quarter.

Kim settled into the command chair. *"Can you identify them, Mr. Klein?"*

"Just a moment, Captain." His eyes narrowed as he waited for the returns to clear.

"Assume the worst," she said. *"Ahead full. Collision stations. Shields up. Where's our escort?"*

Truth is like nudity: It is on occasion indispensable, but it is dangerous and should not be displayed openly. It is truth that gives life its grandeur, but the polite fictions that make it bearable.

—RANDLE ABRAM, *Letters to My Son*, 241

In the morning Kim ate breakfast with Cole, thanked him for his hospitality, checked her bag through to Terminal City, and caught the shuttle to Sky Harbor.

Interstellar maintained its operations division in the lower hangars on the Plum Deck, so called because of the color of the walls. Kim showed up at the service desk and asked if she could speak with Walter Gaerhard. She gave her name and sat down to wait. A few minutes later a muscular man with skin the color of black ivory opened the door and looked in. "Dr. Brandywine?" he asked.

"Mr. Gaerhard."

He smiled and offered his hand. "You wanted to see me?"

"For a few minutes."

"I'm not buying anything."

"It's nothing like that. Can I take you to lunch?"

He was looking closely at her, trying to imagine why she was there. "It's early, Doctor. But thank you. What can I do for you?"

"How good's your memory?"

"It's okay." He led her into a side office. "Are you from Personnel?"

"No. I'm not connected with the company."

He offered a chair and took one himself. "So what did you want me to remember?"

"I want to go back twenty-seven years."

"That's a few."

"You did some repairs on the jump engines of a yacht owned by the Tripley Foundation. The *Hunter*."

His features hardened. "Don't remember," he said. "Twenty-seven years is a long time."

"Interstellar must keep records. Would it help to consult them?"

"Not that far back."

"You don't recall working on the *Hunter*? At all?"

"No." He stood up. "How could you expect me to? What's this about, anyway?"

"I'm doing research on the Tripley Foundation. The *Hunter* is a key part of that history. It was Kile Tripley's personal yacht."

"I just don't remember anything that long ago." He was leaning toward the door, anxious to be away. "Anything else?"

"I'm not the police," she said. "I'm not suggesting anything's wrong."

"I'm sorry to cut this short but I really have to get to work." And he literally bolted from the room, leaving her staring after him.

The crash that had killed Kim's parents was one of those anomalies that isn't supposed to be possible. People died in accidents: they fell off mountains and sailed into storms and got cramps while swimming, but the transportation systems were very nearly 100 percent safe. Very nearly.

Afterward Kim's aunt Jessica had taken her in, and among the numerous gifts she received from that fine woman had been an appreciation for mysteries. Although it had taken Markis Kane to introduce her to Veronica King.

On the train home, she dived into *The Parkington Horror*, one of the earlier adventures of that eccentric private investigator. The detective's Moor Island home base was filled with artifacts from the early years of settlement. The atmosphere was gothic, the dramas played out in crumbling ruins along the ocean or in upland retreats whose sloping dormers and gray windows reflected the madness of their builders.

But Kim wasn't able to put the interviews with Tripley and Gaerhard out of her mind. The CEO had convinced her that, if anything out of the way had happened on the last flight, he was unaware of it. And didn't want to know about it.

Gaerhard on the other hand was hiding something. She asked herself what secret he could possibly be guarding? And judging from his reaction, it was a secret that would still get him in trouble, even after all these years. The only thing she could think of was that there had been no mechanical problem with the *Hunter*, or there had been a *different* problem from the one claimed. And that he had faked the reports. Which meant he'd been bribed. If so, it suggested the *Hunter* had returned for reasons other than needing repairs. But what might those reasons have been?

Even if Sheyel was right and there had been a contact, why all the secrecy?

The Seahawk settled into a gentle rocking motion and salt air found its way into the cabin. Occasionally a train hammered past in the opposite direction.

She opened a channel to her office.

"Hello, Kim," said Andra. "How'd the *Star Queen* go?"

"Out of this world," she said. "Are you busy?"

"Sure. I'm always up to my ears. You know that."

"Right. When you get out from under the pile I want you to do something for me. There was explosion in the Severin Valley in 573. Side blew out of a mountain, lot of people killed. You ever hear of it?"

"Vaguely." That meant no.

"It happened at Mount Hope. I want you to find everything you can on the event and lay it out for me: media coverage, police reports, whatever. One of the victims, Kile Tripley, was only a couple of days back from an interstellar mission on board the *Hunter*. Two other members of that crew, two women, vanished at about the same time." She gave her their names. "Get whatever you can on them, what they did with their spare time, who their friends were, anything you can find. And Kile Tripley too. He was the CEO at Interstellar. And I'd like to know if anybody was ever arrested or charged with anything."

"Okay. May I ask why?" Her voice dropped to a conspiratorial whisper.

"Not sure myself yet, Andra. Can you get everything together this afternoon?"

"If that's what you want."

"Please. And send it to my place. I'll be going directly home. And Andra—?"

"Yes?"

"There's an archeologist at Wheeling Bay. Her name's Kane. Tora Kane. See if you can arrange for me to stop by there tomorrow and see her."

Kim leaned back, the e-book resting on her lap, and closed her eyes. A shiver of excitement rose up her spine.

When she got home she found a note from Matt congratulating her on what was, "from all reports, an outstanding effort." She also had a three o'clock appointment next day with Tora Kane at something called the Colson site, along with a code locator for the cab.

Other than Kane's ex-wives, his only known relative, and the only person with whom he'd maintained a close relationship, was his daughter Tora. Tora Kane had been quoted in the record to the effect that her father had never been the same after the Mount Hope event, that he had tried to stay on at Severin Village, hoping the town could rebuild. But everyone had given up. Too many bad memories. And then the news had arrived that the dam would have to come down.

The ex-wives had all built other lives for themselves. They seemed to harbor no ill will toward Kane, but it was evident that all had made a clean break after the marriages had expired.

She was watching visuals of the daughter when the files on Emily and Yoshi and the Mount Hope event arrived.

Kim collected a dinner of cheese and fresh fruit, and carried it into the living room. She set it on the coffee table, went back for wine, and told Shepard to begin.

Most of the information Andra had gathered about Emily was well known to her, of course. Where she'd gone to school, that she'd written some articles, that she'd been a junior executive for Widebase Communications Systems before landing with the Foundation.

But as she read the articles, looked at the pictures, glossed over comments about her by her colleagues, she began to realize that she'd never been close to understanding the real Emily Brandywine.

An extract from one typical essay revealed the depth of Emily's commitment:

> Somewhere, other eyes than ours watch the stars. Let there be no doubt about that. Were it not so, we would have to confess there is little point to our existence, other than to eat, drink, and procreate. We have come to life on the shore of an infinite sea. Whatever power has designed this

arrangement surely intended that we not be alone, that we set out to map its currents and its deeps, explore its islands, and ultimately embrace whatever other sailors we encounter.

Unfortunately, the islands are farther apart than we could have imagined. Many among us suggest we should simply give it up and stay home. Be content under our own warm suns. Hang around on the beach. But I would suggest to you that if we take that course, we will lose that part of us which is most worth preserving: the drive to push into the unknown. If we are true to ourselves, the day will surely come when we lift wine in the company of brothers and sisters born beneath strange suns.

It was a little overwrought, but there was no doubting her sincerity. Emily had not been trained as a scientist, so she tended to draw conclusions based on emotional need rather than on evidence. The human race could not be alone because the universe was so *big*. Because we needed to have someone to compare notes with.

The reality, of course, was that the appearance of life on Earth seemed to require a set of circumstances so unusual and so fortuitous that it might very well have been a unique event. It was quite possible that the human race was the only intelligent species in all those billions of light-years. In the dark of the night, Kim suspected that was precisely the true state of affairs. She would not have admitted it, not even to Solly. She'd been riding point for too many years, trying to engender enthusiasm for Beacon, which was the only Institute project that seemed to have the capacity to get people excited.

Yoshi Amara had left no written work behind, save her doctoral thesis, which dealt with atmospheric thermodynamics. She was still in her early twenties when she joined the Tripley team. Her flight on the *Hunter*, as far as Kim could determine, was the first time she'd been away from the home world.

She ran some videos of Emily urging the Algonda Chamber of Commerce to get behind a public funding for elderly citizens; conducting a leadership program for managers at All-Purpose Transport; speaking to the class of '71 at Mellinda University, saying all the things one usually says to graduates; participating in a symposium on the topic "Where Do We Go from Here?"—which was about population loss and not space exploration— and arguing strenuously for a concerted effort to persuade people to have more children.

She switched over to her Tripley file and watched Kile at the charter meeting of the Foundation, trying to explain why it was essential to pursue the search for celestials. It never seemed to occur to him that they might not exist. He struggled a bit. It was, after all, not an easy argument to nail down. Someone in the audience commented that we all know how humans behave and if there are celestials out there and they operate the way we do, maybe finding them wouldn't be such a good thing. Let them be, he said.

By midnight she'd concluded that Emily's companions on the *Hunter*—Tripley, Amara, and the pilot, Kane—were everything they purported to be. It might be true that all but Kane edged into fanaticism, including Emily, but there was no doubt that, had they succeeded in their attempt to find evidence of other civilizations, had they actually encountered something alive beyond St. Johns, they would have broadcast it to the world.

That meant Sheyel was wrong. Had to be. Yet there was a good chance the shoe from the villa had belonged to Yoshi.

And Gaerhard was hiding something. He'd done what the records indicated was a routine repair job almost three decades ago. And when she mentioned it he knew immediately what she was talking about.

Andra had provided several hundred accounts of the Mount Hope explosion and its aftermath.

Kim studied pictures of the area *before* and immediately after the explosion. The crater was there, of course, a kilometer and a quarter wide, looking as if someone had dropped a nuke. Trees for vast distances had been scorched and blown down. The valley had been decimated.

There were literally hundreds of pictures of the destruction, buildings wrecked, fires burning, rescue workers pouring in, dazed survivors wandering through the carnage.

Investigators had estimated the yield at several kilotons. But there was no radiation. A government commission had finally labeled the incident "due to cause or causes unknown."

No record could be found of a vessel that had lost fuel cells, or of improper disposal of spent units. Of course it would not have been in a perpetrator's interest to get caught, and records were not difficult to falsify.

Authorities pursued independent investigations of both the disappearance of the women, and of the explosion. Neither ever came to anything.

■   ■   ■

The Mighty Third Memorial Museum was dedicated to the exploits of the Third Fleet during the brief but bloody war with Pacifica. Theory had once held that interstellar war would never happen because of energy consumption limitations, the problems inherent in subduing a planetary-sized hostile population, the impossibility of bringing an opponent's interstellar force to combat should they wish to avoid it, and the fact that nothing one might steal was worth the effort to carry it off.

All this reasoning broke down because it assumed war was a rational exercise, carried on for rational purposes.

Historically, few leaders have calculated a cost-benefit ratio before plunging into combat. Kings often provoked conflict for the sole purpose of feeding their troops at someone else's expense. Or to get tens of thousands of malcontents out of the country and pointed somewhere else, as happened during the Crusades, and again on Tigris during the Andrean Wars.

Historians were still arguing over details of the slide sixty years before into the war between Greenway and Pacifica, the only one ever fought between star systems. It was a war that neither side wanted. The critical factor seemed to have been everyone's conviction that armed conflict was impossible. Both governments therefore had felt free to engage in threats and posturing.

The shooting began when a PacForce destroyer mistook a cruise ship for an intelligence-gathering mission and fired on it, killing 212 passengers and most of the crew. When they refused to apologize—the liner apparently had been off course—the steps to war had followed swiftly one after another.

The conflict eventually raged for eighteen months. There were several major battles. Embargoes were placed on third parties, raids against military targets spilled over and killed tens of thousands, and electronic warfare had constantly shut down power grids and computer systems.

Markis Kane became one of the celebrated names during the war. He began as an escort captain and ended as the commanding officer of a squadron of destroyers. He was decorated half a dozen times. He avenged the worst atrocity of the conflict, the terror attack on Khatalan, which killed sixty thousand people, by destroying the battle cruiser *Hammurabi*, which had led the assault. His best-known exploit, however, was at Armagon, where his squadron disrupted an attacking line of destroyers. His own vessel, the escort *376*, had been badly damaged and was for a time thought lost. He brought it back full of holes, its guidance systems gone, its weapons blown out, half its crew dead. But it had arrived in home skies with all flags flying.

The exploit had entered story and song. Books had been written, and there were few children on Greenway who had not played at being Markis Kane on the *376*.

The Third Fleet had been Greenway's principal attack arm. It had won most of the victories, and absorbed most of the casualties. Its commander in chief had risen to the premiership on the strength of his performance, and its veterans still gathered in meeting places around the world.

The Mighty Third Memorial Museum was located on a peaceful hilltop on the western edge of Seabright, where, according to tradition, women and men from Earth had made their first landing on Greenway. The site looked down on a reflecting pool and a carefully cut green lawn and a series of walkways. Landing pads accommodated hundreds of visitors daily.

Kim stepped out of her cab and strolled up a gravel path that wound beneath a clutch of ancient oaks. Two of them were supposed to have been planted by the crew of that first lander, launched by the *Constellation*. But the descent had been six hundred years ago and the oaks couldn't be more than half that old. Nevertheless it was a pleasant legend and no one bothered to dispute it.

The day was gorgeous, full of sunlight and the smell of the sea. Kids, tourists, and students were everywhere. She went inside, checked the guide, and walked into the east wing. An entire section was given over to the *376* and to Markis Kane.

There were photos of the hero, parts of the ship itself, and a mock-up of the flight deck. The actual command chair was encased behind a glass wall. One of the ship's laser cannons pointed down a hallway. Personal articles of the crew were laid out, including a jacket that had belonged to Kane. The original logs were there, contained on two disks that gleamed like diamonds on the arm of the command chair. Copies were on sale in the museum store. And there was a strip of bloody cloth that the ship's engineer had used to tie down the fuel leads after the *376* had taken a hit.

Kim read a copy of a letter sent to the parents of one of the crew killed on the mission.

She entered the VR tank and went through the flight, watching everything through Kane's eyes. She emerged shaken, impressed by the courage and tenacity of the man.

Kane could not possibly have been part of a hoax. Not under any circumstances she could imagine. Therefore, if he'd told Sheyel nothing had happened, that should end the matter. And yet—

"Ah, Kim." She turned and looked into the amiable features of Mikel Alaam, the museum director. "It's good to see you again."

"Good morning, Mikel." She embraced him and offered her cheek for a kiss. "How've you been?"

Alaam wore his hair shoulder length. He had the sort of professional aloofness one usually finds in museum directors, fiction writers, and morticians. "Quite well, thank you. What brings you to the Mighty Third?"

"I'm interested in Markis Kane."

"Ah, yes. He's a fascinating man. He was here for the dedication. Even functioned as an advisor when we put the exhibition together." They had pictures from the event: Kane drinking coffee with a couple of the technicians, Kane wielding a boltlight, Kane laughing with somebody's kids.

"Really? When was that?"

"Oh, a long time ago. I was only an intern then, but I actually got to meet him. In fact I shook his hand." He gazed soulfully at his palm.

"What can you tell me about him?"

"Not much. He was a friend of Art Wescott, who was the director at the time. I thought he seemed embarrassed by all the fuss. But we were delighted to have him. That was when they'd just dedicated the museum."

"So it was—?"

"Around, what, 575. Sure, that was our first year." He looked at the flight deck mock-up. "Yes," Alaam continued. "He walked around, talked to everybody, signed autographs. Decent man. Not like some of these people—"

The room was bright with sunlight. Like Kane's reputation.

Kim's cab moved north up the coastline through a gray sky.

Ahead, Mount Morghani stood directly astride the shore line, overlooking Wheeling Bay. Morghani had provided a string of dictators with a natural fortress during the long years of their rule over the island empire. Esther Hox had carved from its slopes the Black Hall, a stronghold from which she directed military operations against the bands of rebels who tried unsuccessfully for four decades to unseat her.

Today, Morghani and its fortifications and the harbor it guarded provided Seabright with a stunning backdrop. The Black Hall was a major tourist draw. And a prime archeological site.

The structure was four hundred years old, built during the dark age that had followed hard after Greenway established itself formally as an independent political entity. Guns, lasers, and missile launchers were still in place in the surrounding mountains, and the control room from which Hox personally oversaw defenses was still visited annually by tens of thousands.

The Black Hall had become one of the prime symbols of that age, and therefore, in an inexplicable manner, of the romance of the period. Kim loved the place, which was maintained by the Seabright Historical Union. Much of the old fortress was off-limits because it wasn't safe. But troops in the uniforms of those bygone years were still marshaled twice daily in the main courtyard. The imperial quarters were also open to visitors, as were the art gallery and the library. Hox and her successors had commissioned much and stolen more. Today, it was all on display.

At the foot of Morghani, the ocean was restless. The surf pounded the rocks, gulls moved in everlasting circles, and along the stony beaches, children collected shells.

The cab crossed the face of the Black Hall and sailed in over the bay. Here, piers and docks pushed into the water, and warehouses lined the shore. Civilization had moved south after the wars, so the structures were crumbling and largely unattended. Some of them were built atop ruins that dated back half a millennium. Vandals and thieves had been at work for centuries, but teams of archeologists were now trying to retrieve details of everyday life during the age of the dictators.

The vehicle dropped low toward the water, skirted the shoreline moving west, and set down finally among a cluster of modular shelters beside a couple of battered flyers carrying the markings of the Seabright Historical Union. Kim opened the hatch and dropped down onto a surface of hard-packed clay and sparse grass. A damp, cold wind blew in off the sea.

Several people were working around the edges of an excavation pit, from which they'd hauled timbers and broken concrete and steel beams. A couple of the males looked up, appraised her, and exchanged approving glances.

A young man, probably a graduate student, had been brushing earth from a piece of electronic equipment. He broke off and came over. "May I help you, ma'am?" he asked.

"I'm looking for Dr. Kane," said Kim.

He punched a button on his link. "Tora," he said, "you have a visitor."

A female voice responded: "Be right there." Moments later a woman wearing a wide-brimmed hat and coveralls came out of one of the shelters and walked toward her. The grad student accepted Kim's thanks and went back to his brush.

"Dr. Brandywine?" the woman asked, holding out a hand. "I'm Tora Kane." The hat, Kim noticed, carried a Glory logo. Tora followed her gaze. "The *Arbuckle*," she said.

The *Arbuckle* was a freighter that had gone down on Glory almost five centuries earlier, making it one of the oldest artifacts in the system. Kim knew that the crash site was a preserve, and that only certified scholars were allowed to go near it.

Tora was about Kim's height, with auburn hair drawn back, full lips, full breasts pressing against the coveralls. She had her father's dark, intense eyes. Looking into them, Kim could almost focus down, eliminate everything else, and believe she was seeing the old starship captain. "I appreciate your making time to talk to me," she said, taking the outstretched hand.

"My pleasure." Tora glanced from Kim to the taxi. "Have I won something?"

A gust of wind blew across them. "I was wondering if I could ask some questions about your father," said Kim.

"Ah," she said, as if she should have realized. "May I ask what your interest is?"

"Emily Brandywine was my sister."

Muscles worked in her throat. "I should have recognized the name. And the face."

"I'd like very much to find out what happened to her."

"Of course." Tora turned back toward the bay entrance and Kim could not see her expression. "I wish I could help. But I just don't know anything. When they came back on the *Hunter*, my father stayed on board to see to the entry procedures. The other three got off, and he never saw them again."

"Are you sure?"

"Yes, I'm sure."

"Please don't take this the wrong way, but may I ask *how*?"

"Because he *told* me. Don't you think he was upset by it all? Everything happened at the same time, the disaster at the village, the loss of Tripley, the missing women." The wind tried to push them toward the excavation. "Why don't you send the cab away and come inside?" she said.

Kim did and Tora led the way back to the shelter. "It's not very comfortable," she observed, "but it's out of the cold." She opened the door, and Kim stepped into a flow of warm air.

It was musty and cramped. One room plus a washroom. Maps of the waterfront area covered the walls. Two tables were stacked with jars, electrical artifacts, coins, tools, candles, toys, small pieces of statuary. "How's it going?" asked Kim.

"Not bad. We think we've uncovered Gabrielli's private residence."

"Gabrielli?"

"One of Hox's advisors. If it's true, we may finally be able to find out why they had Rentzler murdered. Well, you don't care about that." She held a heated cloth to her face, offered one to Kim, and sat down in a canvas chair. "Kim," she said, her tone suddenly regretful, "we all lost people in that business. I won't pretend that what happened to my father and me compares to losing your sister the way you did, but his life disintegrated too."

"In what way?"

"A lot of people were dead. There was talk about antimatter. Everybody else who'd been on the mission vanished. It all sounded like a conspiracy. And people like to have someone to blame. He was the only one left alive, at least the only one they could find. So they blamed him."

"It doesn't appear in the record."

"His friends got cold. People he'd known for years backed away from him, looked the other way when they met on the street. Some tried to get up a lawsuit but there was no proof. Eventually he left the valley, but it followed him. Forgive me, but people like you would show up asking questions. No accusations, but the implications were always there.

"My father was a decent man, Kim. He'd never hurt anybody, and he wouldn't have been part of any of the things that were being talked about."

"Like stealing fuel cells."

"Yes. Like stealing fuel cells." Tora got up, poured a couple of cups of coffee, and held one out to Kim. "I'm afraid I just don't know anything that would help."

Two people came in, got introduced, went back out. Kim said: "You don't think there's any connection between the return of the *Hunter* and the Mount Hope event?"

"I don't. I can understand why people want to tie them together. But they checked the *Hunter*. *All the antimatter that should have been there was there.* Everybody forgets that. My father did nothing wrong. He had everything he wanted in life. He had no reason to steal fuel cells. Or anything else."

"So what do *you* think happened?"

"I don't have a theory. I know my father was ruined by it all. He never piloted another ship. Did you know that?"

"Yes," she said. "I did."

"With Tripley dead, the Foundation halted its flights, and nobody else would hire him. Oh, they didn't mention Mount Hope. Just don't need any captains right now, thank you.

"Look, Kim, I know it hurts. But if you want my advice, let go."

"You had a call from Dr. Flexner, Kim."

She took off her jacket and dropped it over the sofa. "Okay, Shep. See if you can reach him."

"It was just a few minutes ago. He was in his office."

She picked up a glass of apple juice and slipped into her comm-chair.

"He seemed upset," Shepard added.

"In what way?"

"Irritable. Angry. Anyway, we have a connection."

The walls vanished and she was sitting in Matt's office. He did indeed look a trifle mussed. "Hi, Matt," she said.

"Hello, Kim." He was seated behind his desk, writing. "I've got a question for you," he said, not looking up but putting the pen down.

"Go ahead."

Now his eyes rose to meet hers. "What did you do to Benton Tripley?"

"What do you mean?"

"I got called in by Phil this morning. *He* apparently got a call from Tripley. Tripley is in a rage."

"Why?"

"It wasn't exactly clear *why*. But it has to do with you. When you were making the presentation, did you ask him about the Mount Hope incident?"

"We talked about it."

"Did you imply that his father was involved in criminal activity?"

She tried to remember the conversations. "No," she said. "Why would I do something like that?"

"That was going to be my question."

"It didn't happen."

"Good. Because whatever benefit we got from giving him the Morton Cable Award, we've more than lost."

"Matt—"

"Did you *really* break into his house?"

"No!"

"He says you did."

Kim felt her temper rising. Take a deep breath and don't lose control. "I looked at the property in the Severin Valley. But it's not his place anymore. That whole area's abandoned."

"Are you sure about the details? Did you check out the ownership before you went in?"

"No—"

"That's what I thought. The director had to apologize to him this morning."

"Apologize?" Tripley's image took shape in her mind. He was smiling. "What for? Whatever the paperwork says, the place is abandoned."

"Tripley thinks the Institute's sticking its nose into his business." Matt sighed. "Kim, we've assured him there's a misunderstanding somewhere, and that the matter is ended. I don't know what this is all about. But it *is* ended, right?"

"Matt, this is something I've been doing on my own."

"*No*, Kim. *You* don't do anything on your own. You're a representative of the Institute. For God's sake, you speak for us a couple of times a week." His gaze hardened. "You will back away and not go near any of this again. Do you understand?"

She returned his stare. "Matt, I talked to one of the Interstellar technicians yesterday. About the repairs made on the *Hunter* after they came back. He lied to me."

"How do you know?"

"I could see it in his face."

"Good. That'll hold up if anybody questions you—"

"Listen, if there's nothing to any of this, why is Tripley so bent out of shape? What's he hiding?"

"That's easy. A lot of people died out there. In the explosion. If it were to be shown that his father was in some way liable, there'd be a hundred lawsuits against the estate."

"After all these years?"

"I'm not a lawyer. But, yeah, I'd say he stands to lose quite a lot if you were to find something that makes his father culpable."

Somebody apparently entered the office. The interruption was behind her, so she couldn't see who it was. But Matt glowered over her shoulder at the visitor. She heard the door shut, and his attention returned to her. "Matt, I don't see how I can just walk away from this."

He cleared his throat. "Kim, I have a pretty good idea what this means to you—"

"Matt, you have no idea what it means to me—"

"All right. I'm sorry. I hear what you're saying. But the problem is there's no proof anywhere to support an investigation. All that's going to happen if you persist is that the Institute will get burned, you'll wind up out on the street, and nothing will have been accomplished."

She took a minute to get control of her voice. "How do we get evidence if we don't look?"

He looked pained. "I don't know, Kim. But you have to realize that you represent the Institute. Round-the-clock. Whatever you do reflects on us." He braced both elbows on his desk and set his chin atop his clasped hands. "I understand that we're not being fair to you. But you have to understand there's just too much at stake."

"Money."

"A lot of money."

She let her eyes close. "Anything else?"

"No. That's about it."

"Thanks," she said. And broke the connection. Her living room re-formed around her. She got up, retrieved the jacket, and walked out onto the deck.

The sea looked cold and gray.

O come with me to the misty veils
Beyond the sunset, west of St. Johns. . . .
—CRES VILLARD, *West of St. Johns*, 487

The big push at the Institute was to lay out a strategy for exploiting interest in Beacon. Matt had already arranged interviews with the crew of the *Trent*. It was awkward because the hypercomm signals required time to make the round-trip. Journalists had, in effect, to submit their questions and come back the next day for the answers. So much for spontaneity, or for playing off a scientist's response and letting it lead naturally to the next question.

Consequently nobody really wanted to talk to the *Trent* crew. No one from the media had accompanied the mission, because travel time was excessive and it just wasn't perceived as that big a story. It was too far away. And nobody took celestials seriously anymore. The interest was not generated by the reason for the experiment, but by the fact that we had demonstrated we could trigger a nova.

Consequently, the Institute's public information group decided to concentrate on that aspect of the story, and the benefits the human race might eventually derive from the capability. Unfortunately no one could think of any. Improvements in magnetic bottle design, maybe. We *were* getting better at antimatter containment. And maybe gravity deflection systems, which allowed electronic devices to function in ever-more-concentrated gravity fields.

Cray Elliott, a public relations specialist who was a junior member of the team, nodded and wrote it all down. Kim showed her disquiet. "We are forever trying to sell science because somebody somewhere will get a better toothbrush," she grumbled. "Whatever happened to sheer curiosity?"

"You have to be practical," Cray said. He was bright, ebullient, cheerful. She really didn't want to have to deal with *cheerful.*

Nevertheless it was all there if one wanted to look: long-range star travel was rendered more efficient, the cells that provided fuel to heating and lighting systems for entire cities would increase their capacity, and safety would be enhanced.

"But," said Kim, "star travel is being cut back everywhere, we've already got more power than we can possibly use, and there hasn't been any kind of accident, that *I* know of, involving fuel cells. *Ever.*" Other than Mount Hope, probably.

"It doesn't matter," Matt said. "Those are just details. Nobody notices *details.*"

Maybe he was right. It wouldn't be the first time they'd stretched things a bit. Two years before, the Institute had not challenged rumors that a breakthrough in antigravity was imminent, even though no such thing was in the works, and in fact every physicist that Kim knew of thought antigravity an impossibility. The story retained credence because people believed that if you could induce artificial gravity, you could surely nullify its effects. But it was a different matter altogether. One didn't need to bend time and space, but only to establish magnetic fields, to create the condition that allowed people to walk about in starships.

Kim thought that the public relations division might even have *started* the rumor. When she'd mentioned it to Matt, he had piously denied everything. Piety was always how you knew Matt was lying.

Now she listened to his instructions and wondered why she didn't just walk out. The money was good, the Institute was a decent cause, and the truth was she got a lot of satisfaction simply from the fact that she was so talented at what she did. But as long as she stayed here, the career she'd wanted, dreamed about, prepared for, would not happen.

She recalled the defensiveness with which she'd told Sheyel what she was doing. *"It's not the field I'd have chosen."*

And he'd been embarrassed for her. *"One never knows how things will turn out."*

It was always like that. She was among those who never went to reunions.

Back in her office she found a communication from Shepard. *"There's a response to your message to St. Johns,"* he said.

"Onscreen, please, Shep."

"Yes, Kim. Please note I have adjusted all dates to Greenway Central Time."

From: Chief, Records Branch
To: Dr. Kimberly Brandywine
Date: Monday, January 15, 600
Subject: *Hunter* Flight Plan

Per your request, following information is provided re: EIV4471886 *Hunter* flight plan, filed February 11, 573.

Depart St. Johns Feb 12, 573 0358.

Arrive QCY4149187 April 17, 573, to begin general survey Golden Pitcher.

Projected departure from Golden Pitcher was to have been reported when known, but was expected at approximately June 1, 574.

J. B. Stanley

Records Chief

The entire mission was to have lasted fifteen months. Kim pressed Solly's key.

"Hi, Kim." His image brightened the screen. "How'd the meeting go?"

"As usual. Got a question for you."

"Go ahead."

"I should have asked this before: When the *Hunter* left St. Johns, would they have inspected the jump engines?"

"You mean the station?"

"Yes."

"Only if asked. The engines should have been looked at by the Foundation's own people before leaving Sky Harbor. If you're asking me whether a breakdown is likely early in a voyage that was going way out into the deeps, I'd think not. But it happened. And to be honest, jump engines take a beating. It doesn't take much of an oversight to cause a problem."

"What happens if the engines die while they're in hyperspace?"

"Bye-bye, baby," he said. "Unless they can make repairs."

"What about communications?"

"They won't have any. The ship has to make the jump back into real-space first before they can talk to anybody."

"That doesn't show a great deal of foresight."

He shrugged. "Realities of basic physics, m' dear."

"Has it ever happened?"

"Don't know. We've lost a ship from time to time." He watched for a reaction, but she didn't provide one. "Why? What have you got?"

"Not a thing," she said.

She put the projected route on her screen, drawing a line between St. Johns and the *187* target star. Somewhere along that line, the engines had shut down and they'd come out of hyperspace, made temporary repairs, and returned to Greenway. So they'd gotten nowhere close to the Golden Pitcher. In fact, since it was approximately a forty-day flight back to Sky Harbor from the closest points along that line, they couldn't have been much more than a week out of St. Johns when the problem developed.

A week.

That was still a long distance. A starship would cover about 270 light-years in a week.

She marked off the line at that point. Somewhere between the mark and St. Johns, the engines had brought them out of hyper.

"So what?" said Solly, who seemed to be reading her mind. "I mean, we've known all along they broke down. What difference does it make where it happened?"

"Let's go back to square one," she said.

"What's square one?"

"'We struck gold.' Sheyel's convinced there was a contact of some kind. Let's assume he's right. That the *Hunter* saw something out there. So the question becomes, where were they when it happened?"

"You tell me: Where were they?"

"Near a star."

"How do we know that?" asked Solly.

"Has to be. If contact was made either with a ground entity or with an orbiter of some kind, we have ipso facto a star system. If it was made with a vessel, you'd have to ask yourself whether the vessel was in a star system or whether it was out in the void. If it was in the void, what could it have been doing out there?"

"Repairing its engines?" suggested Solly, seeing the point.

"Right. What are the odds against two ships suffering breakdowns and showing up at the same empty place? No, whatever happened, it had to be close to a star."

She looked at the *Hunter*'s course. "I count seven stars within a reasonable range along their course line. If they ran into something, it would have been in the neighborhood of one of those seven."

Solly shook his head. "Okay," he said. "Suppose you're right. Suppose there *was* an encounter of some kind. It was twenty-seven years ago. You think the celestials are still going to be hanging around out there?"

"It doesn't have to have been another *ship*," she said. "They may have discovered a living world."

He sat down on the edge of his desk and considered the possibility. "Yeah," he said. "That could be."

"There are only seven stars," she said again. "*Seven.*"

"I hope you're not telling me you're going to ask for a mission."

"No."

"Good," he said.

"Matt would think I'd gone over the edge."

"That's right. And I'm not sure he'd be far wrong. Look, Kim, this is all guesswork, and you don't have anything more persuasive than a shoe and a crew member who calls home with a cryptic message that may not mean anything at all. That may have been misunderstood for that matter. By the way, did it occur to you that Yoshi might have been talking about the Golden Pitcher?"

"They didn't get to the Golden Pitcher. They didn't get anywhere close."

"Okay." He shrugged. "I mean, if they found, say, a tree out there, or a *city*, why not say that? What's the big secret?"

She had no answer.

He looked at the time. "Got to go. I have some reports due."

She could see he felt relieved. He'd expected her to go in and make a fool of herself trying to persuade Matt that the Institute should send out a survey team. "Solly," she said, "when a ship's logs get sent to the Archives, does anyone actually review them?"

"Under normal circumstances I can't imagine why they would. But if you're asking whether anyone has seen the *Hunter*'s logs from the Golden Pitcher flight, I'd say almost certainly."

"Because of the disappearances."

"Right. The police would have looked for any indication that something unusual had happened on the mission. The fact that there doesn't seem to have been a follow-up, that no one searched Tripley's place, seems to indicate they didn't find anything."

"They might have been bought off."

"It's possible." A long silence drew out between them. "Kim," he said, "Matt's right. Why don't you give this a rest?"

She'd have liked to. Kim had no appetite for challenging her boss, for taking on Tripley, for encouraging Solly to think she had become obsessed. But Emily was lost out there somewhere, and somehow it all seemed to be connected. "I can't just walk away from it," she said. "I want to know what happened. And I don't care who gets offended, or who gets sued."

Solly looked at her for a long minute, and nodded. "Let me know if there's anything I can do," he said.

"There is. How can we get a look at those logs?"

He took a deep breath. "We'd have to bribe somebody," he said.

Bribe? "Isn't there a way to do it without breaking the law?"

"None that I know of. So I think where we are is this: You need to decide whether you're as serious as you say. If so—" He shrugged.

Kim had never knowingly violated the law. "We can't do that," she said.

"I didn't think so." Solly looked out of the screen at her, trying to suggest everything would be all right. "Gotta go," he said.

The screen blanked. She sat staring at it, pushed back in her chair, activated it again and brought up the *Autumn*. Emily with those wistful eyes looked back at her.

Where are you?

She thought about the terrible days after her disappearance while they waited for news. Her parents had tried to protect her, to reassure her that Emily was coming home, that she'd taken a trip somewhere and they'd be hearing from her at any time. But Kim had seen the hollowness in their eyes, detected the strained voices. She'd known.

They must have assumed from the beginning that she would not be found alive. Murders were extremely rare in Equatoria, seldom exceeding more than a half dozen annually, in a population of six million. Homicides were usually domestic, but there was still the occasional maniac. The St. Luke killer, so named because of his penchant for leaving biblical verses pinned to the bodies of victims, had rampaged through the northwest during a two-year spree in which he'd murdered seven people. He had been the worst of modern times.

What must have surprised her folks was that the mystery was never solved. No body was ever found.

Set against that, what was a little bribery?

She punched in Solly's code and he appeared onscreen, not looking as surprised as she'd expected.

"Can we arrange it?" she asked.

He looked at her disapprovingly. "Is my lovely associate running amok?"

"Yes," she said. "If that's what it takes. Can we do it?"

"I know somebody," he said.

"How much will it cost?"

"I don't know. Probably a couple of hundred. Let me make some calls, and I'll get back to you."

Kim was scheduled to have lunch with a representative of the Theosophical Society, a Brother Kendrick. This time, her objective was not to solicit contributions, but to reassure the Society that there would be no long-term deleterious effects from Beacon, thereby persuading them, she hoped, to remove their outspoken opposition to the Institute.

They ate at Kashmir's, which specialized in cuisine from the Sebastian Island chain. Brother Kendrick expressed the Society's concern that the series of novas would make an area of approximately eight million cubic light-years permanently uninhabitable.

Kim pointed out there were no human habitations anywhere close to what the technicians called the target box.

"What about nonhuman habitations?" he asked.

The question stopped her cold.

Brother Kendrick, like almost everyone else on Greenway, was of indeterminate age. But he was inclined to lecture rather than talk. His attitude embodied a barely concealed condescension, his eyes never left her, and it was clear he was speaking through a controlled anger. He wore a neatly trimmed black beard and his hair was cut long. The Theosophists were not among those who adhered to trends.

"There are none in the region," she said. "We did an extensive survey to assure ourselves—"

"—How many star systems are in the affected area?"

"Several hundred," she said.

"Several hundred." He made the number sound as if it bordered on sacrilege. "And we examined the worlds in all these systems?"

"Not in all," she admitted. "Most of the systems have multiple stars and can't maintain planetary bodies in stable orbits. Others don't have worlds in the biozone—"

"Dr. Brandywine." He drew himself up until he seemed all beard, eyes, and backbone. "The truth is we still don't know very much about the origin of life, so it would seem to me somewhat presumptuous to pretend we can state with any degree of certainty what the required conditions are. The only thing we can be sure of is that several hundred systems will receive an extensive radiation bath over the next century or so. We might destroy the very thing we say we're looking for."

The waiter appeared. Kim settled for a salad. She had little appetite for these confrontations. Her companion ordered a dish of steamed rice and cabaña eel.

"Brother Kendrick," she said, "we were aware of the danger from the beginning, and we worked extensively over fourteen years to assure ourselves that nothing would be harmed."

His voice softened. "I know you would like to do the right thing, Dr. Brandywine. But it seems to us that we're far too cavalier with these efforts." The waiter brought calder wine and Kim offered, as a toast, the Theosophical Society. Brother Kendrick hesitated. "Under these circumstances, I think that might be inappropriate. Let us drink instead to your health, Dr. Brandywine."

The wine tasted flat. "I can assure you we did everything within reason," she insisted.

"Except stop the event." Kendrick wore a white shirt with a gray ribbon tie and a gray jacket. His eyes were of the same hue, and there was in fact a general grayness about the man that suggested he'd given up on human nature and was now beyond being shocked. Kim felt the full weight of his moral judgment. "When they tested the first hydrogen bomb," he said, "there was some concern that the explosion would set off a chain reaction. Blow up the entire planet. Scientists felt the chance of such an occurrence was slight, so they took it. Risked everything we ever were, everything we might ever become." He examined his drink, and then downed it in a swallow. "Dr. Brandywine," he said, "how is that action different from what the Institute has done?"

"There's no one in the area," she said again. "No one we could possibly harm."

Bars of sunlight fell across his stern features. "Let us hope you are right."

■　　■　　■

She was glad to get back to her office. When Matt asked her how the luncheon had gone, she complained that Brother Kendrick had been immovable. No amount of argument about the conditions that had to exist before organic molecules could appear had any effect on him. "He said that anything short of a physical search, *everywhere*, was inadequate."

"I'm sorry," said Matt. "But we had to make the effort."

"*You* can have him next time."

"I had him last time." He tapped his desktop. "I thought maybe he'd be receptive to feminine charm."

"You owe me," said Kim.

He nodded. "I'll treat for lunch tomorrow. By the way, Solly was trying to get hold of you."

Solly was in a seminar at the moment, and she had to wait till the end of the afternoon to speak with him. His image appeared in her office as she was getting ready to go home. "No luck," he said.

"With the Archives? I thought you knew somebody."

"They've got a big integrity push now. Apparently caught one of their people diverting the Archives's funds into her own account." He shrugged. "I'm sorry."

She had dinner that evening on Calico Island with a young man she'd met through the Sea Knights. He was of the class of persons who neither pursued a career nor dedicated themselves to a life of unbridled leisure. A substantial number of people were taking that middle route now, staying away from anything that put routine demands on their time, and instead indulging in a range of academic or other interests. They spent their lives engaged in drama, or chess, or wallball. They toured the world's beaches, if their resources permitted. Life was short, her date argued, although it was now longer than it had ever been. He had dedicated himself to locating the *Marmora*, a maglev brig lost somewhere in the middle northern latitudes on the far side of the world.

"Find the *Marmora*," he said, "and my life will have counted for something."

He sounded like Kile Tripley.

Like Emily, now that she thought of it.

Maybe like herself.

Men are so slow-witted and give themselves so easily to the desires of the moment that he who will deceive will always find a willing victim.
—NICCOLÒ MACHIAVELLI, *The Prince*, II, 1513 C.E.

Kile's widowed mother, Sara Tripley Baines, lived in Eagle Point now, had lived there at the time of the event. A search turned up several hits and a couple of recent pictures: She liked to dress formally, and was quite striking even by the heightened standards of the age. Her bearing demonstrated that she was fully aware of her charms.

Sara was the president of an architectural club which annually awarded a prize for best executed design for a public building. She was on the board of directors of Tupla University, and she remained an active participant in competitive gymnastics. Kim watched a VR of her appearance at a benefit dinner where she tried to persuade the attendees to back a building project. Her delivery was a trifle stodgy, Kim thought, but dreadfully sincere.

Kim consulted the directory for her number, picked up one of the Institute's virtual projectors, and went to a public booth to ensure she could not be connected to the call. She selected a model from the projector's inventory, a tall, redheaded, aristocratic woman, and then punched in Sara's number, audio only, which was, of course, correct practice when calling a stranger.

The house AI answered.

"Hello," said Kim. "This is Kay Braddock calling. I'd like to speak with Sara Baines, please?"

"May I ask what your business is with Mrs. Baines?"

Kim hesitated. "I'm working on a book about the Severin Valley," she said. "I understand she was an eyewitness to the Mount Hope event, and I wondered whether she would be willing to spare a few minutes to provide some details."

The AI asked her to wait, and Kim squirmed. First bribery, now this. What was going to be next? Burglary?

She recognized Sara's voice. "Kay Braddock?" she said, with perfect diction. "I don't believe I've heard of you."

"I'm probably not well known," said Kim. "Mrs. Baines, I appreciate your talking to me."

Kim's visual signal lit up. An image of the aristocratic redhead had just appeared in front of Sara. "Why did you choose *me*?" Sara asked.

"I watched you speak to the Tupla alumni last year about the expansion project. You seemed to be very observant, and very concerned about the welfare and history of the community."

"Thank you," she said. "That's kind of you." Sara blinked into view. She was seated in a gray Polynex chair, with a black cat coiled in her lap. She was tall, clear-eyed, no-nonsense, accustomed to being in charge, but pleased at the possibility of appearing in a book. "What kind of book are you writing? It's hard to see what anyone could add to the material that's already been assembled about Mount Hope."

"A woman's perspective. I'm interested in the long-term effects of the disaster on the families of the victims."

"Oh," she said. And there was a catch in her voice, which did nothing to assuage Kim's rising sense of guilt. "I can tell you about *that*." She cautioned Kim that she had *not* actually been an eyewitness, that she'd flown down immediately after the event, arriving while the fires were still burning. She described those first hours in general terms, the agony she'd witnessed, the bodies, the hysteria, the sheer empty-eyed shock. She avoided describing her own emotions while facing the increasing probability that her son had been lost.

"Yes," she said, "I knew Kile was back. He called me from the house. In the past, he'd usually spent a few days in Terminal City after completing a flight. He'd get together with people from the Foundation to review the mission. And probably to celebrate a little bit. That's how he was. He liked people, and he had a lot of friends. Pity he didn't do it this time; he wouldn't have been there when the mountain blew up."

"You went first to your son's home?" Kim asked.

"Of course."

"Had it been damaged?"

"There was some water damage. They were wetting everything down. But other than that, no. The villa came through intact."

"But it *was* empty?"

"Oh yes." Her voice dropped to a whisper. "He was gone. Poor Kile. They never did find him." Her eyes clouded. "His flyer was gone too. He must have been in the air, somewhere near the explosion. He used to do that, fly up into the mountains to relax."

"I'm sorry, Mrs. Baines." Kim watched her check her blouse, looking for something to adjust. The blouse was green, embroidered with a white design suggesting musical notes. Quite pretty, really.

"It's all right. It's been a long time." She dabbed her eyes.

For the first time in her adult life, Kim saw that she was being cruel. But she pressed ahead. "I wonder if you'd care to tell me what you were thinking, and feeling, when you first went into the villa."

"I'm sure you can guess, Ms. Braddock."

"You were frightened."

"Of course."

"Did you find anything that suggested where he might have gone?"

"No."

"Anything unusual at all?"

Sara shot her a suspicious glance. "No," she said. "Considering what was happening outside, the villa was quite normal. Save that my son was missing."

"This was how long after the explosion?"

"Two hours, I guess. No more than that. Emergency teams were still arriving." She paused, shook her head. "These things happen," she said. "He was a good son. He had a lot to offer."

"Mrs. Baines, did you notice whether he'd left any notes or records about the mission? Anything that would help—" She stumbled, unsure how to proceed.

Sara's face hardened. "—I've heard all the rumors, Ms. Braddock. I can assure you if anything out of the ordinary had happened out there, I'd have been first to know. There was nothing connected with the flight in the house. At least nothing that *I* saw. No records. No visuals. *Nothing.*"

"I see."

"I'm glad you do." She had recognized Kim's ulterior purpose, but she hadn't really taken offense. "When it was over I tried to sell the villa.

But I was asking for too much in the beginning, and the chance to get rid of it passed. After a while I couldn't give it away. Eventually I donated it to a religious group. I understand they still hold the title. Waiting for the valley to come back, I suppose."

"You must have salvaged his belongings."

"His books. A few other things. I gave some of the furniture away. But I left most of it." She grew pensive. "There was a sculpture of a couple of hawks that I knew Mara would like—"

"Mara?"

"Benton's mother. And I kept a lamp. I'd given it to Kile for his birthday. And a set of bookends and a model starship for Ben."

"The *Valiant*," Kim said.

"Yes. How did you know?"

Kim smiled as a wild thought struck her. *Why would anybody manufacture a model of a starship and forget to include the propulsion tubes? Was it possible that Tripley had taken a set of visuals of a strange spacecraft? Had used the visuals to build a scaled-down replica? It would be a delicious irony if Tripley was sitting there with the big secret propped up on his bookshelf, staring him in the face.* "I have a passing acquaintance with Ben," she said sympathetically. "I know the model meant a lot to him."

"Yes." Sara's eyes were wet. "That's really all there was. Not much left out of a lifetime."

Kim wanted to ask flat out whether she'd seen any evidence that Yoshi had been there, any indication of a woman staying at the villa. But she could think of no way to do it without alienating her. Sara would not have admitted to any such thing anyhow. "Thank you, Mrs. Baines," she said at last.

"What's the title going to be?" Sara asked.

"Of what?"

"Of your book?"

"Oh." She thought it over. *"Aftermath."*

"You *will* be sure to send me a copy, won't you?"

"Yes," said Kim. "I'll be pleased to do that."

The National Archives was located at Kaydon Center in Salonika, the capital of the Republic, in the lake country 120 kilometers west of Seabright. Salonika was a trophy city, a showplace of skywalks and fountains and marble monuments commemorating the history of Greenway.

Here was George Patkin proclaiming the birth of the Republic. And there was Millicent Hodge turning the first batch of salmon loose into what would later be known as Lake Makor. And in Liberty Green, the onetime astronomer Shepard Pappadopoulo, for whom Kim's household intelligence was named, launches a missile against Henry Hox, the dictator's son, at the battle of the Twin Rivers.

The Archives was a long, two-story utilitarian structure, fronted by a mall and a reflecting pool. The pool was surrounded by spruce trees. Walkways curved through the manicured grounds, and broad marble steps led up to the main entrance, which was guarded by a statue of Erik Kaydon, the first premier.

Kim sighed and looked once again at the picture of her target. Manville Plymouth, Assistant Commissioner for Transportation Records. Since Plymouth knew Solly, it was up to her to do the dirty work.

She was wearing a silver wig and contact lenses to change her eye color.

At the end of the day, he always comes out through Freedom Hall, Solly had told her. Solly had looked uncomfortable during the preparations, had used the term *obsessed* several times. Had urged her to think about what she was doing. Had suggested she think of their careers, both of which were being put at risk. Had even threatened to walk away from it all. That would have left her without much chance of success, and he knew that. In the end, when he was convinced that she'd try no matter what, he'd stuck with her.

Freedom Hall was actually the structure's central rotunda. Here were the great documents of the Republic: the Instrument of Individual Rights, which denied the absolute power of Gregory Hox, the fourth and last in the line of dictators; the Articles of Governance, which established the mechanisms of government and defined the rights and duties of citizens; Joseph Albright's Statement at Canbury, which, in the darkest days of the revolution, gave new fire to the rebels.

There were numerous other journals, letters, diaries, and artifacts from the 327 year history of the Republic: Stanfield welcoming Brodeur when Earth lifted its century-long embargo; Amahl's handwritten notes detailing the sacrifices of the doctors at Dubois; the captain's logs from the *Regal*, the Republic's first interstellar vessel.

Kim casually circled the gallery, pretending to study the objects in the illuminated cases.

The Hall, Solly had said, was the only place in the building where they have serious security. Surveillance here was round-the-clock. But the routine nongovernment records were kept in the east wing. They'd never had any kind of problem, so they didn't worry much about thieves. But you have to get *into* it. And to do that, a scanner has to identify your DNA and then approve admission.

That was where Manville Plymouth came in.

She waited only a few minutes before the man himself appeared from the east wing and entered the Hall. He closed the door behind him and walked briskly across the rotunda, glancing neither right nor left. She checked her picture again to be sure, and fell in behind him, following him out onto Republic Avenue.

Plymouth was a fitness nut. He went every day, seven days a week, to an athletic center called the Blockhouse.

She followed him through the fading sunlight. The area was filled with public buildings, city hall, the courthouse, the licensing commission, the board of trade, the national legislature, the National Art Gallery. Plymouth moved swiftly, and his long legs gobbled up the ground. Kim had to hurry to keep up. Once she glimpsed Solly standing unobtrusively beside a tree.

But Plymouth wasn't heading in the right direction. He was walking north, away from the Blockhouse, up one avenue, across a park, past a fountain. Eventually he turned into a clothing store. Moments later he came out with a plastic bag, and stopped again to buy something at an electronics outlet.

Plymouth's muscles rippled while he walked. He was *big*, in a world full of big people, with an extraordinarily narrow waist and wide shoulders. Once he glanced back, and she pretended to be gazing into the treetops. Then he was moving again, this time walking south, past the Klackner Museum, where he turned onto a long pathway that led directly through a patch of wood to the Blockhouse. Reassured, she now dropped back and stayed discreetly out of sight.

Despite its name, the structure was flared and curved, three stories high in front, lower in back, with a lot of dark glass. A dozen wide steps led up to a portico. Plymouth took them two at a time and disappeared inside.

She strolled casually in behind him. He was gone, into the men's locker room. But she was reasonably sure she knew his ultimate destination.

There were probably twenty people in the women's area, changing clothes and showering. Kim claimed a locker, picked up a towel, switched into a gym suit, and, following Solly's instructions, went into the Total Workout section. There were a dozen people of both sexes using the machines. Plymouth was not one of them.

She did a few knee-bends to loosen up while she waited. Presently he emerged in shorts and a pullover, with a towel draped around his neck. He glanced at her and she smiled, inviting his approach.

"Hello," he said. "I don't think I've seen you here before."

"First time. Thought I'd try it."

"It's a good spot." He offered his hand. "Name's Mike." She knew he didn't like *Manville*, and never used it.

"Hello, Mike," she said, taking the hand. "Kay Braddock."

"You new to the area, Kay?" They picked a couple of the duroflexes and climbed onto the tables.

"Just moved in. From Terminal City."

"You'll like Salonika," he said. "It's a good cultural city. There's lots to do here. It's a little less *commercial*—" He hesitated, suddenly worried that he might be giving offense, but he'd gone too far to back off. "—Less *commercial* than most other places."

She understood he'd intended to say *than Terminal City*. Not too quick on his feet, this guy. Just as well. She reassured him, set the timer for twenty minutes, and climbed on board. If he was still in the duroflex when the time expired, she'd simply extend it.

The machine adjusted to her dimensions. Coils settled around her wrists and ankles. Pads pressed against thighs and buttocks.

"Do you do this regularly?" he called over to her. It was difficult to carry a conversation while the machine was in operation, but he wasn't going to be discouraged.

The duroflex began to move, gently at first, tugging at arms and legs, rolling her shoulders, squeezing her knees, massaging her buttocks.

"Yes," she said. "I like to work out."

Kim listened to occasional remarks about theaters and museums, how he'd come to Salonika at the end of the war, had found a home, and wouldn't live anywhere else, and how good the weather was. Eventually he got around to inviting her out to dinner. "There's a great place on the lakefront—"

He was likable enough for her to overcome her prejudice against bureaucrats, notwithstanding the fact that she was one herself. And he did have a modicum of charm.

"Sure," she said. "I'd like that." Yes. Dinner would not be a major sacrifice. That satisfied him and he quieted, surrendering himself to the machine.

So did Kim.

The duroflex gradually picked up the tempo. It stretched whole groups of muscles and ran a series of sit-ups at a reasonably fast pace. It chimed to warn her of a change in routine and then she was touching her toes.

She just rode with it for the most part, eyes closed, relaxed, feeling the glow that comes with moderate exercise. Kim was not an enthusiast of the machines; she preferred to get her exercise the old-fashioned way, but this system did indeed have its advantages. It was almost possible to sleep while you did push-ups.

It went on until she began to ache. Sensing her discomfort, it slowed somewhat, but not enough. Then she was aware that Plymouth's machine had stopped. He was climbing down, covered with sweat, wiping his head and neck with his towel. "Meet you in the lobby?" he asked.

The device was putting her through a series of knee-bends. It wasn't conducive to maintaining her dignity, or even at this point to getting out an intelligible answer. So they both laughed, and he glanced at her timer, which still showed six minutes. She nodded. She'd be there as soon as the system shut down and she'd changed.

"That's good." He tossed the towel in a bin, offered her a broad smile, and strode out of the room. As soon as he was gone, she hit the STOP button. The duroflex coasted to a halt and released her.

She would have preferred to lie quietly in the mechanism and wait for her back and shoulders to stop hurting. But there was no time for that. She climbed down and limped over to the bin, trying to look casual. The room had emptied somewhat and none of the three or four people rocking back and forth in the devices seemed to be paying any attention to her. She held her towel over the bin, retrieved Plymouth's, and dropped hers.

Ten minutes later, she handed a container to Solly in the lobby and then turned back to wait for her date.

By evening's end she felt uncomfortable about taking advantage of Mike Plymouth.

The restaurant he selected was a quaint little bistro called The Wicket. It had a lovely view of a lake and hills. It was all candlelight and soft music and logs on the fire. The food was good, the wine flowed freely, and Mike exhibited a wistfulness that first surprised her and then captured her imagination.

Born on Pacifica, he'd been in the war.

"*Their* side—" she said.

"Of course." There was an intersection here: He'd been on board the *Hammurabi* when Kane's small squadron blitzed it. He was cast adrift in an escape capsule, and had been rescued after eleven days by a "Greenie" patrol boat. "I never went home," he explained.

"Why?"

"I'm not sure. I made friends. Liked where I was. Everyone accepted me." The experience in the capsule, he added, had changed him.

"In what way?" asked Kim.

"I think I got a better idea of what I wanted out of my life. What counts."

"What *does* count?"

"Friends." With a grin: "Beautiful women. And good wine." His eyes drifted to the candles burning overhead in a wall rack. "The smell of hot wax."

This was a guy she could really learn to like.

My God, she told herself, he's a *bureaucrat*. Worse, he works for the government. He's an exercise nut. Probably has this basic routine he uses on everybody.

He reached across the table and shyly touched her hand. She caught her breath, felt her pulse begin to pick up, imagined herself swept away by him, carried off to an island somewhere. She pictured them walking on a moonlit beach.

Right. He'd really be interested in a woman who's playing him for a fool.

She briefly considered abandoning the project. But she couldn't. No way she could do that. It was too late anyhow. She'd already lied about her name.

Nevertheless she wondered what Solly would say if she didn't show up tonight at their hotel.

They left The Wicket and strolled for an hour along the lake's edge. The conversation became intimate in the sense that she saw longing in his eyes, and heard the subtext to his comments about his job at the Archives or the three mixed-breed dogs he owned. "I enjoy sailing," he said. "I've a boat on Lake Winslett."

"Ever dive?" she asked.

"No. But I'd like to try it. You?"

She nodded. "You seem out of place in a government job." She realized immediately it was the wrong thing to say and wished she could call it back.

But he shrugged and smiled as if he was used to it. He explained he wasn't in it just to supplement his income. He had a taste for statistics and for order. He liked being responsible for dividing history—of which, he said, there was nothing more chaotic—into journals and diaries, into investigative reports and records of transaction, and then storing the documents in coherent form. "Cataloging events gives me a sense of control. And I know how that sounds."

Under other circumstances it would have struck her as a hopelessly mind-numbing career. But there was a lilt in his voice when he talked about it. And he seemed to understand exactly what she was thinking, that it was the work of a dull intellect. So he shrugged and laughed in a self-deprecating way that left her almost helpless. "Born to be a librarian," he said.

Holding up her end of the conversation was no mean feat. Having manufactured a false name, she was forced to construct a series of lies. She was a teacher, she explained. Of mathematics. She'd secured a position at Danforth University and would start in about two weeks. At first she had a hard time recalling that her name was Kay. A general sense of confusion seemed to have set in.

Toward the end of the evening she was having trouble remembering what she'd said, what branch of math she specialized in, the name of the school in which she'd worked in Terminal City, the exact date she'd arrived in Salonika. Had that question even come up? She was sure it had.

Where was she from originally?

"Eagle Point."

"My brother lives there, Kay. What part of Eagle Point?"

What part did she know? She had to make up a name. "The Calumet," she told him, hoping he wasn't familiar with the town either.

"Oh yes." His reaction implied he knew the place well. Was he playing with her? Or was he being less than honest?

She began to realize that this was an evening she would always remember. And she visualized herself years from now recalling Mike Plymouth and wondering with a pang what had become of him.

"I should be getting home," she said finally.

"It *is* getting late," he agreed.

He insisted on escorting her, so she named a hotel, not the one she and Solly were actually using, and the cab took them there. As it drifted down through the cloudswept sky toward a landing pad, they fell silent.

"Will I see you again?" he asked, as though he'd detected something, knew there would not be a second evening.

"You can reach me here at the hotel, Mike." There was another quiet stretch after that. The lights rose up around them, and she understood that they were both embarrassed, but only she knew why. The cab touched down, and she climbed out into a brisk wind. He joined her, and they stood holding hands, gazing at each other. "Mike," she said, "I had a lovely evening."

"Is something wrong?" he asked.

"No. I'm just worn out, I think. Been a long day."

He kissed her lightly. Her body stiffened and he smiled sadly at her, sensing the distance. "I'm glad I met you, Kay," he said.

He squeezed her hand, looked in the direction of the elevator and back toward his cab. "I'd like very much to do something like this tomorrow."

"Yes," she said. "That would be nice." But she didn't want him calling during the day. Maybe find out she didn't live here after all. "Pick me up at nine?" she said.

"Count on it."

"Good. And maybe you should let me have your number. Just in case."

"You're a lovely woman, Kay," he said. Then he was standing by the cab while she followed the ramp to the elevator bank. She got in and punched the button for the lobby. He waved, she waved back, and the doors closed.

You're an idiot, Kay.

"How'd it go?" asked Solly.

She shrugged. "Okay."

"He didn't show any sign of catching on, did he?"

"No. He has no idea."

"Good. I got the package off to Alan. He's not happy."

Alan was Solly's buddy at the Institute lab. "Well, he knows we're doing something illegal and if we get caught he's going to be in the soup too."

"He knows we wouldn't blow the whistle on him."

"Wouldn't matter," she said. "It wouldn't take a genius to figure out who was helping us." She really didn't like the way this was turning out.

"I'm done for the day," said Solly. "We should get everything back tomorrow, and we can go in tomorrow night."

"Solly," she said, "I'm beginning to wonder if it's worth it."

He let her see that he wasn't surprised. "You know how *I* feel. Say the word and it's over. I don't think there's anything to be gained by all this. I don't believe you're going to learn anything you didn't know before. I'll concede that Yoshi might have been at Tripley's place, but there's a relatively innocent explanation for that too. I mean it should be no surprise that he might take her home for a few days if she's willing."

"She was supposed to be going to the hotel with Emily."

He shrugged. "There's never been any proof they *both* got into the taxi. They used Emily's ID. So Yoshi went with Tripley to his place for a couple of days. And got caught in the explosion. And she's still up there somewhere. Since they didn't know she was there, they didn't look that hard for her."

But they'd have found her body in the general search.

"If you want to quit," he said, "this would be a good time."

And an odd thing happened: She realized that Solly wanted her to give it up. But he'd be disappointed if she did.

She realized something else too: She couldn't back away. That would mean spending the rest of her life wondering about the truth.

11

In every honest man there lives a thief but give him sufficient spur.
—DELIA TOMÀS, *Caribee Annals*, 449

The package arrived at midafternoon. They checked the contents, a single filmy glove which was carefully packed in a translucent case. Kim put the case, with the glove still in it, in the pocket of her jacket.

They spent the day sightseeing, although Kim was too nervous to enjoy it. She picked at her meals and, as the sun began to fade, they took one of the moving skyways into Kaydon Center. The temperature was dropping and the wind had risen.

The Archives looked bleak in the hard dusk. The last visitors were filing out, their coats pulled tight around them. The pebbled walkways and the landing ramps had been swept clear of snow. A cab was lifting off as they approached from the direction of the reflecting pool. A thin layer of ice had formed on the surface. Solly was uncharacteristically subdued as they walked.

"You're sure there's no visual surveillance?" she asked, for the third or fourth time.

"I'm sure," he said. "Only in Freedom Hall, or if the system doesn't like your DNA."

She considered what getting caught would do to her career. Indeed, she'd thought of little else for the past day. And she'd have felt better if they had a flyer available, in case they needed to leave in a hurry. But parking a flyer on the pad might draw attention. If things went wrong, Solly had insisted, it wouldn't matter anyhow. The authorities would know who they were before they could get out of the building.

"You still sure you want to do this?" he asked yet again.

"What do you think they'll do to us if we get caught?"

"Work farm for several months. Probably a couple of days in the cube." The cube was a transparent cell located in a public place, so that everyone who knew a convicted criminal could observe the sad state to which he or she had fallen. Relatives, family members, and friends were all notified, and they could come in person or watch the humiliation from their living rooms. It was, she thought, a particularly cruel mode of punishment for a supposedly enlightened society.

She could see the headlines: INSTITUTE SPOKESWOMAN ARRESTED IN BURGLARY. EXPERTS PROBE: WHY DID BRANDYWINE TURN TO LIFE OF CRIME?

They approached the front entrance and turned right onto a pathway that circled the building. "There's no point in both of us going in," said Kim. "I know what I'm looking for. Why don't you wait outside? I mean, we're—"

"—I've come this far," said Solly. "You may need me."

They turned off at a secondary entrance, climbed a ramp, and stood before a glass door. Inside, a corridor was lined with offices.

The reader clicked open and a line of instructions appeared: PLEASE PLACE YOUR FINGERTIPS ON THE LENS. DO NOT MOVE UNTIL PROCESS IS COMPLETE.

Kim glanced around to be sure no one was watching. She took the container from her pocket, lifted out the glove, slipped it on, pulled it tight, and showed it to Solly.

"Perfect," he said.

She placed her fingertips on the designated spot. The lock clicked and the door opened. She and Solly stepped inside, and the door slid shut behind them.

The corridor was long and shadowy, lined with doors, its high ceiling gray and in need of repairs. The doors were translucent. Digital numbers and designators blinked on as they approached to identify what lay behind each. They passed Standards, Personnel, General Maintenance, Scheduling, Security, Special Operations.

No one else seemed to be in the building. "There are only nine or ten employees in the whole place," said Solly. "During regular work hours."

"The assistant commissioners."

"Right. And a few directors. And systems analysts. Everybody has a title. All the routine work is automated. As far as I could determine, nobody hangs around after closing time."

It was of course the cue for contradiction. They'd gone only a few meters farther when a lock clicked behind them, in the direction of Freedom Hall. They watched an office door open. A man in a green worksuit stepped into view and looked curiously at them.

Kim felt her heart stop. Her natural impulse was to bolt.

"Walk naturally," whispered Solly, taking her firmly by the arm, inspecting one of the designators, nodding as if he'd found what he wanted, and turning directly toward the worker.

The man frowned. He was olive-skinned, with wide shoulders, and an expression that suggested he'd been having a difficult afternoon.

"Hello," he said. "Can I help you?"

Solly waved an ID in his general direction. "Security check," he said. "Everything quiet here?"

"Far as I know."

"Good." Solly glanced meaningfully at one of the office doors. "Thanks." He pushed gently against it and nodded his satisfaction that it didn't open. Kim took the hint and tried one on the other side of the corridor. They proceeded past the man in the worksuit, and strolled down the passageway, continuing the process of periodically testing offices.

He watched them until they reached a cross corridor and turned out of his field of view. "What do you think, Solly?" she asked.

"I don't know. I don't think we were very smooth." They listened for footsteps. When they heard none, she peeked around the corner and saw that he was letting himself out of the building. "I think we're clear," she said.

Solly consulted his notes and led her down to the next cross passage and turned left. They came to a section marked RECORDS, and found a door whose designator read INTERSTELLAR NONCOMMERCIAL.

Solly produced a batch of universal keys in a wallet. They were plastic chips, each coded to fit numerous interior locks then in service. He had to try four or five in the dex before the lock moved and the door opened.

"You'd have made a good burglar," she told him.

He looked pleased. "They just don't worry about break-ins. Not back here. Out front, where the Instrument is, yes. If a mosquito gets in, alarms go off, guards come running, the doors come down. But back here, it's a whole different game. Nobody cares about old files."

They went in and closed the door behind them.

It was a cubbyhole. A small window looked out into a tiny courtyard. Kim sat down at the lone terminal and brought up the menu. She needed less than two minutes to locate EIV 4471886 *Hunter*, Arrival Date 30 March 573, Command Log.

"Got it," she said. She inserted a disk and instructed the computer to download.

Solly held a finger to his lips. Footsteps outside. He moved behind the door so he'd be out of sight if anyone looked in. Kim scrunched down behind the desk.

Voices.

Two people, talking, and then laughing. They moved on.

Kim was surprised to discover a sense of elation. She squeezed Solly's shoulder. "What?" he asked.

"We should do more of this," she said.

Sheyel adjusted the cushions in his dragon chair. "Kim, it's good to hear from you. Do you have news?"

"Probably not. I wanted to thank you for tracking down Yoshi's shoe size."

"It was nothing. Now will you tell me why you asked?"

"We found a grip shoe at Kile's villa. Fits the size."

"Oh?"

"That's all we have for the moment. And it probably doesn't mean anything."

He was silent.

"I need more information."

"Of course. If I have it."

"Was there anything artificial about Yoshi's body? Anything that a sensor might detect?"

His eyes slid shut. "I don't think so."

"Any kind of artificial enhancement, maybe? Or something that had been repaired?"

"No," he said. "Nothing that I know about. She had an accident once playing wraparound. Had to get a couple of her teeth capped."

"I don't think there's anything there we can use. Okay, Sheyel. I'll see if I can find another way. In the meantime, if you think of anything, give me a call."

He nodded. "Thanks, Kim. I appreciate what you're trying to do."

She switched off, poured herself a drink, glanced at a code she'd written on a piece of paper, and punched it in.

"Hello?" Mike Plymouth's voice. She left the visual off.

"Hi, Mike." She made her voice as soft as she could.

"Hello, Kay. I *thought* I'd hear from you."

"Yes. I'm sorry. I can't make it tonight."

"Oh. Well— You *are* all right?"

"Yes. I'm fine."

"Another night, maybe?"

She'd pushed Solly out of the room. Now she wished he were there. "I don't think so. There's really no point."

"Oh." He was fumbling for something to say. Something to retrieve the situation. Or save his pride.

"I'm sorry." She thought about making up a story. Something to spare his feelings. *I'm already committed. I was cheating yesterday.* But she let it pass. "I'm just really tied up right now."

"I understand." The room grew still. "Goodbye, Kay."

Then he was off the line and she was staring at the link. "Goodbye, Mike," she said.

They arranged to have the hotel deliver some cheese and wine and settled back to watch the *Hunter* logs. Kim put the disk into the reader, set it for the screen, sampled the cheese, and turned to Solly. "Ready?" she asked.

He nodded and she started the program.

Titles appeared, identifying the ship, setting the time and place, listing commercial cargo ("None"), and describing the general nature of the flight. The date, translated to Seabright time, was February 12. Date of departure from St. Johns.

The early visuals were from the out-station, depicting technicians and maintenance staff working on the *Hunter.* Solly described what they were doing, these checking life support maintenance, those topping off water supplies.

"We'll get two sets of records," he explained. "One will be the data flow from the various shipboard systems, life support, navigation, power plant, and so on. The other will be a visual record of what's happening in the pilot's room. The imagers will only record movement. If the room is empty, or if the pilot's asleep—" he held out his hands, palms up, "—nada."

"How much work is there for a pilot to do, Solly?"

"It's a tough profession, Kim. It takes a high level of intelligence, extensive knowledge, great reflexes—"

Her eyes closed. "Solly—"

"Trade secret?"

"Go ahead. You can trust me."

"You could jettison the pilot at any time and be perfectly safe."

"Really?"

"Sure. The pilot does three things: he talks to the ground, tells the AI where to go, and takes over if the AI blows up. Which never happens."

"That's it?"

"That's it. And the AI can talk to the ground." He fast-forwarded past the technicians. They whirled through their tasks, and then disappeared and the screen went blank. The clock leaped forward two hours. The next sequence gave them Markis Kane coming into the pilot's room.

This was Kane more than forty years after the war, but there was of course no physical difference between the man who sat in the cabin of the *Hunter*, and the man whose image was prominently displayed at the Mighty Third Memorial Museum. This later version might have been a little less lean, and his features might have been a trifle harder. Otherwise, he was the same person.

He wore a blue jumpsuit with a shoulder patch depicting the *Hunter* orbiting a ringed planet, with the motto PERSISTENCE. His black hair was cut short and he was clean-shaven. He had a natural youth and vitality that rendered him quite attractive, Kim thought. He was a war hero, and he had the soul of an artist. Quite a résumé.

The pilot's room was not radically different from the one she'd seen during her inspection of the *Hunter*. The two chairs were different, the carpeting was lighter, the walls darker. But the instrument layout did not seem to have changed.

Kane sat down in the left-hand chair and picked up a notepad. Kim watched him go methodically through a checklist. The procedure lasted about ten minutes. When he'd finished, he got out of his chair and left the room. She recalled the layout of the *Hunter*, and knew that the pilot's room opened onto the upper level of the rotunda. The imager stopped recording. The clock jumped ahead sixteen minutes and Kane reentered, eased into his seat, and began touching blinkers.

"*Hunter ready to depart.*"

"*Hunter, you are clear to go.*"

He touched a stud on the chair arm. "*We are thirty seconds from departure, folks. Buckle in.*" His own harness came down over his shoulder and locked in place. The chair moved to face forward.

At the time of the *Hunter* flight, St. Johns was on the edge of known territory. That was still true. No deeper outpost existed. Several hundred missions had gone beyond, but that was a trivial number spread against so vast a region. There was an ongoing argument among the Nine Worlds about who should bear the financial burden of maintaining the outstation. Traffic had fallen precipitously, and the station no longer supported itself. There was talk of closing it down.

The *Hunter* edged forward. Kim watched the umbilicals detach. The dock began moving past on the overhead screen and in the windows, moving quicker, and then it dropped away. The acceleration pressed Kane back into his chair. He spoke briefly with the operations people, and noted for the record that the ship was clear, on course, and all conditions were nominal.

Solly moved the record forward. Kane remained alone in the room, watching his instruments, occasionally talking to the AI. Then, about a quarter-hour into the flight he spoke into his intercom again: *"We are going to initiate acceleration to jump status in five minutes. Emily and Kile know about that. Yoshi, once it begins you won't be able to move. It'll last roughly twenty-five minutes. Anything you need to do, this is a good time to take care of it."*

"The jump engines feed off the mains," Solly explained. "Most systems require almost a half hour of steady one-gee acceleration before they can lock in enough power to make the jump to hyperspace."

Kane got on a channel that was probably private and told Kile Tripley that *Hunter* should be scheduled for a general overhaul on her return. Kim fast-forwarded the record until a bank of green lamps lit up the console. *"Going hyper,"* Kane said.

Lights blinked, dimmed, brightened, blinked again.

Kane looked at his instruments and, apparently satisfied, told his passengers that the jump was completed. He asked each of them to check in, and informed them they were free to walk about as they liked. He got up, stretched, and left the room. The imager shut down.

The clock ran off seven minutes and he was back in with Tripley. The mission leader had been rethinking the destinations, and was considering going *here* instead of *there*. A larger number of old class Gs in one area, too much radiation thrown off by nearby young supergiants in another. Here was a new order of places he'd like to visit. They'd still go to their initial series of targets. But after that he wanted to make the adjustment. Could Kane manage it without undue difficulty?

The captain suggested he leave the list. *"I don't see any problem, Kile,"* he said. *"We'll need to work out what it'll do to the duration of the flight. Otherwise—"* He held out his hands to indicate he'd go along with whatever Kile preferred.

During the balance of that first day, and for much of the time following, the pilot's room was empty. The clock leaped forward over durations of several hours at a time. The calendar began to click off numbers. At precisely 8:00 A.M. daily, Kane entered, sometimes alone, sometimes with one or another of the crew, and studied the control panel. He talked to the AI, in effect asking it whether there were any anomalies, whether it foresaw any difficulties, whether there were anything it wished to call to his attention. The interactions acquired a ceremonial quality.

"It's a precaution," Solly said. "Required by the regs. They've built in a lot of redundancy, so it's hard to imagine any sequence of events that could lead to trouble without alarms going off in plenty of time. Still, we all go through the same routine. Truth is, I think it's intended to make the pilot feel as if he's got something to do."

Here for the first time Kim saw the living Yoshi Amara. She was vibrant and alive and full of enthusiasm for the mission, absolutely convinced that they would not come home without success. She was, Kim thought, a gorgeous young woman. Dark hair, dark eyes, offset by a gold chain and a gold bracelet.

"She must have had money," said Solly.

Kile Tripley seemed to enjoy the pilot's room. Other than the pilot, he spent more time there than anyone, often slumped back in the right-hand chair, his long legs crossed, usually reading, sometimes making notes. When Kane was present, or one of his colleagues, he tended to talk about what it would be like to round the curve of a new world, gliding into the night, and see patches of light across its continents. Kim understood that he'd made that run countless times, and that the night had always remained unbroken. As it had through the whole of human history.

"Can you imagine what it would mean," Tripley said over and over, *"if we can find them?"* Not *whether they're there,* but *if we can find them.*

Kim saw what Tripley apparently did not, that Kane did not believe there was anything to find; or if there was, that it was so thoroughly lost among the stars that there could be no realistic hope for success. We could continue crossing the terminators without result, his dark eyes implied, until we get tired of it and find a more useful outlet for the Foundation's resources.

But he must have seen no point in actively discouraging his employer. Yes, he said, the Golden Pitcher's rich with class Gs, yellow suns like Sol and Helios. Travel time among them would be relatively short. They could cover a lot of ground in a year.

We *will* cover a lot of ground, Tripley would say. And: *"We're going to do it this time, Markis. I know it."*

Kane inevitably responded with a nod and an abstract gaze, agreeing with Tripley but informing Kim that this was the conversation they always had. And nobody had ever found anything.

She was looking for an indication of tension between the two, but there was nothing to imply they did not get along, even though the personalities of the two men were vastly different: Kane was cool, deliberative, skeptical, methodical. Tripley was a believer, inclined to follow his emotions. But his instincts were good, and he was generally rational, other than his fixation on celestials. He had his own vision of the world and did not allow reality to intrude. Had he been devoted to religion, he would have been among those who argued that there *was* a God and a heaven, because otherwise what would be the point of life? Kim's overall impression was that he was a man who had never quite grown up. But it was clear he was utterly devoid of malice. She discarded the possibility that he might have killed Yoshi. Or anyone.

She glanced at his record. He had completed twenty-nine missions in search of his grail, totaling almost twenty-five years off-world. That qualified him as a fanatic, an *Ahab*. No wonder *Hunter's* motto was *Persistence*.

Later, to Emily, Kane delivered a more realistic assessment: *"We'd need a hundred of these boats,"* he said. *"A thousand. Headed every which way. Then there might be a chance."*

Emily too had understood the odds.

This was the first time Kim had seen her sister in private interactions. They were three days into the flight before she came into the pilot's room and Kim was finally able to observe her. Kane was already there, doing his morning routine. She strolled up behind him and *squeezed* his shoulder. Kane looked back at her and Kim understood that the presence of the imager, recording everything, was an impediment to them.

Solly glanced over at her but said nothing.

Emily slipped gracefully into the right-hand seat. She wore the mission jumpsuit, open at the neck just enough to reveal the curve of her breasts.

Kane commented that everything was going well. It was a nondescript remark, small talk, but his voice had dropped an octave. "They're lovers," Kim said, more to herself than to Solly.

There was nothing overt, of course. Kane and Emily gazed at each other with the kind of forced indifference that can only be displayed by people in love who are trying to hide the fact.

Yoshi was just out of her teens. Her grades had suggested promise, but she too was caught up in chasing the *Dream*. Kane took time whenever the opportunity offered to caution her that the missions had gone out many times. That it looked easy when there were hundreds of class Gs within a narrow field. That, despite the assumption that it was just a matter of finding the right one, there was no guarantee that there *was* a right one. No assurance that *any* star anywhere, other than Sol, had produced life. Accept the possibility, he told her. *"We may be alone."*

"It could not be," she said. *"It's a basic scientific principle that nothing is unique."*

Kim noticed that the crew of the *Hunter* never talked about finding an *amoeba*. Judging from all the conversation about how to handle a first encounter, what kind of technology to look for, what dangers might be posed by an immensely advanced celestial, she saw that the discovery of a blade of grass, everybody else's ambition, would have been a distinct disappointment to this outfit. At the very least, they hoped to unearth ruins somewhere, evidence that another intelligence had existed.

"Until we show that it can happen somewhere else," said Kane, *"we have to accept the possibility that the human race was divinely created."*

She laughed at the idea, but Kane smiled back. *"How else would you explain it?"* he asked. "The universal silence?"

She had no answer.

Kim listened as they discussed their strategy. First step was to calculate the area of a given sun's biozone, and then to find the elusive blade of grass. Once they had done that, had found a living world, then they would proceed to hunt for evidence of intelligence, past or present.

It was all very optimistic. But after all, Tripley said at one point, that's what makes it worth doing. *"It wouldn't really be very sporting, would it, if there were life in every other system?"*

■   ■   ■

By four A.M. Kim and Solly had reviewed the first six days of the mission, looking for hostility among the members of the research team, for indications of anything that might lead eventually to murder. It might have seemed a handicap that they were barred from overhearing conversations anywhere other than the pilot's room, that in fact those who spoke for the record knew they were doing so, yet it was evident that the crew members got along well. Kane was almost always present during these dialogues, and there was never more than one other person with him, except on one occasion when Yoshi and Tripley arrived with sandwiches and beer.

There were some differences of opinion, minor and unavoidable among a group of people who talked politics and history, science and philosophy, apparently ran a book discussion group, and engaged in virtual gaming. Kim and Solly were never privy to the games, but they judged by what they heard afterward that they included a fair amount of sexual byplay. There was, however, no evidence of tension between Kane and Tripley, or between the women. Apparently there was an arrangement, but Kim couldn't sort out its precise nature.

Solly had fallen asleep. Kim was weary but she wanted to hang on until she found out what would happen. If indeed *anything* would happen. She'd begun to fast-forward through the conversations, planning to come back later and listen more closely. Sometimes Kane was alone in the pilot's room, reading, writing in a notebook, occasionally doing sketches on a pad which he kept on a side table. She thought she detected an early version of the *Autumn.*

She was moving quickly through the record when she saw, for the first time, an *empty* pilot's room. A klaxon was sounding and lights were blinking. She noted the time: 11:17 P.M., February 17, the fifth day of the mission.

The picture went to a split screen, adding a shadowy area that she recognized as the engine room.

She woke Solly.

"Problem with the jump engines, looks like," he said.

"But they're in flight, right? Coasting. The jump engines aren't actually doing anything at this point, are they?"

"They're still online," Solly explained, "and any of a number of things can go wrong." He brought up the data stream and examined it for a few minutes. "Auxiliary feed system," he said. "It's a redundant safety feature.

Monitors the antimatter flow controls during the jump. If there's a problem, it takes over."

"You mean the engines would still work okay without the system in place?"

"Oh, sure. But you don't want to do that."

"Why not?"

"Because antimatter is a cranky fuel. It has a tendency to blow out controls. If the secondary system isn't there, and you get any kind of overload at all, you can kiss your baby blues goodbye."

Solly switched back to the visual record in time to see Kane come down the stairs into the engine room. Emily, wrapped in a robe, was right behind him. He paused before a console, touched it, and the alarms died. *"It's okay,"* he told her. *"We're not in danger."*

He sat down at a monitor and was paging through schematics when the others arrived. *"It's the auxiliary feed system,"* he said. *"We're going to have to abort the mission."*

"Abort?" Emily looked stricken. *"Is it really that serious? Can't we fix it?"*

Kim knew *she* would have asked whether they were in trouble.

"I can jury-rig it temporarily. But we don't want to be running around the Golden Pitcher with a busted AFS."

"Why not?" asked Tripley. *"What exactly is the risk?"*

"Hard to put a number on it. It's a safety device that we won't need unless we need it. If you follow me. But my opinion doesn't matter. The regs require us to head back."

"Who'd ever know?"

"I would. We die out here, it'd be my responsibility." He took a deep breath. *"It's not the end of the world, Kile. There'll be another day."*

"Yeah." Tripley glared at the engine as if it had deliberately betrayed him. *"Okay, what do we do now?"*

"I need a few hours to work on it. Make some temporary repairs. We'll get out of hyper and do the job. When I'm finished, we'll jump back in and head for home."

"They have to get out of hyperspace," Solly explained, answering the question he saw in her face, "in case something goes wrong. It's a precaution against getting stranded."

"Bingo," said Kim. "This is where the encounter happens."

"Home?" Tripley said. *"Why not St. Johns? Why go all the way back home?"*

"It's a major job. Not the kind of thing they do out there. They'd do

what I'm about to, put together a patchwork solution. But to get recertified for flight, we need Sky Harbor."

Emily gazed up at Tripley. *"I'm sorry, Kile."* She made a sympathetic face.

"Okay," he said. *"Do it. Goddammit."*

Kane opened a channel to the AI. *"Hunter, abort TDI. Take us out."*

"Wait a minute," said Kim. "Are they near a star?"

"Don't know," said Solly. "Depends how you define *near*. If you mean inside a planetary system, I'd say it's *real* unlikely."

"Then this isn't right. They have to go sight-seeing. They have to decide to come out near one of the seven stars."

Solly shook his head. "It's not going to happen."

She watched Tripley leave the pilot's room, watched Emily and Kane belt down. The AI counted off the minutes, and then they sailed out of hyperspace. They were in a heavily populated area of Orion, and the sky was filled with great clouds of stars. She couldn't see enough of it to determine whether there was a nearby sun.

They fast-forwarded. Kane used two hours to make his repairs. Then he alerted the others they were ready to go, and they began the acceleration toward the jump. Twenty-five minutes later they slipped uneventfully back into hyperspace and started the long journey to Sky Harbor.

The eastern sky was beginning to brighten, and a brisk wind rattled the windows. "I just don't believe it," she said.

He shut off the computer, glanced meaningfully at her, slid back on the sofa, and closed his eyes. "Looks like it was all a false alarm," he said.

Her commlink woke her. "Kim?" It was Matt's voice. Flat. That set off alarms. "Where are you?"

"In Salonika," she said.

"Were you planning on checking in any time soon?"

"I assumed you'd call if you needed me, Matt." She kept it on audio.

"I need you."

She sighed. "Okay. What are we doing?"

"A delegation of physicians and surgeons is coming in tomorrow. We've offered them a tour of the Institute."

"Okay. I'll be there. What time?"

"Ten."

"I'm on my way."

"It's an opportunity to do some good public relations. Media will be here. And Johnson."

World's leading cosmologist. Guarantees lots of attention.

"We're going to spring for lunch. I'd like you to accompany the tour and talk to them over the salad."

She listened, said she'd take care of it, and started to disconnect.

"I'm not through yet."

"What's wrong, Matt?"

Solly knocked softly and stuck his head into the room. She waved him in.

"Have you been nosing around Sara Baines? Asking questions?"

"Sara Baines? Who's Sara Baines?" She looked desperately at Solly.

His lips formed the words *Deny everything.*

"Tripley's *grandmother*, for God's sake. We got another complaint from him. Says somebody was out to interview his grandmother for a book. She can't remember the title. But I don't guess Tripley trusts you very much. He showed her your picture."

"And?"

"She says no. But Tripley thinks it was you. Was it?"

"I guess I did it, Matt."

She heard him let out his breath. "Kim, what am I going to do with you? Are you determined to lose your job? We've been through this before, and it's not going to happen again. You will keep away from Tripley. Do you understand me?"

"I understand you."

"Don't take that tone with me. This is your career you're playing with. If there's a third round of this nonsense, I'm going to be forced to put you out on the street."

"Matt, I don't really have a choice—"

"You damned well do, Kim. I don't mean to sound unsympathetic, but your sister's a long time gone. Ease up, okay? For everybody's sake."

She was staring up at the imager. "Matt, we may have found one of Yoshi's shoes in Tripley's villa. At Severin."

That got a long pause. Then: "You got a DNA match?"

"No. All we have is that it's her size. But it's a *grip shoe.*"

She could hear Matt thinking it over. "That sounds like lawsuit country. Kim, we're talking about something that happened a long time ago. You're grasping at straws."

"I know," she said. "See you tomorrow."

"He's right," Solly said.

She looked at him. "We need to find the body," she said.

"Yoshi's? How do you plan to do that?"

"It might not be all that hard. She wore gold."

12

And I would have, now love is over,
An end to all, an end:
I cannot, having been your lover,
Stoop to become your friend!
                    —ARTHUR SYMONS, "After Love," 1910 C.E.

Kim caught the red-eye back to Seabright and addressed the physicians and surgeons at the Institute breakfast. That went well, but Matt remarked quietly that it was good to see her again. His tone was simultaneously worried and accusing. He was always good at making her feel guilty. She explained that life had got hectic, and got away before he could press her. Afterward she went directly to the station and took the first train to Wakonda, home of the University of Amberlain. Solly was waiting for her in the physics department, where he'd borrowed a handheld sensor unit that the technicians were configuring to scan for gold.

When asked by the lab people if she'd uncovered a vein, Kim nodded and observed that she and Solly were about to acquire some serious wealth.

The unit tested to a range of about thirty meters for the quantity of gold one would expect to find in a bracelet roughly equivalent to the one Yoshi had been wearing.

Afterward, they caught the Snowhawk, which connected a half dozen cities across the central tier of the Republic, from Seabright on the east, through Eagle Point, to Algonda on the west.

They retired into a first-class cabin and were back reviewing the *Hunter* logs minutes after the train left the station.

The sun was already down as they eased out of Wakonda Central, picking up speed until the landscape blurred and eventually faded into the darkness. Solly sprawled leisurely in a padded chair; Kim sat on a cross bench, her arms wrapped around drawn-up knees.

They went back to the point at which the *Hunter* had dropped out of hyperspace, and watched Kane work on the AFS.

They ran the segment again, slower this time.

Kane finished up, notified the AI, and disappeared offscreen. Forty minutes later, scrubbed down and in a fresh uniform, he arrived in the pilot's room. Emily came up and they surveyed the enormous star-clouds.

"*In there somewhere,*" Emily said, dreaming of celestials.

"*Maybe,*" said Kane. He was invariably more forthright with her than with Tripley. "*But unless you're damned lucky, you'll need more than a single lifetime to find them.*"

She sat down in the right-hand seat.

"*Eight minutes to jump,*" said the ship.

Kane pushed back and let his eyes half close. "*We've been fortunate,*" he said. "*This is the first serious technical problem we've had in, what, a dozen or more missions? That's not bad.*"

She looked across at him, her spirits visibly sagging. Emily did not want to go home. "*A lot more than a dozen. Markis, how long do you think it'll take to make the repairs?*"

He considered it. "*They'll pull the unit and replace it. A couple of days. No more than that. But the ship needs some general maintenance too before it goes out again.*"

They continued in that vein while the AI counted down. The minutes ticked off and the conversation subsided while Kane turned his attention to the console. The power buildup that routinely preceded a jump became audible.

At thirty seconds, the main engines shut down and *Hunter* went into glide mode.

"There's nothing here," said Solly, somehow disappointed, as if they hadn't already seen the sequence, didn't already know nothing was going to happen. The jump procedure was now too far along to stop. If a celestial had pulled alongside and waved, they could have done nothing.

When the *Hunter* made its transition to hyperspace, Emily was staring out the window at the stars.

The Snowhawk was passing through a valley. Two of Greenway's moons were in the sky, drifting among wisps of cloud. Dark slopes rose on either side. Treetops swayed in the blast of the passing train. Away to the north she could see the glow of a town. *"Can't really expect to hit it right away,"* said Markis. *"You have to be patient."*

"We've been patient."

"Okay," said Solly. "That does it for the celestials. Now we're just look-ing for a motive for murder." He looked at her. "You think if someone killed them, Yoshi and Emily, he wouldn't have taken the gold?"

"If it was a burglar, something like that, sure he would have. But Tripley's the prime suspect. You think he'd kill over some jewelry?"

"You really think Tripley did it?"

"No. But I can't bring myself to believe they were killed by a robber. Wherever Yoshi is, she's wearing her gold."

Kim and Solly fast-forwarded through more conversations, all routine, mundane, what they would do when they got home, how they would spend the unexpected time. Tripley made it clear that he planned to mount the next mission as quickly as time permitted, and that he hoped to retain the services of the current crew. They didn't hear him say it explicitly, but that the sentiments had been delivered beyond the range of the recording devices was apparent from the conversations in the pilot's room. Everyone planned to return.

All this took the edge off the frustration, particularly for Yoshi, who'd come as an intern and who must have been worried that she might not be invited back. The weeks passed, and the general morale recovered and was reasonably high when they returned at last and docked at Sky Harbor.

Yoshi told Kane that she would stay the night with Emily at the Royal Palms in Terminal City, and then spend some time with her family until they were ready to try again. There was no indication, no nonverbal sig-nal, that she was not telling the truth.

Tripley promised to hustle the repairs along. He estimated a relaunch in about a month. Was that satisfactory for Kane?

It was.

Tripley informed him that he would receive a bonus for his perfor-mance. Then he left Kane alone in the pilot's room.

The captain spent a few minutes with the instruments, collected his sketchbook, and left. The imager blinked off.

It was over.

"No matter how many times we run it," said Solly, "it's going to keep coming out the same way. Nothing happened."

The flight home had required forty-one days. They went back and looked again, with no idea what they were hoping to find. When Tripley spoke of Yoshi, he showed a genuine affection for her. And he seemed far too gentle to perpetrate either physical or psychological violence against anyone. His clone-son, thought Kim, was a different order of beast altogether.

They reviewed Kane's conversations with the other crew members, listening, moving on. Kim watched Emily as the days ran down, thinking how luminous her sister looked, how energetic she was, how driven by the great search. And she was within days of losing her life.

But gradually an inconsistency emerged. She watched the interplay between the captain and Emily, went back to their conversations in the first part of the mission, and compared the earlier with the later. "Do you see it?" she asked Solly.

He leaned forward and squinted at the screen. She'd frozen the images, a few days from the end of the voyage. Kane and Emily had been talking about getting more serious about their physical conditioning programs on the next flight.

"What?" said Solly. "I don't see anything."

"What happened to the passion?"

"*What* passion?"

"Do they sound like lovers to you?"

"They *never* sounded like lovers to me."

"Solly, they were hiding it before. Maybe from the others, or from the imager. Maybe from each other. Now it's just not there."

"Maybe they had a fight. We can't really see very much, you know."

"No, it's not like that. There's no tension between them on the return flight. This isn't the kind of behavior you'd see in the aftermath of a breakup. It's simply a cordial relationship between congenial colleagues. Not at all the same thing."

The train was pulling into the outskirts of Eagle Point.

"What are you saying?" he asked.

Kim shut down the program but she stared at the screen until the train stopped moving. "I'm not sure," she said.

They checked into the Gateway and Kim stayed up most of the night replaying the conversations between Kane and Emily. Outbound, the captain's depth of passion was quite evident. He loved her sister. She could see it in his eyes, in his tone, in his every gesture. She wondered what the interaction between the two was like when they were away from the recording devices.

But it had changed during the return. Not because, as Solly had suggested, they'd had a falling-out. In that event they'd have been cold in each other's company. The body language would be exaggerated. She'd see resentment in one or the other. Or both.

But none of that was present. Their mutual regard was precisely what one might expect from good friends. Nothing more, nothing less.

Again and again, she listened to their final conversation, recorded during the approach to Sky Harbor:

"Thanks, Markis."

"For what?"

"For getting us back. I know we put some pressure on you to continue the mission."

"It's okay. It's what I would have expected."

They were on the night side of Greenway. The space station looked like a lighted Christmas ornament. Its twin tails were also illuminated, one reaching toward Lark, the other dipping into the clouds.

"As always, Markis, it was nice to spend time with you."

Kim shook her head. The remark was artificial; the voice contained all the passion of a cauliflower.

"You too, Emily. But I guess we'll be back at it in a couple of weeks."

"I hope so. I'm getting tired coming home empty all the time."

The station grew larger in the screens and then the *Hunter* was approaching one of the docks. People were visible in the operational sections and a spacesuited technician waited for them with an umbilical. There was a slight bump as the ship came to rest. A bank of console lights blinked furiously before settling on amber.

"Time to go home," said Kane. They unbuckled and left the pilot's room, Emily leading the way. If they said anything else to each other, it was lost.

Solly had come out of his bedroom during the last minutes. He was wrapped in a muted yellow robe. "So now," he said, "Kane stays with the ship for a few hours to take care of the paperwork. Then he goes down to Terminal City and checks into a hotel. Tripley flies home. Yoshi and your sister flag down a cab, tell it to take them to the Royal Palms, but they don't arrive."

"That's the scenario."

"But we think Yoshi somehow or other got to the Severin Valley. Which probably means Emily was there too."

"Probably."

"Okay." It was still dark outside. "If we're going to go looking tomorrow, we'd better get some rest."

They used the network to rent diving gear and a collapsible boat from the Rent-All Emporium, and a flyer from Air Service. Then they went down to a late breakfast. The flyer, with the equipment inside, was waiting for them when they finished.

Kim tied the gold sensor to an input jack, through which it would interface with the onboard tracking systems, displaying results on an auxiliary screen.

At a few minutes after noon they lifted off the roof of the Gateway and turned south toward Severin. The day was cold and cloudless.

"How'd it happen," Solly asked as they flew through bright skies, "that both Kane and Tripley lived in the same small town?"

"Tripley didn't *live* there," Kim said. "Severin was a tourist spot, and he vacationed there. He also used it as a retreat during the off-season. He liked the solitude.

"Kane moved there in 559, when he inherited a villa from a relative who'd admired his war exploits. He was already beginning to make a name for himself as an artist, and he decided it would be an ideal place to work. The town only had a thousand or so people then, so it's no surprise that the two eventually met. When Tripley went looking for someone to pilot *Hunter*, Kane was at hand."

Mount Hope dominated a group of peaks to the southwest. They were coming down the Severin, flying low, barely a thousand meters off the ground. This stretch of the river wasn't navigable: it descended toward the dam through a series of cataracts. On either side, thick forest advanced to the water's edge. They saw an occasional farmhouse, inevitably dilapidated. The landscape was deep in snow.

Kim watched a freight train moving west. It was gliding just over the treetops, and the trees reacted to its passing in the manner of a bow wave, parting in front, closing behind. It was headed toward the Culbertson Tunnel, which would take it through the solid wall of mountains. The tunnel wasn't visible from her angle, but she saw the train begin to slow down as it made its approach.

She hadn't been able to give the flyer the exact coordinates of Tripley's villa, so she switched to manual as they glided out over Remorse. The lake was a sheet of glass.

Solly activated the sensor. The display gave them groups of configuration data, blanked, and then went green. Negative return.

Ahead, Tripley's villa sat on its lonely hilltop.

The place felt as if it were pinched off from the real world, like a black hole, a singularity where the laws of physics were slightly warped. Where footprints vanished.

They descended to treetop level and moved in directly over the roof. The display remained green.

The utility building showed nothing.

She circled the immediate area, keying off the villa. Most of the old Tripley property was new-growth forest and heavy underbrush. Its fences were down, and a group of spruce trees on the east side looked dead.

Next she extended the search several kilometers west, flying a crosshatch pattern, scanning as far as the ridge that had protected the town on the night of the explosion. She checked along the summit, surveyed the far slope and the woods beyond until the ground got rocky.

Using the map, she came back and flew over the town. The center of Severin Village was in the water. She went down until the treads got wet. The display remained green.

"You didn't really think the killer would hide her near city hall, did you?" asked Solly.

"If he was a maniac," she said, "who knows what he might have done?"

A killer would have been likely to throw the body into the lake, which had been much smaller then; or into the river. Or he might have buried her north of town, in ground that was now at the bottom of Remorse. In either case, she'd still be in the water. So Kim flew systematically over the lake surface, marking off squares until, after an hour and a half, they'd covered it all.

That eliminated, Kim thought, the most likely places.

She took them east along the southern shoreline. Almost immediately the screen began to blink. "Got something," said Solly. The rate varied back and forth as she jockeyed through the sky.

Down there.

Just woods. "I see an iron fence," said Kim.

"And some headstones." They were overgrown by thick brush, hidden by trees.

And a pair of wrought iron gates.

"Cemetery," said Solly. He got a fix on the hit so they wouldn't lose it when they moved out of the scanner's range.

Kim set down in a glade about a hundred meters away. There was a short argument about who would go and who stay. "It's my party," she insisted.

Solly shrugged. "Keep talking to me."

"I'll be fine," she said.

She sealed her jacket, climbed down from the flyer, and plunged into the woods. The day was cold and hard and very still. Snow crackled underfoot.

She wasted no time getting lost and had to double back. Solly's line of sight provided shortest distance to the target, but did not allow for fences, thick shrubbery, creeks, or other obstacles. On her second try she found the gates. An arch was inscribed with the words JOURNEY'S END.

"These people weren't much for subtlety," she told Solly.

"What do you mean?"

"I'll explain later."

"Okay. Are you inside?"

"Yes. Give me a bearing."

Solly checked the map he'd made and compared it with her position. "To your right, about sixty degrees."

There were a lot of headstones, and the cemetery was overgrown. She headed off in the indicated direction.

"Good," said Solly. "Keep straight."

She glanced at the markers as she went by. Some were two centuries old.

"You got it," said Solly. "You should be right on top of it."

She was looking up at a stone angel. "Nothing here except a grave," she said. "*Old* one. Husband and wife. Both buried at the beginning of the last century."

"That's got to be it. It's down there."

She looked at it. Looked at some elms and a couple of mausoleums and more headstones half hidden in the underbrush. "Can't be," she said.

"Sure it is. It's ideal. Nobody'd want to dig it up."

"But the killer would have had to disturb the original grave. Somebody would have noticed." Maybe the couple had been buried with their wedding rings. "This is not where you hide a body, Solly. You put it in the woods, or weight it and drop it in the lake."

She walked back to the flyer and they took off again and resumed the hunt along the southern shore, and then off to the east. They broke out pork slices and apples while the AI executed the search pattern. The afternoon wore on.

By twilight, Solly had given up. "I don't think we're going to find anything," he said.

"Where haven't we looked?"

"Tripley had a flyer."

"Yes."

"If I had a flyer and I wanted to get rid of a body, I don't think I'd dig any holes. It's too much work, and you're too likely to get caught."

"We've looked in the lake."

"To hell with the lake. I'd fly it out to sea and dump it."

"If he did that," she said, "we're out of luck." She tapped her index finger on the instrument console. "The explosion occurred three days after they arrived. We have to assume things were happening fast and he had to get rid of it locally." The sun was touching the crest of Mount Hope.

"Top of the mountain?" he suggested.

"It's all granite up there. No way to bury it."

"The river," said Solly. "But upstream. The other side of the dam."

"Why would you put it there?"

"The water was deeper up there. Look at your map."

Large sections of the dam were still intact. Sluices had been left open. The river rushed through them, and through gaps in the concrete, and roared out the south side, crashing down fifty meters into the lower canyon.

They flew low over the structure and were rocked by the wind. Kim yowped and the flyer warned them belatedly that turbulent conditions were common in the area. *"We should exercise caution,"* it added.

The wreckage reminded Kim of the remnants of a monolithic altar, or perhaps a vast jawbone left in the river.

The onboard AI apologized for the rough ride, assured them it would strive to be more careful, but complained that they had imposed a ceiling which prevented it from rising to a more comfortable altitude.

They looked down at the dam. On its upstream side, the river was a patchwork of water alternately rough and tranquil, of wakes and eddies, of sandbanks and splintered trees. It rushed at the shattered dam, crashed through it, and fell about forty meters into a canyon, which carried it into Remorse.

Solly instructed the AI to take them lower, but it complained that the action wouldn't be prudent. *"High winds,"* it said. *"Best to stay where we are."*

Solly sighed. "Kim," he said, "change seats with me."

She shook her head. "Going to manual won't do any good. If it doesn't like what you're doing, it'll override."

"Change seats," he said.

She complied and they climbed over each other while the flyer asked for instructions. When he was seated again, Solly looked to his left, found a panel marked A-DATA and opened it.

"What are we doing?" asked Kim.

"Taking out the AI." He showed her a yellow-coated cable and disconnected it from a black box. The flyer momentarily lost headway and started to sink. Solly threw a couple of switches, and a yoke snicked out of the deck and locked in place. He tested it, pulled back on the stick, and leveled off.

"I never knew you could do that," said Kim.

He grinned. "Learn something new every day. You ready?"

"For what? You weren't planning on dropping us into the river, were you?"

"Have no fear," he said.

"Right. Into the hands of God—"

He picked out one of the larger dam fragments and took them down the north face until they were just over the water. The descent was smoother than she'd expected.

"Good," she said.

He nodded. "Nothing like having a professional—"

The screen began to blink.

"Bingo," said Kim.

"Right at the foot of the dam, looks like." That made sense, of course. Throw an object in anywhere along this stretch of water, weigh it down, and if it moved at all, it would end up wedged in here.

Solly looked at the darkening sky. "It's late to push this any further tonight," he said. "Why don't we come back tomorrow? Work in full daylight?"

"When we're this close? It'll only take a few minutes. Let's get it done. Find out what we have."

Solly frowned. "Wouldn't take much for the river and the concrete to beat up a diver pretty good."

"It just means we have to be careful," she said. "Anyhow, it's not as dangerous as it looks."

"It *looks* pretty dangerous."

They surveyed the area for a place to set down.

"There," said Solly. He was looking at a slab, a piece of the dam that had been hewn off and dumped. It was lying almost flat in the water, one end submerged, the other angled up at about ten degrees. Just enough room for the flyer.

"That the best we can do?" asked Kim.

"There are better landing sites—" he was looking at a couple of beaches, "—but we'd have a hard time getting out into the river."

The slab, in fact, was perfectly situated, if they could manage the landing. Solly lowered the aircraft cautiously, arranging his approach so that the treads were parallel to the angle of incline, with the forward end *up*. "Hang on," he said.

He was feeling for the concrete, much as a person reaches for the next step down in the dark. A burst of wind drove them off. He took it up, came back and tried again.

Kim found herself willing the aircraft down, behaving as if *she* were at the controls, telling herself *easy*. *Easy*. They touched, lifted, and touched again. Solly maintained power. The aft section settled, and it suddenly seemed as if the angle was steeper than it had looked, that they were about to slide back into the river.

And then they were on the slab.

He let the engine run for a minute. When nothing happened he shut it down and took a deep breath. "Nothing to it," he said.

Kim let her heartbeat return to normal. "I knew you could manage it."

Solly opened the door, climbed out, and leaned upslope. "It's slippery," he warned.

One of them would have to stay with the sensor, to direct the dive. Kim started to remove her earrings. Solly watched her and then shook his head. "*You* stay put."

"Why?"

"Take a look at the river." He had to shout to get above the wind and the roar of the water.

Kim got out, planted her feet on the wet concrete, and nodded. "It *is* a little rough," she said. "Which is exactly why you need to stay here."

"How's that?"

The target area was just a few meters out from the slab. Not bad. She held up a tether. "If you go in and get into trouble, I'd never be able to pull you out. We need the muscle *here*."

His eyes drilled into her. "That's a dumb argument."

"Who says? Anyway, this is *my* project. And Solly, I'd feel a lot better knowing you were up here ready to lend a hand if you have to, than down there where I couldn't help worth a damn if something happened."

He stared at her and she saw his irritation grow. Because he knew she was right. She pulled her suit out of the back of the aircraft. "Let's just get it done."

"I really don't like this."

A pair of iron clamps jutted out of the concrete. "Relax," she said. She fixed the tether to one of the clamps and clipped the other end to her belt. "If anything goes wrong you can haul me out."

They argued for another few minutes. Then he gave in and she looked at the rushing river, watched it surging across the lower end of the slab, and wondered briefly whether this was a good idea after all, whether they should not have waited and maybe got a diving team together. She was about to back off when Solly shook his head, lowered the radio receiver into the water, and glowered at her. "Dumb," he grumbled.

"It's no big deal."

He grimaced, apparently uncertain what she'd said, but she shrugged and spoke into her mask radio. "It won't be bad once I get down a couple of meters."

He nodded and mouthed the word *dumb* again.

She tugged on her flippers, connected the jets to her belt, strapped a lamp on her wrist, and pulled her converter over her shoulders.

He gave her a pained expression. "Good luck."

She returned a smile that was meant to be reassuring, pulled the mask in place, and slipped into the river. "It's not that bad," she told Solly.

"The slab's breaking it up. That won't last."

She ducked under, heard the converter kick in and begin extracting oxygen from the water. Competing currents pushed at her, carrying her first one way and then another. She ran a radio check. Solly responded, she turned on the lamp, and started down, feeling her way along the smooth face of the slab. The water was murky and she couldn't see. She kept descending until she felt bottom. It was thick with mud and rock.

"Straight ahead," said Solly. "About twelve meters, looks like."

At first the water was relatively calm. She moved out away from the wall, trying to keep contact with the bottom. She worked her way past debris, drowned trees, pieces of machinery, concrete chunks. The rush of water pushed her one way and then another, then bore down on her until she lost all track of direction.

But it didn't matter. Solly had both the diver and the target blip on his screen. "Drifting right," he told her.

The current kept getting stronger. She had to use a burst from the jets to compensate. Dangerous, that, when she couldn't see.

"Drifting right again. Eight meters dead ahead."

Another burst carried her forward. The river tore at her, tried to carry her away. She anchored herself to an engine housing and caught her breath.

"How's your visibility, Kim?"

"A half meter."

"Okay. You should be right on top of it."

The lamp was no more than a soggy glow. "I don't see anything."

"It's right there."

"It could be buried."

"Wouldn't surprise me. Why don't you come up? We'll get a team and the right equipment and come back tomorrow."

The light reflected against something. Off to her right. Reluctantly, she dug in her heels, let go of the shrubbery, and crawled forward.

It was a piece of plastic. Sticking out of the muck. "We might have something, Solly."

"What is it? What do you see?"

Inside the plastic. "A shoe."

"You sure?"

"Yes."

She pulled at it. "Solly, it's a *foot*."

"Okay. Go easy."

"It's *somebody*."

"You can see a corpse?"

"I think so."

"Man or woman?"

"Are you serious? I've got a leg. That's all."

"Okay. You all right?"

She knew what he was thinking. "I'm fine."

"What's it look like?" All business again.

"It's small. I guess it *is* a woman. Or a child." She removed a line from her belt to fasten it to the plastic. But she lost her balance and the river caught her and sent her tumbling.

Solly's voice stayed calm. "Status, Kim? What's going on?"

She crashed against something hard, but found a handhold.

"Kim?"

"Current caught me." She was hanging onto a tree branch.

"You want me to come down?"

"No," she said. "My God, no."

The current tried to jerk her mask off. She grabbed hold of it, got it back in place, and listened to herself breathe.

"I think this would be a good time to come up, Kim. We can alert the authorities in the morning and let them do the rest."

"Which way's up?" she demanded. The question wasn't entirely facetious. She needed guidance getting back so she didn't pop out of the water at the wrong place and get sucked through the dam.

"You need to go about six meters right. Do that and you'll come up directly in front of me. Calmest water in the area."

Which wasn't saying much.

But it was hard to follow directions in the river. And she was getting tired. How long had she been down?

She used the jets to move right.

"Hold it," said Solly, alarmed. "You're going the *wrong* way."

But the river caught her. She seized something, a piece of iron, and hung on. "What's happening, Kim?"

She knew immediately. Communication breakdown: her right wasn't his right.

"I'm sorry," he said, figuring it out. "My fault. You okay?"

"I'm fine."

"You don't have to worry about going anywhere you don't want to. I've got the line."

Her shoulders ached. She'd drifted into an eddy and she took advantage of it to rest for a moment and let the river carry her forward. The current seemed to be getting stronger and suddenly she was tumbling and being swept along. She banged into something. Lights flashed behind her eyes and the tether yanked at her hip. The river rushed past her, dragged her mask up onto her forehead. She swallowed water and slammed into a tangle of branches. Pieces of iron or wood stabbed at her belly and the river tried to drag her clear but she hung on.

The torrent roared in her ears. It pounded her and pressed the breath out of her.

She got the mask back on and used the purge valve to clear the water. But it wasn't happening fast enough so she blew it out herself. The mask immediately began to fill up again.

"Kim!" Solly sounded far away. "Are you okay?"

She tried to answer but only swallowed more water. The purge valve didn't seem to be doing anything and the river was pouring in around the lens.

"Kim, what's happening?"

She cleared out her mask again, tried to push off from the tree. But the tether brought her back.

The tether. It was fouled.

And the river had become too strong, or she too tired. She couldn't fight it, couldn't even think about making headway.

"—stuck—" Solly was saying. "If you can hear me, I'm on my way. Hang—"

She wanted to talk to Solly, tell him to send for help, to stay away. But she couldn't get the water out of her mask, couldn't talk, couldn't even scream.

She tore it off, disconnected the hose, bit down on the mouthpiece, and sucked in a lungful of air. It allowed her to retreat inside her head, away from the rushing river—

Can't stay here.

She tried to free the tether, get clear of the branches, but every movement was fighting the torrent.

Solly would be following the tether down. But he'd no more be able to survive this than she was.

Something crashed into her ankle. The current dragged at her, and her shoulders hurt, and she almost lost the mouthpiece. She kept one hand clamped down on her belt, holding the tether lest it be torn away; the other held the mouthpiece in place.

Theoretically she could last for days. As long as the converter kept working she could just wait for Solly to bring help. But Solly wasn't bringing help; he was coming himself.

If she did nothing, they would both die down here. Or at least, *she* would.

Her lamp went out.

She tried to untangle the tether from the tree, but it was hopelessly snarled. She made her decision, unclipped it, and let it go. Then she pushed clear.

She rose in the torrent for a brief moment, and it slammed her into a wall. Her mouthpiece was torn away. The wall had openings, culverts, and she was dragged into one. It squeezed down on her, scraped her converter, wedged her into a narrow space. She felt around frantically for the mouthpiece.

She was jammed in headfirst and the mouthpiece should be in front of her, *had* to be in front of her, but she couldn't find it.

It was a sluice. A spillway. But it was partially blocked with debris. The converter, which was mounted on her back, was caught against mud and concrete.

She found the mouthpiece, gratefully put it between her lips, and took a deep breath. The air tasted very good. But she was fighting panic.

She would not get out the way she came in, and she could not squeeze through. As long as she tried to hold onto her breathing system, she was going to stay right where she was.

She tried again to wriggle free.

How far was it through the dam and out the other side? How far *could* it be? Surely not more than twenty meters.

She took a deep breath, removed the mouthpiece and released the converter clip. The torrent threw her against the straps but she struggled out of them and the river tore her away from the unit, thrust her deeper into the spillway. It swept her along, forcing her against walls and rock. She tried to protect her face and head. Once, for a few desperate seconds, she was caught again, but the obstruction broke loose almost immediately.

The flood carried her through the dark. She raised her head periodically hoping to find trapped air, but there was only water and concrete.

She crashed into something metallic, a screen, a grate perhaps. She felt her way past it and was moving downstream again, reminding herself that the water was only passing through the dam, that the lower river lay just ahead. That she'd be out in seconds.

A curious kind of tranquillity settled over her. As if some deep aspect of herself had given up, had accepted the darkness and the river.

And suddenly the pressure was gone and she was falling.

The fall went on and on. The river torrent turned to mist and she caught a glimpse of the river below, of white water and shadows. She gulped down lungfuls of air, straightened out and hit feet first, sinking into quiet depths. Then, delighted that her parts still seemed to be working, she kicked back to the surface.

13

I don't believe the truth will ever be known, and I have a great contempt for history.

—George G. Meade, 1871 c.e.

History is bunk.

—Ascribed to Henry Ford, 1915 c.e.

It was close at both ends.

When Air Rescue finally got to Solly they found him pinned against a gate in the powerhouse penstock. He had been in the water almost four hours.

He was not happy.

Nevertheless he and Kim were both on the scene next morning when police brought up a mummified corpse. It was wrapped in a plastic sheath.

The salvage operation was directed by a tall, dark-skinned, dark-haired official who introduced himself as Inspector Chepanga. "Tell me about it," he said.

He wore a black pullover sweater with a rolled collar. His beard was trimmed to a point, and he studied Kim with a world-weary attitude, suggesting that he fished corpses out of the Severin with depressing regularity. In that age of general prosperity and respect for law, the numbers might actually have run to once every few years.

"It's Yoshi Amara," Kim said. Solly was trying to signal her to be quiet, but she could see no point in that. She had no reason to protect Tripley or to hinder any investigation that might take place.

"How do you know? How did you know she was here?"

Kim explained about the shoe and the gold, and how they had conducted the search.

Chepanga listened, nodding occasionally, frowning frequently. At last he looked over at Solly, as if he at least should have known better. "You two are damned lucky to be alive," he growled, suggesting he'd have been just as happy if Kim hadn't created a problem for him.

The body had been weighed down with rocks. There wasn't much left except teeth and bones. And a bracelet and a necklace.

"Tripley's place?" asked Chepanga.

"Yes."

He stared out over the river. "The trail's a long time cold."

Solly and Kim celebrated their escape from the Severin by treating themselves to lunch in the most expensive restaurant they could find. They toasted each other's courage and good fortune, and Kim sat back to relish the moment. She assured him that he had behaved heroically, even if the rescue hadn't gone as planned. She was genuinely touched by this new evidence of his willingness to put himself on the line for her. He seized the first opportunity to grumble about her foolhardiness and she admitted she'd been less than prudent. But there was much that was charming in his insistence that next time he'd appreciate it if she'd try listening to him for a change. She smiled and squeezed his hand and insisted on refilling his drink from the decanter. Solly looked at her as severely as he could manage. He was, in his own way, the most charming person she knew. Well, maybe not quite as charming as Mike Plymouth. But Solly was unique.

Toward the end of the meal, one of Chepanga's assistants called to confirm it *was* Yoshi Amara.

Afterward they returned to the hotel, and she tried to reach Sheyel. The reception wasn't good, trouble on the lines somewhere, and her old teacher's image, when it finally appeared, lacked definition. It was fuzzy around the edges, particularly up around his shoulders, and occasionally he faded to near-transparency. Add his gloomy demeanor, and the result was spectral.

"I'm sorry," Kim said, the words inadequate as always even though the victim had been dead almost three decades.

"Murdered?" he asked.

"The police are looking into it. But, yes, I'd say that's a safe assumption." Kim had given few details, had in fact few to give.

"In a river," he said.

"I'm sorry." She didn't know how else to respond.

"Thank you, Kim. I appreciate what you've done." He looked *empty*. She realized that until that moment he'd never really given up hope.

"What will you do now?"

"Wait for the results of the investigation."

"I don't want to sound discouraging, Sheyel, but with the principals dead, I doubt there'll be much of an investigation."

The picture cleared up. "Surely they'd want to establish the truth about this," he said.

"Maybe. I have my doubts."

"I see." The image faded again, down to a silhouette. "Kim," he said, "have you finished?"

"You mean, do I plan to pursue this any further?"

"Yes. That is what I mean. Because I honestly don't understand—can't imagine—what happened. I've done a lot of research on Tripley and Kane. I mean, I've looked at everything that's available. I just don't believe either of them is capable of murder."

"Those are my thoughts exactly."

"So are you going to continue?"

"To the extent that I'm able."

"Then I want you to be careful. Yoshi's killer may still be out there."

"After all these years?" She tried to sound skeptical.

"You have someone up there with you?"

"Yes," she said. "A colleague. Solomon Hobbs."

"Good. Stay close to him."

Chepanga conducted a virtual interview that afternoon. He asked Kim to repeat her story in tedious detail. When she was finished he asked why she had become interested in the case. "End of the century," she told him. "It got me reminiscing about the sister I'd lost."

He had clearly hoped for more. He asked Solly whether he had anything to add.

Solly did not. "I was just trying to help a friend," he said.

"How did she die?" Kim asked.

"Her neck was broken."

"And what do you plan to do now?"

"We'll conduct a thorough investigation, of course. Although we have to face the reality that it's been a long time. A case of this nature—Well, we'll do what we can." He thanked her and blinked out.

"I think he's telling us it's over," said Solly.

"He thinks Tripley did it, and Tripley's dead. At least he's legally dead."

"Yeah, that's my guess." Solly fixed her with an odd look.

"What?" asked Kim.

"You promised Sheyel you'd press on. How do you go about pressing on?"

"I don't know. There ought to be something we can do." She still felt exhilarated after her derring-do in the river. Who'd have ever thought little Kimmy had that in her? "How about going out on the town?" she said.

"Absolutely." He made drinks for them, swallowed his, excused himself, and went back to his bedroom. Minutes later he reappeared in a lemon-colored jacket. "The new *me*. What do you think?"

"Dazzling."

"Bought it last week. For a special occasion."

"Good. It should put us in the right frame of mind for taking the next step."

"*Us?* How do you mean *us?*"

She canted her head and gazed steadily into his unblinking eyes. She was sending out a subliminal call for help and she knew it and Solly knew it. "I wouldn't put any pressure on you, Solly," she said.

"Of course not. And what," he asked cautiously, "would the next step be?"

"To find out what happened to the relationship between Kane and Emily."

They went to a show. Dancers, live music, a celebrity troop of singers, a comedian. The place was packed. Afterward they strolled along the skyways, enjoying the fountains and the bistros.

They stopped by the Top of the World for dinner. But they'd hardly been seated when a text message came in from Matt: *We understand police found Amara's body in Severin. Some of us are wondering how it happens that Institute personnel are involved.*

"Some of us" translated to Philip Agostino, the onetime physics whiz who'd realized his tastes ran more to power than to science and who was now director of the Institute. "I suspect," Solly said ominously, "there'll be some fallout."

After the experience in the river, trouble with her boss seemed of minor consequence. Kim ordered a bottle of wine far more expensive than she could afford, filled both glasses, and raised hers to Solly. "For all you've done," she said.

Later, back in the hotel room, she looked again at the final conversation between Kane and Emily, as the *Hunter* approached Sky Harbor. The lights were dimmed in the pilot's room, and they spoke in the casual manner of longtime colleagues.

"Thanks, Markis."

"For what?"

"For getting us back. I know we put some pressure on you to continue the mission."

"It's okay. It's what I would have expected."

"As always, Markis, it was nice to spend time with you."

She stopped it there, backed it up, went to get Solly, who was trying to read in another room, and reran the line.

"As always, Markis, it was nice to spend time with you."

"Okay." She went to a split screen, Emily and Markis again, from a conversation seven weeks earlier, shortly after *Hunter* had departed St. Johns. "Watch."

Neither spoke. Emily squeezed Kane's shoulder and slipped into the right-hand seat.

"We're right on schedule," he said.

She leaned toward him, as close as the restraints would permit. *"Maybe this'll be our time."*

"I hope so, Emily. I really do."

"Listen to his voice," Kim said. "Watch the body language."

The two sat several minutes, talking about incidentals. But the *manner* of it, the tendency of each to reach out and touch the other broadcast their mutual passion. Kim froze the picture at a moment when they gazed soulfully at each other.

"I don't know," said Solly. "What are you trying to prove?"

"Inconsistency."

She replayed the conversations in her mind and stared out at the skyline.

"Let me change the subject," said Solly. "The Institute called a while ago. Harvey's asked for some time off. They need a replacement pilot."

"For—?"

"Taratuba."

The black hole near the Miranda nebula. The genesis candidate. The

Thomas Hammersmith was scheduled to leave in eleven days.

There was a suspicion, but little hard evidence, that Taratuba had created a false vacuum, had collapsed into a new big bang. A baby universe. The event, if it *had* in fact occurred, would have erupted into a different space-time continuum, forever separated from this universe. But theory held that if it were in fact happening, Kung Che radiation would be detectable around the hole. It might be a chance to *touch* the fires of creation. To make some progress on precreative conditions.

"You'd be gone quite a while," she said.

"Several months." He looked at her. "What do you think? Does it make a problem for you?"

"No. Of course not."

"I mean, this thing has lain fallow for thirty years."

"Of course."

"You think there's anything to it?" he asked.

"To what?"

As if he'd been reading her thoughts: "Alternate worlds. A place where you and I are sitting in this same room, having this same conversation, except maybe we've figured out what's going on."

She shrugged. "Not my field, Solly. But I'd like to compare notes with the other Brandywine."

He looked at her for a long moment. "I wonder," he said suddenly, "if there's a place out there where we're lovers?"

He blurted it out, as if he had to say it before some prohibition intervened. He looked uncomfortable in the wake of the remark, and she knew he would have called it back if he could.

She took his hand, not knowing quite what to say. There'd always been an unspoken understanding between them, a distance created by the knowledge that they would not risk a long friendship to a sexual encounter. But there were occasional hints, suggestions from Solly that he wasn't entirely comfortable with the status quo. Still, he was all the family she had, and she did not want to lose him. "I'd hope so," she said cautiously, smiling, but using a neutral tone.

While Solly called the desk and booked tickets on the Snowhawk in the morning, Kim parked herself in front of the display and began running the *Hunter* logs again.

Emily and Kane.

I love you, the early encounters said, the passion reciprocal. There was no way to miss it.

And: *"As always, Markis, it was nice to spend time with you."*

The nonverbal cues were almost *professionally* correct, no suggestion of sexual tension, no touching, no wistful smiles. Nothing. Even the voices were friendly but detached. *Pass the coffee.*

"It's all wrong," she said aloud.

"If you figure it out," said Solly, stretching, getting up from the sofa on which he'd been spread out, "let me know. I'll see you in the morning."

Kim put up her split screen again, Kane and Emily from early in the mission on one side, Kane and Emily saying goodbye on the other. She ran both sequences forward at normal speed, then backed them up and ran them again at one quarter. And then she saw it.

My God.

She reversed it and watched it again. There was no question.

She knocked on his door. "Solly."

He came out with a sigh, securing his robe, wearing an expression of infinite patience. "Yes, Kim?" he said, emphasizing the aspirate.

She killed the sound and ran it for him. "Watch the seats," she said.

He lowered himself onto the sofa. A table lamp burned steadily beside him. "What am I looking for?"

On the left side, the early conversation, the encounter coming to an end and Emily shifting her weight and beginning to rise. Kim stopped the picture.

On the right, the talk also winding down. Again Emily shifting her weight and getting up. Kim restarted the sequence, both images synchronized, both in slow motion. In each, Emily flicked the harness open with a graceful left hand and used the other to push off the chair arm.

She hit the *pause* function. "Do you see it?"

"I give up," said Solly.

"Look at the seat." The polymod fabric in the early sequence contained the unmistakable imprint of a human bottom. On the right, it was perfectly smooth.

"That's strange," he said.

They ran other sequences. Whenever *anyone* sat in the right-hand chair, the seat showed the imprint afterward before returning gradually to its own shape.

Anyone except Emily. Emily on the return flight.

But outward bound, she always left the imprint. Kim looked at the first conversation on the return flight:

"Can't really expect to hit it right away," said Markis. *"We have to be patient."*

"We've been *patient."*

"I know."

Emily sat silently for several minutes. Then unbuckled. *"Gotta go."*

Kane nodded as she rose.

Kim stopped the picture.

No imprint.

"Tell me what I'm thinking, Solly. You're good at that."

He scratched his head. "I'd say that on the return flight we're looking at a *virtual* Emily."

"So the logs are faked."

Solly took a deep breath. "Yeah, I'd say so. But a missing crease in a seat isn't compelling. Maybe the light wasn't right."

"How hard would it be to do this? To falsify a ship's log?"

"It wouldn't be easy. You have to get all the visuals right. You also have to make sure the data streams reflect the story you're telling. When the *Hunter* makes a jump, the instruments have to show that."

"Could you do it?"

"Fabricate a log?" His teeth glittered in the lamplight. "Yes. I think I could manage it. Given some time and the cooperation of my colleagues."

"So why would they use a virtual Emily?"

"Because the real one wouldn't cooperate."

"—Or wasn't functioning." They stared at each other.

"It could be," said Solly. "Look, no fraudulent log can stand up to a serious investigation. So, if you're right, we should be able to show it convincingly. Everything on the visual record has to be consistent. The lighting is always *about* the same, but it changes as people move around in it. You'd have to match that up. There are too many details and there's just no way to get them all absolutely right."

She turned away from the screen and looked out at the city. "Kane?"

"Oh yes. It would *have* to be Kane. Have to be somebody intricately familiar with the ship."

"Which brings us to the bottom line: *What* happened to Emily?"

"Let's go slow, Kim. Let's have the lab do an analysis and make sure you're right."

She nodded, sat down at the phone, and brought up the directory.

She was looking for the Customs Service office at Sky Harbor. When she found it, she called through.

A uniformed officer appeared onscreen. "Greenway Customs."

"Hello," Kim said. "My name's Brandywine. May I ask a hypothetical question?"

"Of course, ma'am."

"Arriving passengers," she said. "If anyone is supposed to be on a ship, but isn't, you'd know, right?"

"Yes, ma'am. They have to pass physically through customs."

"How about crew members?"

"They do too."

"You have a manifest, then, and you check everyone against the manifest. And if someone doesn't get off—"

"Oh, I'm sorry. I misunderstood you. If a person doesn't get off, we don't really care. We're only concerned with people seeking entry onto Greenway."

She decided to try another tack. "Does Customs keep a record of persons debarking from arriving vessels?"

"Yes," he said.

"Do you interview everyone?"

"Not in person. Customs declarations are usually taken electronically."

"If I were on the manifest, and I submitted a declaration, but I did not get off, would you know?"

"No, ma'am. We would not."

Kim thanked him and disconnected. "I'm beginning to understand why Emily never got to her hotel." She poured herself a drink but only stared at it. "She never got off the *Hunter*, did she?"

"We don't know that."

"Solly, what's the penalty for falsifying logs?"

"It can be criminal, depending on circumstances. The very least penalty would be disbarment. Logs are sacred."

"So it's not something you'd do without a very good reason."

"You got it."

"All right, let me ask another question. If you created a bogus set of logs, what would you do with the originals?"

Solly's brow wrinkled while he thought about it. "It would depend," he said. "If I'd murdered somebody and thrown her out the air lock, then I'd certainly lose the originals. But if somebody *else* had done something, if my only participation in whatever this is about was as, say, part of a cover-up, then I'd *keep* the original logs in case I eventually needed to prove I didn't do the murder."

"That's exactly the way I see it. Solly, who can we get to do an analysis of this thing? Somebody discreet?"

"I have a friend," he said.

"In Seabright?"

"Yes."

"Take it to him tomorrow, will you? Swear him to secrecy, but see if you can get confirmation. How long do you think it'll take?"

"Hard to say. Depends how busy he is. How much we're willing to pay."

"Okay. Make it worth his while. Call me when you get a result."

"What are *you* going to do?"

"Hang around here for a bit. See what else I can find out." She opened a line to the desk and canceled her reservation on the morning train.

Many demons are in woods, in waters, in wildernesses, and in dark pools. . . .

—MARTIN LUTHER, *Table Talk*, DLXXIV, 1569 C.E.

"Of course I remember you." Jorge Gould smiled pleasantly and held out a hand while she watched him try frantically to recall her name. "You're the sister of Markis Kane's model." He waved an index finger at her as if to say *who could forget?*

"Kim Brandywine," she said. "I wanted you to know how pleased I was with the Kane you sold me."

"Oh yes. Yes, that was quite a good buy, Ms. Brandywine. You did well for yourself." He came out from behind the counter and glanced around at the stock. "Were you interested in looking at more of his work?"

"Perhaps another time," she said. "There *are* one or two others that I'd like to add to my collection."

"No need to wait." He rubbed his hands together. "We have a very liberal payment plan. Which ones did you want to see?"

"Yes," she said, ignoring the question, "Kane does marvelous work."

"He does indeed. Did I tell you I knew him personally?"

"You mentioned that."

"So what can I show you?"

"Jorge, I don't plan to make a purchase today. I don't like to pile up debt. Buy outright, I say. Wouldn't you agree?"

"Well—"

"I'm sure you do." She mentioned *Autumn* and *Night Passage*, and implied that she would shortly be in the market for both. "Marvelous compositions," she said. "He's a genius."

"Sometimes it takes time before the world recognizes this level of talent."

He insisted on showing her more of Kane's work. *Candlelight* depicted a couple having dinner on the observation deck of an interstellar. A candle glitters beside a bottle of wine, thick violet drapes cover the wall, and a waiter stands over them with a tray. The couple are handsome and absorbed in each other. Above, through a sheer overhead, the orange and red ring of a recent supernova casts an eerie light across the scene.

In *Passage*, a survey ship is silhouetted against a pulsar, caught in the moment that the star's beam sweeps past.

"These would be excellent additions to any collection," Gould said.

She agreed. "How marvelous it must be to have known him."

"Yes. He and I were quite good friends, as a matter of fact."

"I envy you." She delivered a smile of pure innocence. "What sort of home did he have? I think when I was here before you said he lived in Severin?"

Gould offered her a chair and they both sat down. "Yes," he said. "That's right. That's where he lived. My wife also lived there at the time." He repeated the details while Kim listened patiently. Finally he asked whether she knew he was a war hero.

"I know," said Kim. "Tell me about the villa."

Gould recalled that the living room had been coldly formal; that Kane had lived in his den, had entertained his friends there. "Sometimes," Gould said, "people he'd served with, in the fleet, came to town." He shook his head. "Kane and his friends knew how to party."

"It's beautiful country," said Kim. "He must have had a lovely view."

"He had a deck on the side of the house where you could sit in the evenings and watch the sun go down behind the mountains—"

They continued in that manner for several minutes until Kim felt ready to ask the one serious question she'd brought with her. "Did I hear you say there was a secret room?"

"Secret room?"

"Yes. When I was here before, you told me that during his last couple of years there, he sealed off part of the house. Wouldn't let anybody see it."

"Oh yes. I'd forgot. That was the den. After the Mount Hope business, he stopped using it for guests and switched to the living room."

"Why do you think he did that? Was he restoring it, maybe?"

"No, I don't think so." He made a face, signifying he was thinking hard. "You could see Mount Hope from the den. Maybe he didn't want to look at it anymore. Or maybe he'd just developed an eccentricity. Artists are like that."

"I suppose," she said. "He wouldn't let *anybody* in there?"

"Not as far as I know."

"I wonder if it might have been that he'd begun to work there? To paint?" *Or whether he'd hidden something he didn't want anyone to get near. Like the* Hunter *logs?*

"I doubt it. He had a workroom toward the front of the house."

"Where was the den?"

"At the rear."

"You never saw it again after he sealed it off?"

"No. Never did." He looked at her and at the two Kane's. "Now, why don't we arrange for you to take one of these little beauties home?"

Kim had to pay the Rent-All Emporium for both the wet suit, which had been torn, and for the mask and converter, which were still in the river. They asked no questions, but snickered at her when she told them she wanted to rent a rubber boat and another wetsuit. It would require, they explained, a substantially heavier deposit.

An hour later, in her rented flyer, she lifted off the Gateway pad into a cold gray afternoon and once more turned south. For a few minutes she ran above a train, but it quickly distanced her and lost itself in the craggy countryside.

She had not told Solly what she intended to do because he would have insisted on coming. That would have been comforting, but she was anxious to have the results on the *Hunter* logs. And she felt a compunction to confront her fears about the local demon. After her experience in the river, she told herself, she feared nothing that walked.

She looked up the train on the schedule. The Overland. Hauling dry goods, electronics, lumber, and machinery from Sorrentino to the coast. She liked trains. Always had. She'd have preferred at the moment to be aboard one.

She'd circled the location of Kane's villa on her map of the village. It had been on the north side, in an area now in deep water.

She traced bearings from the Kane home to the dam, to the city hall (which was in fifteen meters of water, but whose tower still rose proudly out of the lake), and to a onetime flyer maintenance facility atop a low hill that had become an island when the dam came down.

The river looked cold in the somber light. She glided out over the lake and, minutes later, descended on Cabry's Beach.

The flyer came to rest with one of its treads in the water. She watched the edge of the forest while changing into her wet suit. The tree branches swayed gently in the wind coming off the water. No blue jay fluttered through that sky; no deer came down to the shoreline to drink.

She opened the hatch and eased down onto the sand. It crackled underfoot. The wind was cold. She turned up the heat in her suit and tugged a woolen hat down over her ears. The sky was heavy and overcast.

She pulled the boat out of the back seat, hit the inflater, mounted the motor, and dragged it into the water. It had a transparent bottom. She tossed in a paddle, her flippers, and the converter. And her packet of pictures of Severin Village circa 573. She added forty meters of line, marked at two-meter intervals, and used a rock to make an anchor.

She strapped a lamp and an imager to her wrist, and looped a belt around her waist. She attached a utility pouch to it, and put in a compass and a laser cutter. Satisfied that she had everything, she launched the boat and started its waterjet engine.

The surface was choppy. Although she had a remote, she sat in the rear, steering by hand, headed out into the lake.

She moved onto the bearing with the dam and followed it until the city hall and the flyer repair facility lined up. Then she killed the engine and looked down through the bottom of the boat. The water was clear and she could see a bench. Nearby lay an abandoned flyer. Beyond the flyer she could make out a group of poles. A children's swing set. The swings swayed gently as she passed overhead.

The boat rose and fell.

She saw a house, but it was not Kane's, not the right shape. Her pictures indicated it was probably his neighbor on the south, a physician who'd performed well during the disaster.

She continued straight on until she saw what she was looking for: an arched pavilion, a stone wall, a Thunderbird house.

That was it. It had angled wings and courtyards and a long central spine. The roof, with its crests and ridgelines, was unmistakable.

Kim dropped her makeshift anchor over the side and watched the line play out to fourteen meters. *Deep.* She secured it to the gunwale, pulled on her gear, and slipped into the water. She immediately felt safer, as though she were no longer exposed.

She turned toward the bottom and rode down on her jets.

Gray light filtered through the surface. The water grew cool and then warm again as she passed through alternating currents. An eel glided past. She switched on her lamp and a few fish quickly retreated. The boat was a dark shape above.

She leveled off in front of the second floor, eye-to-eye with an oculus window. The interior was thick with silt. But she could see a bed, a dresser, a couple of chairs. A fish glided out of a venting pipe, turned toward the lamp, and then disappeared out of the room.

She descended to the front door. It had no power, no knob, no easy way to open it. She passed by, moved along the front of the building, found a gaping window, and swam in.

Her lamp picked out a couch, a fireplace, and a flatscreen in the down position on one wall. This, she thought, had been the formal living room Gould had described.

Amazing. Kane had apparently not bothered to move his furniture when he left, had simply given in to the rising water.

She passed into the central hallway. A staircase rose on one side, assorted chairs and tables were tumbled about, and a couple of beams lay in the debris.

Kim pushed across to the opposite wing. She had to struggle to get the door open. Inside, she looked into what seemed to be Kane's work area. A wooden table was turned over, its legs sticking up like those of a dead animal. Several rolls of what might once have been canvasses were scattered in the silt. Artists' brushes lay everywhere, and pieces of an easel.

She could make out sketches, or parts of sketches, on the walls. Women's faces, mostly. Framed by trees, lanterns, a vestibule. But always the woman was prominent.

They were incomplete, as though he were trying out ideas. The expressions were inevitably wistful, melancholy, mournful. No life of the party here. The hairstyles were different, the hair itself sometimes cut short, sometimes shoulder length, inevitably in the fashions of the 570s. But it struck her, as she passed along the wall, examining the figures in the glow of the lamp, that each was an aspect of *Emily*.

Or herself.

Kim's scalp prickled.

She drew the imager out of her utility pouch and began taking pictures. She tried to record everything.

She had come hoping to find the original *Hunter* logs. The possibility suddenly seemed remote, but the table had a drawer, so she opened it. It contained only a couple of rags.

There was a door at the far end of the room, leading to an enclosed porch, beyond which lay a washroom. She went through the door, and saw plastic containers and flowerpots on the porch floor. She found a medicine cabinet in the washroom and opened it. One of the containers still had air trapped inside. The container floated out and rose to the ceiling.

She went back the way she'd come, through the formal living room and on into the far wing.

She opened drawers, broke into cabinets when hinges wouldn't work. She searched everywhere, and then went upstairs and prowled through bedrooms and washrooms. A broken pot or two remained in the kitchen cabinets. She was shocked to find several of Kane's trophies in the mud, including the Conciliar Medal of Valor, the highest award the Republic had to give. It seemed odd that no one had been here before her and claimed the treasure.

Tora should have it. She wiped it off and put it in her pouch.

She felt movement in the water.

And sensed that she was not alone.

She listened, heard nothing, and surveyed the room for another way out. She'd have no choice but to go through the window if she had to, risking the glass shards still jutting out from the frame. She turned abruptly, as if to catch someone watching her. But the room was empty save for shadows drifting around the walls.

Dumb.

It was not at all hard to imagine that the spirit of Markis Kane lingered about the place. Had she been in sunlight, she'd have smiled at the notion and dismissed it with contempt. But down here—*There must be a part of us,* she thought, *that's wired to accept the paranormal. Science and the experience of a lifetime don't count for much when the lights go out.*

She returned to the hallway, swept it with her lamp, and started toward the rear of the house, stopping to examine a cabinet and a small desk. She'd acquired an escort of fish, long, rainbow-colored creatures that moved with her but darted back whenever she turned toward them. She was pleased to have their company.

Another bedroom opened off left. Here the furniture was still more or less in place. Clothing, or possibly bedding—it was impossible to know—lay in gray piles on the floor.

She continued down the corridor to the last doorway, which was on the right hand side of the corridor.

The sanctum sanctorum.

Its door was closed.

She pushed on it, gently at first, and then with as much force as she could muster. It did not budge. She took out the laser and cut a hole big enough to pass through.

Within, she saw a desk, a credenza, some cabinets and tables. And a chair.

She passed inside.

There was a closet across the room. Drapes covered the wall on her right. Two of the other walls had large windows. *This* window, she thought, looked north toward Eagle Point. The one on her left opened onto Mount Hope. She visualized Kane seated in here, watching the sun drop behind that scarred peak. What had he been thinking?

She rifled everything, breaking into cabinets, opening drawers, trying not to spill their contents, as if that mattered, searching the closet, which contained more clothes and several unopened packages of sketch paper. When she'd finished she drifted back into the center of the room, allowing her lamp to point where it would.

The beam touched the drapes. Still in place after all these years.

They covered an *interior* wall.

She thought of the sketches of Emily in the west wing, and the murals Kane had done for local libraries. Her converter came on, startling her. It murmured gently as it went about its business of renewing her air supply.

What was behind the drapes?

She raised her lamp. There must have been something jerky in the movement because the fish accompanying her vanished. Kim floated in the center of the room, fighting the natural buoyancy that kept lifting her toward the ceiling. She approached the curtains, touched them, tried to grasp them, to draw them back. But they dissolved in her hands. She tried again and brought another section away.

There *was* a sketch on the wall.

A ringed world.

She pulled the rest of the drapes down.

It was hard to make out in the uncertain light. But the planet was part of a mural embodying a woman. Another *Emily*. No question: her own image, brave and resigned, smiled out at her. She looked as she had on the *Hunter*, wearing the blue jacket open at the throat, her hair shoulder length, her eyes pensive. The ringed world was in her left hand.

And there was *something* in her right.

Kim went closer with the lamp, trying to make it out.

It looked like a turtle-shell.

She stared at it while the chill from the water crept into her bones. A flared teardrop on an elliptical platform.

The toy warship.

The turtle-shell vessel from Ben Tripley's office.

It was the *Valiant*!

There was more: Although most of the sketch had faded during its long immersion, the background had been filled with star fields and— what? Roiling clouds? Impossible to be sure. But there, in one corner was the unmistakable image of NGC2024. The Horsehead Nebula.

Horsehead and ringed world and turtle-shell and Emily. All she could think of was *Turtles all the way down.*

The water seemed to have gotten colder and the suit's automatic heating function wasn't keeping up. She adjusted the control a couple of degrees, and then started taking pictures.

The most logical explanation was that the *Valiant* had been a real ship, and that Kane had once served on it. But it seemed unlikely that Ben Tripley would not be aware of that piece of information, would not in fact be conversant with every known make of starship. That was, after all, his business.

She moved in close and peered at the vessel.

No propulsion tubes. Just like the model.

What kind of ship didn't have propulsion tubes?

She caught her breath: Was the bookshelf model a reproduction of a vessel from another civilization? A *celestial*? The Horsehead was in Orion, and would have been visible along the projected course of the *Hunter*. If there had in fact been contact, Kane and Kile Tripley might each have recorded it in his own way, one in a painting, the other by using a tech shop to build a reproduction. Her earlier guess that Ben Tripley's model starship was a replica of a vessel from another place suddenly looked quite prescient.

Something caught her eye, a movement, a flicker, outside the range of her lamp. Over near the hole she'd cut in the door. A fish momentarily passing through the light?

She put the imager away, wondering if it would be worthwhile to arrange for a team to come in and recover the wall, to bring it out into the sun. The villa had been abandoned, so surely she could do that without legal consequences.

The thought drained away as she became aware that light was coming from the passageway. It was dim, barely perceptible, but it was there.

She shut off her lamp and backed into a corner. Marine life. It had to be: a luminous eel of some sort, probably. Nevertheless, she edged toward one of the windows. The frames were jammed with broken glass.

She did a final survey of the room, refusing to be rattled, and was rewarded with the sight of a mug all but buried in the silt. When she picked it up and wiped it off, she saw that it was emblazoned with the designator and seal of the *376*. She added it to the Medal of Valor.

The illumination grew brighter. A soft green glow, like phosphorous.

She pushed off the wall and drifted easily across the room, getting an angle so she could look out into the passageway without getting too close.

A pair of eyes stared back. Great, green, unblinking eyes. They locked on her.

Intelligent.

Mad.

She could see no head, only the eyes, floating almost independent of one another just outside in the corridor. They were *big*. Enormous. Too large to belong to any creature that could have reasonably fit into the hallway.

Her heart exploded and she almost lost her breather. She dived back away from the door, crossed the room, turned on her jets, and crashed through the broken frame, taking wood and glass with her.

She made for the surface, thinking, there had been nothing attached to the eyes, no body, no corporeal presence of any kind.

It was dark when she broke the surface. Kim looked around, located her boat, and raced to it, half expecting to be seized from below and dragged beneath the water. She hauled herself quickly over the gunwale, cut loose the anchor, tore off her breather, and started the engine.

The boat moved away with maddening deliberation.

She didn't know where the flyer was. The sky was full of stars but the shore was featureless. She forced herself to slow down. She checked her compass and brought the boat around to a southeastern heading.

Behind her, something snorted. But nothing showed itself.

When she got close to land she had to cruise the shoreline, past forest broken up by buildings and strips of beach. Occasionally she saw flickers of light in the trees, moving in conjunction with her as though she was being tracked.

Then her lamp picked out the welcome shape of the flyer. She turned the boat quickly inshore, ran it onto the beach, abandoned it, and made a dash for the aircraft. Once inside, she directed the vehicle to take off.

"Where?" it asked.

"Anywhere," she said. *"Up."*

15

I got no way to go to Draco.
—GEORGE THOMAS & LIVIA HOWE,
The Arcturian Follies, Act II, 600

"**Y**ou should never have done that," said Solly. He was furious. "Not alone. You know better."

"Yeah," she said. "*Now* I do." And: "Never again."

A long silence this time. Then: "Kim, it has to have been an eel or something."

She was still in Eagle Point, in her robe, on the sofa with her legs tucked under her. A virtual Solly sat in a virtual chair in the projection area. Behind him, she could see a window and a view of the ocean. He was at home.

"It wasn't an eel," she insisted. "And it wasn't in my head." And to her everlasting embarrassment, tears ran down her cheeks. "It was *really* there, Solly. So help me, it was *really* there."

"Okay," he said.

"Whatever it was, it was there, and it wasn't human. But the eyes *were* intelligent. It looked right through me."

"Okay," he said. "We don't go in the water anymore, right?"

She was swallowing, trying to get control of herself. "Right," she said. Her voice trembled.

"Couldn't have been a squid or something, could it? Something that followed you in?"

"The lake's fresh water."

Solly didn't say anything for a long moment. Then: "Did you get a picture of it?"

"No," she said. "I was a little busy."

"So what do *you* think it was?"

"You want to know what I think? Really? I think Sheyel is right. I think they brought something back with them. And I know how crazy that sounds, but I know what I saw, I mean I *don't* know what I saw, but it *was* there, and it wasn't a *squid*."

"You want me to come up?"

"No. I've had enough. I'll be on my way back in a couple of hours."

Solly looked relieved. "You don't have any plans about going back into the lake."

"No." She managed a laugh. "No way that's going to happen."

"What about the boat?"

"I told the rental shop where it is. They're charging me for the pickup, but that's fine. I don't mind."

"All right." He was visibly relieved. It was a reaction that pleased her. "Think about it a minute. How could a *thing* have got past customs? How would it get down in the lift?"

"I don't know. Maybe it was *inside* somebody. Maybe it took over *Emily*. Maybe that's why they couldn't show her on the logs."

"Kim—" His eyes went briefly out of focus. "What've you been reading? Do you have any idea how that sounds?"

"Solly, I don't have any answers. I just know what I saw."

"All right." He was appraising her. "You're sure you're okay?"

"I'm fine." Sure she was.

"I don't suppose," said Solly, "you found the *Hunter* logs? The real ones?"

She looked out the window. Sunlight glittered on the peaks. It was a normal world out there. "No," she said. "But there *is* something." She held up one of the pictures of the sketch on the wall.

He leaned forward. Squinted. "My God," he said. "It's *Emily* again."

"She seems to be his favorite model."

"I'd say. What's she holding in her hands?"

Kim produced close-ups, watched him study the planet, and the ship. He frowned at the *Valiant*. "What *is* that thing?" he asked. "A turtle?"

"It's a ship of some kind. What's weird is that Ben Tripley has a model of it in his office."

"The same design?"

"Yes."

"What the hell is it doing in the sketch?"

"Solly, it *might* be a celestial. Maybe it's what they saw out there." She took a minute to rearrange her cushions. "I think they came out of hyper near one of the seven stars, and they saw *this* thing." She shook the photo. "We've got to do a search, see if any ship that looked like this has ever existed. Tripley didn't know about it, so I'd bet not. Anyhow it has no propulsion tubes, at least the model doesn't—it's hard to tell with this—" she meant the sketch. "As far as I know everything *we* make has propulsion tubes. If I'm correct, the ship is either fictitious or a celestial. If it's fictitious, why would it appear simultaneously in Kane's mural and as Tripley's model?"

Solly tapped his fingers on his armchair. "Why would Tripley—Kile Tripley—*want* a model?"

"I don't know. Answer that and maybe everything else becomes clear."

"Okay," he said. "Another subject—"

"Yes."

"You were right. The log's a complete fabrication. Or at least, it is from about the point where they have the engine breakdown."

"Maybe that becomes the first question. Did they really experience a breakdown?"

"Probably. If not, and if there was a contact, it would imply a rendezvous. That seems like stretching it. No, I think we can assume the engine problem was legitimate."

"Okay. If what we saw on the log was accurate, would it have been enough to bring them out of hyperspace?"

"Oh yes. *Any* kind of problem with the jump engines, you get out before you start monkeying with it. That's SOP. Because if you don't and something goes wrong, nobody ever hears from you again."

"So we're making some progress. The logs look good until the problem develops. And the virtual Emily shows up at about the same time."

"So what's our next step?" Solly's voice got a little deeper, signaling that his testosterone was pushing him in a direction he really didn't want to follow. "How about if *I* go up to Severin and see if I can get some pictures of the thingee?"

"No. It scares me, Solly. I don't want to have anything to do with it."

"That's not a very scientific attitude."

"I don't care."

"Okay."

She could see he was uncomfortable, that he thought he should argue a little, maybe even insist on going. So she changed tack: "Have you decided to take the Taratuba assignment?"

"Not yet. Why? Did you want to come along?"

"I'm going to try to talk to Matt and see if I can borrow the *Mac*. If I can get it, I'll need a pilot." The *Mac* was the *Karen McCollum*, one of two Institute interstellars currently at Greenway.

"Why do you need a starship? Where do you want to go?"

"I think it's time to bite the bullet."

"You're getting dramatic. What does that mean?"

"Find out whether a meeting between the *Hunter* and a celestial really happened."

"How do you propose to do that?"

"Go out and look at the neighborhood."

"Kim—" He was studying her, trying to make sense of the proposal. "We're talking about something that happened almost three decades ago—"

"If they found a civilization, it won't have gone anywhere."

"But we seem to be talking about a *ship*. We don't think they'd still be hanging around after all these years, do we?"

"Maybe not. But it doesn't matter."

"Why's that?"

"Their traces would still be out there."

She got off the train at Blanchet Preserve and took a cab to Tempest, home of Orlin University. It was the first time she'd been back since graduation, and she was struck by the degree to which the town had changed. The MacFarlane Recreational Complex looked abandoned, much of East Campus had become a public park, and all of the buildings, with one or two exceptions, appeared weather-beaten.

It was nevertheless good to see it all again, maybe because the old scenes were mundane, laid out against the midafternoon sun, part of a solid, predictable world. No specters need apply. She took comfort from it, from the Thompson Astronomical Center, which received a steady stream of images from observational facilities throughout the Orion Arm; from the Picacci Building, which housed the student center and cafeteria; from Palfrey Park, where she'd often done her reading assignments when the weather was good. Off to the north in a cluster of trees she could almost see her old apartment.

And *there*, at the end of a quiet lane, stood the house in which Sheyel Tolliver had occasionally gathered groups of graduate students and other faculty members for lunches and wide-ranging discussions. *Never look for complexity in diplomatic decisions. With very few exceptions, actions always devolve—and that's the exact term—from someone's self-interest. Not the national self-interest, by the way. We are talking here about individual careers.*

She hadn't believed that at the time, had assigned it to the natural growth of cynicism in an aging instructor. Kim had been an idealist then. Now, although she retained a strong belief in the essential decency of the average person, she was convinced that those whose tastes run to personal power could never be trusted to act save in the pursuit of their own ambition.

The last meeting of Sheyel's informal discussion group had occurred two days before graduation. It had been a farewell, and the students had brought the goodies for a change, and had given Sheyel a plaque, which had read FOR UNRELENTING ADEQUACY. The reference was to his assertion that the standards in their group were so high that *adequacy* constituted a singular achievement.

The house was stone and glass, in the Sylvan style, with a rooftop garden and a large bay window overlooking a country lane. A portico dominated the eastern side, and a pool occupied the rear. A postlight had been turned on to welcome her.

She recalled standing by the pool at that last meeting, sipping a lime drink—how odd that that detail would stay with her—in a group with Sheyel and another instructor and two or three students, and the subject had turned to the sorry state of human history: its long catalog of blood, desperation, corruption, missed opportunities, oppression, and often suicidal policies. And Sheyel had commented on what he perceived as a root cause:

There is, he'd said, *an inverse correlation between the amount of power a person has and the level at which his or her mind functions. A person of ordinary intelligence who acquires power, of whatever kind, tends to develop an exaggerated view of his own capabilities. Sycophants gather. There is little or no criticism of decisions. As his ability to disrupt the lives of others advances, these tendencies become stronger. Eventually you end with Louis the Fourteenth, who thinks he's done a good job for France, although the country he left behind was ruined.*

The front door opened and Sheyel stepped outside. He looked up and waved at the descending cab. She waved back. The taxi eased down onto the pad and he came over to help her out.

"It's good to see you, Kim," he said. "I can't tell you how indebted I am to you."

"I'm glad I've been able to help."

They stood in the bright afternoon sunlight, studying each other. He wore a dark blue loose-fitting shirt with long sleeves, and light gray slacks. She detected a pallor that hadn't been apparent in the virtuals.

The cab lifted off. "What are your plans for the balance of the day?" he asked. "Can I entice you to stay for dinner?"

"That's very kind of you, Sheyel," she said. "I wish I could, but I'm on a tight schedule."

"Pity," he said, making way for her to go inside. Kim couldn't remember the details of the furniture, but the book-lined walls were still there and the glass doors leading out onto the patio. And the framed copy of the Magister Folio, whose principles had formed the basis of the Articles.

"I was reminiscing about the times you had us over," she said.

He seemed puzzled at the remark, and she wondered if he'd forgotten that he used to open his home to his students. "Yes," he said finally. "I don't do that anymore."

"I'm sorry to hear it," she said. "It was a good experience."

"They have rules now that prevent off-campus gatherings." He shrugged it away. "What can I get you to drink?"

She settled for a dark wine and they retreated to his study. "I'm sorry we don't have more answers about Yoshi," she said. "The police say they're looking into it, but as I told you, I'm not confident."

She wasn't certain what he'd mixed for himself. It was lemon colored but it smelled of mint. "I understand, Kim. Did you learn anything about your sister?"

She hesitated, not sure what she'd learned. *Something*, certainly. "No," she said. "Still no trace."

"Are you feeling all right?" he asked. "I read the accounts. You almost lost your life."

"It was a wild ride," she admitted.

He sipped his drink. "We always wondered whether Yoshi had been injured in some way, wandered off, who knew?"

There were two framed pictures of her in the room: one as a child of about four standing outside in the patio, holding Sheyel's hand; and a graduation photo, displaying all her elegance.

"For whatever consolation it may be," Kim said, "it appears she died quickly." The preliminary police report had not yet been officially released, and Kim really didn't know whether Yoshi had suffered. Nevertheless it seemed like the right thing to say.

Sheyel gazed at her through watery eyes. "It's a terrible thing to be cut down so young."

Kim said nothing.

He gazed steadily at her. "I take it you didn't just come to see how I was getting on. What have you to tell me?"

She looked steadily at him. "I have a question first."

He leaned forward.

"When you originally came to me with this, you told me there was something loose in the Severin woods. That if I doubted you I should just go up and spend a few hours in the area."

"Yes. I probably said something like that."

"After dark, I think you said."

"I don't recall the conversation in detail."

"'I've felt it. . . . Go look for yourself. But don't go alone.' That's what you said."

"Okay."

"I've done that, Sheyel."

A chill settled into the room. "And—?"

"You were right. There *is* something there. What do you know about it?"

"Only that the area is oppressive. I saw lights in the woods a couple of times. There was never anything I could lay hands on though." His eyes dropped to the floor. "There were some accounts that that was the real reason people left."

"How could anyone have stayed in the village?" asked Kim. "They were taking down the dam."

"They decided not to repair the dam because people were clearing out. It wasn't the other way around." His eyes were hooded. "There's a lot of history about it. Check any of the sources." He went to his shelves and took down several volumes. He tapped his finger on one with a gray cover and artwork depicting a moonlit phantom. "I especially recommend this: Kathryn Kline's *The Specters of Severin*." The phantom looked nothing at all like the apparition Kim had seen.

He went through the others, commenting in a similar manner, laying them before her. "People tend to get overwrought. But the evidence is striking."

She glanced through them while he refilled their glasses. "I was up there several times. This was *years* after I'd talked with Kane. The dam was long gone and the place was deserted. You've been there, you know what I'm talking about.

"It's disquieting. Maybe because I *knew* it was connected with Yoshi's disappearance. I thought I could feel things moving in the dark. The valley scared me. I don't think I scare easily, but that place did the deed." He seemed to withdraw into himself. "Why don't you tell me what it was *you* saw?"

"Not really anything," she said. "It's just very *quiet* out there. You understand what I mean?"

He nodded. "Have you learned anything about the *Hunter*? *Was* there a contact?"

She showed him the pictures. "I think they encountered another ship, and I think this might be what it looked like."

He leaned forward, opened a cabinet drawer, and took out a viewing lens. He held it over the images. "You *really* think so?" he said. The moroseness which had marked the conversation to this point was swept away by a wave of excitement.

"Yes. I think so. There's no proof. Probably not even strong evidence. But yes, I think it happened."

His eyes widened as he gazed at the mural. "Why," he said, "that's Emily."

The Conciliar Medal of Valor glittered in the midday sun. Tora Kane held out her hand, took it from Kim, and studied it. She read her father's name from the obverse. "Where did you get it?" she asked.

"In the Severin Valley."

Tora's mood visibly darkened. "You can't leave it alone, can you?"

"I thought you'd want to have it."

"That depends."

"On what?"

They were standing on the beach at Wheeling Bay, at the same point where they'd talked before. Kim's hands were pushed into her jacket pockets. The tide was out, and a few gulls patrolled the wet sand. "It depends on what else you have to tell me. When you're done with all this poking around, are you going to be making accusations against my father?"

"Do you think he did anything wrong?"

"Look, Kim—" Her teeth bit down on the name. "Markis wasn't perfect by any means. He had a short temper, and he wasn't very tactful, and sometimes he forgot he had a daughter. But he was essentially a decent man, and I know he wouldn't have been mixed up in anything ugly."

"Did you ever see the inside of the villa?"

"The one in the valley? Sure."

"Were you inside it at any time after the Mount Hope explosion?"

"Yes," she said. "I visited my father from time to time. I lived there while I was growing up. When I came of age, my parents let the marriage lapse. But I went back when I could."

"May I ask when that was?"

"I left the villa in 569. After that I visited occasionally, once or twice a year."

"Did you happen to notice whether there was a mural in the den?"

"In the *den*? No, not that I recall."

"Would you have seen it if there had been?"

"Of course. Listen, what's this about?"

"There's a mural there now."

"So what?"

"The woman in it is my sister."

"Oh." She gazed briefly into the sun. "Well. It's hard for me to see what inference can be drawn from that."

"Dr. Kane, my understanding is that your father sealed off part of the house after the last *Hunter* mission. Did you know anything about that?"

"Part of the house?"

"The den."

"That was his private space. There was nothing unusual about that."

"Did you have access?"

Kim could see her considering her answer. "No," she said at last. "Not in the later years. He kept it locked."

"Did he say why?"

"No. I really didn't concern myself with it. And I don't see what business any of this is of yours anyway."

Kim nodded. "Thank you," she said.

"Now if you don't mind—"

"I'm sorry," said Kim. "Listen, I know you don't approve of me very much."

Tora remained silent.

"For what it's worth, I admire your father."

"Thanks."

"I don't think you need fear for his reputation."

Tora took a deep breath and turned away.

Kim watched her walk. She was reasonably sure she believed what she had just said.

She had an afternoon engagement next day at the Mariners' Club, which had nothing whatever to do with boating, but was rather a group of older citizens. The name referred to the members' view of themselves as persons who had sailed through life, and who had now arrived at safe harbor, and who planned on enjoying the time they had left.

The club seal, displayed on a banner, depicted an anchor and five stars, one for each of the club's guiding principles, and its motto *Keep the Wind at Your Back*. Kim had taken time to read the guiding principles and she wove them into her remarks. They were mundane feel-good truisms, like *Always walk in the surf*, and *The only real failure is failing to try*.

The Institute is a lot like the Mariners, she told them. "It's about stretching horizons and splashing around in the cosmos. And we don't always succeed on the first try. Life is like that. Science is like that. Like the Mariners, we're not afraid to fail, and in fact that's the way we learn."

As usual, she played her audience well and when she was finished she got an enthusiastic ovation. The emcee thanked her heartily for coming, a number of individuals lingered to ask questions or deliver compliments, one tried to ask her out, and the organization's president took her aside: 50 percent of the proceeds from the Mariners' spring fund drive, he explained, were customarily donated to a worthy organization, usually an educational institution. He wanted her to know that he had been impressed by her presentation, that the other board members shared his feeling, and that the Institute could expect to be the recipient of this year's gift.

It would be no small amount, she knew, and she was delighted to carry this piece of good news back to the Institute.

■   ■   ■

Matt was waiting. Kim knew it wasn't good news by the general mood in the office. Something had happened. She suspected her coworkers didn't know the details, but they felt the boss's tension.

"You wanted to see me?" she asked, standing in his doorway.

He'd been talking to the AI, something about anticipated cost-benefits, and they continued the conversation while he waved her in. He managed not to look at her while doing so, but his voice took on a cooler note. When he'd finished he turned, shook his head in a gesture that suggested he lived in a universe that was out to get him, signaled for her to close the door, and without a word started the VR.

Kim sat down as an image of Ben Tripley took shape.

"This was received about an hour ago," Matt said.

Tripley was seated on the edge of his desk. He looked unhappy. "Phil," he said, apparently speaking to Philip Agostino, the director, "I asked you to request Dr. Brandywine to stop involving herself in my affairs. She has now caused a police interrogation, and has unfairly called the character of my father into question." Over Tripley's shoulder, Kim could see the forward section of the *Valiant*. "I have to inform you that I am reevaluating my support for the Institute, as your organization seems to have too much free time on its hands, and a propensity for chasing down discredited rumors. Be advised that if any damage comes to either my property or my reputation as a result of this incident, I will regrettably have no choice but to seek legal redress."

It blinked off.

"Want to see it again?" Matt asked.

"Yes," she said. "But kill the sound."

He stared at her, taken off guard, waiting for her to cancel the request. When she didn't he reran it. She went over to the desk where she could stop it at the point she wanted.

"The director has instructed me," Matt said angrily, "to ask for your resignation."

"Tripley's a crank," she said.

"He's an important crank, Kim."

She froze the image, Tripley leaning forward, mouth open, index finger jabbed in their general direction. "Matt," she said, "look at this." She tried to adjust the image so they'd get more of the *Valiant*, but it was already full frame.

"Yeah. Looks like a bookend. So what?"

"It's a model starship."

He shrugged. "And—?"

"Matt, I'm pretty sure the *Hunter did* have an encounter with a celestial."

"Kim—"

"I can't prove it, but I'd bet on it." She pointed at the *Valiant*. "And *this* is what it looked like."

"The model."

"Yes. Look, I know it sounds goofy but I'm almost positive it's so."

"If it's so, why is Tripley keeping it quiet?"

"I don't think he knows anything about it. Not about the mission. Not about the model. I think his father had it made in one of the local tech shops immediately after he got back. After the explosion, Ben's grandmother found it at the villa, thought it was only a toy and gave it to him."

Matt looked as if his shoes were too tight. "What evidence do you have?"

She told him about the fraudulent log and showed him the pictures of Kane's submerged wall. She said nothing about the vision in the passageway.

"How do you know the log is fraudulent?"

"We had it analyzed."

"By whom?"

"By experts."

"You don't want to tell me."

"Not really."

He stopped to catch his breath. "Kim, I'm sorry. You're a valuable member of the organization and I'd have preferred not to lose you, but you don't really give me any choice. I want you to go back to your office and write out your resignation. Make it effective thirty days from now. That way I can give you a month's pay. But don't come back." He stared at her across the top of his desk. "You know I'd change this if I could, but I warned you, damn it. I *did* warn you this was going to happen."

He scowled and waved her out of the room. But when she started for the door he stopped her. "Kim," he said, "if you need a reference, make sure it's addressed to me personally and not to the organization."

The words didn't register. "Matt, this isn't fair. I haven't done anything wrong. I've violated no procedure—"

"You disobeyed a directive. I told you to stay away from this—" He stuttered a couple of times and waved one hand in a frustrated circle.

She glared at him. "Don't you *care* what the truth is?"

"Okay, what *is* the truth? We've got one woman dead and one missing. If Kile Tripley did it, it doesn't much matter because he's also gone to a better world. So it's not as if we're looking for justice.

"You find a bookshelf model and a sketch on a wall and on the basis of that you think somebody met a celestial. If they did, why the goddamn hell didn't they tell somebody? *Anybody?*"

"I don't know, Matt. But if there's nothing to the story, why'd they gundeck the logs?"

"I don't know that they did."

"You can check them if you want. When you do, and when you find out that what I've told you is true, I'd like very much to borrow the *McCollum.*"

His eyes widened. "You're a remarkable woman, Kim, I'll say that for you. But maybe you didn't hear me earlier: You're not working for us anymore."

"How'd it go?" asked Solly.

"They fired me." She had a blowup of Tripley's *Valiant* taped to her wall.

"Goddammit, Kim, I told you that would happen."

She was trembling, with anger, frustration, with a sense of the sheer injustice of it all.

"Maybe it'll blow over," he said. "Just sit tight for a bit. Give them a chance to calm down until they discover they need you."

"No," she said. "I don't think that's going to happen."

They embraced and neither spoke. "Look," he said at last, "I have some friends at Albestaadt." Albestaadt was a major research facility on Pacifica. "I can't promise anything, but I could put in a word. I think there'd be a decent chance. And you could go back to being a researcher."

"Thanks, Solly. Maybe later. I've got a point to make first."

"You're going to continue to push this thing?"

"Might as well. I've nothing to lose now."

"You could get sued. Anyhow, what more can you do? Where can you go from here?"

"I'm going to prove the encounter happened."

"How will you do that?"

"The *Hunter*'s radio, Solly. It was omnidirectional, remember? With a booster."

She saw his features brighten. "You really think it would work?"

"Why not? All we need is the right equipment."

Solly's eyes met hers. "You'll need a starship. I don't guess Matt agreed to let you have the *Mac*?"

"No. Not exactly."

"So— How do you plan to manage it?"

"I was thinking about *stealing* it."

"Kim—"

"I mean it, Solly. I'll do what I have to."

"I believe you would."

"Solly, I can't just walk away from this. If we're right, it'll be the prime scientific discovery of all time. We'll be famous, immortal, whatever you like."

"Rich?" said Solly.

"I'd guess rich beyond imagination."

"Yeah. Well, rich is good. But the risk is a little high. You're going to have to count me out, Kim. I'm sorry, but I draw the line at grand theft. Which is what this would be." His features were flushed, his lips pressed tight together, his eyes hard. "I'm sorry. But this is way out of line."

Yeah. How could she have expected anything else? "I understand, Solly."

"How about chartering a ship? Better yet, rent one. I'll pilot."

She'd considered it. But she needed the specialized communication equipment of the Institute vessels.

"I'll help you pay for it," he said.

"Won't work. We need FAULS." That was the Flexible Array, Unified Long-range Sensing System. If somebody did a radio broadcast a hundred light-years out, FAULS would pick it up.

"Kim," he said. "Let it go."

Hyperyacht, Inc., had an assortment of interstellars ranging from sleek executive models to economy-class buses. But the cheapest were not licensed for voyages outside the Nine World bubble, and the better ones were impossibly expensive. Worse, even if she could somehow meet the cost and persuade the Institute to let her have the communication gear, it couldn't be installed.

She put it aside and went home to stare at the ocean.

And to send out résumés. They went to a dozen research institutions around the globe, but she had little hope any would respond favorably. There wasn't much to put in the *Current Projects* and *Recent Accomplishments* blocks.

I am on the verge of making contact with an intelligent species.

Sure I am.

She could have undoubtedly gotten a job somewhere as a fundraiser, but she didn't want to spend the rest of her life pleading for money. Might as well simply retire to a leisurely existence like the majority of the population. Accept her monthly government allotment and sit on the porch.

She took to haunting the shoreline. The beach was especially appealing in winter, and its bleakness fit her mood. There was rarely anyone else out. Dressed in an insulated suit, she circled the island every day, moving at a rapid clip, stopping occasionally to look at the shells.

A seacoast is a special kind of place, she thought. It's like the edge of a forest, or the foothills of a mountain range, where we stand at the rim of our daily existence, looking out at something quite different. Occasionally Kim would stay out past twilight, watching the tide run, letting the night roll into her soul. The beach was a sacred place to her, one of those areas where the infinite touches down.

She was in the presence of *two* oceans, one of water and one of spacetime, and they somehow tended, after dark, to get mixed together. Pick the right spot, where the only real sound is the murmur of the surf, and it was possible to stroll along the damp sand and feel her blood run in sync with the tides.

An ocean's edge is by definition a meeting place between the magnificent and the mundane. We listen to seashells and hear our own heartbeat.

When she got home each day, there was a message waiting from Solly: *You okay? How's everything going? I've talked to the people at Albestaadt. They've got a position for you if you want it. You'll have to interview for it, of course, but the fix is in. I've told them about you and they're excited at the prospect.*

She responded by thanking him politely: *Thanks for your efforts but I don't think so.*

The Moritami Orbital Research Center surprised her by inviting her in to interview for an entry-level researcher's position. It was conducted at their administrative offices in Marathon and she did well. Interviews were one of her specialties. When they informed her she'd have to live off-world, she knew she had the job. They told her they'd call her and she came back out into the hard sunlight with mixed feelings. But the bright side was she'd be doing astrophysics again.

Again.

Truth was, she'd never really functioned within her specialty.

When she got home, Solly was waiting.

"How'd it go?" he asked.

She wasn't surprised that he knew. The world community of physicists and astronomers was tight-knit. Information usually got around pretty quickly. "Okay," she said. "I think they're going to take me on."

He was dressed in seagoing casuals, and wore his captain's cap with its anchor emblem. The cap was pushed over to one side, an affectation he indulged only in her presence because he knew it made him look ridiculous and inevitably cheered her. "So you finally got what you want."

"Yes."

"No more fund-raising."

"Nope."

"Maybe this thing'll turn out to be a blessing."

There was something about the phrase, or maybe his tone, or maybe simply his presence. Because suddenly she was angry and her eyes were damp. She wanted so desperately to follow the track of the *Hunter*. To find out what was out there. To find out what had happened to Emily.

"It's okay, babe," he said. He pulled her close and stroked her hair.

"You're getting your cheek wet," she said.

He held onto her until she calmed down. Then he stepped back and his blue eyes grew intense. "Listen." He took off his cap, ran his fingers through his hair, and put it back on. Straight, this time. "If you're still up to it, we can take the *Hammersmith*."

She looked at him, not sure she'd heard correctly. "You talked them into letting us use one of the ships?"

"Not exactly," he said. "But I guess maybe we could *take* it."

Twenty minutes later, she called Moritami. "Thanks for considering me," she told them. "But I'm going to be unavailable for awhile."

16

So grab up your pack and come on with me
And we'll hop a fast freight to the stars. . . .

—BUD WEBSTER,
"The Ballad of Kansas McGriff," 1998 C.E.

"**D**o you know," asked Solly, "how long it would take to get out into the area where the *Hunter* was?"

"It's forty days, seventeen hours, and twenty-six minutes to the target site."

"I'm impressed. You've done your homework."

"Thank you."

"Now all you need is a means of transportation." His gaze turned inward. "If we do this, we're putting everything on the line. Career, freedom, reputation, you name it. So my question to you is, are you sure?"

"Solly," she said. "It'll work. I *know* it'll work."

"That wasn't the question."

"Am I sure I want to do whatever's necessary to get at the truth? Yes. Absolutely. Am I sure we're on the right track?" She had to think about that one. But the cold mad gaze of the thing in the water had imprinted itself in her soul, where it exercised a dual effect: something *had* happened out there, and part of it has infected the Severin Valley; but she wasn't sure she wanted to get any closer to it. This was a truth that she'd just as soon avoid.

And yet.

"Yes," she said.

"Okay then. We'll do it. Fortunately the *Hammersmith* is prepped, groceries on board, water tanks full, and ready to leave for Taratuba."

She watched him breathe. "Solly," she said, "it'll be okay. We do this, they'll get upset for a while. But we'll bring back evidence of a *contact*. They'll meet us with a brass band."

Taking the *Hammersmith* should have been childishly easy. The Institute was meticulous about having its maintenance routines performed early. Solly, who'd been assisting with logistics for the mission, had already seen to stocking the vessel, so it should just have been a matter of walking on board, powering up, passing a satisfactory story to operations, and launching. But Worldwide Interiors had offered to redesign the living and working quarters on the *Hammersmith*, gratis, and several of their people were still on the ship when Kim and Solly arrived, twenty-two hours prior to scheduled departure for Taratuba.

Kim had never before been on the *Hammersmith*. After a quick inspection, Solly admitted that Worldwide had indeed improved the interior. "Although there was plenty of room for improvement," he added.

Four workers were laying carpet, installing furniture, and redesigning cosmetics throughout the ship. Even the cargo hold had acquired a fresh coat of mahogany paint.

The Institute's fleet, which consisted of five vessels, was maintained at the Marlin Orbital Dock. They'd ridden over from Sky Harbor in a shuttle, picked up their bags at the service desk, and walked them on board, past the Marlin crew chief and a couple of operations people. As Solly had assured her would happen, no one asked any questions.

She'd gotten a look at the *Hammersmith* from the approach shuttle. It was a reconverted yacht, a boxy vehicle with three levels. Living quarters, including the pilot's room, were located on the top floor; labs, more living quarters and recreational areas were in the middle section; the utility deck, housing cargo, life support, and storage were below. Engineering occupied the lower two levels at the rear of the craft.

Whatever ambiance might have existed in its luxury days had later been sacrificed to the gods of utility. Despite the new paint and the new carpets, *Hammersmith* felt like a small hotel that had been let go and was now being refurbished for a new buyer. There was something essentially *threadbare* about it that no amount of restoration could hide.

The hull was crowded with antennas, sensor dishes, and a host of other devices of whose use Kim had no idea. Its name and designator were imprinted forward, and SEABRIGHT INSTITUTE, in large black letters, ran the length of the ship.

Solly told her to choose any compartment she liked. There were eight dedicated to passengers, each designed for two people. The middle units on either side of the hall comprised the pilot's room and a mission control center. A conference room occupied the rear of the top floor.

She said hello to a man installing stained panels, and saw several others working in the rec room. She picked her quarters, just aft of the pilot's room, and stowed her gear.

Solly was in the hallway, munching toast. "How are we doing?" she asked.

He held out his hands in a helpless gesture. "Ready to go, as soon as Worldwide gets off."

"When's that going to happen?"

"Hard to tell. They don't seem to be sure themselves."

"Can't we ask them to leave?"

"Not without raising some eyebrows."

She punched in a request for cheese and coffee. "How many are there, Solly? Workers?"

"Four Worldwide people, plus one technician from Marlin." He looked at the time. "They'll probably all shut down in a little while for lunch. If they do that, we'll clear out."

She looked doubtfully at the food dispenser. "What happens if this thing breaks down?"

Solly went into mission control and opened a panel in the back wall, exposing the automated kitchen. "We can do it manually if we have to." He smiled at her. "How about some toast to go with your cheese?"

"No, thanks," she said.

"We can make twenty pieces at a time," he observed.

"We have enough food for four months or so?"

"Have no fear. We'll eat well. *Ham* is stocked for seventeen people for a half-year." His expression turned serious. "But there *is* something we should talk about."

"Yes?"

"I know we're assuming your idea's going to work, and that coming back here with big news is going to get us off the hook for stealing this little buggy."

"It'll happen, Solly." She picked up her coffee and cheese.

"Maybe. But my experience is that nothing ever goes according to plan. Especially something like this." They crossed the corridor and looked into the pilot's room. Three chairs, some consoles, an overhead screen, two auxiliaries each left and right. Two big screens which would act as windows in the left-hand wall. "To be honest, I'm not optimistic. I suspect we're not seeing something clearly, and I just can't believe we're going to go out there and accomplish what you think we will."

"Okay." Kim would have liked to have his confidence, but she'd known all along that he was skeptical. No surprise there. Still, hearing it like this: Had he come simply because she needed him? "It'll be there," she insisted.

"Okay. Maybe it will. I hope so. But in the meantime we'd be smart to develop an alternative plan."

"For what happens if we come back with nothing?"

"For what happens if we discover it would be a good idea not to come back." He took a deep breath. "Look, Kim, neither of us is going to want to face a court."

"Solly," she said, "you can still back out if you want."

"If I did, what would you do?"

She stared silently at her coffee cup.

"Right," he said. "So I'll do it—"

"Thanks."

"No. Not for you. I'm not that crazy. But there's enough of a chance that you're right to make it worthwhile. I wouldn't want to spend the rest of my life wondering. So I'm willing to gamble. But if it doesn't work, Kim, I have friends on Tigris."

"Okay."

"I've made arrangements with them. Just in case."

She nodded.

"If things don't go the way we want, we'll retire to a mountaintop on Tigris. They have an extradition treaty with Greenway but it only covers capital crimes. So we'd be safe."

The Marlin technician went to lunch, but the Worldwide people broke into shifts and the noon hour came and went with no opportunity to leave.

In midafternoon a young beefy man showed up with his luggage. "Uh-oh," Solly said.

"Who is it?" asked Kim.

"Webley. He's a cosmologist assigned to the Taratuba team." They heard him talking in the passageway and Solly went out to greet him. Kim followed.

One of the technicians was pointing Webley in the direction of the living quarters. He wore a self-important smile and when he saw Kim his gaze swept past her as if she were of no consequence. "Solly," he said, "good to see you. Are the others here yet?"

Solly did the introductions first, and then informed Webley that no one else had yet arrived.

Webley wore a jacket of the type favored in the Kalipik Islands, white shirt with fluffy collar, dark slacks, and a red neckerchief. His voice seemed set quite low so that one had to strain to hear him, but his manner implied it was well worth the effort. He had an unkempt red beard, of a slightly different shade from the neckerchief. "Is everything on schedule?" he asked.

"Yes," Solly said briskly. "To the minute."

"Good." He adjusted his sleeves and checked the time. "May I ask which room is mine?"

"Unit eight," said Kim. End of the passageway.

When he was gone, Solly turned a worried gaze on her. "This isn't going so well," he said. "We may have to cancel."

Kim shook her head. "Let's not give up too easily." She walked down the corridor and passed Webley's door. Music had begun to play within. Heavy classical stuff. Vorwerk, probably. Or Benado.

She needed to get rid of the workmen first.

The Worldwide crew were still mounting trim, touching up window frames, hanging curtains in the conference room, bolting down a table in the rec area, and installing cabinets on the bottom level. The one who seemed to be in charge was an older man, a candidate for membership with the Mariners.

"How we doing?" she asked casually.

"We're getting there. We're a man short on this job," he said, wiping his sleeve against his mouth. He looked overheated. "Happens every time. They let something go to the last minute and then somebody decides to take time off."

"Why'd they wait until the last minute?" asked Kim.

He made a face. "Uh, well, you know, these things happen." His eyes never met hers and she understood he was lying. The truth, she guessed, was that no money was passing hands. This was a tax write-off job, not high on Worldwide's priority list.

"Will you be finished by five?" she asked.

"Hard to say." His expression took her into his confidence. "If we don't make it, it's overtime, you know?"

Across the room, the Marlin technician closed a panel and began gathering his gear together.

"Done?" she asked.

"That's it." He asked her to initial his work order. He'd updated the VR equipment. She signed; he thanked her and left.

She turned back to the Mariner and asked what his name was.

"Leo Eastley," he said.

She put on her best executive demeanor. "Leo, you and your crew have done a good job, but we're going to have to proceed as is. Leave things where they are. We'll finish up."

He looked at her. His silver hair was hanging in his eyes.

"No time left," she explained.

"Why's that?" he asked. "I thought we had all day. We're not finished."

"We have to run some tests."

"Go ahead. We won't get in the way."

"No, you don't understand. These are precision mass-acceleration tests. The presence of extra people will skew the results."

"You're sure?"

"Yeah. Sorry, but we don't have any choice."

"We won't be coming back. Job's supposed to be finished today."

"It's okay."

He produced a notepad. "You'll have to sign that everything's done and you're satisfied. "

"Sure. I can do that."

"I'll make a notation here about what happened. Warranties may be affected."

She smiled at him. "It's okay. We can live with it."

She signed and initialed the notation. Leo rounded up his crew, and Kim watched them exit through the air lock and start up the tunnel. As the last of them vanished, a luggage cart approached. *"This the* Hammersmith?" it asked.

"It is," said Kim.

The cart scanned the bags. *"Where would you like me to put them?"*

"Where are the owners?"

"My last information is, they were headed for Happy Harry's."

"Happy Harry's?"

"A cocktail lounge."

"On Sky Harbor?"

"Yes."

"Thanks," she said. "You can leave it right here."

"In the tunnel?"

"Yes. It's okay. I'll take care of it." When she was alone she called Solly. "More coming," she said, looking at the name tags. "Wentworth, Little Deer, Moritami, Henderson. They stopped at a bar."

"They could be here any time," Solly said. "We have to get rolling, or forget it."

"Webley's still back there. You want to take him along?"

"Do you think he'd want to come?"

"Not likely."

"Then do something."

"I was about to." Webley was a familiar type. He belonged to the relatively small subgroup of researchers who believed with all their hearts that no one had ever seen more clearly into the interior of the atom, or whatever, than they had. That nothing in life was of more importance than their corner of scientific knowledge and the recognition by others of their place in it. Like children, they believed that they were the center of the cosmos. That fact outweighed everything else, and also constituted their prime weakness.

He opened to her knock and gazed at her as if trying to remember who she was and what she was doing in his doorway.

"Professor Webley," she said. "We're scheduled to run some engineering tests during the next hour or so. It's going to get loud, and there'll be a fair amount of vibration."

"Oh? They never had to do that before."

"You probably never arrived this early before."

"Oh yes, madame, as a matter of fact, I have."

"Whatever. We're going to have to go through the basic engine shakedown, and it makes a terrible racket. I was going to head up to the Domino to get away from it." She inhaled slightly, tilted her head, and summoned the most captivating smile she could manage. "I'd enjoy your company if you'd care to come."

"Really, Dr. Brandywine, I don't think—"

"I'd like very much to hear what you're currently working on."

Webley's brow creased. "I thank you for your interest, but I really am a bit pressed just now." He gazed at her as if she were a recalcitrant child, and then he wished her good day and closed the door.

She bowed slightly, turned, and left. "So much for my charm," she told Solly a minute later.

He grinned. "The temptress strikes out, huh?"

"I guess so. He looked annoyed."

"Ham," he told the AI, "start the mains. Prepare for departure."

"Confirm," said Ham, in a female voice.

Kim frowned. They did *not* want to kidnap this guy.

"The six o'clock shuttle is in," Solly said, responding to her unasked question. "If Moritami and the others are on it, they'll be here any—" He stopped and pointed at one of the displays. Three men and a woman had appeared at the far end of the approach tunnel. "Speak of the devil—"

"Solly, what do we do?"

"We need something that'll burn," he said.

"Burn? Why?"

"Ask questions later. What have we got that's flammable?"

Starships weren't good places to look for combustibles. Clothes, panels, furniture. Everything was fireproof.

"Hold on a second," he said. He got up and went into the mission control center. She heard him open the panel to the kitchen. Two minutes later she smelled smoke.

"Toast," he grinned. "Twenty pieces. Now, go down and stand outside Webley's room. When things start to happen, help him leave."

God, this was going to be one of Solly's finest moments. She started back down the passageway as a Klaxon began to sound. The intercom switched on. "This is the captain. There's no reason to panic, but we have a fire in the forward compartments. All passengers please leave the ship immediately. This is the captain. I say again, we are not in immediate danger. Do not panic—"

Webley's door opened and he put his head into the corridor, looked both ways, saw Kim and scowled. He was about to say something when he spotted wisps of smoke leaking into the passageway behind her. The smell of burnt toast had become pretty strong.

"We're on fire," Kim said.

"For God's sake, young woman," he complained, "how could *that* happen?"

"Let's talk about it later, Professor. This way out." But he turned back into the room, threw open a suitcase and started scooping his clothes into it.

"You haven't time for that," Kim said, letting her voice rise. And then, inspired: "This whole place could blow at any time."

That was enough for Webley. He threw the lid down, hefted the bag under one arm, grabbed some clothes, and banged out of the room. "Incompetent," he snarled. "Everywhere I go, people are so goddamn incompetent!"

"This way, sir." Kim pointed him to the boarding tunnel. He disappeared into it.

Outside, an alarm had begun to sound.

"All clear," she told Solly.

"Good. Close the hatch."

"How?"

"Let it go. I'll do it from here. Come on up and strap in. We'll be leaving in a minute."

"But Webley hasn't had a chance to get clear."

"Is he in the tunnel?"

"Yes."

"He'll be fine. The tunnel seals automatically when we button up. Don't worry about it."

Moments later she slipped into the pilot's room and sat down beside Solly. "It strikes me," she said, "that when this is over, I'm going to owe apologies to a lot of people."

"Including me," he said.

Kim got up again and looked at the seat. "See." She pointed. "You *can* see an imprint."

"Control," Solly told the mike, "This is *Hammersmith.* We have an emergency departure. Request instructions, please."

"*Hammersmith,* Control. State the nature of your emergency. We just got a report of a fire."

"Negative that, Control. The report resulted from a communication problem at this end."

"What is your emergency?"

Kim reclaimed her seat and the harness came down around her shoulders.

"Taratuba's false vacuum has gone premature."

Kim looked at him, surprised, and mouthed *What?*

"Wait one, *Hammersmith.*"

"Solly," she said, "do they even know what Taratuba is?"

"I doubt it. It's better that way. Fewer questions."

She scanned the bank of screens, which provided a 360-degree view. They were free of encumbrance save for a forward utility line. All Solly had to do was make the disconnect up front and there was nothing to stop their leaving. "Why don't we just go?" she asked.

"We could hit something," he said. "And anyway somebody would immediately call the Patrol. Moreover, if we somehow escaped being jailed for theft, it would guarantee my loss of license."

"*Hammersmith*, Control. Departure is authorized. Data is being fed now."

Solly acknowledged, watched his array of lamps flicker with the download, and then spoke to the ship's AI. "Ham, disconnect mooring and let's go."

"*Complying*," said the ship.

" '*Let's go'?* That's all there is to it? '*Let's go'?*"

The ship began to back away from the Marlin facility.

"I guess I've just revealed a trade secret, Kim. And when we get where we're going, I'll tell it 'okay.'"

"Seriously—?"

"Seriously, human pilots are only on board to deal with problems. Emergencies. And probably to soothe the concerns of passengers, who've never been happy with the idea of purely-automated vehicles."

"Taxis are pure automation," she said. "Nobody minds those."

"You know how to fly the damned thing yourself if you have to."

They were easing away from the orbiter, lining up with their marker stars. "*Acceleration will commence in one minute*," said the AI.

"*Hammersmith*, Control." It was a new voice, deeper, with authority.

"Go ahead, Control."

"This is the supervisor. You are directed to return to the dock."

"Solly." Kim pointed at one of the displays, on which a long ominous greyhound of a ship was moving in close.

"I see it."

"They know."

"Sure they know. Our passenger has been talking to them." He opened the mike: "Control, we are unable to comply."

"Solly—"

"Ham," he said, "proceed with programmed acceleration."

"*Proceeding*."

Kim felt a gentle push into her seat as the ship swung around to its heading and began to move forward.

"We'll be okay, Kim," he said.

The push became more pronounced and the station slid off the screens.

Another new voice, female, irritated: "*Hammersmith*, this is Orbital Patrol. You are directed to return to port immediately."

"Hang on," said Solly. Acceleration was increasing.

"We better make our jump, right?"

"The jump engines feed off the mains. We need to build more reaction before they'll kick in."

"How much? How long are we talking?"

"About twenty-five minutes."

"*Twenty-five minutes?*" That was ridiculous. "Damn Worldwide and its paneling. Solly, we don't *have* twenty-five minutes."

"*Hammersmith*, return to the station or we will take appropriate action."

"Do they have any way of actually stopping us?"

"Short of blowing us up?"

"Yes. Of course."

"Only a Tursi field."

"The damper."

"Right. It would shut down our mains. But it's a bluff."

"How do you know?"

"Rev up an engine and then turn it off, just like that, you risk an explosion. Damn near a fifty-fifty chance. They won't use it without getting permission first from the Institute. And that'll take time. Anyway Agostino would never agree to it. He doesn't want to lose a ship."

The comm system was crowded with incoming voices: the Patrol warning them again to stand down; the supervisor at Marlin insisting they return; and, oddly, Webley, demanding what in God's name did they think they were doing?

"Just relax," Solly said, "and enjoy the ride. In the meantime, it wouldn't be a bad idea to tell me precisely where we're going."

"Zeta Orionus. Alnitak. Or rather, I want you to pick a spot twenty-seven and a fraction light-years from Alnitak." She dug in her pockets and pulled out a data disk. "Here," she said. "Put us anywhere on the bubble."

"Alnitak," he said. The easternmost star in the belt of Orion. "Why? A guess? Or do you know something you haven't told me?"

"You remember asking if I knew how long the trip would take?"

"Sure. You gave me a fairly specific answer."

"Forty days, seventeen hours, twenty-six minutes. It's the total elapsed return-trip time on the *Hunter* logs."

"The *bogus* ones?"

"Yes. But I couldn't imagine any reason why they'd change the elapsed time from the originals. The time frame, if it's correct, gives us Alnitak. And there's something else." She showed him a blowup of Kane's mural. "See this?" She pointed at the Horsehead.

"Yep."

"It's visible from Alnitak."

The Patrol moved into a parallel course on their starboard side, at a distance of only a few hundred meters.

Solly shut down the comm system and the voices died. "Makes me nervous," he said.

"You think that's a good idea, right now?"

"Depends on whether you want to listen to the threats."

He set the timer to count down to jump status. Kim stared at it, willing the numbers to hurry along.

They were still several minutes out when the AI announced an incoming transmission from a new source. From one of the satellites. *"From the Institute."*

"It'll be Agostino," said Kim.

"You want to talk to him?"

"No," she said. "We'll talk when we come back. When we have something to negotiate with."

The patrol vessel was still there when power began to flow to the jump engines, and Solly took them out of their range.

17

It is difficult to know at what moment love begins; it is less difficult to know that it has begun.
                    —HENRY W. LONGFELLOW, *Kavanaugh*, XXI 1849 C.E.

Solly's analysts thought the *Hunter* logs were accurate to the point where the vessel experienced engine trouble. Allow approximately a day or so for Kane's repair work, and that puts Tripley and his party at Alnitak roughly February 17 or 18. Those estimates also fit with the timing of the return to Greenway. "If all that's correct," said Kim, "then getting proof should be easy."

It was now January 28 in Seabright. Assuming February 17 as the base date for the event, for the contact between the *Hunter* and the celestials, and assuming further that radio transmissions would certainly have been involved, she had calculated precisely where the radio waves would be at this moment, and had derived an intercept course for the *Hammersmith*. All very simple.

"There's really only one feasible scenario," she told Solly. "They ran into another ship out there. That means there would have been at least an *attempt* at radio communication."

"You're hanging an awful lot on the fact that the turtle-shell showed up in the mural. There could be other explanations. They might have found a ground-based civilization. Maybe preindustrial, no lights, no radio, nada. Just torches and the local equivalent of horses. In that case—"

"It couldn't have happened that way," she said. They were seated in the mission control center, chairs angled toward each other, drinking coffee.

"Why?"

"Alnitak's too young, for one thing. It's not ten million years old yet. So no local life. And it puts out too much UV. Millions of times what Helios does."

"Oh."

"Right. It would fry everything in sight. Anybody they ran into out there would have had to be star-travelers."

A survey ship had looked at Alnitak two centuries before. As planetary systems went, it didn't have much: one world, a captured gas giant far out in the boondocks.

"It's been a long time for a radio transmission," Solly said. "You get a lot of spread over three decades. FAULS is a good system, but it might not be good enough to pick up a signal that weak. Or to sort it out from the general babble."

But Kim had spent time with the specs for the flexible array. "If it's there," she said, "we'll find it."

They spent the first day housekeeping, arranging their quarters, exploring the ship. Solly was already familiar with it, of course, but he enjoyed showing it off to Kim. She wondered whether her initial failure to be impressed with the vehicle might have insulted him. But it *did* remind her of the Institute's Special Quarters, where non-VIP visitors were housed.

They wandered from floor to floor, and he demonstrated the features of the recreational facilities and the VR section. They inspected the two sets of engines, the mains, which propelled the *Hammersmith* through realspace, and the Transdimensional Interface, the jump engines. The TDI was small enough to hold in her hands.

Kim was pleasantly surprised to discover that the transition into hyper had come with no side effects.

She'd never experienced transdimensional flight as an adult. She was aware, as she hadn't been as a child, that some people got ill during the jump; that others experienced changes in perspective, that walls seemed less solid, that the grip of artificial gravity lessened or tightened, that people claimed to become aware of the thoughts of those around them. There were accounts of unearthly dreams and severe bouts of depression and of sheer exhilaration. Solly told her there was some truth to it. All interstellars, he said, carried a generous supply of antidepressants and sedatives. He had seen people stricken with severe headaches, stomach cramps, toothaches, all deriving from no discernible physical cause. "But it's never been more than an irritant," he said. "Like seasickness.

"Some of the effects, though," he added, "can be eerie. Dreams can be extraordinarily vivid. And I've seen other odd stuff. I remember a woman who thought she'd regressed to her childhood, and a man who claimed to have seen through to the end of his days. Alternate personalities show up sometimes. One elderly passenger swore she'd become possessed. Another insisted he'd been followed on board by a werewolf."

"A werewolf?"

Solly's blue gaze locked on her. "You haven't been seeing anything out of the ordinary, have you?"

"I'm fine, thanks." She was quietly proud of herself.

"Tell me about Alnitak."

Kim pushed back in her chair. "It's a class O. Pretty hot, about thirty-five thousand times as bright as Helios."

"Wear your sunglasses."

"I'd say. It has two companion stars, both a long way out, but close enough to ensure that planets will probably never form. Or if they do, that they'll be unstable."

"But you said there *is* a planet."

"*Captured,*" she reminded him.

"*Alnitak.*" He tasted the word.

"From the Arabic for 'girdle.'"

They took over the briefing room for their first onboard dinner and put out a few candles. The windows, had they been *real* windows, could have revealed nothing other than the glow of the ship's running lights, had Solly chosen to put them on. Instead he programmed a view of the Milky Way as it would have appeared to an approaching intergalactic vehicle.

The meal itself was quiet. Solly usually carried more than his share of the conversation, but he had little to say that evening. The candles and the wine and the galactic disk provided an exquisite atmosphere. The food was good. Yet Kim felt the weight of her decision, and worried that she might be wrong, that she might have overlooked something, that she might have destroyed Solly's career. And her own. They were probably swearing out warrants at this moment. "I wish," she said, "that I could come up with any kind of explanation why they would have kept it quiet. I mean, contact would be the story of the age."

"Don't know," said Solly.

She looked up from a piece of corn. "We've more or less assumed that everybody feels the same way about celestials that we do. That everybody wants to find them if they're out there. Except maybe Canon Woodbridge and probably the Council. But there might be a lot of people who'd prefer the status quo. Who'd just as soon we *not* discover that we have company."

Solly's face was framed by the candles. "I'm one of them," he said.

"You're kidding."

"I never kid. Look, Kim, life is pretty good right now. We have everything we could possibly want. Security. Prosperity. You want a career, it's there. You prefer lying around the beach for a lifetime, you can do that. What can celestials give us that we don't already have? Except things to worry about?"

"It might be a way to find out who we are."

"That's a cliché. I know who I am. And I don't really need philosophy from some *thing* that may in fact look on me as a potential pork chop. There's a real downside with this, especially considering your experience in the Severin. And I'm sorry, but I can't see much *up*side. For you and me, maybe, if this pays off. But I think the human race, in the long run, would not benefit."

She pushed back from her food and stared at him. "Considering how you feel, I can't understand why you came."

"Kim, if they're out there, then it's just a matter of time before we meet them. I don't like it, and I'd stop it if I could. But it has the feel of inevitability about it. If it happens, it'll be a big moment. I'd just as soon be there. And we're probably better off if we know it's coming."

"Hunter instinct," said Kim.

"How do you mean?"

"Hide in the bushes. Kill or be killed. Are those the kind of conditions you really think would exist between interstellar civilizations?"

"Probably not. What I said was, it *could* happen. And since things are pretty good right now, I can't see why we'd want to change anything. Why take chances? Leave well enough alone."

"Solly, why do you think we went to Mars?"

He dipped a roll into his soup, bit off a piece, and chewed it thoughtfully. "We went to Mars," he said, "because we recognized that exploitation of the solar system would have long-term economic benefits."

"You really think that was the motivation? Long-term economic benefits?"

"It's what the history books say."

"The history books say Columbus headed out because he wanted to establish trade routes to India."

"Last I heard, that was the explanation."

"It was a *cover* story, Solly. It was intended to help Isabella make the right decision. To hock her jewels, have an argument ready for her councilors, and at the same time to follow the call of her DNA."

"The call of her DNA?" He looked amused. "You always did have a talent for poetry, Kim."

She waited patiently while he finished his wine.

"So," he asked at last, patting his lips with his napkin, "what was the call of her DNA?"

"It wasn't trade routes," said Kim.

"So what was it?"

"Outward bound," she said. "Exploration. To set foot, either in person or by proxy, in places that have never been seen before."

"I hear what you're saying," said Solly. "But we've done that. We've set foot in a lot of places over the last few centuries. What's that have to do with celestials?"

"We've accepted the notion we're alone."

"We probably are." Solly reached for the decanter and refilled their glasses. "Maybe there's somebody out there somewhere, but they're probably so far away it'll never make a difference. Yes: for practical purposes, I think we can proceed as if we're alone."

"The problem with that," she said, "is that we've become complacent and self-satisfied. Bored. We're shutting down everything that made us worthwhile as a species."

"Kim, I think you're overstating things."

"Maybe. But I think we need something to light a fire under us. The universe has become *boring*. We go to ten thousand star systems and they're always the same. Always quiet. Always sterile."

"Is that why Emily was on the *Hunter*? Is that the way she felt?"

"Yes," said Kim. "She tried to explain herself to me when we used to go down to the beach."

"You remember *that*?"

"She asked me if I knew why ships always traveled along the coast? Why they never put out to sea?"

"Oh," said Solly. It was because there was nothing there. Just water for thousands of kilometers, until you'd rounded the planet and arrived at the western side of Equatoria. Back where you started.

"That's where we are, Solly. On the beach, looking out at an ocean that doesn't go anywhere. As far as we know." Her eyes slid shut. "But if there's really nowhere to go, I don't think we have much of a future."

After dinner they watched *On the Run*, an irreverent chase comedy in which several unlikely characters discover they're clones of some of history's arch criminals and find themselves the targets of a desperate manhunt. An interactive version was available, but they were both tired and satisfied just to sit and watch.

She fell asleep toward the end and woke after midnight, alone in the room. The projector had shut itself off, Solly had apparently gone to bed, and she sat for a time staring at the Milky Way.

For meals, they eventually took over the mission control center. It was small and consequently more intimate than the dining area. They spread a tablecloth over one of the consoles and discovered it worked very nicely.

Solly varied the views in the windows. Sometimes she looked out at star fields or at generated worlds, sometimes at waterfalls or a mountainscape or even downtown Seabright.

"What's it really like outside?" she asked.

"Utterly black," he said. "No stars, of course. Ship's lights seem to lose some of their intensity."

"Anybody ever actually been outside during hyperflight?"

"No," Solly said. "Not that I know of."

There was no sense of movement in this environment, which seemed more like a condition than a *place*. Seven weeks to Alnitak. It would be a long time to spend cooped up with a single person. Even Solly.

Vessels traveling in hyperspace were completely cut off from the outside world. They could receive no sensor information, no communications, no data of any kind. Nor could they transmit. Solly could have brought them out to satisfy their curiosity as to whether the Taratuba mission had got off okay. He thought they'd have used the *Mac*. And they were curious whether the theft of the *Hammersmith* had been made public, whether the Institute was trying to communicate with them. But it would have taken time, they'd have had to adjust the clocks, and Kim would have had to correct the program to get the calculations right for the intercept. So they let it pass.

One of the more curious aspects of hyperspace was that time seemed to run at an indifferent rate. Timekeeping devices on a transdimensional flight always had to be reset later. Sometimes forward, sometimes back. No one knew why this was so, but fortunately the differential was never more than a bare fraction of a percent, so that it did not unduly interfere with navigation. This was essential because TDI flights could navigate only by dead reckoning.

They fell quickly into a routine. They ate breakfast whenever they got up, and took their other meals at regular hours, ending with a late-night snack. Kim read through the mornings, a wide diet that included political and scientific biographies. She devoured two classics that she'd been meaning to get to since college: Blackman's *Beyond Pluto*, an account of the cultural changes which flowed from the penetration of distant systems; and Runningwater's *Narrow Horizons*, a history of the decline and eventual collapse of organized religion. She added some novels and some essays. And, of course, she read extensively in her specialty.

After lunch during the early days of the flight they often played chess, but Solly won all the time so they gave that up and substituted poker, with three or four virtual opponents. And they participated in virtual seminars with Julius Caesar, Isaac Newton, Mikel Kashvady, and other classic personalities. One of the highlights of the early weeks came from watching Henry Mencken and Martin Luther talking past one another.

On the sixth day out they tried a Veronica King interactive, "The Laughing Genie." Kim's taste ran to the King adventures because they were much more than whodunits. Rather, the emphasis was on solving puzzles in which crimes may or may not have occurred. When a victim died, she was inevitably in a locked room, or asleep under the watchful eye of a security system that detected no perpetrator. In "The Laughing Genie," an archeologist has spent a lifetime looking for the tomb of Makarios Hunt, the second century Numian dictator and mass murderer; he finds it; but uses explosives to reseal it and refuses to tell anyone its location, or what he has seen.

They enjoyed it so much that the following night they tried "The Molecular God," the story of a physicist who comes into possession of the lost diaries of Embry Sickel, whose work led to the development of the jump engine. The physicist, now in possession of an exceedingly valuable historical document, proceeds to burn it and apparently leaps from a seventh-floor office.

In each case, witnesses and documents are made available to the detectives, played, of course, by Kim and Solly. They switched the roles back and forth. Kim particularly enjoyed portraying the giant bodyguard Archimedes Smith.

They spent much of their time lounging in virtual environments. Kim preferred artscapes, settings that never existed and never would, where colors and images assumed impressionist designs, where fountains floated in midair and sprayed tactile light into azure skies. Solly was more conservative: he liked seascapes, mountains, and had a special taste for the Egyptians, favoring pyramids and the great temple from the Valley of the Kings. Sometimes the temple was portrayed as a ruin; sometimes it was seen as it appeared during its glory days.

Neither was inclined to be alone, but since Solly tended to lose his color among Kim's abstractions, she gave in and settled for the more mundane surroundings.

She had plenty of time to think, and she spent much of it trying to persuade herself that she'd done the right thing. She fretted over Solly, and came to realize that she desperately wanted him not to come to grief because of her.

She owed him a considerable debt. He'd helped her through some bumpy times, including the loss of the only man she'd ever thought she loved. He'd gone off with an accountant, leaving her a note wishing her a good life. Kim understood now that the relationship would never have worked, but the experience, even after several years, still gnawed at her. Solly and his then-wife Ann had almost adopted her during that period.

Later, when Ann chose not to renew, Kim had been there when he needed to talk, and had even fixed him up with friends.

They had a lot of good memories and prided themselves in thinking they were closer, in many ways, than most lovers. They'd celebrated together, supported each other, and enjoyed one another's victories. When Kim's wildeye team had won an amateur championship two years earlier, Solly, who was bored silly by team sports, had been in the stands.

They'd grown closer after Ann left. But there was a line between them, and they both respected it.

But Kim had begun to fantasize about Solly. And one evening, midway through the third week, she decided the time had come to make an offer.

It was her turn to choose the evening's entertainment. She selected *Raven*, a historical romance set in Equatoria's second century, when law, order, and civilization had all broken down. The Raven was a dark jewel, supposedly a relic from an unknown and possibly nonhuman technology, which falls into the hands of Clea, a young woman who must transport it through a host of perils to present it finally to its rightful owner. She is pursued by all manner of pirates, scavengers, corrupt government officials and, most feared of all, the bandit chief Aranka.

The program incorporated a nudity selector, which Kim set at a modest level. When they were ready, when the drinks had been poured and the snacks set out, she started the entertainment.

Clea of course wore Kim's appearance. *Was* Kim.

She has just rented a flyer and is preparing to cross a rain forest on the last leg of a trip home when a wounded man staggers out of the trees barely ahead of a mob of pursuers. The pursuers have guns and are blazing away. The fugitive sees her and turns in her direction. Clea is his only chance.

She hesitates and throws open the hatch. He leaps on board in a hail of lasers. The flyer bucks but lifts off and they are away.

But the man is bleeding profusely.

Clea examines him and sees quickly that he's dying. She does what she can. In the meantime, another flyer takes off in pursuit. In a spectacular sequence, she leads it into a tunnel where an oncoming train takes it out. But the aircraft has also suffered damage and is forced to land.

"What happened?" she asks her passenger when they are on the ground. "What did they want?"

He produces the Raven. Minutes later he is dead and she detects movement in the trees around her. She hides the artifact under a seat. Nomads emerge from the woods and take her prisoner.

They talk of selling her into slavery. Clea tries to win the favor of her captors by performing a torrid torchlight dance. It is this sequence which had prompted Kim to select *Raven*. The viewer never quite gets a good look at the dancer: everything is firelight and shadow, tempo and drum. Passion and temptation.

While her doppelganger writhed and spun, Kim sat back with a mix of satisfaction and nervousness. It was, after all, not very subtle. If Isabel's

DNA had opened the way for Columbus, hers was now performing a similar service for Solly. A smile formed on her lips: the eternal female, real or virtual, civilized or barbarian. The game never changes.

Solly watched the shadow play, but kept his eyes averted from *her*.

He knew of course what was happening and it was evident he was trying to play his own game, pretending to be objectively amused by the scenario. But she saw the tension in his face.

She lost track of the narrative at this point. The entire world—curious that she would think in that term, given that the entire world, in this reality, consisted exclusively of the interior of the *Hammersmith*—the entire world squeezed down to Solly's eyes, narrowed, looking straight ahead, aware of her all the same.

"I don't think," he said finally, still avoiding her glance, "this is a good idea."

She let almost a minute pass. They might have been frozen in place, illuminated only by the flickering glow of the VR. "Okay," she said at last. "Whatever you think."

Solly touched the remote and shut down the projector. The room went dark save for the soft glow of security lights along the base of the wall.

Nobody moved.

"Kim." His voice was low and seemed to come from far away. "I think I love you."

And there it was: finally out in the open.

She got up and stood before him, entwined her arms around his neck and drew him to her.

"I've always loved you," he said.

"I know." It was what made the moment particularly frightening. And particularly joyful.

He pulled her down beside him. Their lips brushed lightly, withdrew, came back. "This wasn't supposed to happen," she said.

She could feel his heart beat. Or maybe it was hers. It was getting hard to tell.

His cheek was hot against hers and she clung to him, reveling in the passion of the moment. She felt him shudder. But he still seemed tentative.

"It's okay, Solly," she said.

Inhibited by the behavior pattern of more than a decade, he drew just far enough away to look at her. "I'm not sure about this," he said.

"Be sure." She took his hand and placed it against her breast.

■　　■　　■

The bunks were not portable, nor were they big enough to accommodate two people, so after the first couple of nights, which were spent in a tangle on the floor of the rec room, they retreated to their individual quarters after their passions had been satisfied. *Ham*, Solly remarked, had not been designed for lovemaking.

Kim found the arrangement eminently unsatisfactory. Solly agreed and removed the mattresses from two of the beds, added some cushions, took over a third compartment, and turned it into their sleeping room. It worked quite well.

As one might expect, morale on the spacecraft soared. Solly revealed to her, under prodding after an offhand remark, that in his view she'd spent much of the first week in a general funk. Reviewing her moods, she realized it was probably true. Despite his presence, she'd felt alone because it was *she* who had pushed the project, she who had insisted it was worthwhile to hang their careers out to dry. She who would bear the responsibility if they found nothing. And then she had learned that Solly thought it would be *better* if the mission failed.

Well, now at least Solly had come on board. So to speak.

Kim began to think of those days as the happiest of her life. By the end of the fourth week, she was wondering how she could possibly have waited so long to take him.

At midnight on the thirty-second day of the voyage, February 30, the second nova would be triggered. "If we get lucky," she said, "Beacon will be obsolete before they've blown Ozma." Ozma was scheduled to be the last star in the series.

Despite the exhilaration that came with giving herself free reign with Solly, she had begun to develop an irritation at being cut off from the outside world. "It isn't just the newscasts," she explained. "It's like being in a cocoon."

"You need more candlelight and music," Solly said. "It's probably the same effect that causes hallucinations in the liners. There, it's less pressing because there are a thousand or so people on board. They run casinos and gossip shows and all kinds of things like that, but even then the sense of extreme solitude affects people. Here there are only the two of us."

"I recall," Kim said, "reading an account once about a woman stranded on a world for three months before help came. She had all she could do to stay sane, knowing she was the only person on the planet."

Solly nodded.

"Do *you* feel it?" she asked.

"Sure," he said. "The ship has echoes. It's like an old house. But look, if it's getting to you, we can jump back into realspace and at least talk to somebody. You could ask Phil Agostino how he's doing."

"How long would that take? To talk to somebody at the Institute?"

"Several days for the transmission to make the round-trip."

"Not really worth it, is it?"

"It is if you need to do it."

"No," she said. "Let's keep moving."

That night, at midnight, they toasted the Beacon Project. They did it with mixed drinks and crystal glasses that Kim had brought aboard, and Solly expressed his fervent hope that, when the light from the novas reached Greenway in several centuries, people would still remember Kim Brandywine.

She blushed. "Why *me*?"

"It would be a reminder of a time when the human race thought it was alone. Before Brandywine opened the door."

"I'll drink to that," said Kim, refilling both glasses.

"I've something more important for you to drink to."

She laughed and put down her glass and kissed him and rubbed her breasts against him, warming to see the light come into his eyes. "What could be more important?"

"Kim," he said, "I know this is a special circumstance, and I don't want to read more into it than what's there. But I want you to know that, when we go home, wherever we go from here, I'm not going to want things to go back to being the way they were."

It was the moment she'd both feared and hoped for. "I don't think we ought to make any decisions like that out here," she said.

"Why not? Or is that a *no*?"

They were sitting on their impromptu bed, both in underclothes. A Nelson adventure was running, full-masted naval warships blazing away at one another. They'd turned off the sound and reduced the images so that the vessels simply floated in the middle of the room.

"No, it isn't. I just don't think we should rush into this." She wondered why she was saying something so at odds with what she was feeling.

"Okay," he said.

"Solly, let's let it go for now. Enjoy what we have."

"Okay." He looked unhappy.

"I mean, hey, how long's Ann been gone?"

"Seven years."

"That's how long you waited to make your move." She was surprised at her own sudden anger. Where the hell had *that* come from?

Solly said nothing for several moments. Then he excused himself and left the room.

Goddamn it. A lover's quarrel.

It hadn't taken long.

18

We could never know who we truly were until we heard the whispers of the stars.

—CHANG WON TO, *Mind and Creation,* 404

Never go to bed angry.

They slept together that night as they had every night since *Raven.* But the lovemaking was perfunctory, reserved, cautious. One might almost say *politic.*

"Are you okay?" she asked, when they'd finished and lay quietly, aware that the tension had not eased.

"I'm fine."

"No, you're not. Solly, I don't want you angry with me."

"I'm not angry."

And so it went. The odd thing was she'd never seen him this way before. She'd known him to sulk, to take offense, and even on occasion to turn cold. But there was something deeper here, a degree of resentment that both surprised and hurt her.

It might have been that he also regretted the lost years, and that he was holding her responsible. Being bottled up in the ship didn't help. Everything was too closed in. There was too much solitude.

In the morning things were better. He apologized and agreed that of course they should wait, should not rush into commitments that maybe neither of them was ready to keep.

During the days that followed they supplemented their impassioned evenings by creating love by proxy, staging romances in which their alternate selves indulged in exotic exploits. But only with each other. No outsider was permitted to join the party.

The climax of the first phase of the flight came during the late afternoon of March 7, the thirty-ninth day. The *Hammersmith*'s automatic systems warned them that transition into realspace was imminent. They'd been waiting in mission control, drinking coffee, full of anticipation for the hunt.

"*Five minutes,*" said the AI.

Kim brought the harness down over her shoulders.

"Zero hour," said Solly. "Good luck."

The ship was always alive with the sound of power, of ongoing maintenance, of life support, of the engines even when they were in an inactive mode, which was most of the time. Kim had quickly become inured to it and heard it only when she deliberately listened for it, or when the tone changed. Now, as they approached their destination twenty-seven light-years off Alnitak, the jump engines began to build and power flowed through the walls.

Kim's eyes drifted shut. She imagined herself going home with the evidence, showing Agostino proof that an encounter had taken place, calling press conferences, accepting the congratulations of the world. A thousand years from now people would still speak in hushed tones of the flight of the *Hammersmith*.

The *real* challenge, she suspected, would be to create a *second* meeting.

It all seemed very promising, and she was luxuriating in the glory to come when the jump engines took hold and they crossed back out into realspace.

"Okay," said Solly. "That's it. We've arrived." He brought the forward view up on the overhead screen. It was filled with stars.

"Time to get to work," she said, so anxious she could scarcely contain herself.

He reached over and clasped her hand. "We should have thirty hours or so before the signal will be arriving here. But since we can't trust the clocks, let's get to it."

Constellations tend to dissolve when one moves a considerable distance toward them. Stars that appear in home skies to be close to one another are seldom so in reality. But Orion's Belt was a brilliant exception. Its three superluminous components remained in their classic relationship to each other, except that here, at a range of less than thirty light-years rather than the approximately fifteen hundred across which humans customarily saw them from Greenway, they dazzled the eye and utterly dominated the night.

Mintaka, "The Belt," is the westernmost. It's officially Delta Orionus, the least brilliant of the three, with a luminosity 20,000 times that of Sol or Helios. It has a relatively dim companion, not visible at this range, which orbits at about half a light-year.

Epsilon Orionus, in the middle, is also known by its Arabic name *Alnilam*, "Belt of Pearls." Its luminosity is twice that of Mintaka. A haze surrounds it, caused by the irregular nebulous cloud NGC 1990, glowing in the way that cloudy skies do when they reflect light from cities.

And finally, on the east, Zeta Orionus. *Alnitak.*

The Girdle.

She watched it move to center screen in the mission control center as the *Hammersmith* turned toward it. Alnitak too had collected a haze, contributed by the Flame Nebula and the emission nebula IC434.

"*We are on course toward Alnitak,*" said the AI. "*And accelerating to thirty-four kilometers per second.*"

"Very good, Ham," said Solly.

The ship's normal operating antennas locked on the giant star. Others emerged from wells around the hull and lined up along the central axis.

"It really amazes me," said Kim.

"What's that?"

"I'd always thought of the ship's captain bent over consoles, punching buttons, making adjustments, doing stuff. You could sit here with a good book and nobody'd know the difference."

"We've got good public relations," he said. "Maybe you should think about going to work for the pilots' association."

The engines shut off and they began to coast.

"*Acceleration complete, Solly,*" said the AI.

"All right, Ham. Launch FAULS."

Twin ports that had originally been designed to accommodate probes ejected a pair of communications packages. Eleven minutes later a second pair were launched. And then a third, until sixteen of the devices had been released.

They waited several hours while the packages arranged themselves into a vast field, aimed at the target star. Then they unfolded, one at a time, great white blossoms opening up.

Kim never left the mission control center during the deployment, save for a couple of trips to the washroom and a quick meal. At around eleven P.M., Ham announced that FAULS had come online. They now had a radio dish whose effective diameter was roughly equivalent to that of the orbit of Greenway's outermost moon.

Solly smiled at her. "Do you want to give the command?"

"Oh yes," said Kim. "Ham, activate FAULS."

Lamps blinked on. *FAULS activated.*

A storm of low-volume static spilled out of the speakers.

An auxiliary screen on Kim's right powered up. The system ID blinked on and stipulated it was working.

"Activate program search," said Solly.

"Activated." The static volume lessened.

"Now what?" she asked.

He looked up at the overhead monitor, which was locked on Alnitak, and increased magnification until the star became a disk. "We wait," he said.

She diverted the input to her earphones and listened for a few minutes. The void was alive with radio waves, a cacophony of whimpers and squeals and murmurs, the fading shrieks of stars plunging into black holes, the staccato clatter of pulsars, the murmur of colliding hydrogen clouds. The FAULS search program would sort out anything that might be a coherent signal. If *Hammersmith* succeeded in picking up a broadcast from the *Hunter* (or by wild chance from something else), the AI would immediately sound an alarm.

Solly instructed Ham to kill the sound.

Kim wondered about the range of possibilities, whether they might not be able to travel one day to remote places and collect historically significant radio broadcasts. Of course, they'd have to get closer to home. At fifteen hundred light-years from Greenway, and *sixteen* hundred from Earth, no radio transmissions would yet have reached this far. It was fascinating to think what they could see if they had a telescope capable of looking at Earth, where at this relative moment Henry VI sat on the British throne and Joan of Arc was a schoolgirl.

Solly got up. "That's as much as we can do for now. Want to go back to the workout room for a while?"

She was surprised he was willing to walk off at a time like this, even though the high-probability period was still hours away. "No," she said, "I think I'll hang on here."

She was still there when he came back two hours later with sliced beef and fruit.

They lay awake talking long through the night, listening for the alarm. Now that they were here, on station in a place where she could see countless stars, *clouds* of stars, but no sun, she lost confidence. Silly to do that: she'd checked the math any number of times; the equipment was equal to the task; physical law was very precise about how radio waves traveled in a vacuum. But *Hunter* seemed so long ago, in human terms. And what evidence did she really have other than Kane's sketch and a bogus set of logs?

Solly, who'd lived all his life in a star-traveling fraternity which assumed that the cosmos belonged exclusively to humanity, tried to encourage her, but his tone gave him away.

They spent most of the next day huddled over the instruments. Kim listened to the cosmic noise and watched the clock. She skipped lunch and tried to read, opening one book after another. Solly busied himself calibrating instruments that probably needed no attention.

They ate a light dinner and put on another King mystery. Just to watch, without participation. But Kim couldn't keep her mind on it. They did not go to bed. At midnight Kim was sprawled on the couch, one arm thrown across her eyes, listening to the silence.

"It might take a couple more days," Solly said. "Maybe even a week. Out here, we can't be all that precise about where we are." On the screens, the void rolled out forever. He was about to say something more when Ham spoke to them: *"We have a hit."*

Kim came wide awake.

"Transmission acquired 12:03 a.m. No visual. It is an audio signal only. On standard frequency."

"Run it," said Solly. It was 12:06. "From the beginning."

Kim sat up.

The speaker delivered a single *blip.*

Then, moments later, a pair of blips.

"Is it *Hunter*?" Solly asked the AI.

Three blips.

Four.

"Uncertain. It is artificial, with better than ninety-nine percent probability."

Hammersmith had *Hunter*'s transmission characteristics in its files. Given time, and a sufficient sample, it would be able to establish identity beyond question.

"It couldn't be anybody else," said Kim, elated. "We've *got* them."

She listened intently for more, but the speakers remained silent. Solly asked, "Is that all?"

"Yes. The signal arrived four minutes ago."

"Ham, if you get any more, pipe it directly through."

"They counted to four," Kim said.

It started again.

One. Two.

"What the hell is that all about?" asked Solly.

Three.

"They've seen something."

Four.

Kim wanted to scream for pure joy. "Something they can't talk to. They're trying to say hello."

And again. One—

"What kind of *hello* is counting to four?"

"It's the only common language they have. If it's really a celestial, it can reply by counting to *five*." She pressed her palms together and whispered a prayer to whatever power controlled such matters. Then she threw herself into his arms. "Solly," she said, "It's *really* happening."

"Let's hold on before we start to celebrate—"

The signal stopped. Kim let him go, pressed her palms together, and waited.

"If they've really got somebody else out there," she said, "we'll only get one side of the conversation." That was because the other vehicle would almost certainly be using a directed signal, as opposed to Tripley's omnidirectional broadcast.

"Do you think they're getting an answer?" asked Solly.

It began again. Same pattern.

"No," she said. "Not yet." Her heart was pounding. The sequence stopped. And started again.

One. Two. Three. Four.

"Characteristics of the signal have been analyzed," said the AI. *"Confirm it is the* Hunter."

She visualized the scene: somewhere near Alnitak, the Tripley vessel was busily making repairs, *had been* making repairs—it was at the moment hard to separate past from present—when they'd encountered *something*. The flared teardrop. The *turtle*. The *Valiant*.

One. Two. Three. Four.

"Come *on*," she pleaded.

Solly watched her. "You still figure they're getting no answer?"

"I think so. As soon as the other ship responds, they'll switch to something else."

"What would they switch to?"

"I have no idea, Solly. Anything—"

One—

"Why doesn't the celestial answer?" she demanded.

"Maybe they don't know *how*." Solly too was caught up in the confusion between past and present. They had, in a sense, retreated into time.

"They'd *have* to know, Solly. How could they *not*?" She prayed for a visual. Had *she* been onboard *Hunter*, she'd have taken the *Valiant*'s picture and sent it across to the other ship, inviting the stranger to do the same. A nice friendly gesture. One that would put an image into the transmissions. And tell her without any question what was going on.

The four-count continued to come in. The durations between individual blips varied, indicating they were manually tapping out the signal. The complete count usually ran about eight seconds. The sequences were divided by almost a minute.

"Are we using the multichannel?" Kim asked. Just in case the celestials transmit and their antenna *happens* to be pointed in the right direction, Ham would be able to hear it.

"Yes. We've got them covered. But don't bet the lunch money."

They were between signals. Kim tried to imagine the state of mind in the *Hunter*, and wondered what they were seeing in their scopes, what they had found. Had it been possible, she would have cheerfully killed Markis Kane. Hadn't it occurred to them that an event like this might generate future interest on the order of a later intercept of the original signals? That therefore they should provide for posterity?

Solly looked at the timer. "They're late."

The silence stretched out. It went to five minutes. Seven minutes.

"Maybe they gave up," he said.

"No." That couldn't happen. You don't give up if you're sitting there looking at a celestial. "They wouldn't do that."

"They might if the celestial took off."

Her stomach sank. It was a possibility she had never considered.

She'd assumed that a star-faring species would necessarily show the same raging curiosity in this type of situation that she would. Call it the Brandywine Fallacy.

But if there had been a meeting, and if it had been terminated abruptly, it wouldn't explain the subsequent events. No, it couldn't be that simple.

"They're probably trying something else," she said. "Something that's not showing up in a transmission."

"For example?"

"If I were there and I got no response on the radio I'd start flashing my lights. There's even a possibility that a connection has been made, that they're getting ready to exchange gifts and pledge mutual friendship. Maybe they've opened hatches and are waving at each other. None of *that* would show up on FAULS."

"That last is a possibility you can discard. There hasn't been time for anybody to get into a pressure suit." He looked into her eyes and frowned: "Are you all right?"

"If this goes on, Solly, I'm going to be an emotional wreck." She stared hard at the image of Alnitak as if by an act of will she could make out what was happening. At this moment, hidden in the light show coming in from the giant star, were the images of the *Hunter* and the *other*. "Got a question for you," she said.

"Sure."

"Would there be a way to know whether there are life-forms on another ship? That is, if we ran into something, but it stayed quiet, do we have sensors that could reach in there and determine somebody's on board?"

"No," he said. "Any ship in close to Alnitak would have to be heavily insulated against radiation. The *Hunter* would have no way of knowing directly whether it had a crew, or whether it was automated. The only way to be sure is to talk to them. And even that wouldn't tell you definitely because you could be dealing with an AI." He thought about it some more. "I think you'd have to go over physically and shake hands." He grinned. "Or shake whatever. Until then it's strictly guesswork."

At first she didn't remember where she was. *Hunter* was sending again. *Blip. Blip. Blip*— The pattern now was one-three-five-seven. Inviting the other vessel to send a nine. Did the fact that they'd changed the sequence mean they'd gotten an answer?

She was back on the couch. Solly had thrown a spread over her.

"They've been at it for about two hours, I think," he said.

"You think?"

"There was a break in midsignal. It continued for fourteen minutes. They may have gone behind something. Maybe that gas giant you mentioned."

It was after four A.M. Four hours since they'd picked up the *Hunter* signal. "Do you want to go back and get some sleep?" she asked.

"Yeah. I think I've had enough of this for one night. How about you?"

"I'm going to stay with it."

"Okay." He got up, bent over her, kissed her lightly. "I never would have thought they might actually have discovered something but got ignored. *Hey, we found a bona fide celestial out there, but they wouldn't talk to us. Where'd they go? No idea.*"

"Well," she said, "I hope we get more than *this*." She looked at the monitor, which was blinking out the new count. "I can see myself sitting in Agostino's office with a recording that does nothing but produce blips from the *Hunter*."

Solly stopped in the hatchway. "If nothing else," he said, "we can prove beyond any doubt that Kane faked the logs. Whatever these transmissions might really be about, none of them were recorded." He started to peel off his shirt. "Call me if anything happens—"

Then he was gone and she was yawning, snuggling back under the spread, listening to the radio noises. One, three, five, seven. Over and over.

But she was awake now. She got up and got some coffee. Mission control was always cooler than the rest of the ship. Life support wasn't quite correct. "Come on, *Valiant*," she said. "Answer up."

She drank the coffee. The *Hunter* group kept transmitting.

The bearing on the radio signal pointed directly to Alnitak. They'd come out of hyper somewhere near the star, as she thought, probably in the neighborhood of the gas giant. And there they'd met another sightseer.

The incoming signal changed.

One. Two. Three. *Five.*

Five?

Then *eight.*

Kim flicked on the intercom. "I hear it," said Solly, from his quarters. "What does it mean?"

The system went silent.

"It's a new series," she said. "A little more complicated. Solly, I think they might have got a response."

"Why?"

"Why else veer from a simple series?" She was conjuring up the scene on board: jumping up and down, clapping one another on the back, screaming congratulations.

"So what's the next number?"

"Thirteen," she said. "If it's really happening, that's what they're listening to right now. Thirteen blips from the other ship."

"It would be nice if we had something a little more concrete to speculate with." But he came back to mission control in his pajamas and squeezed her hand. "I hope you're right." The squeeze developed into an embrace.

She *was* right. She was sure of it. And in that moment she was supremely happy.

Solly held onto her and rocked her back and forth while they waited for the next series.

When it came, she counted eleven. That was all: eleven blips.

"What is it this time?" asked Solly.

"Who knows?" she said. "Eleven's a prime number. But it should be a response to something the other ship sent."

"Such as?"

"One, two, three, five, seven. All primes. Or maybe they sent the first five odd numbers."

Solly shook his head and eased himself into a chair. "Kim," he said, "we don't really have *anything* here."

"Well, what did you expect?" she demanded, pushing away from him. "We knew it would be a one-sided conversation. Short of pictures, this is as much as we could have asked."

Again the system was quiet. They waited and the silence stretched out past fifteen minutes. "Maybe they're trying to decide what to do next," she said.

"What would *you* do?"

"Face-to-face. I'd go visual. If that went okay, I'd try for a physical meeting. Send out the lander."

Solly nodded. "You think there could be a problem with the visual exchange?"

She thought it over. "Yes."

"For example?"

"What happens if they're stomach-churners and they see us reacting? Or if *we* arouse visceral reactions in them? But at some point you have to try it."

The AI broke in: *"We have video reception,"* it said in its mellifluous voice.

Solly's eyes caught her and a world of emotions passed between them. He switched the feed to the overhead display.

"Enhancing."

"On-screen," said Solly.

They were looking at the *Hunter* seal, the ship and the ringed world. After a moment it dissolved to Emily! She sat in an armchair. Kim felt a pang of regret. How young she looked. And she was radiant with emotion. Her hair was pulled back, she wore a loose-fitting white blouse, and she smiled happily at them. *"We know you can't understand any of this, but (not recoverable) hello anyhow. Greetings from Greenway. Can (not recoverable) you?"*

Kim's heart pumped furiously.

One by one, each of the *Hunter*'s crew came forward and talked. Tripley gushed. He was, despite the physical resemblance to Benton, quite unlike him. A softer man, more enthusiastic, more *alive*.

Yoshi was gentle, lovely, with luminous eyes and a ravishing smile. She wished her new friends good fortune, and expressed her hope that this would be the beginning of a new era for both their species.

"I think we're in business," said Solly.

Kim shook her head, wondering how the images would be interpreted by the occupants of the other ship. If they could see them at all. What was the likelihood their equipment would be sufficiently compatible to receive visuals?

"That's fairly straightforward technology," Solly said. "They'd almost *have* to have the capability."

And finally Kane. He spoke from the pilot's room, and his manner was perfunctory but not gruff. He said he was pleased to meet the occupants of the other ship. That remark sent Kim into another round of celebrating.

"Congratulations," Solly said.

Kane asked whether the *Hunter* could assist. He was somehow the only one of the four who managed to keep the pomposity naturally generated by such a moment out of his voice.

Kane gazed out of the picture directly at them for about a minute. And then he was gone. The screen flashed the *Hunter* seal again, and the picture blinked off.

"End of reception," said the AI.

Kim was still standing up, far too excited to sit. "I'd do anything to see the answer to *that*," she said.

"Find the original logs," said Solly.

She nodded. "We have to do that when we get back. That's our first priority."

Solly folded his arms and stared at the screen. "I hope Kane didn't destroy them."

"I'm sure he didn't. This is the most dramatic moment in human history. There's no way he'd have destroyed the record. None. He's hidden it somewhere."

"But where? Why?"

"I don't know. We'll figure it out."

It was taking a long time for the next transmission to come in. "You know," said Solly, "one of Kane's questions keeps coming back to me. Why do you think he asked if *Hunter* could assist? Is it possible the celestial is disabled? In trouble?"

"Could be. Damn Kane anyhow. We shouldn't be caught up in all this guesswork."

"I think you should show more appreciation."

"Why's that?"

"If he'd done everything by the book, done what he was supposed to do, this whole matter would have been settled twenty-seven years ago. And you would never have gotten near it. Instead, he's saved you a juicy puzzle and a chance at immortality. Be thankful."

"Visuals," said the AI.

Emily reappeared. *"Hello again,"* she said. *"Would you like to come on board?"*

"What's *that* all about?" asked Solly. "They don't expect anybody hanging around out here to speak *English*, do they?"

"It's not the words," said Kim. "It's the tone. The nonverbals. But I wouldn't think a truly alien culture would be able to read our nonverbal cues."

The image went to a split screen and *Hunter* materialized beside Emily. It floated against a river of stars. A dazzling burnt orange planetary ring arced across the sky behind it. The cargo door opened and lights came on, illuminating the interior. Emily's side of the split screen vanished, and Yoshi blinked into existence in her place, beckoning to the open door so the occupants of the other vessel couldn't possibly miss the point.

"That's not bad," said Kim.

Solly pursed his lips. "I'm not sure I agree."

"Why?"

"If we were looking across, say, a few hundred meters of empty space at a ship that was not manned by *people*, that was in fact operated by God knows what, and they opened a door and invited *me* in—" He held out his hands to heaven. "Not very likely."

"Solly," she said, pretending shock, "where's your spirit of adventure?"

The *Hunter* repeated its transmission.

And repeated it again.

"The whatevers are thinking it over," said Kim.

Solly nodded. "Tripley's pressing his luck. He should leave it alone. Offer once and drop it."

A slice of starry sky was visible past the hull of the *Hunter*. "Solly," she asked, "how would you think they're producing those pictures?"

He thought for a moment. "Easiest way would be to use the feed from one of the scopes." He glanced at the starfield glittering in their windows. "Then do an overlay of the *Hunter* just as they've done with Yoshi."

"Then that's the way the stars would actually have looked, on that night, from their position?"

"Probably. Sure."

"Would you guess the *forward* view?"

"Maybe. That might be the natural way to do it. Why? What difference does it make?"

"Probably none. But it *does* give us a course heading during the contact." She filed the information away in her head.

"What time of day would it have been when all this was going on?" asked Solly.

Kim had been keeping track. The first radio signal had been transmitted from *Hunter* at 11:42 A.M., February 17, 573, Seabright time. It would now be 4:12 P.M. on the *Hunter*.

"What they should do," said Solly, "is just go back to the radio and keep talking. Try to establish a next step."

The FAULS screen was blank again. "Well," she said, "I don't think the invitations are working."

There was nothing more for almost two hours. Then *Hunter* transmitted the open-door image again, this time with Tripley. But he merely waved to the viewer and made no effort to point at the cargo area.

"I guess they're at a standstill," said Solly.

Kim exhaled. "I'm surprised."

"In what way?"

"That they'd spent so many years trying to accomplish precisely this and been so little prepared for the event."

"You mean the open-door pictures?"

"I mean the whole thing has a kind of spontaneous feel, doesn't it? As if they were all taken by surprise. It makes me think they never really *expected* to succeed."

"What *should* they do?" asked Solly.

"The bottom line is that Emily and her friends can't do very much. And they need to recognize that. They aren't going to be able to master a new language; they can get only so far with number games; and it's obvious that establishing a sense of mutual trust with, say, giant spiders is going to be a tricky business. I'd say it would take a team of specialists to get much beyond saying hello."

"Therefore—?"

"Therefore they should concentrate on *one* thing: establish a date for a second encounter. If they could do that, they'd have achieved as much success as anyone could wish."

"How would you go about it?"

"They've got a planet handy. They could use the planet to make a date. Show them, say, a couple hundred revolutions. Six months. *We'll be back in six months.* The meaning would be plain enough."

"You make it sound easy," Solly said. "Too bad you weren't with them."

She drew up her knees and put her arms around them. *Emily was with them.*

Solly was showing signs of frustration. "How about some breakfast?" he suggested.

"No, thanks. I want to stay here."

"You won't miss anything. I don't mind getting it."

"That's okay," she said. "I'm not hungry. Really."

He shook his head. "I'm going to exercise my prerogative as captain and insist. This might go on for another twenty-four hours or so, and I don't need you getting sick out here."

She looked at the status panel. At the glowing lamps. "All right," she said.

He brought out two plates of ham, biscuits, and pineapple slices. Kim ate quietly, subdued, annoyed at the apparent inability of the *Hunter* to create an effective strategy. Solly suggested the celestials might have been scared off by the open door. Or that they might have a cultural bias prohibiting them from befriending a different species. Or—

"How could *that* happen?" she asked. "These critters have spaceflight. Since they're in the vicinity of Alnitak, they must have FTL. Surely they wouldn't be afflicted with preconceptions about another sentient species."

"Maybe they'd have a religious problem about us," he said. "Maybe we're not supposed to exist, and we've trashed a theological system."

"I don't think you'd find that kind of thinking among space-travelers."

"Really? We had Christians and Muslims arguing all the way out to Carribee. Even the Universalists are inclined to look down on anyone who doesn't subscribe to the official theology."

"Which is that there *is* no official theology."

"Doesn't matter. The same tendency is there. I don't know. Maybe the celestials don't come in a lot of packages the way humans do. If there's basically only one type of critter, it would never have been required to deal with anything *different*."

Solly slowly ate through his breakfast, let his head drift back, and fell asleep. After an hour or so he woke up, went to his room, showered, and changed. When he came back he looked neater but still fatigued. "I can't believe they're just sitting there doing nothing," he said.

"Maybe they've launched the lander," suggested Kim. "It's possible they're trying a meeting."

"No. There'd be radio traffic. The *Hunter* would need to tell them— *show* them—what they wanted to do."

During the course of the morning the screens remained quiet. Solly and Kim went over the same ground again and again. By midafternoon Kim thought the quality of the signal had probably disintegrated to a degree they were simply not acquiring it anymore.

"It's possible," said Solly. "But not likely."

They went down to the rec room and worked out. Neither said much and when they were finished, had showered and changed, Solly asked whether she thought it was over.

"Probably," she said.

"So what do we do now?"

"We listen some more. If we don't hear anything, we move to another intercept site and listen to it all again. That'll allow us to take a second bearing and pin down their location."

"How long do we stay here?"

The *Hunter* had been in the Alnitak area almost two days. "Let's stay put through midnight tomorrow. If we haven't heard anything by then, we'll clear out."

That evening he came to her with a tenderness and a passion that overwhelmed her. "I'm glad you got what you wanted," he told her after the first flush of lovemaking had passed. "We don't have all the details yet, but at least we know it happened."

"Kiss me, you fool," she sighed.

The night filled with laughter and a few tears, and she didn't know why, couldn't explain the tears either to herself or to him, but just let them flow.

"I'm in bed with an immortal," he said.

And she knew it was so. Eventually they'd sort everything out, get the answers, learn what had happened to Emily and find out how Yoshi ended up in a river and what had blown the face off Mount Hope. It was just a matter of time, and kids a thousand years from now would be learning how to pronounce her name.

She had never, *ever*, felt more alive than she did then, and she attacked Solly with a will, laughing when he finally slumped back exhausted, pleading with her to give him a rest.

Somewhere around five A.M., lying on her back with Solly's left arm thrown over her, she decided that she would keep him, she would do whatever she had to. Moreover, Solly was part of this whole marvelous event and she was going to hold onto all of it. They had been wedded by the sheer joy of the experience. The ceremony, when it came, would be only a recognition of what had happened in this most glorious of starships.

They slept late in the morning, ate, watched a VR, and wandered down to mission control, where the FAULS screen was still blank. They had gone more than twenty-four hours without any further interceptions. It now seemed clear, for whatever reason, that the party was over. But they waited anyway. They hurried through dinner, anxious to concede the issue, to be off to their next station, to outrun the radio transmissions, to race across the void and jump back into realspace and take a new bearing on Alnitak.

"But I'm not hopeful," she said, down considerably from the previous day's high. She was thinking of the old axiom that if you want people to believe extraordinary claims, you must present extraordinary evidence. Did she *have* extraordinary evidence?

She remembered the telescope she would have turned on Henry IV, and wished with all her heart she had such an instrument to point at the ringed world in the Alnitak system. She'd be able to *see* the two ships, *see* what was happening. It frustrated her to know the photons were all around her, the disassembled truth of whatever had happened to the *Hunter* and the *Valiant*, flowing past, accessible to the proper instruments.

At midnight she sighed. "Time to go."

19

. . . Every individual existence goes out in a lonely spasm of helpless agony.

> —WILLIAM JAMES, *The Varieties of Religious Experience*,
> VI 1902 C.E.

The *Hammersmith* passed into hyperspace at 12:41 A.M., Saturday, March 10. The plan was to go back outside the expanding bubble of radio signals. They would remain in the plane of the Alnitak system, but their new bearing on the giant star would be at right angles to the first one. They would be traveling roughly thirty light-years, and would arrive at their destination just after eight P.M.

They slept late. Kim woke up excited, anxious to get through the day, and to launch the second round of FAULS devices. But she could find nothing to occupy her, and ended by playing chess in the rec room with the AI, whom she set at a beginner's level and proceeded to hammer.

Solly, with his inimitable sense of what was needed, put together another candlelight dinner. She drank a bit more than she should have, and she was a bit woozy when the *Hammersmith* returned to realspace.

This time, because the jump had been much shorter, they arrived closer to their ideal site, and within an hour they were listening again to the *Hunter* trying to open a conversation with its invisible companion. Shortly after the intercept had begun, however, they lost the signal. They were gratified to see it appear fourteen minutes later, precisely on schedule. That seemed to confirm the speculation that it was passing behind the gas giant.

They knew there'd be several hours of futile signaling by *Hunter* before *Valiant* responded. So they settled in, alternately reading and napping, and occasionally cavorting like adolescents. "This is the way star travel was meant to be," Solly told her.

Four hours after the first signals, the four-count, had been sent, the *Valiant* had apparently responded. *Hunter* replied with thirteen blips. Emily and her shipmates appeared onscreen, and sent greetings. And showed their open door.

As before, there was no further transmission.

But they had their second bearing. They compensated for stellar movement in the interim, and the lines intersected at a point three hundred AUs from Alnitak. Right on the orbit of the gas giant.

They waited nevertheless through two more days. Finally, there could be no question that the show was over, and Solly put a disk into the recorder and directed the AI to copy the intercept record from both sites. When it was completed he gave it to Kim. "With luck," he said. "It'll keep us both out of court."

"We'll see." She looked at the disk. "It might be easier for someone to argue the entire crew of the *Hunter* went over the edge rather than that they actually saw something. That might be stretched to account for the missing women, as well. What we really need is a glimpse of whatever it was they saw." She took a deep breath. "Okay, I guess it's time to go to phase two."

"The scene of the crime?"

"Yep."

"Why bother? What's the point? They're all long gone."

"Solly," she said, "put yourself in the place of the other ship. Look, for reasons we don't understand, our people came back and didn't say anything. Maybe there was a fight on board, a disagreement on how to handle the announcement, on who was going to get the credit—"

"—That doesn't make sense—"

"Okay. But something happened. Maybe the experience scared them off. Maybe they saw something so terrifying it drove them all out of their minds—"

"—And we want to go there?—"

"We'll be careful. And we won't be taken by surprise. Look, the point is, *both* ships knew there'd been contact. It had to be as big an event for the celestials as it was for us. So what did they *do* afterward? What would you and I do?"

He propped his chin on one hand and gazed steadily at her.

"Assuming no real conversation took place and the other ship just took off, we'd post a surveillance."

"Can you see any possibility we *wouldn't* do that? That we'd just ignore the incident?"

"No," he said after a moment's pause. "No, although we *did* ignore the incident. But I'd have expected we'd have put science teams out there right away."

"And they'd have stayed for years, right?"

"I suppose. But *twenty-seven* years?"

"Well, maybe not *that* long. I don't know. But we'd leave some automated systems in place."

"Sure," he said. "We'd establish a presence and keep it indefinitely."

"Right. So all we have to do is show up at Alnitak and let whatever they've left behind get a look at us. We head for the gas giant and we do whatever we can to draw attention to ourselves. We look for anything that doesn't belong there. And if we're lucky, who knows what might show up?"

At three hundred AUs, the world was eight times farther out than Endgame was from Helios, or six times Pluto's distance from Sol. It had seventeen satellites and a ring system divided into three sections. A permanent storm of the kind often associated with gas giants floated in its southern latitudes. It required roughly twenty-three centuries to complete an orbit around the central luminary, which even at this extreme distance, was fully a third as bright as Greenway's noontime sun.

Solly set course toward the planet.

"The system," said Kim, "has been surveyed once. That was a hit and run, in-and-out. They spent two days here. There are no really unusual features, unless you're talking about the atmospherics." She meant the vast interstellar clouds, cradles for new stars, turbulent and explosive, illuminated from within and also by Alnitak. The nearby nebula NGC2024, stretching for light-years across that restless sky, was a kaleidoscope of bright and dark lanes, of exquisite geometry, of glowing surfaces and interior fires. Enormous lightning bolts moved through it, but it was so far that they seemed frozen in place.

"Slow lightning," said Solly. "Like the mission."

Kim looked at the nebula. "How do you mean?"

"We've known for a long time that contact might eventually happen, maybe would *have* to happen, and that when it did it would change everything, our technology, our sense of who we are, our notions of what the universe is. We've seen this particular lightning strike coming and we've played with the idea of what it might mean for at least twelve hundred years. We've imagined that other intelligences exist, we've imagined them as fearsome and gentle, as impossibly strange and remarkably familiar, as godlike, as incapable, as indifferent. Well, I wonder whether the bolt is about to arrive. With you and me at the impact point."

On the other side of the sky, a long luminous bar, IC434, stretched away into a glorious haze. Presiding over it was the great dark mass of the Horsehead Nebula.

"It's a place for artists." She stood by a window looking out at the vast display. The brilliant rings of the gas giant angled past her field of vision, a glowing bridge to its family of moons, all in their first quarter. She looked again at the blowup of Kane's mural. It was impossible to know whether this world was the one in Emily's hand. But she'd have bet on it.

There were two other suns in the system, one too remote to pick out, the other bright enough to provide reading light. The nearer was approximately 1300 AUs from Alnitak. It too was superluminous, though not in the same league with its companion. "People used to think a binary star couldn't have a planetary system," she told Solly. "We know better now, but the planets tend to get tossed around a lot, and often thrown out altogether. Especially when both components are massive and there isn't a lot of space between them." She eased herself into a chair and gazed steadily at the rings and moons. "It won't stay in orbit long. It's just a matter of time before something jerks it loose."

The planetary disk had an autumnal coloration. The storm was a darker splotch, a circular piece of night. "About one and a half Jupiters," he said, using the standard measurement for gas giant mass. "I'm beginning to understand why they decided this was the place to stop while Kane did his patchwork."

"It *is* spectacular. I looked over the records of Tripley's previous voyages," said Kim. "He was here before. Wanted to see the Horsehead."

Solly stared at the clouds and the world for long minutes, and then turned to her. "What do we do first?"

Good question. "We go into orbit. And then we wait."

"Kim," he said, "we were a little critical of Tripley for being unprepared to run a contact scenario. Are *we* ready? If something happens?"

She drew herself up in her professorial mode. "Be assured," she said, "nothing will happen." They both laughed. In fact, Kim had prepared a visual program to transmit in the event there was an encounter. It included pictures of the *Valiant* and the *Hunter*, of herself and Solly, of interiors of the *Hammersmith*. There were pictures of Greenway's forests and oceans, of people lounging on beaches. There were anatomical charts of humans and several dozen animals and plants. And finally there was an image of three *Valiants* and three *Hammersmiths* silhouetted against the rings of the Jovian; and the Jovian itself followed by four hundred lines divided into tens. She showed it to Solly.

"We meet back here when the planet has turned on its axis four hundred times."

"Good," he said. A day on the gas giant lasted between seventeen and eighteen hours. So they were talking roughly one year. Enough time to outfit an expedition, work out their strategy, and return. "Kim," he asked, "how do you want me to program the sensors? What exactly are we looking for?"

"Set for maximum sweep and range. And we should look for *anything* that wouldn't normally be out there. Processed metal. Plastic. Anything that isn't gas, rock, or ice. Or anything that moves on its own."

The original survey gave few details for the gas giant. Kim knew it had an equatorial diameter of 187,000 kilometers, and a polar diameter of 173,000 kilometers. Average density was only 1.2 times that of water, indicating a high proportion of the lighter elements, hydrogen and helium. Its axial tilt was 11.1 degrees.

Its most striking feature was the rings, which were coplanar with the equator. They had an overall diameter of 750,000 kilometers, and were divided into three distinct sets. The innermost reached down almost to the cloudtops. They were barely one kilometer thick, so when the *Hammersmith* passed them edge-on they all but vanished.

Two of the satellites were larger than Greenway; one minuscule worldlet at the outermost extremes of the system was only a half-dozen kilometers across. It orbited almost at right angles to the equator.

"It would help," said Kim, "if we knew precisely where the incident took place."

"How do you mean?"

"Altitude. Orbit, if possible."

"Don't see how we can determine that," said Solly. "We can see the rings in one of the sequences, but the planet's not visible at all."

"But we know when everything happened," said Kim. "We know now right to the minute." Contact had been made February 17 at 11:42 A.M. shipboard time. "We have a picture of the rings during the event, and we have a starry background."

"The stars would look the same from anywhere in the system," he objected.

"The *stars* would," she agreed.

But not the moons. And surely there was at least one moon in the picture.

There were *two.*

They ran the sequence again, *Hunter* floating against the midnight sky, the cargo door opening and lights coming on, splashing out into the void. How warm and inviting the interior looked, Kim thought, especially when Yoshi's smiling image appeared and invited entry. There was something almost blatantly sexual in all that, and she wondered what the celestials had made of it.

They surveyed the satellite system until they had its mechanics down. Once they'd accomplished that, they ran the orbits backward to 4:12 P.M., February 17, the moment that the open door image had been transmitted. They matched the positions of the moons against the angle of the rings.

"Okay." Solly put a graphic on one of the auxiliary monitors. "In order for everything to appear as it does in the picture, the *Hunter* would have had to be *here.*" He showed her the point, eleven degrees north of the equatorial plane, at an altitude of 45,000 kilometers. "But we only have a couple of minutes on the image, and it's not enough to track a complete orbit."

"We've got a second picture," Kim reminded him. The *Emily* image, which had been taken two hours later.

Solly brought it up, found more moons, three this time, repeated the process, and smiled triumphantly. "I think we're in business," he said.

She was delighted. "Good. Let's get ourselves into the same orbit. But I want to move a bit faster than the *Hunter* would have."

"Why?"

"So that we'll overtake anything that might be traveling at *Hunter's* velocity."

Solly frowned.

"Just do it, okay?" she said.

"Okay, Kim."

"And let's do as thorough a search as we can."

"What exactly do you expect to find?"

"*I expect nothing,*" she said, feeling like Veronica King, who always said that. "But the possibilities are limitless." The hope that she entertained, that she did not want to describe, was that the celestial was still here somewhere, a derelict. It was *possible.*

Solly passed instructions to the AI. "We'll be going into orbit," he told her, "later this evening. And we'll need roughly twelve hours to do a complete search along the orbit."

There was something in Solly's voice. "Anything wrong?" she asked.

"I thought about this before we left but it didn't really seem like something I wanted to bring up at the time."

"Tell me, Solly."

"We're not armed," he said. "Has it occurred to you that if this thing is here, it may not be friendly?"

"I don't think that's likely."

"Why not?"

She looked out at the star-clouds. "Solly, even if they were an aggressive species, there wouldn't be any point shooting at someone in a wasteland like this. What's to gain?"

"Maybe they just don't like strangers. *Something* happened to the *Hunter.*"

"We have to assume they're rational, Solly. Otherwise they couldn't have gotten here in the first place." She enjoyed being with him, alone in all this vast emptiness. It was different now that they could look out the windows and know that what they were seeing was really there. "They didn't shoot at the *Hunter.* Or if they did, they're not very dangerous because the *Hunter* got home safely."

"It's possible," said Solly, "they're at war against their own kind. Maybe Ben Tripley got the name right, calling it the *Valiant.* It could have been a warship."

"Solly," she said patiently, "*they got home all right.*"

"Did they? Who knows? Maybe they were taken. Maybe something else went back." He made a scary face and hummed a few notes from the old horror series *Midnight Express.* She laughed. But a chill ran through her nevertheless.

■　　■　　■

Shortly after dinner they settled into *Hunter*'s orbit, which was roughly equatorial, varying only a few degrees above and below the line.

The rings dominated the sky, a vast shining arch beneath which the copper-gold clouds rolled on forever. Lightning bolts cruised through the depths and occasionally they saw the fiery streak of a meteor.

It seemed a place of infinite serenity and beauty. One might almost conclude it had been designed specifically to please the human eye and mind.

It was, she thought, a reason in itself to pursue starflight. Even if we were truly alone the mere existence of this kind of world and its magnificent star-clouds should be enough to summon the race from its ancestral home. There was something decadent in what was happening now, in the general retreat back to comfort and routine and familiar surroundings. In the lack of interest in all the things that had once been counted as noble and worth accomplishing.

We had begun to lead *virtual* lives.

No one had to work, so few did anything more than pursue quiet leisure. Kim had always thought herself ambitious. Yet during her entire life she had never felt an urge, even when the opportunity was there, to move beyond the home worlds. People complained about long weeks locked up in spartan accommodations, at getting ill during the jumps, at the expense of interstellar travel. And they settled for imaginary images, lovely little technological fireworks displays, created in the warm comfort of their living rooms. Throw a log on the fire and visit Betelgeuse.

She started to explain to Solly how she felt, looking at the star-cradles glowing in their windows, at the Horsehead, at the rings. The presence of another intelligence seemed not quite as important as it had a few hours before.

"Welcome to the club, Kim," he said when she'd finished. "Those of us who make a living out here have known that for years. It really doesn't matter all that much whether there are celestials in Orion. There's just too much to see to complain about the details. And if it does turn out that we're the only part of the universe able to see what's around us, that's okay."

She'd always felt that Solly tended to neglect the more intellectual aspects of life. He didn't read as much as he should, and he'd seemed to be too interested in the practical and the mundane, a man who seldom considered the philosophical issues. He'd surprised her several times on this trip, particularly with his remarks about the slow lightning. Ask Solly what the purpose of existence was, and he could be expected to reply that it's a good lunch with good friends. Or a good woman.

She'd had a confused notion that life had something to do with expanding one's intellectual horizons. And with achievement. Now she looked out the window and decided that whatever her purpose was, she'd fulfilled it when she arrived *here*.

And if she could choose a place to meet another intelligence, this would surely be it.

Below her, the upper atmosphere caught the light from the distant sun. It looked *warm* down there, and it was easy to imagine broad oceans and continents lying beneath those shimmering mists. In fact the temperature at the cloudtops was a terrestrial -17° C, the heat generated internally. Not all that bad if you could breathe hydrogen and methane.

Solly concentrated the scanners along the arc of the orbit, but he maintained a full search bubble out to more than six thousand kilometers. That took about 30 percent off the range and definition of the main search, but it was a price he was prepared to pay to avoid being surprised. Kim didn't argue the point.

They were circling the planet every hour and twenty-two minutes. It had gotten late but no one showed any inclination to retire.

During the third orbit the alarm went off.

"Organic object ahead," said the AI.

They went to the pilot's room and Solly put the hit onscreen and went to full mag. They were on the dark side of the planet, in shadow, and consequently he could get nothing more than a marker. But the analysis had already begun.

Calcium.

"Object is rectangular, approximately two meters long, less than a meter wide."

Carbon.

Range was twelve hundred kilometers.

Solly relaxed a bit. He laid in an intercept course. Kim felt the engines come on. The ship began to accelerate.

Potassium.

Below, the great arc of the rings was mostly in shadow, but a couple of moons gave them some light.

Hydrochloride.

Ahead, the sun was coming up. That wasn't going to help visibility either.

"Won't take long," he said.

Kim felt a darkness gathering at the pit of her stomach.

They sat silently, sufficiently chilled that Solly raised the temperature on the flight deck.

Nine hundred kilometers and closing.

They flew into the sunrise.

Sodium.

The marker seemed to change its aspect, growing alternately brighter and dimmer. "It's tumbling," Solly said.

They raced toward the sun, passed under it, eventually got it behind them and were able to get a clear visual.

It was a body.

She was barely breathing now, gripping the arms of the chair, conscious of Solly watching her.

"You all right, Kim?"

Six hundred kilometers.

It wore a dark blue jumpsuit with a shoulder patch. She couldn't make out details of the patch, but she knew what it said. PERSISTENCE.

Kim watched the body tumble down its lonely orbit.

Emily.

By the time they caught her, they were on the dark side again. Solly instructed the AI that they would take her on board through the cargo lock. Then he turned to Kim. "You sure you're—?"

"Yeah," she said. "I'm okay."

He nodded. "Stay here. If anything unexpected happens while I'm gone—"

"What do you mean *unexpected*?"

"If we get jumped—"

"Oh."

"Don't hesitate to tell Ham to get us out of here."

"It'll obey *me*?"

"Sure."

"Solly, be careful."

"Count on it."

"You're not going outside, are you?"

"No farther than I have to." He switched on the cargo hold imager so she could watch the recovery. Then he held her for a moment and went downstairs. Several minutes later he walked into the cargo bay, wearing a pressure suit and a jetpack, and waved at her.

"Kim," came his voice, "can you hear me?"

"I hear you, Solly."

"I'm in the process of decompressing the hold. As soon as we're ready, we'll open up." He was standing in front of the cargo door, which was half again as high as he was, and about six meters wide.

"What do you need me to do?"

"Nothing," he said. "I'll handle it from here."

"What about if you fall out?" She wasn't entirely joking.

"Can't fall out," he said. "I'm tethered."

The engines slowed. Instead of a steady pulse, *Hammersmith* was now modulating its approach with occasional bursts from its turning thrusters.

The object came within range of their lights and she got a good visual. It *was* Emily, without question.

"I just don't believe this," Solly said. "Why in God's name would they leave her out here?"

"Because they didn't want to have to explain how she died." Kim's blood began to race. The sons of bitches had killed her after all.

Why?

The corpse drifted to within a hundred meters. Kim watched through the external imagers as the cargo door opened. She saw Solly framed in the light, silhouetted against the Jovian's rings.

The thrusters kicked in again. *Hammersmith* rolled slightly, and slowed almost to a matching velocity with the body. It passed out of the forward view and appeared off to port.

"You okay, Solly?"

"Yeah. I'm fine. I'll have her in a minute."

She watched him lean out the open door. A moment later he hauled the body inside, laid it gently on the deck, placing it so it was out of the view of the imagers.

"Let me see her," said Kim.

"You don't want to," he said.

But she insisted and Solly moved her.

The body had withered and caved it on itself. Yet the uniform was sharply pressed. She wore black grip shoes and white ceremonial gloves.

Her black hair still framed her face, which even in its mummified condition registered bewilderment and shock. Death, Kim thought, had come on her suddenly and unaware.

"*Kim,*" said the AI, "*I have movement. At nine hundred kilometers.*"

"What kind of movement?"

"*Non-orbital.*"

"Coming our way?" Her hopes soared. Not unmixed with a dash of apprehension.

"*Yes. It is closing at almost one kps.*"

"Close the door and repressurize, Ham. Solly, you hear that?"

"Yes, I did. Ham, is it on an intercept course?"

"*I would describe it as a* collision *course, Solly.*"

"Is it slowing down? Maintaining speed?"

"*It is accelerating.*"

"Okay. Prepare to leave orbit."

"Wait a minute," said Kim. "We don't know that it's hostile."

"It's sure as hell behaving that way. If they want to talk to us they can get on the radio."

"Solly, for God's sake, this is why we came. If somebody's out there and we run for home, what good will it all have been?"

"Kim, trust me. It's coming after us."

He was right. She knew he was right, and it filled her with fury. What kind of stupidity was she facing?

Run.

"Ham," she said, "can you put the object onscreen?"

"*Negative, Kim. It's too far away. But I can tell you it has no identifiable propulsion system.*"

Kim jabbed a fist in the air. "You hear that, Solly? No tubes. It's the same technology. The *Valiant* is the real thing."

"I hear it, Kim. You've been right all along. But it's still dangerous. Ham, are we ready to move out yet?"

"*In fifteen seconds.*"

"Come on, Solly. Think what you're doing."

"I *am* thinking."

"Look how *small* it is."

"That's what bothers me, Kim. Mines are small. Nukes are small. Ships with friendly celestials are *not* small."

"Solly—"

"Trust me. I'd like to make this work the way you want it to. But we don't want to get killed over it. Ham—?"

"*Ready, Solly.*"

"Take us out of here. Accelerate at two gees for the moment. Take best course away from the object." And to Kim: "If that thing's directed by a friendly intelligence, it'll recognize we're scared, and it'll pull off. If it continues to charge, that'll tell us everything we need to know." He opened one of the cargo containers, put the body inside, and secured it.

"They might not think the way we do," she objected.

"Nobody friendly would launch something without trying to talk to us first. Ham, are we getting any kind of radio traffic?"

"No, Solly."

"Put me on the multichannel," Kim said. Solly threw her a pitying look. "It might be a misunderstanding of some sort," she added.

Solly sighed loudly enough for her to hear. "I'm lost out here with a mad scientist," he said.

She spoke into her throat mike: "Hello. This is Kim Brandywine on the *Hammersmith*. We come in peace."

Static.

"Is anybody out there?"

"Just us goblins," said Solly. "My guess is that the whole operation is automatic. You fly in, trigger the alarm, they shoot."

"That couldn't be. It's stupid."

"Maybe it is, but I'll bet you that's what's happening. I'd say these people are a pretty ugly bunch."

Kim tried several more times before giving up. "Where's the object now?" she asked Ham.

"Closing fast. Range sixteen hundred kay."

Solly waited impatiently, trapped in the hold while it repressurized.

"Solly," she said, "Why don't we take a chance here?"

"Kim, they are *hostiles*. What does it take? We'd better admit the reality." A bell dinged and he pulled off his helmet and hurried out of camera range. "Ham," he said, "what else can you tell us about this thing?"

"Its casing deflects sensors, Solly. Regrettably, I can offer little additional data. I can report, however, that it has adjusted course and velocity and continues to gain on us, although it is now doing so at a constant rate. It is still on a collision course."

Kim listened with growing dismay. The thing had all the appearance of a missile. How could they be so goddamn dumb? Like everything else in this business, it made no sense.

Solly came into the room, sat down, and buckled in. "Exciting, huh?" he said.

"I guess I was wrong."

"I guess so." He looked up at the image of the pursuer on the overhead. "Okay, Ham, let's rev it up. Go full ahead."

The *Hammersmith* leaped forward.

"How long until we can make the jump?" asked Solly.

"Twenty-one minutes, ten seconds. Object is still closing."

Estimated time to intercept blinked in the right-hand corner: 17:40. "We can't do it," she said. "We might as well turn around and try to talk to them."

"Talk to a *torpedo*?"

She tried to think. "Don't we have any defensive systems at all?"

"We could go outside and hit it with a stick." Solly looked unhappy. "I wish it were burning fuel."

"Why?"

"It's small. It would run out quickly. What kind of power plant does it have?"

"I can speculate," said Kim

"Go ahead."

"Magnetic force lines is one possibility. Antimatter's another. Maybe quantum cells."

"How do they move without thrusters?"

"Maybe they're using the same kind of technology we use to produce artificial gravity. Except in their case, the field forms *outside* the vehicle. In whatever direction they want it to go. So they just fall into it."

"In either event," said Solly, "they're going to have long-range capability."

"Oh yes," she said. "Certainly. But they might not be able to keep up with us. Keep pouring on the coal."

"You're more optimistic than I am. The damn thing's at seven hundred kay, currently closing at forty-eight per minute. That closure rate's been a constant regardless of our acceleration."

"How about maneuvering?"

"We can try that when it gets closer."

The object was close enough now to have acquired definition. It had hyperbolic lines. In fact, it looked like a flying *saddle*. It even had a horn and side panels that resembled stirrups. Ham drew bar scales to show its size: thirty centimeters long, half as wide. Four centimeters thick. It was *smaller* than a saddle. The exterior was a smooth gray shell, save for a row of black lenses set along the side of the seat. It was white, and she could detect no markings. "It doesn't *look* like a bomb," she said.

"Glad to hear it."

"Can we make a run for the rings? Maybe hide behind something?"

"We're too far away. But I'll tell you what we *can* do."

"Yes?"

"Send a subspace transmission to St. Johns. Copy to Matt. Tell them what we found and what's happening."

"I'm not sure I want to tell the world what we're doing."

"Why?"

"Because we lose control of the discovery if we do that."

Solly looked at her. "I'm beginning to understand what might have happened to the *Hunter*."

"If we get chased off, go back with nothing, somebody else will be out very quick. I'll tell you what, Solly. Let's prepare the package, compress it, and have it ready to go. If it looks as if the worst is going to happen, we'll send it. Okay?"

He agreed and she instructed Ham what was to be done, what the message would say. It was to include a description of everything they'd done so far, especially the discovery of Emily's body, and would recommend that anyone else coming to Alnitak be equipped with defensive systems.

When she'd finished, Solly attached visuals of the object and Ham squeezed everything into a hypercomm transmission that would require less than a second to go out.

Kim had meanwhile been watching the images on the navigation screen. The object continued to close.

"Five minutes to intercept," said Ham.

"Maybe it's a heatseeker," she said. "How about cutting the engines?"

He shook his head. "Our first sighting was at nine hundred kilometers. That's too far out for a heatseeker. Anyway that would be pretty primitive stuff for somebody who doesn't need reaction mass. No, this thing has a visual lock on us. Best we keep running."

They had two clocks posted, one keeping track of time to intercept, and the other, about three minutes behind, the time till jump capability came on line.

"We could try the lander," she said.

"Abandon ship?" He looked at her. "If we do that, the best we can hope for is to spend the rest of our lives here."

"Why in God's name," demanded Kim, "would they do this? The damned thing can't be all that dumb."

"Don't know," said Solly. "I'm not up on my celestial psychology."

Time to intercept clicked inside two minutes.

"Ham, on my command, we'll execute a thirty-degree turn, mark fifteen, to port."

"Solly, at this acceleration, you and your passenger will be subject to extreme stress and possibly even a degree of hazard."

"Thank you, Ham. I appreciate your concern."

"I am always concerned for the welfare of crew and passengers."

The object was fifty kilometers out. One minute away. Solly watched the clock tick down to a final ten seconds. "Ham," he said. "Execute."

The *Hammersmith* rolled hard left and the nose lifted sharply. Kim was thrown to her right. Her organs jammed against one another while the seat shoved up against her. Her heart hammered and her vision got dark and she was afraid she'd black out. The rumble of power in the walls increased, and she tried to concentrate on the blip.

"It went by us," Solly said. And then he looked at her. "You don't look well."

"I'm doing fine," she said.

"Object has commenced to turn," announced Ham.

Kim sat with her eyes closed. For the moment she almost didn't care.

"We bought a minute or so," said Solly.

She shook off her stupor.

"Still closing."

Its image dominated the overhead. It was a preposterous object. Goddamn silly saddle.

"Coming up the tailpipe," said Solly.

And then Ham: *"Sir, it is decelerating. Moving to port."*

It slipped off the screen, appeared again moments later as one of the other imagers picked it up.

"The object is running on a parallel course. Still decelerating."

"Hard right, Ham."

This time it stayed with them.

"Maybe it's not hostile after all," said Kim. "It could have blown our rear end off if it wanted."

"Maybe."

The range finder put it four meters off the port side.

Four.

"It has matched course and speed," said Ham.

The jump status indicator signaled they'd be ready in two minutes to go into hyperspace. "Hold off, Solly," Kim said. "Give them a chance."

"You have a suicide complex, sweetie. But we'll play your game."

"Object at two meters," said Ham.

They watched its image growing larger. Then it was offscreen.

"Where'd it go?" asked Kim, after a long, damp silence.

"It's in close. The sensors aren't picking it up."

"Object," said Ham, *"has attached itself to us."*

They sat without moving, without talking, without breathing.

Kim gripped the arms of her chair, thinking how you really couldn't predict what a celestial might do. "What happens if we make the jump now?" she asked, in a voice so low that Solly had had to lean forward to hear her.

"Hard to say." He also was whispering. "We might get rid of it. Or it might come with us."

Kim's pulse was in her throat. "You still think it's a bomb?"

"What else could it be?"

"Jump status achieved," said the AI.

"Hell," said Kim, "let's go."

Solly didn't need to be persuaded. "Where?" he asked.

"What do you mean?"

"Greenway? Or Tigris?"

"Solly, this is probably not the best time for a discussion group."

"Your call."

"Greenway," she said.

"You're sure?"

"Yes."

Solly looked momentarily thoughtful and then directed the AI to take them home.

The jump engines took over and the lights dimmed. Then the screens were blank, Alnitak was gone, the ringed world was gone, the star-clouds were gone.

"Jump successfully completed," said Ham.

"The object?"

"It's still there."

20

What is it in the cast of a dying moonbeam that suggests a pair of eyes, a watcher in the shadows?

—SHEYEL TOLLIVER, *Notebooks,* 591

"If it were going to blow us up," said Kim, "I'd think it would have done so by now."

"You're probably right. So we should be safe. For the moment."

"How do you mean, *for the moment?*"

"We can't very well take it home."

"Why not?"

"It might be a tracking device."

"You don't really think that's so?"

"What else would it be if it's not a bomb?"

She thought it over. "It could be a gift."

"Like at Troy?"

"Solly, we may be getting a little paranoid here."

"Yep. Of course, there's nothing necessarily wrong with a little paranoia when you're being chased. We've no idea of their capabilities. And so far their intentions don't seem especially friendly."

"Okay," she said. "Let's get rid of it."

Solly nodded. "My thought exactly."

The object clung to the hull, not far from the main air lock.

Solly got up and started for the door. "I'll take care of it," he said.

"What are you going to do?"

They left the pilot's room and walked downstairs. Solly opened a closet in the main floor entry. "Only thing we can do. Go outside and shoo it away." He frowned. "It's probably not dangerous, Kim. If they'd wanted to attack us, they'd have done so by now. Chances are, they're hoping we didn't notice we've got a piggyback."

She nodded. "What do you want *me* to do?"

"Stay put and keep warm." He selected an insulated bar and hefted it. "This should work."

"How about if *I* go out this time?"

"How much EVA experience do you have?"

"How hard can it be?"

"It isn't hard. But it helps to know what you're doing." He kissed her.

"Solly," she said, "why would they put something on the hull that we can just go outside and remove?"

"You're suggesting they didn't."

"That's right. I'm suggesting it isn't going to come loose."

"Let's find out."

Kim had played enough chess to know the basic credo: always assume the opponent will make the best possible move. "I don't like this," she said.

Solly managed to look as if everything were under control. "It might be just a mind game. If it's anything more, if something happens out there, tell Ham to head for St. Johns, okay? Don't go home. If we have to risk losing something, let's make it the outpost and not Greenway."

She felt drained watching him climb into a pressure suit. And she thought suddenly of the Beacon Project. *Here we are. Come get us.* But no, it really couldn't be like that. It was not reasonable.

"What irritates me about all this," she told him over the link as he finished dressing and climbed into the air lock, "is that I never seem to be able to do anything to help."

"So far you've done it all, Kim. Now sit tight and I'll be back in a half hour."

They ran a radio check, shut off the gravity, and turned on all the portside exterior lights. Minutes later the panel indicated the outer door had opened. She directed the AI to watch Solly with whichever imagers it could bring to bear.

"*Kim,*" said Ham, "*he also has a camera atop his helmet.*"

"Can you activate it?"

"*Of course.*"

"Do so."

Pictures appeared on three screens, a side view of Solly, one from the rear, and the view from his helmet. A fourth imager locked on the object.

Solly attached his tether to a safety ring just outside the air lock and strode purposefully across the hull, secured by magnetic boots.

There were no stars, and consequently no sky. Space and time existed in this nether-universe, though the latter seemed to run at a variable rate, and the former was squeezed. This did not resemble, say, a night under thick clouds; because even the clouds would have been *visible*, sensible objects whose presence was *felt*, whose weight pressed down on an observer. This was a true *void*, an absence of everything, a universe which theory held to contain neither matter nor energy, save that which occasionally penetrated from outside, through the agency of jump engines.

It reminded her of the terrifying moments in the spillway, when the world had closed down on her, *buried* her. When the only light, cast by her wristlamp, had faded into a darkness of mind and spirit that might have gone on forever.

Solly moved among the antennas and sensors and housings littering *Hammersmith*'s hull. She watched him draw close to the object, watched him turn his light on it.

It had come to rest between a service hatch and a sensor mount.

"What do you think, Kim?" he asked.

"Don't know," she said. "Be careful."

He touched it with the tip of his bar. There was no reaction. "I'm going to give it a poke," he said.

"Gently," she advised.

"Poking."

She saw no reaction.

"It's on pretty good," said Solly. "Probably magnetized."

He stooped down and tried to wedge the bar *beneath* it. The saddle seat irised open. Kim jumped.

So did Solly.

It was as if a dark eye looked up at them.

"Solly," she breathed.

"I see it." The opening was as wide around as her hand was long. The darkness was palpable, a couple of centimeters deep.

"Be careful."

Solly waited to see whether anything else would happen. When it didn't, he went back to trying to work the bar under the object. Kim's view was poor: everything was a mix of shadows and bright lights and

Solly's arms. She wished they could bring it inside, look at it, but even that seemed dangerous.

Who would have believed it? They had obtained an apparently genuine extraterrestrial artifact, and they were going to throw it away.

She wanted desperately for this to be over and Solly to be back inside.

He worked the bar in and was grunting loudly as he pushed down. And suddenly the hull and the sensor mount, half-seen in the uncertain light, seemed to *ripple*.

The effect came and went so quickly that she wasn't sure she'd really seen it.

The object came loose.

"Okay," Solly said. He got his right hand under it and peeled it off like a man removing an orange skin. When it was clear, he lifted it high, held it for her to see and the imager to record, turned it a half dozen ways so they missed nothing. Then he flung it away. She watched it spin out into the dark.

"Good show, Solly."

"Thanks."

Solly pushed the bar into his belt and retreated into the air lock. He switched over to the AI's channel. "Ham, where's the object?"

"Still outbound, Solly. At three kilometers per hour. Showing no sign of internal power."

She glanced up at the screen dedicated to Solly's helmet imager and watched the lights come on in the air lock. The door swung shut and gravity returned throughout the ship. She could see the bench opposite the one he was sitting on. And part of the control panel, a blinking amber lamp, a hand rail, and one of Solly's feet.

"Ham," he said, "Track the object as long as you're able. If there's any change, let us know."

"I'll do that, Solly."

The amber lamp would continue to blink until air pressure reached normal. Then it would turn green.

Kim was wrestling with the problem. It was possible the *Hunter* had blundered the first contact, and it might be that she was now doing the same thing. "We might wind up being a laughingstock for future historians, Solly," she said.

"I just don't like any of this, Kim. We've established there's something here. Now I think we need to turn the whole thing over to a team that can come out here prepared to—"

The amber light dulled.

And brightened.

It wasn't supposed to do that.

"—To do the thing systematically," Solly concluded.

Behind the lamp, the wall and the control panel *wrinkled.* In the way of a strip of pavement on a hot day.

It was gone almost before the sensation had registered. "Solly," she said, "are we having an imager problem?"

"No," he said. "I saw it too." The silence in the ship was overwhelming. She left the pilot's room and was waiting by the air lock when it opened. Solly came out.

She put all the lights on in the entryway and looked into the air lock. Everything seemed normal.

"Ham," she said. "Rerun the sequence from the helmet imager, beginning about four minutes ago. Put it on one of the entry windows."

There were two large windows in the entryway. Both had carried images of the skies as they might have been seen from Greenway. Now one went dark and then lit up with Solly entering the air lock.

"Too recent," she said. "Back it up another couple of minutes."

"It was just a power dip," said Solly.

"Maybe."

She watched him moving rapidly backward, saw the saddle in reverse flight, watched it sail in toward him, saw him put it down on the hull. Use the bar.

Solly-in-the-window worked backward furiously on the saddle. The circular opening in the seat closed.

"Okay," she said. "Stop, Ham. Run it forward."

Solly laid his helmet down, peeled off the suit, and sat down to get out of the boots.

The sensor mount rippled again.

"Ham," said Kim, "hold it."

Solly's brow creased. They ran it several times. Then she took him to the sequence in the air lock, and they watched the amber lamp fade and brighten and the control panel lose its definition. It seemed to fold slightly, and darken, as if something had passed in front of it, as if the space it occupied had changed in some indefinable way.

"Does that—" she stared at the image on the monitor, "—normally happen out here?"

"No." He switched over to the forward hull imager, backed up the record, and they watched the entire scenario from another angle.

The sensor mount was in the foreground. Solly was behind it. And this time, it was *Solly* who rippled.

"I don't understand that," he said.

Kim's heart had picked up a beat. "It scares me, Solly."

When they peeled away her jumpsuit, they saw that something had cut Emily almost in half at the waist. The flesh was charred, the trunk partially severed, but there was no blood.

"They cleaned her up before putting her out the airlock," said Solly, pulling a sheet over the mutilated body.

"What could have happened to her?" asked Kim.

"A laser, maybe." Solly looked puzzled.

They returned the corpse to its container and Kim kept reminding herself that at least now she knew. But it wasn't much consolation.

Analysis of the recordings provided no clue as to what, if anything, had happened on the hull or in the air lock. A trick of the light, perhaps. Or disturbances in the space-time continuum. After all, Solly had been *outside* the ship. Maybe there *were* side effects when you opened up air locks to hyperspace. Indeed, no other explanation offered itself. So they put it out of their minds, as best they could, and resumed their normal shipboard routine.

And as the days passed with no recurrence of the effect, they forgot about it altogether.

Meantime, the conversation centered on the kind of reception they'd receive when they got back to Greenway. Police or a parade? Kim was unwaveringly optimistic. You cannot prosecute the person who answers one of the great all-time scientific and philosophical questions. Solly, who'd been around longer, suggested that their accomplishment would only serve to anger Agostino even more. "We might look good to posterity," he said, "but the locals may take a different view. Remember Columbus?"

"What about him?"

"Died in a Spanish prison."

On the other hand, Kim thought Agostino could be relied on to milk the mission for all it was worth, to make it sound as if it had been an

Institute initiative from the start. In that case, their careers would be safe as long as they cooperated.

Kim believed her interest in the sciences to be generally selfless, spurred primarily by a desire to push the frontiers of knowledge forward, to be part of the collective effort. She didn't think she'd been in it for herself. But she resented the prospect that someone else might try to grab the credit after she'd gone through so much.

Five nights out of Alnitak, Kim, absorbed in these thoughts, was showering for dinner.

Because there were only two people on board, there was no pressing need to conserve the water supply. She had just rinsed her hair and was using a towel to dry her face before opening her eyes. But she sensed movement in the washroom.

"Solly?" she asked.

Once before he'd slipped in while she was in the shower, and had taken advantage of the opportunity, wrapping the curtain around her and fondling her through the translucent plastic.

But he did not answer and when she looked no one was there.

She dismissed the incident and the mild disappointment, dressed, and went down the hall for dinner, which included chicken, a fruit salad, and hot bread. They were talking about inconsequentials when Ham broke in: *"Solly,"* he said. *"I am losing control over some of my functions. They are being rerouted elsewhere. To an alternate manager."*

"That can't be," said Solly. "Are you reporting a virus?"

"It is difficult to say precisely what the cause is, Solly."

"Which systems are you losing?"

"I am having some difficulty with communications, diagnostics, life support. The deterioration is continuing as we speak."

"Ham, what can we do to rectify the situation?"

"I do not know. You might wish to consider going to manual. If the process continues, I will shortly become unreliable."

"Can we do that?" asked Kim. "Can we get home on manual?"

"Oh, sure," said Solly. "It just means we'll have to throw all the switches ourselves. And we might chip a little paint at the dock. Otherwise it's no problem." Nevertheless he looked worried.

They finished dinner, somewhat at less leisure than they'd begun, and went across to the pilot's room. Kim took some of the hot bread with her.

Solly removed a wall panel marked AUTO OFF. "Ham," he said, "I'll check with you periodically. Try to locate the problem and eliminate it."

"Yes, Solly. I am endeavoring to do that."

His fingers touched a pumpkin-colored handle and moved it forward. A row of orange lamps came on. "The pilot finally gets to earn his pay," he told Kim.

"Where do we go from here?" she asked.

"We relax." He gestured toward the navigation console, which was built into a desk. "If you see any red lights and I'm not here, call me."

"If something happened, wouldn't the Klaxons sound?"

"Maybe. If we've got a virus in the system, everything becomes unreliable." He must have seen the doubt in her face. "But don't worry. We'll be fine."

"That's it?"

"That's it. The ship is pretty much still automated. It'll still produce hot water, prepare the food, recharge the power cells. The only difference now is that we're going to have to punch some buttons to make things happen." He paused, considering their situation. "If there's a variance between actual conditions and prescribed conditions, the ship may not notice. Which means we might have to turn up the thermostat once in a while. Piece of cake, other than the inconvenience."

Kim took a long time to ask the question that really bothered her. "Solly," she said, "do you think it's possible—?" She hesitated.

"—That—?"

"—The virus came from the *device*?"

"No," he said, perhaps a little too quickly. "It's a glitch in the programming, Kim." He hesitated. "It happens."

Kim studiously avoided bringing the subject up again. That evening they wandered down to the rec room and watched, but did not participate in, *Party of Five*, a light comedy in which the lead characters discover they are living next door to a group marriage with two husbands and three wives.

Party of Five did not get many laughs, and Kim spent most of her time thinking how cavernous the ship felt. Solly tried to look relaxed, but he kept laughing at the wrong parts.

Before they went to bed, he reactivated the AI, but did not return control of the systems to it. "Ham, have you been making progress with the virus?"

The windows opened out onto an ocean. In the distance, Kim could see a whale spouting.

"Ham?" said Solly. "Answer up."

He glanced sidewise at her and tried again. The AI had always responded within seconds.

Kim got up, put her hands in her pockets, and turned away from the seascape. "It sounds as if it's down altogether," she said.

"Apparently."

"Ever know it to happen before?"

"Never. But this is also the first time I've had to shut down an AI. Maybe it has that kind of effect."

"Ham," she said. "Are you there?"

They went up to the pilot's room and Solly sat down at the console and initiated a diagnostic. "This'll take a few minutes," he said.

The windows opened onto the same seascape, although the whale was gone.

"When we get back," she said suddenly, "you aren't going to walk away from me, are you?"

"No." Solly put an arm around her. "I love you, Kim."

He gathered her in and they kissed.

"Kim—" he said.

"Yes—?"

"Will you marry me?"

It came without warning. "Yeah," she said, carefully keeping her voice level. "I think I'd like to do that."

The diagnostic chimed. It showed no problem. Everything was fine.

"That can't be," said Solly. "I mean, we can't even raise the AI."

Solly broke out the captain's best stock that evening to celebrate their engagement. They made love to candlelight and soft music, starting in the briefing room, where the windows were full-length and provided a glorious view from the top of Mount Morghani, pausing once on the third-floor landing, and continuing with unabated zeal into the bedroom.

Even though they were alone on the ship, Kim always took care to close the bedroom door. On this occasion, however, Solly carried her in and tumbled her among the sheets, and so the door remained open.

The night went on and on, with occasional downtime for him during which they talked of the future. And then Solly came for her again, and she delightedly gave herself to him.

He was inexhaustible that night. Even with a body that was effectively twenty years old, he seemed to be performing above and beyond the call.

But she stayed with him and there came a moment when he was lying with his head toward the foot of the bed and he brought her down atop him, turning her on her back, spread-eagling her.

She luxuriated in the sensation of his body beneath hers, his lips against the nape of her neck, his hands exploring her. The illumination in the ship had dimmed to nighttime levels, which meant the passageway behind her was dark save for the soft glow of the security lights.

Her head was thrown back in ecstasy and she was groaning and sighing, partly because she was inclined to do so, partly because she knew it inflamed him. Her line of vision went through the open door into the corridor.

And she saw something move.

It was a glimmer, a shadow, something at the far edge of awareness. Yet it was there.

She was immediately trying to get Solly to stop. But he was at full throttle.

Something was taking shape back there.

A pair of eyes. From the darkness near the top of the doorway, just outside in the corridor.

Suddenly she was back in Kane's villa, terrified in the cool emotionless gaze of the thing in that *other* passageway. Solly's hands were still holding her, playing with her. She pulled them away and rolled off onto the floor and, without taking her eyes from the apparition, got Solly to understand something was wrong and began feeling around for a weapon. The best she could find was a shoe.

"What's the matter?" he asked, startled.

The eyes were the same emerald color, but flecked with gold. Vertical irises. Cat's eyes. Cool, dispassionate, surgical. Very much like the thing in Kane's villa. But she saw no madness here. Only malevolence.

The eyes were disembodied.

They floated a few centimeters from the ceiling.

Solly was staring down at her but she held a hand against his back, trying to get him to stay still. She found the remote, which was on a side table, and touched it. The lights came on.

Solly looked at her. Looked out into the passageway.

It was empty.

"Kim?" Solly looked down at her. "What's wrong?"

She was weak, unable to move. "It was outside the room."

"Outside? *What* was outside?" He padded into the corridor and looked both ways. "Nothing here," he said. "What did you think you saw?"

She tried to describe it but it just came out sounding hallucinatory.

"All right," he said, when she'd compared it to the thing in the lake. "Let's find out."

She got into her clothes and Solly pulled on a pair of shorts and detached a lampstand to use as a weapon. Then they examined each room on the third floor, Solly doing the actual search while Kim stayed in the corridor to ensure that nothing got behind them.

He looked in closets and cabinets and behind beds. They moved with deliberation, and Kim was pleased to see that, despite the absurdity of her claim, he took her seriously rather than simply trying to argue what he must have thought: that she'd been seeing things.

They went down to the second floor and repeated the process, and then finally they searched the bottom of the ship. Long windows allowed them to see into all of the storage areas and the launch bay. He even climbed down into the lander through the open cockpit. The lander itself was attached to the *Hammersmith*'s underside. They inspected the areas given over to the recycling systems, water tanks, and cargo. They looked in the engine room. When they were finished he turned to her. "Kim, there's no place left to hide."

It didn't matter. "I saw it," she said. It was impossible, and she wanted to put it aside, wanted desperately to believe it was an illusion. A *dream*. A result of the wine she'd drunk earlier in the evening. But she'd been wide awake. Solly had seen to that.

"It was there," she said. "It vanished when I put on the lights."

"Like a reflection would have done."

"Yes."

"But it wasn't a reflection."

"No. It wasn't. Couldn't have been."

There was egress to interior wiring and systems compartments through several access panels. But it would have required time to remove and then replace them. He looked at them, and they were locked down tight.

"I saw it."

"I believe you."

They went back up to their room, walking softly along the carpeted floors, and turned out the lights, returning the ship's illumination to what it had been. Kim looked into the semidarkness, studied the row of tiny security lamps which came on automatically when the ship dimmed down for nighttime running. There was nothing that could have fooled her into thinking she'd seen a pair of eyes.

The most frightening aspect was the thing's resemblance to the earlier apparition. She wondered if it had somehow contrived to follow her out here.

She'd brushed aside the experience in the Severin Valley, locked it in a remote corner of her mind, and convinced herself it had been a trick of the light, or a product of an oversupply of oxygen.

Now she was confronted by it again. And for the first time in her adult life, she questioned her worldview, her assumption that the universe was rational. That it was governed by self-consistent laws. That there was no place for the supernatural.

"You all right, Kim?" He was standing over her, pulling on his clothes, obviously worried.

"I'm fine," she said.

There was another, more likely, possibility.

She sat down at the console and replayed the visuals from Solly's helmet imager, stopping the display when the ripples appeared, on the hull and in the air lock.

The thing she'd seen was connected with the saddle. The object had not been a bomb; it had been a *transport*.

If that were so, she wondered whether she and Solly could even talk to each other without being overheard. Had the celestials mastered enough of the language to eavesdrop?

She told Solly what she thought.

"Okay," Solly said. "We'll proceed on the assumption we've got an intruder. That would explain what's happening to Ham as well."

"There is *this*," she told him. "At least it won't try to murder us in our sleep."

"I don't want to be downbeat on this, but why not?"

"Because it wants to follow us home."

"Kim, I hate to point this out." He lowered his voice. "The course is already set. If it were to get us out of the way, all it would have to do is sit tight and ride old Ham into port."

They were sitting on the bed, staring out into the corridor, which now seemed like strange territory, a passageway from another world. "No," she said. "It probably doesn't know what leg of the trip we're on. It'll want us functioning until we get home. Until it can be sure."

"I hope."

21

FOR COURAGE IN EXTREMITY

—Inscription on the Conciliar Medal of Valor

In the morning, they searched the vessel again, all three floors, the engine room, the lander, and every other space they could think of. Solly removed the various access panels and peered back among the cables and circuits. They found nothing. "It's hard to believe there's anything on board that shouldn't be here," he said.

Reluctantly, she said what they both must have been thinking: "Maybe we shouldn't go home."

They were sitting in the wingback chairs in the briefing room. It was late afternoon; both were exhausted from the long hunt and its accompanying frustrations. "Kim," said Solly, "we can interrupt the flight anytime and call for help. But then what do we do? If it could get aboard without our seeing it, it'll do the same to any rescue ship." He rubbed his eyes. "We've done everything we can to ensure there's no intruder. So either we go home, or we sit out here somewhere until the food runs out."

During the search, Kim had sensed that he was becoming skeptical of her story. In full-daylight mode, the *Hammersmith*'s rooms and corridors seemed less threatening and the danger more remote. The choices, should they determine they actually had an intruder, were stark. Best to write the incident off as the result of dim lighting, heated passions, and too much alcohol. "Look," he said, "at worst, all we have to do is maintain control of hypercomm, don't let it transmit anything, and we don't have to worry. No matter what else happens."

"Are we sure we can do that?"

"I can take a wrench to it if I have to."

■   ■   ■

The return trip remained somber. Kim kept their bedroom door closed, for whatever good that might do. It was, she complained to Solly, like sleeping in a haunted house. The days passed without incident, but Kim knew the thing was there, drifting through coils and corridors, just outside the range of vision. Occasionally, she caught glimpses of it, the eyes sometimes formed of light from a lamp, of steam from a shower. There were movements in the dark, the sense of a cold current brushing her ankle, the sound of whispering in the bulkheads. Even the murmur of the ship's electronics occasionally sounded malevolent.

If Solly picked any of this up, he said nothing.

Unavoidably, the sex became infrequent. When it did occur, it was distracted, stealthy, hurried, as though there were others in the ship who might happen on them at any moment.

The spontaneity drained away. During what she had already begun to think of as the good old days, encounters might begin and eventually be consummated anywhere in the ship. Now, wherever they might start, they concluded behind the closed doors of their sleeping compartment. After Kim had put on the light and inspected it.

She felt exposed and vulnerable when they were both asleep. But when she broached the subject to Solly he looked so dismayed that she did not push for a watchstanding system.

He must be thinking of her as a frightened child, wondering what sort of relationship he'd got himself into. But she *felt* like a frightened child. Were their places reversed, had it been Solly who was seeing things in empty corridors, *she* would certainly be rethinking the relationship. She feared she might lose him over this, and that might be the worst of it. But she couldn't help herself. There was a hazard, and Solly didn't entirely believe her.

She grew resentful, of Solly, and of her own fears. And she acquired an unrelenting hatred for the *thing* that had taken up residence with them. She waited, and literally *prayed*, for it to show itself in some substantive way.

Solly's efforts to get the AI back online produced no discernible results. Occasionally there were nonsense voice responses, asserting that passengers should prepare for acceleration, or that the food preparation system was suffering from an overload and needed a new conduction unit. It suggested course changes and adjustments in mission parameters and wished them good morning at all hours.

"We need somebody who knows what he's doing," Solly grumbled, but he never stopped trying.

Without Ham, he had to get his hands dirty on occasion. He found himself performing routine duties such as managing power flow adjustments. Because some systems had gone down with the AI, he wasn't necessarily alerted when malfunctions happened, nor was there a system to tell him the nature of the problem. So when internal communications crashed, he needed several hours and a lot of crawling around on hands and knees to locate and replace a faulty relay. Self-test procedures run regularly by the jump engines developed an aberration that periodically set Klaxons sounding throughout the ship. He couldn't figure that one out at all and simply shut the alarms down, hoping the engines wouldn't develop a fatal flaw in the meantime.

Solly commented that he was learning a lot this trip.

Kim helped wherever she could, which wasn't often. Electronics was not her forte, but she asked questions and she too was learning.

The closest they came to a serious problem arose during the third week when the klaxons sounded one night at three A.M., signaling that the oxygen–nitrogen mix was exceeding parameters. Solly didn't know what to do about that, and the alarms continued sporadically during the next few hours, warning of a deteriorating condition. He growled that for all they knew the problem was with the alarm system rather than life support, but he continued working on it, replacing every part he could reach until finally the clamor stopped.

Kim's normal high spirits never returned. She no longer wandered through the ship on her own, but rather stayed close to Solly. She read more extensively than ever before, mostly books and articles in her specialty, but also novels and histories and even Simon Westcott, the classic second century philosopher who'd tried to explain how consciousness had developed in a mechanistic universe.

Occasionally, when she was alone, she caught herself speaking to the visitor. "I know you're there," she told it, keeping her voice down so Solly wouldn't overhear.

"Why don't you show yourself?"

Toward the end of the voyage, the debate went underground, where it simmered like a waste-disposal system occasionally leaking noxious fumes. There was simply nothing more to say. During the last three weeks, Kim saw nothing out of the ordinary. She tried to talk herself into dismissing the apparition, or at least into locking it away in a corner of her mind where it could cause no disruption, much as she had the earlier experience at Remorse. But *then* she'd been able to get away from the Severin Valley. Now she was bolted in with the thing.

So there'd been an uneasy moratorium, a studied avoidance of the subject. Conversation necessarily became guarded rather than informative, ceremonial rather than intimate. It was like having a rhinoceros on board, whose presence no one wanted to recognize.

On the last day however, as they approached jump status, Solly broached the subject. "I'm sorry the flight turned out the way it did," he said.

His tone suggested he wasn't holding her aberration against her. "It's not your fault," she said, carefully restraining the anger that began to stir.

"We need to decide whether we're going to report the incident."

Translation: Do you want to admit to having a hallucination?

They were both in the pilot's room. Everything was in order, and the clock was counting down. Solly was waiting for the status lamps to light, after which he would push the EXECUTE key, and they would leap across into their own universe.

"Got a question," Kim said, casually.

"Go ahead."

"When we use the hypercomm transmitter, how do we know it's in use?"

His jaw tightened. "Could you rephrase that, Kim? How could I *not* know I'm using it?"

She tried again. "When we're communicating via hypercomm, does something light up on the status board?"

"Right here." He pointed at a pair of lamps atop the communication console. "*Orange* means Ham's begun the operation, that a channel is being opened, and *green* means it's okay to talk."

"Can you test it?"

"Test what?"

"Test the system. See if it works."

"Kim, why?" He looked puzzled.

"Humor me, Solly. Please."

Ordinarily he would simply have asked Ham to open the channel. Now it was necessary to pull the control board across his lap, consult his manual, press some keys.

"Well?" she asked.

"That's odd."

No lights.

"Problem?"

"The status lamps should have lit up," he said.

"So as things are now, if someone were transmitting, we wouldn't know."

He checked the bulbs. Both were scorched. "How'd you guess?"

She shrugged. "It seemed like a possibility."

He went back to the utility locker and returned with fresh lamps. "This has to do with the intruder, right?"

"I don't like what's happening, Solly." She was suddenly desperately weary, anxious to see real sunlight again, and a real ocean. The virtual expanses of *Hammersmith*'s projection system just didn't cut it. No matter how vast the stretches of sea and beach might appear, she always knew she was inside a chamber. "When do you expect we'll be docking?" she asked.

"About six in the morning."

It was not quite ten A.M., and they were just a few minutes from the jump. "Twenty hours?" she asked. "That seems kind of long."

"It's because of the time differential in hyperflight," he said. "We never know quite where we'll materialize. So we want to be well away from Greenway."

"Sounds good to me."

"Check your harness."

She could hear power gathering in the jump engines. Solly activated the external sensors and telescopes. She sat back, but kept an eye on the hypercomm lamps.

As they clicked down to one minute, Solly sighed. "You really expect something to happen, don't you?"

"I think something just did," she said. "In any case, to answer your question: Yes, I think we should contact Matt as soon as we're able. I want to tell him what's going on."

"So what are you going to say? That you think there's something on board that shouldn't be here?"

"That's right."

He grew somber. "If you do that, we may not get home anytime within the foreseeable future. You'll scare them out of their socks, and we'll spend the next few years on old *Hammersmith*."

"I don't know what else to do, Solly," she said.

The clock ran down to zero and he pressed the key.

A wave of vertigo passed behind her eyes. But she tried to control her breathing and think of other things. Like how good it had been with Solly, despite the problems. Like the fact that Emily's body was downstairs and somebody was going to pay up for that.

The sensation passed quickly and the windows lit up with familiar constellations. Greenway and its moons appeared on one of the auxiliary screens.

"Transition complete," he said.

Kim nodded and kept her eyes on the hypercomm lamps.

Solly opened a channel to Sky Harbor. "This is *Hammersmith*. Approaching on manual. Computer out. Request assistance."

While they waited for the signal to reach Greenway, and for the controllers to respond, Solly looked over his instruments. "Everything seems normal," he said.

Kim couldn't sort her feelings out. She wanted the problem to go away, wanted to get home with her discovery, wanted to enjoy her accomplishment. But she also wanted to be proved *right*, for Solly to see that the apparition had substance. Maybe she wanted to demonstrate that to herself as well. She wanted an apology from *somebody*.

"*Hammersmith*, this is Sky Harbor." A female voice. "We've been expecting you. Patrol will escort you in." They gave Solly a course and speed.

"That doesn't sound good," he said.

He brought the ship around to the prescribed heading and fired the mains. A blip appeared on the long-range navigation screen. "That'll be our escort," he said.

"How far are they?"

"Several hours."

Something caught Kim's attention. A movement, a shift in the light. She looked around the pilot's room. Nothing seemed changed.

"Problem?" Solly asked.

"Don't know." She reached over and touched the hypercomm lamps. They were *warm*. "I think they're out again," she said.

He frowned and tried them for himself. And then scowled. He removed the orange lamp and held it up to his eyes. "They sure are."

"Is there any other way to know whether we're transmitting?"

"Yes." He punched a button. "Patrol, *Hammersmith*. Do you read?"

"*Hammersmith*, this is Patrol one-one. Affirmative. Do you require assistance?" Male voice this time, Bondolay accent. Lots of *r*'s.

"Are we showing a hypercomm transmission?"

"Wait one." He sounded as if he were being patient. Kim wiped her mouth while she waited for the response, which seemed to take an interminably long time. Then the voice was back: "*Hammersmith*," he said, "that is affirmative." He sounded puzzled. How could *Hammersmith* be transmitting and the pilot not know? "Is there a problem?"

"Computer is down," Solly said, climbing out of his chair. "And we're having some other minor malfunctions." He signed off and left the pilot's room in a dead run. Minutes later he was back, his face pale. "You were right, Kim," he said. "There *is* something in the works and the son of a bitch is trying to talk to the folks at home."

"The first thing it'll do," she said, "is tell them where Greenway is. Turn off the transmitter."

"I just did."

"Good."

He opened the channel again. "Patrol, this is *Hammersmith*. Has the subspace transmission ceased?"

"Negative." The voice paused. "*Hammersmith*, what is your situation?"

"I think we ought to tell them," said Kim.

"That would *not* be a good idea. If they believed us, we might just get a missile up our tailpipe."

"I don't believe they'd do that."

"Don't be too sure. This situation has suddenly become very scary."

Suddenly. "Solly. It's *always* been scary." She couldn't keep the note of recrimination out of her voice.

He tried to apologize, but she brushed it away. No matter. It's okay.

It wasn't, of course. But deep down she felt a sense of gratification that she'd been shown to be right.

He talked to the Patrol again, detailing the mechanical problems. "This is becoming a nightmare," he told her. Then he shut down the engines.

"You said something about taking a wrench to it," she said.

"That's what we have to do. But it's on the lower level, back in the woodwork. It'll take a half hour or more. That's too much time."

"So what do we do?"

"Give me a moment." He handed her a wristlamp, told her to turn it on, and opened a closet. He vanished inside and she heard him moving things around, heard the sound of a panel sliding back, and then the room went dark. But it wasn't like the normal darkness in the pilot's room, where one could sit in the glow of the instrument panels. *Everything* died: screens, gauges, status lamps, telltales, the electronic burble of the equipment. The place had gone completely black and silent. She tried to change her position and felt herself rising out of the seat. The artificial gravity was off.

A few security lights, operating on a separate circuit, began to glow. A battery lantern snapped on behind her. "That'll stop it," he said.

"I hate to bring this up." She was afloat now. "Do we still have life support?"

"No. Everything's shut down, except the engines. They're on a bypass. But we'll be okay long enough to disable the transmitter."

They switched to grip shoes and went down to the bottom floor, where long windows looked into the cargo and storage bays. The lamps threw shadows behind stocks of food, esoteric equipment that would have been used in the Taratuba mission, the recycling units, and the gravity control system. Solly opened a cabinet and picked out some tools. Satisfied, he led her toward the front of the ship.

Twin water tanks were housed forward in bays on either side of the passageway. They entered the starboard side and knelt down beside the tank. Solly anchored the lantern, which had a magnetic base, and began removing a panel.

Kim watched him work, got up, and went back into the corridor. She could see the stairway at the rear, outlined by security lights. In the launch bay, in the glow of her wristlamp, the lander's cockpit looked like a fish's head, rising through the floor. Its circular viewports stared back at her.

Solly laid the panel alongside the tank and looked inside the wall at a crawl space. "It'll take a while," he said, ducking into it. "I have to remove some other stuff to get at the transmitter." He took the lantern and was gone.

The darkness pressed down on her.

She could hear the clink of Solly's tools and the occasional scrape of metal on metal. Now and then something banged. The noise lifted her spirits. She stayed close by.

After a few minutes she heard a grunt of satisfaction. "That'll do for the son of a bitch," he said.

At that moment, a circle of illumination snapped on at the top of the staircase and her weight came back with the force of a blow between the shoulder blades. Although both shoes had been in contact with the deck, it was nonetheless like stepping into an unexpected hole in an unlit room. She twisted her knee and yelped. "Solly," she cried, "warn me next time." Her voice echoed off the walls.

"Wasn't me," he yelled.

Lights were coming on everywhere, in the passageway, the individual bays, even in the crawl space.

"Power's back on!" she said.

"I can see *that*. This goddamn thing could have juiced me."

She smelled something burning. Then he reappeared. "One problem settled anyhow," he said. "Nobody's going to communicate with *anybody*."

"Solly." She kept her voice very low. "Why'd the power come back on?"

"Somebody *turned* it on." He was holding the wrench in his right hand.

"What do we do now?"

"We're going to get rid of our visitor."

"How do we do that? We can't even *find* it."

They returned down the corridor and stood at the foot of the staircase, looking up at the landing. The airtight door at the top was open, just as they'd left it.

"We need to get some help," she said.

"That might not be easy. I just finished off the transmitter."

"You mean we can't communicate locally either?"

"Not with anybody outside screaming range. I would have just disabled the hypercomm function if I'd known how. Takes a goddamn engineer to figure some of this equipment out."

"So what's next?" she asked.

Solly put his arm around her and held her for a moment. "Stick with me."

He led the way up the staircase and with noticeable reluctance put his head through the open door and looked both ways along the corridor. "Don't see anything," he said.

The doors to the various compartments were all closed, save for the rec room, which was always open. They peeked in, saw nothing, and climbed to the top floor.

From the pilot's room came the quiet murmur of the instruments. Everything was back on line.

Kim was alarmed to see that the status board was blinking red, but Solly explained it was only a warning that there was no transmission capability.

The Patrol was talking to them, asking what was wrong, pointing out they were off course, urging them to respond, assuring them help was on the way. They would be alongside, they said, in two hours.

Solly went back into the closet and showed her the power cutoff. It was a long black handle. It was *up*, in the white area, designated ON. "That caps it," said Solly. "We *do* have an intruder."

"No way it could trip back itself?"

"No," he said. "It's not supposed to be possible for it to turn itself on or off."

"Maybe," said Kim, "we should blink our lights for the Patrol. Let them know we've no communications."

"They'll figure it out on their own." He slumped into a seat. "It's invisible. But it's solid, right? It has to be. I mean, it turns handles."

"No," Kim said. "We know it's *physical*. That's not quite the same thing as being *solid*."

"Well, whatever, it's time to get rid of it."

"How?"

"Easy." He took two pressure suits out of the utility locker and handed her one. "Put this on."

"Why? What's the plan?"

"We're going to blow it out the door."

At first she didn't know what he meant. And then she understood. "Depressurize," she said.

"Sure. It's the only way I know."

"Brilliant, Solly," she said. "I'd never have thought of it."

He shrugged. "I saw it done in an old video."

She stripped off her outer clothes and got into the suit. It was the first time she'd ever worn one and she needed help to secure the helmet properly. "You okay?" he asked.

She felt as if she couldn't get enough air.

"Just relax," he said. He did something to her backpack. "How's that?"

Better. "Thanks."

"It's okay." He showed her the controls on her gloves, how she could adjust temperature, the air mix, whatever, and pulled on his own suit while she demonstrated she knew how to handle everything. He locked down his helmet and ran a radio check.

"Now," he said, "let's get rid of the pest."

They stowed their personal gear, toothbrushes, soap, clothes, commlinks. Then they walked through the ship, all three floors, opening every interior hatch, and leaving them open. When they'd finished they returned to the pilot's room and sat down. Kim looked around, could see nothing else that required their attention. "I think we're ready," she said.

Solly nodded, turned off the blowers, and shut down the air supply.

Kim punched the stud on the arm of her chair, and the harness settled over her. "All set," she said.

Solly leaned over the console and his fingers flashed across the keyboard.

"What's going on?" she asked.

"I have to override the safety routines. But we're in business now."

The Patrol voice asked again whether *Hammersmith* was receiving. "Please blink your lights if you hear me," he said. And a moment later: "We have traffic for you from the Seabright Institute. Please respond if you are able."

"Solly," she said, "did you hear that?"

"Business first."

"Okay," she said.

"Opening up."

She heard a hatch downstairs turning on its bearings. Then a murmur that escalated rapidly into a hurricane of sound. Wind swirled around her and tried to suck her out of the chair. Loose objects sailed past.

It lasted about two minutes. Then, as quickly as it had begun, it subsided, and the ship fell silent.

"We've got vacuum," said Solly.

They unbuckled and went downstairs to the air lock and looked out. Helios was behind them. The three bright stars of Orion's Belt glittered in the night. "What do you think?" he asked.

"It should have worked. There's no life-form *I* ever heard of that can resist a total depressurization."

"How long should we leave it open?"

"I'd give it a couple of hours. I don't suppose you saw anything unusual go out?"

"No."

"Pity."

They went back to the pilot's room where Solly blinked the running lights.

"Please inform us if you can hear this transmission," came the reply. "One blink for yes. Two for no."

Solly blinked once.

"Are you in imminent danger?"

Solly blinked twice. Not that it made any real difference, as far as Kim could see. She doubted they could get here any faster.

The Patrol asked whether the pilot had control of the vehicle.

Solly blinked once.

Could they go to a new course?

One blink.

They set the directed course and speed. Then they began responding to queries about *Hammersmith*'s condition. Finally the Patrol vessel pronounced itself satisfied there was no immediate crisis and put the Institute on the circuit.

"Hello." It was Matt's voice. "Solly, are you okay? Kim? Is everyone all right?"

Solly blinked once and heard the Patrol relay the answer. "*Yes.*"

"They tell me you've got problems with the radio and can't respond." He sounded relieved. "But they think you're doing okay, and they'll have you out of there pretty soon. We're glad to see you back home. I don't think the official powers are happy, but they've got their ship back. Maybe they won't prosecute. I'm leaving in a few hours and I'll meet you at Sky Harbor. Did you have any luck?"

"He sounds subdued," suggested Solly. "How do you want me to answer him?"

"Tell him *yes.*"

Solly blinked once.

"Do you mean you *found* something?"

Yes.

"Intelligence?"

She was thinking this was not something they'd want to discuss in public and Matt knew it but he couldn't restrain himself.

Yes.

"I'll meet you when you dock."

He signed off. "Prosecution," said Solly, "probably depends on whether Phil is happy with the results."

"He won't be happy," said Kim. "We met a celestial and we killed it." She was quiet for a while. Then: "Why not try the AI? Let's see if it's back."

"Ham," said Solly, "are you there?"

"*I'm here, Solly.*"

Another good sign. Solly let out his breath. "Thank God," he said.

"Are you fully functional, Ham?" asked Kim.

"*Yes. I believe so.*"

"Do you know what happened to you?"

"*I was—*"

"Yes?"

"*—taken over—*"

"Go ahead, Ham."

"*By an intelligence.*"

"Artificial?"

"*I do not know.*"

"Is it gone now?"

"*I do not detect its presence. Although I suspect it could hide itself from me if it wished.*"

"What can you tell us about it?"

"*It is not listed in the catalog.*"

"Was it biological?" Kim was asking the questions while Solly listened.

"*I don't think so. I believe it was molecular, and that it was powered by electrical fields, possibly generated by accelerated quantum activity. It was quite a unique presence. It seems to have been designed for a specific purpose.*"

"What purpose?"

"*I would say to seize a starship.*"

"I wonder," said Solly, "if it was supposed to grab us before we left the Alnitak system?"

"It's possible," said Kim. "It would have had to be pretty quick to do that."

"*I think there was an alternate function. With respect to us.*"

"And that was—?"

"*To remain with the ship and inform its—*" the AI searched for a word, "*—inform its supervisor of our final destination.*"

"Who is the supervisor?"

"*I don't know.*"

"The intelligence behind this thing must be a *moron*," grumbled Kim. "Why make a grab instead of introducing themselves?"

"What else do you know of its physical structure?" asked Solly.

"*I detected free hydrogen molecules. Methane. Oxygen. It seemed, however, not to have a coherent physical form.*"

"A ghost," said Kim.

"*I do not understand the connection with folklore.*"

"It's okay," said Solly. "Neither do we."

"One of these things is hanging around Lake Remorse," said Kim.

Solly nodded. "I think you're right."

"*Hammersmith,*" said the Patrol vessel, "are you currently engaged in EVA?"

Solly blinked twice. No.

"You have an open air lock."

If it wasn't gone by now— Solly closed up, reopened the air ducts, and started the pumps. Forty minutes later they had a green board and were able to remove the suits.

"What next?" he asked as he wriggled back into his clothes.

"Go home," she said. "Get a message to Matt. We need the Institute to figure out a way to sweep the ship to make sure the intruder's gone. Then we can turn over the intercepts and wait for world acclaim."

Solly returned a simple *yeah*.

The Patrol vehicle was now within optical range. They watched it move from port to starboard, apparently conducting a visual inspection. It was smaller than the *Hammersmith*, but it looked efficient and deadly. A ring antenna rotated slowly. "*Hammersmith,*" they said, "we will be coming aboard. Blink once to acknowledge."

"That's not routine," said Solly. "They probably have orders to take us into custody."

"It'll get straightened out when Matt—" A puzzled expression had appeared on Solly's face. "What's wrong?" she asked.

He shushed her and cupped his ear. The engines were changing pitch. The mains grew louder and Kim sank back, was *pushed* back, into her seat. They were changing course. *And accelerating.*

"What the hell—?" Solly punched keys on the status board.

The Patrol demanded they return to base course and speed.

"What's going on?" she asked.

"Don't know. Ham, what's happening? *Ham?*"

The mains were still cranking up. "We're moving toward jump status," Solly said.

"That goddamn *thing* is still here." Kim barely breathed the words.

Solly went to manual again and pulled the emergency engine cut-off toggle. Nothing happened. They continued to accelerate.

"It's taking the ship." Kim felt panic rising in her belly. "Heading for home."

"Isn't gonna happen." Solly went back into the closet, where she knew he was going to cut the power again.

She heard him remove the panel, heard him pull the switch. "Goddammit," he said. "It doesn't work. The son of a bitch has killed the circuit."

"What can we do?" asked Kim.

He consulted the status board. "It's going home," he said. "Taking us with it."

"Can we disable the engines?"

"Not if we can't shut down the power. There's not enough time."

She was unbuckling. "How about hitting them with a wrench?"

"They'd probably blow on the spot. There's a safer way."

She followed him out into the passageway and down the stairs. "What? Do these things have a self-destruct mechanism?"

"More or less. All we have to do is cut in the jump engines prematurely. Before they're ready. That's instant overload. Do you have the disk?"

"What? How do you mean?"

"Blow it up, Kim. Come on, let's go."

He meant the intercept disk, the one with the *Hunter* recordings. She stopped to snatch it out of her room. "Get your commlink too," he said.

There were a few other items as well that she'd have liked to save, but it didn't look as if they'd have time to pack.

"Didn't you say there was a safety feature?" she asked.

"I've already overridden it." They were hurrying down to the first level.

"How do we do it without getting killed?"

"From the lander," he said. "But we have to make this fast."

They retrieved Emily's body. Then Solly led the way to the launch bay and stopped in front of a control board. "Never had to do it this way before," he said, typing in a command. Two hatches opened in the lander, one to the cockpit, the other to the lander's cargo hold. They secured Emily in cargo and climbed into the cockpit. Solly took the pilot's seat, and began hitting switches. Power came on. Then he turned and looked at her with a pained expression. "I forgot something," he said. "Sit tight. I'll be right back."

He squeezed her wrist and climbed out.

She watched him dash across the launch bay and out into the corridor. What could have been so important that—?

The hatch closed and clicked. She looked out across the empty bay. "Solly?"

The engine changed pitch again.

She tried to raise him on the commlink. "Where are you, Solly?"

The connecting door between the launch bay and the corridor swung shut. A ferocious fear gripped her. *"Solly!"*

"Kim." His voice came from the link. "Kim, I'm sorry."

"No!" she shrieked at him. *"You can't do this—"*

"I've no choice, Kim. Listen to me—"

"I don't understand."

"I can't detonate *Hammersmith* from the lander."

"But you said—"

"I lied. I'm sorry, I lied. If I hadn't you'd have insisted on staying, and I couldn't allow that."

"Then back off. Let the Patrol do this. They can blow the thing to hell." She was trying to get the door open so she could get out of the lander but red lights were blinking, telling her the air pressure outside had begun to drop. Everything was sealed.

"There isn't time, Kim. They're not going to attack an Institute ship on our say-so. The thing'll get away. It'll go home with the *Hammersmith* and they'll know where we live."

"Please, Solly," she sobbed. "Don't do this."

The lander was moving beneath her, slipping its moorings.

"I can't fly this thing, Solly."

"You don't have to. The initial launch will get you clear. Then just tell the computer to take you to the Patrol. Or wait for them to pick you up."

"Solly, I don't want to live without you."

"I know, babe. Always have."

She banged her fists against the hatch. *"No, Solly. No no no no—"*

"Goodbye, Kim. Don't forget me."

She squeezed her eyes against the flood of tears. Engines surged. The launch gear clicked and whined. Then the lander dropped and she was out among the stars.

Another voice broke into the cockpit. The Patrol. "—Please advise, lander," it was saying. "What's going on?"

"Don't do it, Solly," she screamed. "I'm coming back. Lander, take me back to the *Hammersmith*."

But a brilliant flash illuminated the cockpit. And she heard the Patrol voice saying *"Holy God."*

22

Real friends are our greatest joy and our greatest sorrow. One would almost wish that all true and faithful friends expire on the same day.
— FRANÇOIS FÉNELON, On the Death of the
Duc de Chevreuse, 1714 c.e.

Kim was barely aware of being retrieved by the Patrol. They gave her something to calm her down. They assigned a female officer to stay with her until the trank took effect, and Kim fell into a nightmarish sleep in which Solly was alive and well and talking to her as if nothing had happened, but she knew he was dead, knew it was only a reprieve until she returned to the real world.

She had flashes of being carried on a stretcher, of getting into the lift at Sky Harbor, of being loaded into a flyer.

The real world, when she got back to it, consisted of white sheets, an uncomfortable pillow, and Matt Flexner. And the impression that some-body else was standing behind him.

"How're you feeling, Kim?"

There were blank spots in her memory. She recalled the lander, but not how she'd got on it. She recalled finding Emily, but not how they'd tracked her down. She knew that Solly was gone. But that knowledge was attended by a general numbness.

"Okay," she said. "I'm okay."

"You want to tell us what happened?"

The person behind him came abruptly into focus. Canon Wood-bridge. Casually dressed in black slacks and a gray pullover. She hadn't seen him since the night they'd launched the Beacon Project. He came forward, essayed a smile, pulled up a chair, and said hello.

Kim returned the greeting. Then: "Solly's dead, Matt."

"We know. How did it happen?"

"Where are we?"

"Friendship Hospital. You're okay. You've been released."

"There's something out there. Celestials."

Woodbridge looked at her for a long moment. "What happened?" he asked. "Where did Emily's body come from?"

Everything was coming back now, although details still eluded her. "She was left behind," she said.

"Where?"

"Alnitak."

"*Where?*" demanded Woodbridge.

"It's one of the stars in Orion's Belt," said Matt.

She could see the pulse in Woodbridge's throat. "Please explain what happened, Kim," he said, in a surprisingly gentle voice.

She described everything. She explained that they were trying to find out where the *Hunter* had gone. She told them how they had intercepted the broadcasts between the Tripley mission and an unknown vessel, and she showed them the disk. She described the object that had come in pursuit, and how Solly had gone outside to get rid of it. "But it didn't work," she said. "Something got on board. And it tried to take us over."

"Kim," said Matt, "are you *sure?*"

"Yes, I'm sure," she said. "It's in the ship's record."

"There's not much left of the ship's records," he said softly.

Of course. Her mind was still at quarter speed. The *Hammersmith* had died. And Solly with it.

"It doesn't matter at this point," said Woodbridge. "Whatever happened, it's over."

"You need to warn people about the Alnitak region," said Kim. "Probably about that whole area. Quarantine it. Keep them away."

Woodbridge frowned. "I don't see how we can do that."

"Why not? These things are *malevolent*, Canon."

"That's why we can't do it. Look—" He turned the chair around, moved it closer to the bed, crossed his arms over its back, and braced his chin on them. "It's not that we wouldn't if we could. But we've no way to enforce any such stricture. Not even with Greenway registrations, let alone with anybody else's ships."

"Then issue a warning."

"What do you think would happen if we did that?" He lowered his voice, suggesting he was taking her into his confidence.

"Every private vessel with long-range capability," she said, "would immediately go out there."

"That's right. That's exactly what would happen." He looked over at Matt. "Your colleague here is already thinking he'd like to go himself. Isn't that right, Matt?"

"Not if these things are lethal," he said.

Woodbridge managed a reassuring smile. "What it means is that somebody would eventually give them our address. If your story, and your interpretation, are correct, we have a serious problem."

"So what *are* you going to do?"

"Nothing."

"I beg your pardon."

"Nothing. Not a thing. We want to keep people away from the area. That's our prime concern."

"You've just said you can't do that."

"I said we can't order them to stay away. Or warn them. But nobody ever goes there anyhow. When was the last survey done at Alnitak?"

"Two centuries ago," said Matt.

Woodbridge looked with satisfaction at the ceiling. "My point exactly. The place is remote, nobody cares about it, it's not exactly a tourist spot. If we say nothing about this, nothing to anyone, I think we can assume there'll be no further visits over the short term."

"What about the long term?" asked Kim.

"The government will begin to prepare quietly. I'm sure those preparations will include some automated probes. We should be able to find out what's happening without undue risk. Of course, everything depends on nothing being said about celestials outside this room." He looked at Kim. "We can count on your discretion, I'm sure."

"I was expecting a parade," she said, trying to make a joke of it.

An uneasy smile touched his lips. "I'll arrange something." He got up and turned to Matt. "The Institute of course will want to drop the charges."

"Oh," said Matt. "I don't think Phil would be amenable to that."

"He'll have to be. Bury the incident. The ship wasn't stolen; it was a communication breakdown."

"I'll tell him what you want," Matt said. "How do we explain the loss of the *Hammersmith* to our board of governors?"

Woodbridge pulled on a jacket and started for the door. "I don't know. We haven't completed our investigation yet. Tell Agostino I'll call him this afternoon and let him know what caused the accident. It *was* an accident, by the way." He glanced at Kim, but continued talking to Matt. "When's the next nova?"

"In a couple of weeks."

"That'll be the third one."

"Yes."

"It's the one that will establish the timing sequence. Identical intervals between events."

"That's correct."

"It's what indicates the events are triggered."

"Right."

"Cancel it."

"*Cancel* it?" Matt looked shattered. "We can't do that."

"I don't think the Council would agree, under the circumstances, that advertising our presence is a good idea."

"But, Canon, light from the novas won't reach Alnitak for a thousand years."

"Matt." The room grew intense. "There'll be a court order in a few days suspending the operation for environmental reasons. It'll only say 'suspension.' But you won't want to plan on any more of these explosions."

Matt looked over at Kim and she could see he was assigning the blame to her.

"Something else you should know, Canon," Kim said. "The creature that was on the ship—"

"Yes?"

"There's another one, or something very much like it, in the Severin Valley."

His brow creased. "The Severin Phantom?"

"Yes." She saw him glance at Matt. Too many wild stories for one day. "We'll look into it," he said.

"Canon," she asked, "this didn't happen before, did it? A cover-up?"

He stroked his beard, apparently puzzled. "I don't know what you mean."

"Twenty-seven years ago."

"Oh," he said. "The *Hunter*. No. Not that I know of." He must have read the skepticism in her face. "I wouldn't lie to you, Kim."

"Okay," she said.

He paused in the doorway. "I'm glad to see you're all right. And I'm sorry about Solly."

At home, Shepard greeted her with enthusiasm. He was glad to see her again after all this time. He'd been worried, he said, about reports of her misadventure. And he was dreadfully sorry about Solly, whom he'd liked.

Messages were waiting.

Most were from friends and relatives, some with advice, others saying they were glad to hear she wasn't a thief after all. The Institute had already released its statement, explaining that the entire *Hammersmith* affair had been a misunderstanding. There were a few lawyers who thought she should sue somebody, usually the Institute for operating a vessel with unsafe engines, or for defamation of character. Sheyel expressed his concern, saying that he assumed the incident was connected with the *Hunter*, that he'd been surprised and gratified that she would go to such extraordinary lengths. He was, he added, anxious to hear what she had learned.

The cause of Emily's death, the authorities announced, had been massive abdominal and chest wounds. Possibly inflicted by a particle beam or a laser. Rumors of scandal swirled: There'd been a lovers' quarrel and she'd been thrust out the air lock; Kane and Tripley had been in collusion and had murdered the two women, probably because they refused to cooperate in some sort of bizarre sexual ritual; Life on board the *Hunter* had been orgiastic in nature and the murder had occurred after a wild night of debauchery; Tripley and Kane had been homosexuals who'd wearied of trying to deal with the constant demands of the women, had killed one, and let it serve as a lesson to the other. Authorities promised a full investigation. Meantime, both men's reputations were demolished. And Kim was sorry for that.

So was Ben Tripley, who had been thrown on the defensive by the blizzard of charges that rained down on him. Tora Kane issued a terse statement denying that her father would ever deliberately have harmed anyone. Next day an editorialist commented dryly that any number of Pacifica's defenders had died at his hands during the late war.

The official story moved Emily's death several hundred light-years, well away from Alnitak, so as not to rouse any interest in that area.

Kim still had no idea how or why either of the women had died. She felt responsible for the charges being laid against Tripley and Kane, but for all she knew it was possible the two men had done everything that was now being charged against them. Somebody, after all, had killed the women.

She got a cold reception back at the Institute. Solly's friends, who were legion, wondered, sometimes in her presence, what was so important that it had cost his life, how she had happened to get clear in the lander while Solly was left in a ship with, as the official report put it, an "overload" in the jump engines. They pressed her for answers and found the story she contrived, that they were following a first-contact rumor, unconvincing. She became a pariah.

Agostino rehired her, but refused to allow her in his office when she went up to thank him. She was informed that he blamed her for the cancellation of the Beacon Project. She pointed out to Matt that the project had become redundant.

"Doesn't matter," Matt said. "A lot of people put their life's work into Beacon. And it was a moneymaker for us. Nobody knows that better than you. And the general public doesn't know it's redundant. They think it failed in some way."

When Emily's body was released, Kim arranged a memorial service.

They held the ceremony on a beautiful April afternoon, under a quiet sky. Kim selected a grove not far from the Institute for the service, and the place filled with friends and family. The Sea Knights came out and stood by her, asked how she was, and offered their condolences.

Two days later, a similar event was held for Solly.

The second memorial was conducted on a windswept hillside near the ocean. Solly's family was there, mostly people she'd never seen before. The Sea Knights returned and gathered beneath a flapping banner that carried their insignia, a trident on a white field. The Institute turned out in force. Even Agostino showed up.

Solly's friends, as custom directed, came forward to talk about him. Others simply stood, wiping their eyes.

The wind blew off the ocean. A composer whom Solly had once carried from Earth, and whom he'd befriended, had written a score, "Though Tomorrow Never Come," for the occasion. He'd brought along a vocalist to perform it, and Kim stood listening while tears ran down her face.

Eventually, as she knew would happen, her name came up.

Solly's brother pointed her out, standing with the Knights. "Kim

Brandywine," he said, "the young lady for whom Solly gave his life." They all looked her way, expectantly. "Kim," he added, "why don't you come on up and say a few words."

She'd hoped to be left quietly to herself. But this had been unavoidable, the least she could do, and she'd prepared. She had taken a trank to try to hold herself together, but it seemed to have done nothing to assuage the grief and loss, so her mind went blank and she forgot the lines she'd memorized, and instead talked in a halting tone, on automatic, uttering banal phrases which the wind blew away.

"—Most selfless man I've known—" She could see a sail receding on the horizon and it seemed less real than the seascapes she'd seen in the windows of the *Hammersmith*, with Solly at her side.

The sun was bright and the sky empty. "—I would not be here today—"

She fought back the tears and, at the end, her voice rose over the wind. "God help me, I loved him—" A pair of gulls soared over the surf.

And she heard a child's voice up front: "Then why'd she leave him, Mommy?"

When she finished the brother thanked her politely, took a few more speakers, announced that refreshments were available in the south pavilion, and drew the ceremony to a close.

Kim stood for several minutes, unable to leave. Several of the Knights came over to talk to her and wish her well. Then she was startled by a glimpse of Solly's perceptive blue eyes. They belonged to a young woman with long dark hair.

"I'm Patricia Case," she said. "Solly's sister. I just wanted to get a good look at you." She bit the words off like pieces of ice, fought to hold back tears, and stalked away.

It was the only time in her life Kim could recall seeing naked contempt directed at her. "It's not what you think," she called after the woman. "It wasn't like that—"

The media portrayed her in a similar light: a helpless passenger on a scientific research mission who'd needed rescuing when, shortly after emerging from hyperspace, the engines had run wild.

She received requests for interviews, guest spots on several panel shows, and lucrative offers for exclusive accounts of events on the *Hammersmith*. All of which she declined.

■   ■   ■

Ben Tripley had left a message for her at home. She ran it and was surprised when he looked at her sadly and only wished her well. Her heart sank. She had expected him to take her to task for destroying his father's reputation, to point out he'd warned her something very much like this would happen. But he avoided the recriminations and only said he understood this was hard on everybody. And he expressed his regrets for *Emily*. "I don't know what happened," he said, "I can't *imagine* what happened. But I'm sorry. I wish it could have been otherwise."

How could she respond? You were right all the time? I don't know what happened either, and maybe your father is completely innocent, but the damage is done. Maybe if your father and Kane had spoken up when they came home about whatever occurred out there, everything would have been okay. *It's not my fault.*

After a long time she recorded a message, thanking him, telling him she was confident that when the investigation was complete, his father would be vindicated. She watched it through, decided it was a disaster, and deleted it.

She delayed calling Sheyel because once again she didn't know what to say. She had no appetite for lying to him, but her agreement with Canon Woodbridge prevented disclosure. Still, she needed to talk to someone, and Sheyel seemed to be the only person left.

She punched in his code. Moments later his dragon chair appeared, and then he walked into the image and eased himself into it. "Kim," he said. "It's good to see you." He wore a dark brown robe.

They exchanged pleasantries, although she could see he was anxious to hear about the flight of the *Hammersmith*. He looked more pale and drawn than when she'd seen him last. He was losing ground.

"I can't tell you much," she said. "I just wanted you to know I'm okay."

"I understand." His silver hair and beard had become straggly. She suspected he hadn't adjusted well to the news about Yoshi. "You lost a friend," he said.

"Solly Hobbs. Yes."

"I read what he did. Such friends are rare." He reached beside him and picked up a cup. Steam was rising from it. "What will you do now?"

Good question.

"I think I owe Ben Tripley an apology," she said.

"When are you going to do that?"

"Maybe tomorrow if I can get an appointment."

"You're going up there personally?"

"Yeah. I think I should. Anyway I want to get a closer look at the *Valiant.*"

"The *Valiant*?"

She hadn't meant to say that. But what the hell, he already knew. "The ship in the mural," she prompted. "You remember the model?"

"Oh yes," he said. "How could I forget?" There was, she thought, something very strange in his eyes, but she let it go. Probably the light.

She got through to Tripley's secretary, who said she could make room for her next afternoon toward the end of the day. Kim consented, and put in a call to Tora Kane.

Tora came right on. Strictly audio. "Yes, Kimberly. What did you want?"

The key to the *Hunter* logs, Kim thought, had to lie with the captain's daughter. There *was* no one else.

"I wanted to apologize," she said. "I know this has been a difficult time."

"I really needed somebody to explain that to me." She paused, and Kim could hear the ocean in the background. "Was there anything else?"

"Yes. I wanted you to know that I don't believe your father's in any way responsible for the deaths."

"That comes a little late." Her fury was barely restrained. "You've ruined his name. You know that, don't you? You've destroyed him." With no warning her voice broke. She swallowed, waited, took a deep breath. "Everything he lived for, everything he *did*, it's all gone now. And what they're saying about him is a lie."

"Maybe we can get to the truth."

"Sure we can. You want truth? Stop by the museum and take a look." The voice was pure venom. "Anything else?"

Yes! Where are the Hunter *logs?* "Do you have anything, access to *any-thing*, that might show us what really happened on the mission?"

She paused. Kim wished she could see the woman's face. "No," she said at last. But the hesitation put the lie to it.

"Tora," said Kim, "I can't do this without your help."

"Do me a favor, Doctor," she said. "Don't do *anything*, okay? I just don't need any more of your help." She broke the connection.

Kim walked over to the window and looked out at the sea.

She knows.

■   ■   ■

"Shep?"

"Yes, Kim."

"I want to talk to Solly. How long will it take to—?"

"Acquire the data and assemble the psyche? Not long. And you'll need to fill me in on the details of the mission. But I do not advise the procedure."

"Do it anyway."

"Kim, you've often advised against—"

"How long, Shep?"

"I won't know until I see what's available. If there is online access, you can speak with him tonight."

An hour later she went up the front steps into the Mighty Third Memorial Museum.

It required no shrewdness to guess what she'd find: Another hero from the battle of Armagon had replaced Markis Kane. The attack on the *Hammurabi* was no longer on display. The glass case which had sheltered artifacts from the *376* was empty. Signs indicated that a new exhibition, describing the exploits of fleet physicians, was being prepared.

Even the pictures of Kane helping the museum staff assemble the display were gone.

She went looking for Mikel and found him conducting VIPs through a simulator designed to recreate an attack run against a capital ship in a laser boat. He saw her and signaled her to wait in his office. But she returned to the empty case. She was still standing there fifteen minutes later when he joined her. "I'm glad you're well," he said. "It must have been a terrible experience."

"It wasn't good, Mikel." She watched him sit down, not behind his desk, but on a divan.

"Can we get you something?" he asked. "Coffee, perhaps?"

"No, thank you," she said. "Mikel, what happened to the Kane display?"

"We removed it."

"I see that. May I ask why?"

His eyes widened. "You can't be serious. You of all people. The man's a killer. What would you expect me to do?"

"You don't know that."

"Either he's a killer or he protected Tripley after *he* did it. The details don't much matter." He looked at her accusingly. "I'm surprised that you would object. I mean, that was your *sister* they threw out the air lock. I'd have thought you'd be pleased we took down the display."

"We don't know yet what really happened out there."

"Kim." His voice acquired its bureaucratic tone. "I'm sorry. I don't quite understand your attitude in this. Kane's guilty of *something*, possibly murder, aiding and abetting at the very least, and everybody knows it."

She pushed her hands into her pockets and looked through the office window at the exhibit, at the images of warships, the pictures of the captains. Off to her left a theater was running a recreation of Armagon.

"Children come in here," Mikel continued. "How would it look to have a tribute to a *killer*?"

"Mikel," she said, "when the truth comes out, I think you're going to be embarrassed."

He looked bored. "It's hard to see how that could be. How many people were on the ship? But, okay, if I'm wrong, and it turns out that somehow or other he's innocent, we'll just put everything back up and no harm done."

"No harm done."

"Kim, do you know something I don't?"

"No," she said.

He took a deep breath. "Look, I didn't want this. It was terrible news, learning about Emily. I really didn't know much about Kile Tripley. But Kane— We don't have many heroes. We couldn't afford to lose one. Not this one, especially."

"Then don't give up on him."

"Hello, Solly."

He wore a green shirt, open at the neck; dark blue slacks; and the peaked cap that he usually affected when they were out sailing. Shep had given him his captain's chair from the yacht. *"Hi, Kim. It's good to see you."*

Tears started immediately to run down her cheeks. She knew, had known all along, that this wasn't a good idea. Still, psychoanalysts maintained this was the best kind of therapy after an unexpected loss. If one didn't go too far. "I hate what you did," she said.

"There was no point in our both getting killed." He smiled, and Shep had it exactly right. *"How are you making out?"*

"I've been better." She gazed at him, wishing she could *will* him back. Seize the image, hold him, never let go. It seemed somehow as if it should be easy. As if she could just reach across the room and snatch him into the world.

"How are they responding to the news you brought back? When's the parade?"

"We're keeping it quiet. I've talked to Woodbridge. He's concerned about the possibility of other people going out there."

"I'm not surprised."

"If I had my way, I'd try to find out where the sons of bitches are from, and I'd send the fleet after them."

"That doesn't sound much like the peace-loving Kim Brandywine I've always known."

"I don't feel very peace-loving. They killed Emily. Killed *you.*" He was nodding, agreeing. "Solly, they've taken everything I ever cared about."

"Not everything. That's an overreaction—"

"How can you say that—?"

"Because you have a long future waiting for you. I'm sorry I won't be around to share it. But we took our chances and it didn't work out the way it was supposed to." He rearranged his cap at a rakish angle. *"What did Woodbridge have to say?"*

"He agreed they were dangerous and that we needed to avoid contact."

"Yeah. They're dangerous. But listen. Kim—"

"Yes."

"Woodbridge makes me uncomfortable. He's a little too righteous."

"He's okay."

"You didn't tell him about the Archives, did you?"

"No."

"Good. Don't." He gazed at her for a long time. *"What's next?"*

"I want to try to set things right with Ben Tripley."

"You going out there?"

"Tomorrow."

"Okay."

"You disapprove?"

"He's a jerk. You don't owe him anything."

"Nevertheless—"

"Okay. But be careful around these people. Don't trust any of them."

"Solly, Ben's all right. He's just wound a little tight. Anyhow, I feel guilty. Everybody thinks Kane and his father murdered Emily."

"Maybe they did. Who else was on that ship?"

"I just don't believe it."

"You know what you have to do, right?"

"Sure," she said. "Find the *Hunter* logs."

23

Familiarity and invisibility are sides of the same coin.
—OLAN KABEL, *Reminiscences*, 116

The *Valiant* stood on its shelf, polished and brilliant. Its shining presence, and Tripley's ignorance of its significance, amused her. A mean-spirited reaction, she thought, but nonetheless there it was.

"I wasn't sure," she told him, "that you'd consent to see me." They were alone in his office.

He kept his emotions masked and his tone detached. "Why would I not, Kim?" He remained seated behind his desk, allowing her to stand.

"I didn't intend any of this to happen," she said.

"I know that." He pushed back in his chair. "But we all know about good intentions. You destroyed my father's reputation." His voice remained flat. "He did not *kill* those people. He would never have harmed *anyone*."

"I believe that. I think something unexpected happened during the flight of the *Hunter*. Something that caused the tragedy." She lowered herself into a chair. She'd rehearsed everything she'd planned to say, but it all disintegrated in the heat of his presence. "This is *not* my fault," she said.

"I know. More or less, it isn't. But there's no help for it now. I know you didn't act out of vindictiveness. I'd have preferred you listened to me at the start, when I tried to warn you what would happen. But—" He shrugged. "It's a bit late now."

"Ben, there was no way I could not pursue this. It was a question of finding the truth."

"And did you *find* the truth, Kim?"

Her eyes circled back to the *Valiant*. "Part of it."

"Part of it." His intercom sounded. He broke off, listened, told the machine he'd take care of the matter later, and looked back at her. "What truth have you discovered?"

What truth indeed? That the *Valiant* is a replica of the thing the Tripley mission encountered on the far side of St. Johns? That the *Hunter* was invaded by something unearthly? —How else explain what happened?— She was gazing at the *Valiant* as if it were a sacred object. "Tell me again where this came from," she said.

He looked at it, puzzled. "What has that to do with anything?"

"Humor me, Ben."

He shrugged. "My grandmother gave it to me."

She got up and went over to it, looked at it, and ran her fingers across the shell. "May I?"

"Of course."

She picked it up and gazed casually at it. "I'd like to have one of these made up for my nephew."

He glanced at the spacecraft. "I can get you a sketch if you like."

"I'd appreciate it."

"It *is* a lovely piece."

"I think I mentioned before it belonged originally to my father."

She nodded. "Your grandmother passed it along to you."

Muscles worked in his jaw. "That's correct. I assume *she* told you that."

"I'm sorry about that, too," she said.

"It's all right. You've caught me in a generous mood." He softened. "Why the interest? Why do you care about it?"

"Bear with me a moment and I'll tell you." She held it under a lamp, letting its polished gleam sink into her fingertips. "When you were a boy, did it bother you that it had no propulsion tubes? No main engines? No way to get from one place to another?"

"Kim," he said, perplexed, "what are we talking about here?"

She laid it before him, set it down on his desk, and then held out a picture of Kane's mural. He took it from her, glanced at it, then gazed intently at the turtle-shell ship in Emily's hand. He looked at the *Valiant*, frowned, and turned on a desk lamp. "Where did you get *this*?" he asked.

"It's on a wall in Markis's villa."

His attention moved back and forth between the picture and the replica. "It's the same, isn't it?"

"Looks like it."

"What the hell is it doing in one of Kane's sketches?" Genuinely surprised, he put the picture down, placed both palms under the model's superstructure, lifted it, and stared at it as if seeing it for the first time. She watched him examine it, studying its antennas and sensor dishes and hatches. Here along the lower hull was a long door that might have led to a cargo hold or a launch bay for a lander. *There* was the familiar ring antenna used for hypercomm transmissions. *Here* was a pod that, to a boy, might have concealed a missile cluster.

Then his face changed, grew dark. He hefted the vehicle and his brow furrowed.

"What's wrong?" she asked.

"I don't know." He was staring at the model, weighing it with his hands. "It feels lighter than it used to." He set it down and scratched the back of his neck. He ran his fingertips along the aft section. "That's strange," he said, puzzled.

She watched his eyes narrow.

"The rear hull should have a crease in it. But it's not there."

"I don't follow."

"There was a dent in the hull. Nothing you'd see unless you were looking closely." He stared at the model. "And the *gun*'s different."

Kim noticed for the first time that a short metal stud jutted out of the *Valiant*'s nose. "Different how?"

He touched it with his index finger. "Rounded muzzle," he said.

"And?"

"It should have a rough feel. Whatever was on there originally was broken off."

"You're saying what? That the model's been repaired? Or—?"

"—This isn't mine. It's a replica."

"You're sure?"

"Of course I'm sure." He set it down on the desk and stared at it. "I'll be damned if I can figure *this* out." He picked up the picture of Kane's mural. Then he punched a key on the intercom. "Mary, would you come in a moment, please?"

Mary put her head in the door. She was the dark-skinned female from the outer office. "Yes, Mr. Tripley?"

He directed her attention to the *Valiant*. "This is a duplicate," he said. "Do you know what happened to the original? Did somebody break it and get another one?"

"No, sir," she said. "Not that I know of."

"I'll be damned if I understand that," he said when she was gone. His gaze turned toward Kim. "Do *you* know anything about this?"

"No." She was running her own fingers over the model, trying to find the dent. "Had it *always* been damaged?" she asked.

"As long as I can remember."

"Odd," she said. She glanced at the time and stood. "Well, I don't want to take up your day, Ben. I just wanted you to know that I'm sorry for the trouble I've caused, and that I'm sure when the whole story comes out your father's reputation will be intact."

He was watching her, holding her with his eyes. "Tell me what you know about the *Valiant*."

She shook her head. "I just did. I saw it in the mural. I thought you might know how that happened."

"I've no idea," he said, subsiding.

"I appreciate your time, Ben." She started for the door.

"It's okay." He got up this time. "Thanks for coming by. You'll let me know if you find out what's going on? With my starship?"

"Of course," she said.

She could feel him watching her while she walked to the lift.

Kim rode up to the main concourse, trying to sort it out. Why would anyone steal the *replica*? She got slowly off and joined the crowd moving purposefully along the promenade, where observation areas provided a magnificent view of the ocean world.

Why?

She walked slowly through the mall considering the possibilities, wandering among the shops. The shops were mostly souvenir and clothing stores. There was a Translux, which sold travel packages, on- and off-world. And a cosmetologist. And a Loki's, which specialized in games and puzzles. They'd put a poster in the window, an artist's drawing of the type that twists perspective. In this one a staircase seemed to rise from landing to landing around the inside of a hall, before reconnecting eventually, without a visible descent, with the *bottom* of the stairway. One would climb these stairs forever without getting anywhere. Yet it was hard to see where the perspective changed, how the stairway got back to the bottom.

And she realized why the *Valiant* had been taken. And by whom.

Ten minutes later she was back outside Interstellar's main offices. She opened the door, hoping to see only Mary, but prepared with a story in the event she ran into Ben again.

The assistant was alone at her desk. She looked up as Kim went in.

"Good afternoon, Dr. Brandywine. Did you forget something?"

"A pen," she said, making a show of examining the couch she'd sat in when she'd first arrived. "Oh yes, here it is." She produced one out of her sleeve and held it up where it could be seen.

"Well," Mary said, "that was easy enough."

"Yes." Kim was walking slowly toward the door, apparently fumbling to return the pen to its normal place in a breast pocket. She paused in front of the desk. "Mary, I wonder if you could tell me something?"

"Yes, if I can."

"The business with Mr. Tripley's decorative starship. Is there a security problem here?"

"Oh, no. Not that I'm aware of. That's the first time I've heard of anything being taken. I'm sure it'll show up. Somebody probably moved it during cleaning or something."

"The cleaning crew comes in at—?"

"—Night."

Finally, everything was beginning to make sense. It was all a matter of perception, and she'd been as blind as Tripley. Who would have thought?

She rode the lift down in high spirits, and caught the train to Blanchet Preserve. From there she took a cab to Tempest, giving it Sheyel's address. On the way, she rehearsed what she would say, a mixture of admonition and congratulations. She was in a blissful mood and ready to celebrate, half expecting to see him stride triumphantly out of the house during her approach. He'd know once he saw her coming that she'd figured it out, and he'd be anxious to show her the trophy.

There was, of course, an ethical problem in all this, but she put it aside as the taxi glided through the warm afternoon sunlight. Time enough to think about that later. Anyway it wouldn't be a question of *stealing* anything. Sheyel, like herself, just wanted to solve a long-standing puzzle. And make a point.

And by God were they ever going to make a point!

The treetops opened up and she was circling his house. Inside, the AI would be informing him of the approaching visitor, of the descending cab, but the doors stayed shut.

She settled to earth, paid up, and got out.

The taxi lifted off.

She strode up to the front entrance. The house stared silently back at her. "Sheyel," she said. "Congratulations."

The afternoon was pleasant and still. Insects hummed and a blue jay watched her curiously from the lip of a fountain.

"Sheyel?"

A gentle breeze sighed in the treetops.

She looked at the empty windows. The jay took off and landed on the roof.

Kim tried her commlink. A female voice came on the line: *"I'm sorry. Dr. Tolliver is not available at the moment. If you wish to leave him a message, please do so."*

"This is Kim Brandywine," she told the AI. "I'm doing some work for Dr. Tolliver. He'll want to know about it forthwith. Can you please put me in touch with him?"

"I'm sorry, Dr. Brandywine. But he does not like to be disturbed. When he calls in, I'll be certain to tell him you've been trying to contact him."

And it shut off.

Where was he? She should have called before coming all the way out here, but she'd assumed he'd be home, and she'd wanted to take him unawares. And to help him celebrate his coup properly. In person.

She walked around the house, but saw no one, inside or out.

Where would he have gone?

Only one place she could think of.

Sheyel had always maintained that few actions are driven by reason. People act out of emotion, perception, prejudice. They will believe what they've always believed, filtering out all evidence to the contrary. Until they go too far and run onto the rocks of reality.

If she was guessing right about Sheyel, he was about to run onto a few rocks himself.

She called Shep on the commlink.

"I need you to do something for me."

"Of course, Kim."

"I want you to design an entity."

"Beg pardon?"

"Consider it an intellectual exercise." She described everything she knew about the intruder. And the creature in the lake. Apparent incorporeity. Green eyes. Green tinge. Electrical fields. Free hydrogen molecules. Methane. Oxygen.

"*I can give you a model,*" Shep said after a few minutes, "*but I do not think it would be a life-form that would evolve naturally.*"

Kim had summoned another cab, and she was watching it approach. "Doesn't matter. What have you got?"

"*Uneven charge distribution in individual cells.*"

"Explain."

"*A living system need not be contained within a coherent sheath. A skin cover or shell. It is possible that regions of opposite charges, enclosed for example by a pocket of ionized gases, could function quite effectively by manipulating each other within the system.*"

"It sounds as if you're talking about a living battery."

"*That's an oversimplification. Let me explain in more detail—*"

"No. That's okay. Might such a system achieve intelligence?"

"*I'm not sure how to define intelligence. But I think it could perform fairly sophisticated tasks.*"

"Like piloting a starship?"

"*Probably.*"

"Where would it get energy?"

"*You indicated a greenish tint. Green eyes. That might indicate the presence of chloroplasts. That would allow it to convert light.*"

She directed the flyer to take off. "How would you combat such a creature?"

"*Lure it into an area of extremely high winds. Separate the molecules. Put enough external pressure on it that it becomes unable to maintain its integrity.*"

"Blow it apart."

"*Yes. Precisely.*"

"I might not have a hurricane handy. What else?"

"*It would also be vulnerable, I would think, to short circuiting.*"

She took the cab back into town, to a tech shop, tended by an aging woman in a trim black suit. Her hair was silver and her expression placid. She looked out of place, the sort of culturally resplendent woman one might expect to find discussing art while presiding over a salon. "Can I assist you?" she asked, with perfect diction.

"Yes," Kim said. "I wonder if anyone has recently asked you to make a model starship?" She showed her a picture of the *Valiant.* "It would have looked like this."

The woman studied the picture. "Why, yes," she said. "We *did* do something very much like that. In fact, we still have the template."

Gotcha, Sheyel. "Would you be willing," asked Kim, "to make one for *me*?"

"The same model?"

"Please."

"If you like." She brought up a schedule on her screen. "Tomorrow at about this time?"

"Oh," said Kim. "That won't do, I'm afraid. I'm just passing through. Out on the next train. I hoped you might be able to do it while I wait."

The woman nodded to herself, consulted the screen again. "I'll need about an hour," she said.

"Good. Do it. I'll be back."

"There's an extra charge."

The third edition of the *Valiant* looked as good as either of the others. When this was all over, she promised herself, it would make a fine souvenir.

The proprietor sealed it in a box, accepted payment, and Kim rode to the station, arriving just in time to see an eastbound freight passing. Its lights winked out as her own train appeared around a bend.

The ride from the Preserve to Eagle Point was just under two hours. She tried to sleep, but she was too tense. She gave up after a while and sat watching the countryside begin to grow dark.

At 8:20 local time she walked into the lobby of the Gateway, registered, went up to her room, and activated the phone. "I'll need a flyer tonight."

"Certainly, Dr. Brandywine," came the electronic voice, neither male nor female. *"Did you have any particular model in mind?"*

"The same one I had last time, if it's available."

"It is. Will there be anything else?"

Kim thought it over. "Yes," she said. "A crucifix, a wooden stake, and a silver bullet."

"Pardon me?"

"Never mind," she said. "It's a joke."

Next she called Plaza Sporting Goods and ordered a portable

microwave oven. "I'm going into a protected area," she explained. "Where they don't allow fires."

"*Ah.*" The voice belonged to an automated clerk. "*We have just the thing. What size does madame prefer?*"

"The biggest you have."

"*The family size. Very good. This model is big enough to cook a large game bird.*"

"Excellent. That's exactly what I want."

She just had time for a quick snack, after which the hotel informed her that her flyer was ready, and that her package from Plaza Sporting Goods had arrived. She pulled on her jacket, and took a moment to gaze around the room. The last time she'd been in the Gateway, Solly had been with her. And had urged her not to go back to Severin without him.

She put a laser cutter into her pocket, picked up the spare *Valiant*, and headed for the roof.

Ten minutes later she was south bound, moving through a night sky illuminated by the distant flicker of lightning over the western mountains. It was a beautiful evening, crisp and still. Two moons were rising through a filmy haze. Another was directly overhead.

Kim watched the lights of the city begin to fade. She tried to relax in the darkened cabin, and to anticipate the reaction she'd receive from her old teacher. She expected that he'd be pleased to see her, to show off his trophy. And perhaps to have a witness to the presence that he hoped to entice. But she wasn't sure. Sheyel was becoming unpredictable.

The screens showed another aircraft off to the east, a little behind, moving parallel. It was a black-and-white Cloudrider, a luxurious vehicle favored by VIPs and corporate executives.

She watched it for several minutes until it changed course and veered away.

"*Doctor,*" said the AI, whose name was Jerry, "*you haven't specified a destination.*"

"We don't have one yet," she said. "Stay southwest. Toward Mount Hope."

She had come to the realization that Sheyel wasn't going to want to give the *Valiant* back.

Had she an ethical responsibility to urge its return? To *insist*? Probably. But somewhere down deep she was pleased that he'd gotten away with it. And she didn't really want to see it returned to Tripley. What right had he to a treasure of this magnitude? He'd walked into it by accident, and had never understood its significance.

"We have arrived, Doctor," Jerry said. *"Have you further instructions?"*

She couldn't see anything down there. Even Remorse was lost in gloom. "Circle," she said. "Stay at six hundred meters. Keep just offshore. We're looking for a landed flyer."

"I will tell you if I detect one."

The aircraft moved deliberately around the perimeter of the lake. Kim watched for a light, but saw no break in the darkness. After a while Jerry reported they had done a complete sweep. *"There is no other aircraft in the vicinity,"* it said, *"either aloft or on the ground."*

"Are you sure?"

"Yes. Do you wish to expand the search?"

"No." Sheyel wasn't here yet, but he would arrive before the night was over. "There's some open space in the town. Set down there. But keep the door closed." Not that she had any illusions that a locked door would be sufficient to keep out unwelcome *critters*. But it would make her feel a little safer.

She put a hand on the microwave oven, then made another effort to raise Sheyel, but once again she got only the recording.

Kim was reasonably certain she knew what he planned on doing with the *Valiant*: it was going to serve as a lure, to summon the phantom, the *thing* that had been left over from the Mount Hope incident. Sheyel Tolliver wanted to make first contact. He believed as she had that the creature could be reasoned with. One had only to draw it into conversation.

Deadly naïveté.

The flyer eased down between ruined buildings. The sky was clear and the stars ran on forever.

She turned off the lights but left the engine running.

24

It is odd that those who claim to have a scientific view of the world stoutly deny, in the face of all evidence to the contrary, that ghosts exist, that they make themselves manifest, and that they seem to have a particular interest in oceanfront properties.

—AMY CONN, *Famous Ghosts of Seabright*, 591

The ruined buildings cast long shadows in the moonlight. A cool, sharp wind whipped in off the lake. It howled through the abandoned town and shook the flyer. Kim was embarrassed sitting locked in the cabin like a frightened child. Eventually she opened up and climbed down onto the ground. But she stayed alert.

Somewhat before midnight Jerry broke into her thoughts: *"Aircraft approaching."*

A blip appeared on the screen. Inbound from the southwest. From the general direction of Terminal Island.

She was back in the cabin. "Can we talk to them?"

"Wait one."

Kim felt behind her for the duplicate *Valiant*, brought it up front and set it on the seat beside her.

"Channel is open, Dr. Brandywine."

"Sheyel," she said, "is that you?"

"Kim." He sounded genuinely surprised. And delighted. "Where are you?"

"I'm embarrassed for you," she said. "You took the man's starship."

A long pause. Then: "Yes, I did."

"And what are you planning to do with it?"

"I am going to talk to its pilot. If possible. I'd be pleased if you joined me. Where are you?"

"On the ground. In town."

"There's a strip of open beach to the east. I'm going to set down there."

She saw his lights approaching. "It's not possible, Sheyel. What you want to do."

He sounded surprised. And disappointed. "Why not?"

"Whatever the local goblin is, it's not someone you can talk to."

"How do you know?"

"I know. Take my word for it. It's some sort of disembodied AI. Designed to perform specific functions, as best I can judge. Maybe it's a kind of automatic pilot. But it won't do negotiations."

"Let's not jump to conclusions, Kim." The other flyer had begun to descend. "Everything points to the fact that it's intelligent."

"The thing's deranged, Sheyel. And it's dangerous."

"It's lost and alone. It's been stranded here for almost three decades. You have to start by understanding that."

"Sheyel—"

"You want to say hello to the unknown, there's no way it can be anything *but* dangerous. I accept that possibility. Still, I've never heard of a malevolent AI."

"I have."

"You're letting your imagination take over, Kim."

"No, goddammit. I know what I'm talking about. Let it go, at least until—"

"I think you're running scared, Kim. I'm disappointed in you. But after what you've been through, I can understand—"

"Don't be stupid, Sheyel. This may be the thing that killed Emily and Yoshi. Look, let's take the night to talk about it. Go up to Eagle Point. Hear me out. If you still want to do this tomorrow, then okay, I'm with you."

She watched the lights of his flyer disappear below the trees. "Kim, do you know for sure of anyone it has attacked?"

"No. But—"

"There you are then. We're going to make history tonight, you and I. Are you with me?"

"Sheyel—"

"Do you know what I have on board?"

"Yes," she said. "I know."

"No, I don't think you do. You think I have a replica of the celestial."

"No. You *have* the ship itself."

"Oh." She heard the respect in his voice. "Well done, Kimberly. Well done indeed. How long have you known?"

She was tempted to lie, to tell him she'd realized, as *he* undoubtedly had, from the moment she found out there were identical ships on the mural and in Tripley's office. "I've known for a while," she said. "You didn't tell me the whole truth, did you?"

"You mean about my conversation with Yoshi? Yes, that's so. I did hedge a bit. She told me they'd brought back a ship. But she wouldn't answer any questions. Told me I'd have all the details soon enough."

"What did you think? That they'd hidden it in the outer system somewhere?"

"To be honest, Kim, I didn't know what to think. I suspected maybe they'd brought back something completely different from what we'd expect. And I wasn't sure they hadn't hidden it in the lake. It's why I came here so often." She heard his engine shut off and his door open. "Now, I have to get set up. Come join me if you want."

"I wish you wouldn't do this, Sheyel." She ordered her flyer to lift off, to find the other vehicle and land beside it. It left the ground and followed the shoreline east.

Sheyel's aircraft was down on Cabry's Beach, where she and Solly had landed. "Careful," Kim pointlessly cautioned her own vehicle. There wasn't much room left. And then to Sheyel: "We don't know what this thing might be able to do if it gets access to the microship."

"It won't go anywhere with *this*." He was out of the flyer, dragging a packing case down from the cargo compartment.

"Why not?" Her aircraft settled into weeds and high grass, and she popped open the door and jumped out.

"Because I've scanned it. It has an antimatter power source. But there's no fuel. No antimatter."

"Oh."

"So now we know what blew the face off Mount Hope, right?"

"I guess we do."

He pulled a collapsible table from the flyer, locked its legs in place, and set it on the sand at the water's edge. He pushed on it to make sure it was stable.

Now he opened the case, moved the packing out of the way, and lifted out the *Valiant.* He gazed at it with affection and reverence, and put it on the tabletop.

Kim could have seized it by force. She could have thrown it into the back of her own aircraft and gotten out of there with it. But something stopped her, an inability to defy her old teacher, a need to see what might happen, perhaps simply a reluctance to make the decision.

Whatever the reason, she chose not to act.

He brought out a battery-powered lamp, set it on the table beside the spacecraft, and snapped it on. The *Valiant* sparkled. Kim walked toward it, trying to grasp what she knew to be true: that it was a vessel built by celestials. That it had traveled among the stars. That it had housed an entity like the one that had stalked the corridors of the *Hammersmith.*

Sheyel watched her carefully. For the first time she read distrust in his eyes. "It's beautiful, isn't it?" he asked.

"You said you've scanned it. What's inside?"

"Other than the dimensions, and the propulsion system, or lack thereof, it could almost be one of ours. Control room, individual quarters, pilot's room of some sort. No chairs. Nothing to sit on."

"What about the propulsion system?"

"I can't find one. But that just means we need some experts to look at it."

Kim thought about Kane's offer to assist. "It must have been in trouble when the *Hunter* found them."

"Why do you—?" Something out on the lake caught his eye. She followed his gaze and saw a reflection. Possibly distant lightning. She looked off toward Mount Hope and saw flashes around its summit.

"Do you have pictures of the interior?" she asked.

He was slow to look back toward her. "Yes."

"May I see them?"

"Of course." But he made no move to get them. His attention had returned to the lake.

She saw again the luminous patch. Far out, but brighter this time.

Uh-oh.

His right arm went slowly up in a gesture of triumph.

It might have been a cloud of fireflies, out on the water, but it moved with unnerving precision, a spiral mounting up as she watched, a cloud, a fog, a mist.

Sheyel raised both hands to welcome it.

"Back off," said Kim. "Get into the flyer."

The cloud was alive with tiny stars, floating, moving, swirling.

It was growing noticeably larger. And brighter.

"Coming this way," said Kim.

"Hello," he called. His voice echoed in the night. "I know you can't understand me. But we need to talk."

The cloud was lovely, but its purposeful advance filled Kim with alarm.

"We brought your ship." Sheyel half-turned to indicate the *Valiant.*

The wind picked up and the trees shuddered. Kim was suddenly aware that another flyer was setting down back in the trees somewhere. It was the Cloudrider. Its lights blinked off and the engine died. Sheyel was too preoccupied to notice.

Moments later, three figures, two men and a woman, appeared out of the woods. They surveyed the situation and fanned out. Kim thought she could see weapons. And then a fourth person came out of the trees.

Tripley.

"We want to talk to you." Sheyel continued to address the manifestation. "We are your friends."

The cloud kept coming.

Kim measured the distance between the *Valiant* and her flyer and the angle the intruders had if she decided to grab the starship and run.

Tripley stood watching, his gaze shifting between Sheyel and the cloud. Apparently he wasn't as dumb as she'd thought.

The cloud was now just a few meters off the beach. It floated on the water, almost, she thought, taking sustenance from it. Several patches of internal luminescence formed, distributed randomly through its upper levels, and as she watched they became eyes, the same eyes she'd seen in Kane's sunken villa.

Everyone on the beach froze.

The eyes were deranged. This was not the cool malevolence she'd seen on the *Hammersmith.* This was pure madness.

Kim edged closer to her flyer.

Where the entity touched the lake surface the water misted and swirled, and Kim recalled the missing footprints on her first visit to the area.

Tripley moved up beside her. "My God, Kim," he whispered, "what *is* that thing?" The people who were with him brought weapons to bear. They wore gray uniforms, and they looked efficient. The woman was only a few meters away. Her name patch identified her as BRICKER.

"I think it was the crew of the *Valiant,*" Kim said, recognizing that

Tripley's presence demonstrated that he now knew the truth about his model. She was pleased that her voice sounded almost normal. "I'm glad you brought help."

"Security. I thought the thief might be dangerous."

"You followed me."

"Of course. You have a number of talents, Kim. But acting is not among them."

Sheyel stumbled forward into the water, advancing on it. He was continuing to talk to it, raising his hands in greeting. The emerald glow alternately intensified and faded, as if a great heart were beating somewhere within.

"Get away from it, Sheyel," she cried.

It resembled a *shroud*, diaphanous and pale and insubstantial. As she watched, he splashed toward it and it opened to embrace him. A sudden gust of wind threw the entire structure out of coherence, almost, one might say, out of *focus*. But it drew quickly together again.

Tripley's guards whispered to one another and leveled their weapons.

Sheyel suddenly seemed to realize his danger. He screamed and fell backward. In a single smooth motion, the entity rose around him and engulfed him.

The security people waited for the command to fire. But Tripley hesitated.

She could see Sheyel's silhouette through the folds of the shroud. His body convulsed. Bursts of green light rippled through the thing.

Then he went limp and it dropped him smoking into the shallow water, and flowed up onto the beach. Kim realized it was making toward the table and the *Valiant*.

Tripley gave the signal and his people opened fire. The woods came alive with frightened animals.

The security force had placed themselves well and they had the entity in a cross fire. Laser bolts whispered through the darkness. They struck the creature and bursts of vibrant colors forked through it. It spasmed. Some shots went awry, ripping into trees and the lake. The night filled with steam and geysers and shouts. Then with surprising swiftness it darted to one side and enveloped one of the men.

Kim ran forward to help but Bricker almost casually knocked her flat. "Stay out of this, honey," she said. "You'll just get yourself killed."

Tripley, who did not have a weapon, pulled her out of the line of fire.

The area became a cascade of brilliant light, a gaudy pyrotechnic display. Shouts mingled with the murmur of the lasers and the screech of birds.

Kim recalled her own weapon and broke away from Tripley. She ran back to the flyer.

The struggle raged across the shorefront, illuminated in stark flashes. The shroud let go of its victim, who fell unmoving to the sand, and turned toward Tripley. She thought she saw recognition flicker in the thing's eyes. It ignored the two still firing and flowed toward him. He looked around for a weapon but could find nothing better than a plank.

The two remaining guards threw everything they had at it. It shuddered, and a curious keening rose into the night, but it needed only seconds to overwhelm Tripley, to suck him within its amoebic folds.

Kim pulled the microwave out of its container. It looked like a fold-up tin box. She tugged at it and it opened into a cube about a half meter on a side.

The entity disappeared with Tripley into the trees. The guards raced after it, still firing, the bursts coming a little less frequently and with somewhat less authority as the battery-powered weapons began to wear down. The forest was ablaze with light. A tree trunk exploded and someone screamed. Kim couldn't tell whether it was a man or a woman.

She set the cube down and unwrapped the magnetron. It was an orange sphere about the size of a baseball. She inserted it into its slot.

Behind her, the ruby flashes of the lasers became sporadic. And stopped. Only the slow emerald pulse remained.

The forest fell absolutely silent, save for her own labored breathing.

The green light began moving in her direction.

She thought of abandoning everything, of jumping in the flyer and getting out, but that meant leaving everyone. Leaving the *Valiant*.

The shroud *drifted* through the shrubbery and paused.

Those mad eyes locked on her.

My God.

It knows me.

It thinks I'm Emily.

She dug the remote and the power pack out of the container. She pocketed the remote and manically, irrationally, read the specs on the power pack. The device would generate one thousand watts for about four hours. She started to attach it to the microwave, fumbled it, dropped it, tried to pick it up without taking her eyes off the shroud.

It watched her. Gave her time.

Stupid ass.

As if it had read the thought, it opened up, a vast blossom, preparing to take her. Electricity rippled through its translucent veils.

Kim connected the power pack, drew out her laser, and began cutting a round hole in the oven's front panel. The thing moved close, shut off her air. The eyes were gone, and she felt a sudden flow of warmth and well-being as the mist closed down.

She used her fist to punch the disk out of the front panel, set the oven on its legs, aimed it straight ahead, angled it up a bit, and hit the remote.

The entity jerked convulsively.

She kept her thumb down and the shroud crackled and thrashed. Kim caught an electrical burst on one shoulder, smelled burning flesh, but she bit off the scream and seized the oven in her arms. She turned in a circle and the mist spasmed and retreated from the invisible beam.

The night filled with electricity. The cloud withdrew. It whirled in a dizzying crescendo. Suddenly Kim could see only mist and dying sparks rising into the sky, like the aftermath of a campfire when someone has thrown a bucket of water on the logs.

"Regards from Solly," she said, and continued to fire after it.

The shroud drifted against the wind back out onto the lake.

Against the wind.

The son of a bitch was still alive.

She stumbled after it, splashed into the water, holding the oven clumsily but still firing. The water rose to her thighs and then she stepped in a hole and pitched forward. The microwave went into the water.

She recovered it and lifted it into her arms and tried the remote again. It sizzled and popped and a small cloud of black smoke came out of it.

She dropped the oven, hurried back, and dragged Sheyel out of the water. Then she went into the woods, found Tripley crumpled against a tree, Bricker face down in a small clearing, the remaining guards scattered. All looked dead.

On the lake, the fireflies circled and gained strength.

She collected the *Valiant*, carried it over to the flyer, and put it in the backseat with the duplicate she'd had made up at Blanchet Preserve.

"Jerry," she told the AI, "let's go. Back to the hotel."

The shroud was re-forming. She watched it grow stronger, brighter, as the flyer rose into the air. To her horror, it detached itself from the lake and began to come after her.

"As fast as we can," she urged.

They ascended into scattered clouds. The sky was full of moons.

Below, the shroud trailed tendrils as it rose after her. It was adjusting, changing shape, making itself into a sphere. Mist drifted behind it. It looked like a *comet*.

The thing wants the *Valiant*. All it cares about is the *Valiant*.

Were old memories coming back? She was sure it had confused her with Emily. And it had gone quite deliberately for Tripley, who'd been standing harmlessly off to one side. "Jerry," she said. "Contact Air Rescue."

"Are we having a difficulty, Dr. Brandywine?"

She had to restrain a near-hysterical response. "Minor problem," she said.

Jerry opened a channel and a male voice came on. "This is Air Rescue. Please identify yourself."

"Kim Brandywine. I'm in a Redbird flyer." Jerry flashed the hull number and aircraft description to them. "We're in trouble."

The shroud was coming fast.

"Please state the nature of your emergency, Kim."

"Yes," she said. "That's a little tricky. There are five people dead near the village at Lake Remorse. You won't have any trouble finding them. There are two flyers with them."

That got his attention: "What happened to them?" he asked.

The sensors had picked up the shroud, and she watched its marker blinking onscreen.

"They were murdered."

There was a long silence and then Kim heard a new voice. Female this time. "Kim, this is the supervisor at Air Rescue. Are you reporting a murder?"

"*Five* murders."

"Dr. Brandywine," said Jerry, *"we have an energy source in our rear. I am unable to determine its nature."*

"I'm not surprised."

"Kim, please describe your own circumstance and the nature of the emergency. What happened? Are you injured?"

"It's closing," said Jerry. *"Is it dangerous?"*

"Lethal," said Kim. "Stay ahead of it."

"We are already approaching maximum velocity."

"I'm not hurt," she told Air Rescue. Although her left shoulder was burned and hurt like hell. In addition she'd twisted a knee when she fell with the microwave.

"What happened to the people at the village? Who killed them?"

"It's still closing," said Jerry. *"At current velocity, it will overtake us in approximately ninety seconds."*

"Can't we go any faster?"

"We are at maximum thrust, Dr. Brandywine."

"Air Rescue," she said, "things are getting a bit busy. If something happens to me, you'll need to use a microwave."

"Say again, Kim?"

"Don't have time."

"We have a unit lifting off now. Meanwhile, it'll help us to help you if you can describe your situation. Please try to remain calm."

Kim killed the radio. "Jerry," she said, "can we send them a picture of the shroud?"

"Of the what?"

"Of the pursuer."

"We can do that, Dr. Brandywine."

"Do it," she said.

The lake waters were racing beneath them. The shoreline was lost in the dark. Decision time.

"What are we going to do?" asked Jerry.

The *Valiant* lay in the backseat, black and beautiful. *What places have you seen, little friend?*

She opened the case holding the duplicate *Valiant* and switched on a light to see it better. Even the copy would be worth a small fortune.

"Kim. Be advised I've transmitted the picture to Air Rescue and a record of this flight to my dispatcher."

"Good. We'll see what he makes of it." She picked up the duplicate and placed it on the seat beside her. "Jerry, open the door."

"I'm sorry. I cannot do that. It is dangerous to open a door in flight."

"It's necessary to avoid contact with our pursuer. Open up."

"Please do not take offense, Dr. Brandywine. I know the other vehicle is behaving strangely, but I've only your word that it is a hazard to this aircraft."

She sighed and looked down, searching for the panel Solly had shown her. She found it quickly and opened it. The yellow-coated cable. "Sorry, Jerry," she whispered, and pulled its plug. She recalled the rest of the procedure, threw the same switches Solly had, and took manual control of the aircraft.

The shroud was seconds behind. Kim could see stars in its filmy veils, could in fact see the three giants of Orion's Belt, Mintaka, Alnilam, and Alnitak.

The northern shore was coming up fast. She took the flyer down on the water.

The shroud followed. Kim cradled the duplicate starship in her arms, released her harness, and pushed the door open. The wind howled and tried to slam it shut. She jammed her foot against it, holding it, and sighed. She'd have preferred to hold the starship out where her pursuer could see it—but as soon as she got it through the door the wind ripped it out of her hands.

She watched it tumble into the water.

To her horror, the shroud paid no attention and kept coming.

Either it hadn't seen the bait, or it had detected the deception. Kim muttered a profanity she had never used before and dragged the *Valiant*, the *original*, onto her lap. She tried to pin her position down. A hundred meters from shore. Broken pier on a thirty-degree bearing. Finger of land jutting into the water on her left. And then, heart pounding, she pitched overboard the most valuable artifact known to the species.

The thing *still* did not veer off.

My God, it was after *her*.

She raced across the water and in over the shoreline, barely above treetop level. "You dumb son of a bitch," she screamed, as her door banged shut. "I threw it in the lake."

25

Courage mounteth with occasion.
　　　　　　　　—WILLIAM SHAKESPEARE, *King John II*, c. 1596 C.E.

The flyer was too slow.

The shroud closed on her. It was near enough that she could make out eyes, four of them now, distributed across its forward section, like windows in the cockpit of an aircraft.

It drew close to her tail, filling the aft screen, watching her as though it could see through the flyer's own monitoring system, could see *her*. It *touched* the aircraft, began to engulf the rudders and the rear jets. She yanked hard over and fought for altitude. It tried to follow but the turn was too much and it disintegrated and scattered across the sky. She congratulated herself, leveled off at two thousand meters and turned back toward Eagle Point. At best speed.

Air Rescue was still talking to her, asking what was going on, demanding to know where the bodies were, what the nature of her emergency was, assuring her of dire penalties if the images she was sending turned out to be virtuals.

"It's real," she told them.

"What is it?"

Behind her, the fireflies were beginning to reassemble.

Son of a bitch.

"Kim, *what* is going on?"

"I'm being chased by *something*. I don't know what it is."

"All right. Stay away from it. Help's on the way."

"Tell them to be careful. The thing's deadly."

"What can you tell us about it?"

"I can tell you that directed microwaves will disrupt it."

"Microwaves." There was a brief conversation with someone else. Then: "Where did it come from?"

"I don't know. But it's pulled itself together out there and it's starting this way again."

"We'll be there in a couple of minutes."

Kim saw lights coming from the direction of Eagle Point. "Thanks," she said.

She was several kilometers in front of it now, and it was no more than a fuzzy patch of cloud in the moonlight. But she saw the comet head re-forming, saw it moving against the backdrop of other clouds.

Her sensors told her it was gathering speed. Coming fast and coming faster.

She waited, watched it approach, watched it fill the sky behind her. Its mad gaze stared malevolently out of her screens. And when she could stand it no more, when it was climbing her tailpipe, she turned aside and sent it hurtling once again across the sky.

Stupid goddamn critter.

Trailing filaments *touched* her starboard wing. Lights went off, a red lamp on the console began blinking furiously, and the engine died. The flyer fell. The sky reeled around her and Kim's stomach tried to climb up into her throat. Engine failure was supposed to be something that never happened. But if it did, procedure required taking a minute before trying to restart. Give the automatics time to clear the lines. She held on as long as she could while the flyer dropped through the sky. Then she hit the button. The magnetics caught and the engine came on.

Trees and hills swept past.

She pulled back on the yoke, gained enough to clear obstacles, but stayed low. Keep down in thicker air. That should make it more difficult for the shroud.

It was off her screens, but she thought she could see its remnants, long wispy trails against the stars.

The red lamp was still blinking.

Batteries.

She requested a readout on her power supplies.

AT CURRENT RATE OF USAGE, VEHICLE CAN STAY ALOFT THIRTY-FOUR MINUTES.

"Kim." A new voice. A man's. "Steer northeast and gain some altitude. We'll take it from here."

A police cruiser appeared above off to her right.

"Glad to see you guys," she told them. "Heads up. The thing's bad news."

The shroud was re-forming.

A second unit moved in. Kim scanned for their frequency, hoping to hear what they were saying to each other, but without Jerry she couldn't find it.

The warning lamp was blinking furiously. Get down before you fall down. Ordinarily, she'd have looked for the nearest piece of flat land. But not tonight. She returned to her Eagle Point course.

The police had commenced firing. They were using bolt lasers. Big ones, far more potent than the handheld models with which Tripley's security team had been armed.

Caught in the assault, the shroud rippled orange and white. Sections of it were blown away. Tendrils fountained into the air, and the creature began to dissolve.

The cruiser moved in and attacked at point-blank range.

"—Maybe not a good idea—" she told them.

From Kim's perspective it looked like a minuscule electrical storm. But suddenly the charges stopped, the lights went out, and the aircraft disappeared into the darkness. Moments later, near the ground, a fireball erupted.

The radio was silent.

Power reserves gave her thirty minutes. Getting tight. Where was she going to land that she'd be safe from that goddamn thing?

"Kim." Air Rescue again. "Keep moving. Get out of the area."

"I'm trying to do that." The sky to her rear was dark. "The shooting's stopped back there," she said.

"I know."

Her sensors reacquired the shroud.

"You need something more effective than a laser. You have anything that can transmit concentrated microwaves?"

"We're looking into it. Kim, can you move a little faster?"

"I'm losing power. I'm not sure I can make the city."

"Just as well. Head east. Away from the mountains. Look for a place to set down. We have more units en route."

Head east. "Unless you've got something better than you had last time," she said, "you're just going to get people killed. Me among them. Maybe you should call in the fleet."

"Trust us. We'll take care of it."

Right.

The shroud was coming again. Moving with increasing velocity through the night.

Damned stupid Sheyel. Nobody ever listens.

A string of lights raced across the countryside, westbound into the mountains. The night seemed peaceful, orderly, mundane. Whatever aircraft were coming to her rescue had not yet appeared onscreen. In all that vast stillness, only the train and her pursuer were moving. But she had a substantial lead.

Nevertheless the creature was going to kill her, and there didn't seem to be much she could do about it.

The string of lights started to go out, front to rear. The train was entering the Culbertson Tunnel.

She watched until it was gone. "Air Rescue, how long is the Culbertson?"

"Twenty-six kilometers, Kim. Why do you ask?"

She'd been through it, and she tried to visualize the interior of the tunnel. But all she could remember was that it had been too dark to see anything.

She looked up the train schedules for Eagle Point. There were a half dozen commuters daily and eight long-distance passenger carriers. Freights were more numerous, but the schedules less exact. Three-oh-four was due shortly from Worldend, on the west coast. A freight. This one would be carrying flyers, furniture, building materials. Nine cars. Fully automated. No people on board. Scheduled to arrive in twenty minutes.

She opened her channel to Air Rescue. "Can you check to see whether 304 is running today and whether it's on schedule?"

"Sure." He paused. "Why?"

"Just do it for me. I'll explain later."

She brought up a map of the maglev routes. The freight would be coming in on the western line. Through the Culbertson. Its normal speed through open country approached 400 kilometers per hour. But it would slow down to 220 for the run under the mountain.

"That's affirmative on the train, Kim," said Air Rescue. "They're coming and they're on time."

"To the second?"

"What do you mean?"

She told him what she wanted to do. He caught his breath. She couldn't do that. Too dangerous. It wouldn't be permitted. His instructions were that she was simply to keep running until they could bring down the shroud.

"That's not going to work. Lasers aren't going to kill it and I'm running out of power and I'll be a sitting duck for it on the ground."

"Why is it after you?"

"It doesn't like my political views." Kim glared at the radio. "I don't know." Several sets of lights had appeared in the sky. "Your people are here," she said.

"Okay. Just keep moving."

She counted four more police cruisers. This time they kept their distance, firing from long range, moving away when it veered after one or another of the units. She admired the coordination of the attackers, who kept hitting it from different angles. Nevertheless, the shroud did not seem to be suffering grievous damage.

Kim banked the flyer and made for the tunnel.

Behind her the red and white beams of the lasers flashed like sabers. Then her angle changed and she couldn't see it anymore.

She was riding through the night when the sky behind her lit up.

The Air Rescue channel had been silent for several minutes. Now her contact came back up: "Okay, Kim, looks like you were right. We're going to try something else."

"What?"

"We're going to attempt a midair extraction. It'll be quicker than setting down."

She looked at the forest below. "No," she said.

"It's perfectly safe."

Her stomach turned over at the prospect. "I'm sure it is. But it's after *me*. Not the aircraft. It won't do any good to move me."

"Are you sure?"

"Yes, I'm sure. Look, can we discuss this later?"

"I'm sorry. I know things are a little tense."

"I'd be inclined to agree with that."

"We've just never seen anything like this before."

"Not covered by the operating instructions, I take it."

"Look, Kim. We're doing the best we can."

"Yeah." She softened her voice. "I know. But I'm going to do the tunnel."

"We don't think it's a good idea."

"Offer me a better one."

The talker on the other end was silent.

"I need you to help," she said.

"Wait one."

"Make it quick. Time's getting short."

She saw the southern route as she passed over it, the one used by trains traveling between Eagle Point and Terminal City. It consisted of a magnetized band about as wide as her hand was long. In forest areas it was usually set at treetop level, and was supported by a sturdy metal framework. When the angle was right, the band reflected moonlight.

Had the sun been up, she'd have been able to see the path cut through the forest by the maglevs. Moving at supersonic speeds, they created sonic booms and explosive winds that pushed aside everything close to the track. Trees and shrubbery leaned sharply away on either side, as far from passing trains as they could get. The effect was like that of the parting of the Red Sea, a leafy wilderness this time, divided by irresistible power.

She picked up the maglev route west and began to follow it toward the mountains. Beyond Eagle Point the peaks bunched up into a vast rampart, the tallest range on the planet. They were snow-covered, majestic, impassable without the tunnel. The approaches were scarred from ancient movement: deep canyons, sudden ridges, precipices.

"Hello? Air Rescue, are you there?"

Nothing. She imagined a hand over the mike and people arguing, making calls.

"For a start," said Kim, "you need to turn off any safety devices." Anything that would stop the train if detectors noted an obstruction in the tunnel.

"Go ahead, Doc. If you still want to do this—"

They had her title, which meant they'd checked her out. "Good. Listen, I need some details. How long is the tunnel? Exactly? What are its dimensions? Does it curve? If so, where and how much? And when will the freight enter it? I need to know to the second."

"That might be hard to come by."

"Why? Punch some buttons. It should be easy."

"Not in the time available."

"What's your name?" she asked.

"Tom. Tom Pace."

"Tom, you're all I have."

"Kim," Pace said, "I thought you'd want to know. We've called in the military."

"That's good. When will they get here?"

"Within the hour."

"That might be a little behind the curve. Do you have those numbers for me yet?"

"I'm working on it."

Ahead, a gray wall was rising and she saw the black mouth of the tunnel at its base. She was too early. She turned in a tight circle around toward the north. Buy time and give the critter a chance to get closer.

She checked her power reserve. It was down to thirteen minutes.

"Kim, I have your information."

"Go."

"First of all, the tunnel is straight."

Thank God for that.

"It's nineteen to twenty-one meters wide. Depends where you are. Eighteen meters high, but the track's three meters off the ground, so you really only have fifteen meters clearance. The tunnel is 26.1 kilometers long. The freight will enter the western end at 9:42:45. Give or take thirty seconds. Sorry, that's the best we can do. It'll be down to 220 kilometers per hour on entry. You want me to repeat that?"

She checked the satellite-controlled clock. It was just past 9:31. She punched the numbers into the computer, got her results, and set the timer.

"Kim, this is not a good idea."

"I know, Tom." She could see the shroud coming up from the south, a glowing patch moving against the stars.

She completed her turn and started west again, trying to time her flight so she'd enter the tunnel at exactly 9:35. Her sensors picked up the route and she locked on.

"Good luck," he said. "Safeties are off." To his everlasting credit, he went quiet.

The timer told her she was due at the tunnel in one minute. She looked ahead at the rapidly approaching peaks and estimated she was running right on schedule.

The shroud had made up most of its lost ground and was again closing in. The mountains rose around her and she was committed, no place to go except the tunnel. Her pursuer stayed with her.

At forty seconds, she reconnected Jerry.

It immediately began getting inputs from the flyer's various sensors. *"Kim,"* it said accusingly, *"what have you done?"*

"We have to go through the tunnel," she told it. "I need *you* to do that."

It didn't waste time arguing. It descended slightly, lined up on the entrance, and slowed down.

"There's a train coming in the other end at 9:42:45," she said. "Thirty-second potential deviation."

It did not respond and she assumed it was checking the schedule. *"You're correct. I am filing a complaint."*

"That's okay. Just get us through."

The granite wall blocked off the sky.

"You're aware the train may not be adhering to schedule?"

"It is," she said.

"Zero," said the timer as they roared into the tunnel. Their lights flashed against stone walls. The track raced beneath them.

"I hope you understand that disconnecting the pilot is a misdemeanor, punishable by fine or imprisonment or both."

"Please keep your mind on what you're doing," she said.

"Were you aware that battery capacity is quite low?"

"Yes."

"There seems to have been an accident. How could you have burned out the system?"

"Let it go for now, Jerry. Get us out the other end and I'll replace everything. Promise."

"That's very strange."

"What is?"

"Another vehicle has just entered the tunnel behind us."

"Good." The shroud was going to have a hard time in the flyer's wake. "Got you, you son of a bitch."

The flyer's lights stabbed ahead into the dark. Kim clung to her chair arms, pushing herself back hard in the seat. The walls were slowing down.

She glanced at the gauges. They'd dropped to 170 kph. And they were still dropping. "Jerry—"

"Kim, we cannot maintain stability at this velocity."

"You can't slow down, Jerry. We've got to stay at two hundred klicks. Or we won't get out the other end."

"Can't be done. Not without hitting the wall."

"Jerry—"

"I did not create this situation." The voice was accusing. Petulant.

It was 9:37. They had five minutes to clear the tunnel. "Jerry, we have to *try*—"

"I am sorry. I have no alternative but to slow to a manageable velocity."

They were dropping past 150.

"It's a question of probability. There is none that we can negotiate this tunnel at the minimum velocity you require. There is a slight possibility the train will be late. If it is—"

She pulled the plug on him and tried to take over but the tunnel walls were roaring by too fast, she couldn't control the vehicle and had to drop even more speed, down past 120, past a hundred.

The shroud had fallen well behind, but it was still coming.

At 9:40 she was just barely halfway through.

She touched eighty and steadied. The world was slowing. With a pang of regret she thought of Solly, of dying young, of the mystery she would not live to solve.

The timer counted down to 9:42:45. The freight was in the tunnel, or damned soon would be, the two vehicles bearing down on each other at a combined speed of three hundred kilometers per hour.

Not good.

The guide rail bumped the bottom of the aircraft. Kim held on, slowed more.

Ahead, a light flickered. The single searching beam of the freight's headlamp.

School was out.

She fired the retros and the flyer came down on the track, skidded, turned, pitched over the side into the lower level and slammed into the wall. Kim was thrown hard against her restraints. The cabin lights went out, something crackled and began to burn, and she ended up hanging upside down in her seat.

The tunnel walls, ceiling, guide-rail supports, everything disappeared into the blazing cone of the oncoming headlight.

She was down on the lower level, the flyer jammed in nose first, its tail sticking up in the path of the freight. Kim hit the release and fell out of her seat.

She kicked the door open and scrambled out. The tunnel shook.

She staggered forward a few meters, trying to get clear of the aircraft, and caught a final glimpse of the shroud, which was silhouetted in the oncoming glare.

The track was supported by stanchions, one every ten meters or so. Kim threw herself at the base of the nearest one, grabbed hold, and buried her head. The train boomed past and ripped into the wrecked flyer. She squeezed her eyes shut and tried to burrow down into the concrete as a hurricane of wind and screeching metal rolled over her. The ground rocked.

26

If it is true that artifacts are fragments of lost worlds, it is equally true they are mirrors of our own.
　　　　　—TAIA DELLARIA, *A Brief History of Minagwan Archeology*, 588

She woke up in a pleasant sun-drenched room. Yellow curtains framed the windows, and soft music drifted out of a speaker. A door opened almost immediately and someone came in. He, or she, wore a physician's smock.

Kim couldn't remember how she had gotten here, couldn't remember anything since attending the memorial service for Solly. She tried to concentrate on her visitor, but noticed she had no feeling in her right leg. "Broken, I'm afraid," he said. It *was* a male. Tall, dark skin, deep voice. She couldn't focus on his face. "But you'll be up and around in a few days," he continued.

"Is this a hospital?" she asked.

"Yes." He had dark eyes and seemed pleased about something. "How are you feeling?"

"Not too well." She'd ridden the train to Eagle Point. Yes, that was it: She was in Eagle Point. Looking for Sheyel.

The physician was tapping a pen against a monitor screen, nodding to himself. "You're doing fine," he said. "You'll probably feel a little out of sorts for a while, but you've suffered no serious damage."

"Good," she said.

The battle at the lake shore edged its way into her consciousness.

"Kim?"

Sheyel was dead. They were all dead.

"Kim? Are you with me?"

"Yes, Doctor."

"I'd like to ask you some questions. First, why don't you give me your full name?"

He pulled up a chair and asked about her professional duties, how she had come to get into fund-raising, whether she was good at it. He wanted to know her birth date, what books she had read recently, where she had gone to school and what she'd studied. He asked whether she remembered how she had come to be in the hospital, and when she stumbled trying to answer he told her it was okay, don't worry about it, it'll all come back.

She had fled with the *Valiant*.

He asked her opinion on various political issues, questioned her on whether she owned a flyer, and how she enjoyed living in a seafront home. And he wanted her to explain how it could possibly be that the universe was not infinite.

The police cruiser got too close again. She tried to shake the memory off, assign it to delirium, get rid of it. But it *had* happened.

And then there had been the *tunnel*.

"By the way, there's someone who'd like to talk to you. Asked specifically to be put through as soon as you were awake. Do you feel able?"

"Who?" she asked.

"A Mr. Woodbridge."

Well, it didn't take him long. "Yes," she said. "I can talk to him." She looked at the physician. He smiled at her, took her wrist for a moment, and told her she was going to be fine.

"What happened to the shroud?" she asked

His brow creased. "What's a shroud?"

"The *thing*. The whatever-it-was that was trying to kill me."

"I'm sorry, Kim," he said, "I really don't know anything about that. But I wonder whether you should talk to anyone just now. Maybe you should rest a bit."

She'd thrown the *Valiant* into the lake. My God, had she really done that? "No, it's okay. I'm fine." She tried to raise herself against her pillows. He helped. "Put him through," she said.

"Okay. But five minutes. That's all. Is there anything I can get for you?"

"Something to eat," she said.

"I'll have breakfast sent right up." And he withdrew. She closed her eyes.

The projector came on, and she was staring at a virtual Woodbridge.

He was seated in an old-fashioned oak chair. Because of her awkward position in the bed, the projector was angled. Woodbridge peered down at her from a spot near the ceiling. He looked worried. "Kim," he said, "are you all right?"

"I'll have to do a little healing. Otherwise I'm fine."

"What happened?"

She hesitated.

"It's safe," he said. "We're on a secure circuit."

That wasn't why she hesitated. Tell him about the *Valiant* and it's gone. Either to a government lab for research. Or back to the Tripley estate. Damn. After all she'd been through, the thing should belong to *her*, if it belonged to anyone. Anyway, she couldn't see that she owed any kind of debt to anybody else.

"I got a call from Sheyel Tolliver," she said, "asking me to meet him at Severin." She explained that Sheyel must also have contacted Ben Tripley since Tripley had gone there too. But before she could find out what it was all about, the *thing* had attacked.

She described the assault at the lake and her subsequent flight.

"Curious," said Woodbridge when she'd finished. "Why did Tolliver go out there? Why would he want you and Tripley along?"

"I don't know," she said.

"And why did this *thing* suddenly go berserk? I mean, apparently it was there all these years, right? What was going on?" He frowned at her. "Kim, is there something you're not telling me?"

He tried to dissect her with that Mephistophelian gaze. But she hardened herself and thought how easily she now resorted to deceiving people. "No," she said. "I'm as baffled as you are."

"This *shroud*, I'm informed no trace of it was found."

"Good."

"It strikes me that it has a resemblance to the creature you described from the *Hammersmith*."

"I'm sure it's the same kind of beast, Canon."

"Have we reason to believe there are any others about?"

"Not that I know of."

He looked sternly down at her. "Good. Let's hope not. In the meantime, the local authorities are waiting to talk with you. Be careful what you say to them. No connections to the *Hunter*. Or to the *Hammersmith*. No other-world stuff. Okay? You were meeting friends, and other than that you don't know what it was or why it attacked."

"Canon, why don't you just call them off?"

"Can't," he said. "People would think we were hiding something. You'll be safe, Kim. I have confidence that you won't tell them anything you don't want them to know." He smiled and blinked off.

An attendant came in with breakfast, accompanied by a nurse. "Dr. Brandywine," she said, "there are some people here from the police to see you—"

"Repairing the tunnel's going to cost half a million." Matt Flexner was exasperated. "They'll be rerouting traffic for the next year. You're not very popular right now with the transportation people. Or with the taxpayers."

"I'm really sorry," she said. "It was the best I could do under the circumstances." Aside from the broken bones, she'd suffered internal injuries, some burns, and would have bled to death had it not been for the quick work of Air Rescue, and the good fortune that they'd been able to get to her from the western end of the tunnel.

"Kim, we can do without the sarcasm. Since you're an Institute representative, *we're* taking the heat now."

"Matt," she said, "try to understand: I was running for my life. The Institute's views weren't uppermost in my mind."

He softened. "I know. The problem is that they told you to stay out of the tunnel. But I'm glad you came through it okay."

"I'm delighted to hear it."

He nodded. "I guess I deserved that."

"Yes, you did."

He had a stack of images of the shroud, culled from the media. "What exactly *was* that thing anyhow?"

"It's probably a designer life-form. It was apparently a passenger on the *Hunter*."

His eyes widened. "How can that be?"

Matt wasn't somebody you'd necessarily rely on in a crunch, but he knew how to keep his mouth shut. She needed to be able to talk to *somebody*. Especially if she was going to arrange to have the *Valiant* analyzed.

She was still debating what to do with it after she fished it out of the lake. Take it home and put it in the den? Keep its existence quiet while she tried to learn as much about it as she could? Any other course of action would lose the *Valiant* immediately. "Matt," she said, "I'll tell you everything I know. But first I want a quid pro quo."

"Okay." He folded his arms, as if someone were about to question his honor. "Name it."

"You don't say anything to anybody about what I'm about to tell you without my prior approval. Absolute blackout on this."

"First tell me what it's about."

"No. I won't tell you anything without the agreement."

The muscles around his jaw worked, but he remained silent. "Okay," he said finally. "What have you got?"

"A starship," she said. "A *microship*. From somewhere else."

His eyes went wide. "Are you serious?"

"Have you ever known me to kid around?" She'd never seen him look so confused. "They're telling me I'll be out of here in a few more days." Reconstructive procedures would heal her quickly. "Meet me and I'll show you."

"*Show* me? Where is it?"

"We'll have to rent a boat."

They also picked up some diving gear. Matt didn't swim a stroke, and he worried about what would happen in the event of a problem while Kim was submerged. He feared she wasn't quite entirely recovered yet, but she assured him that she was fine. She needed only not put too much weight on the leg.

He'd drawn the only possible conclusion. "You're telling me it's in the lake," he said, as they put out from the north shore.

"Of course."

"Kim, even if it is, I'll drown trying to get a look at it."

"You won't have to go down."

"You mean it's visible from the boat?"

"I hope not."

"Then what—?"

"Just bear with me a bit." She had a sensor. But in fact it took almost two hours to find the site she wanted. By the time she did Matt had lost all patience. "It's *small*," she told him finally.

He frowned. "*How* small?"

She held her hands a half meter apart. "*Really*," she added. "It's a microship."

The sensor picked it up finally, and she slipped over the side, used the jets to take her down through water that was quite clear, and had no trouble finding it. She plucked it out of the mud, then returned to the surface and handed it over to Matt. He made a skeptical face, took it from her, and stared at it.

"Stop assuming," she told him, "that the celestials have to be the same size we are."

Gradually he came to accept the possibility. On the way back to Eagle Point, he sat with it in his lap, saying things like, *It feels as if it could be.* And *Maybe it's possible.* "But, Kim, God help you if this is a joke."

They bundled the microship in wrapping paper, stowed it in a carrying case, and put it in the flyer. "Okay," he said. "First thing we'll need to do is put together a team to look at it. We'll want to take it apart, find out how it works. Maybe we can figure out what sort of crew it had." He looked pointedly at her. The message was clear: If she was wrong, they were both going to look silly.

"We've got a problem," she said as they lifted off.

"What is it this time, Kim?"

"You start bringing in experts and the word will be out within an hour."

"You're telling me that Woodbridge doesn't know about this."

"If he did, do you think we'd be sitting here with the microship?"

His jaw muscles worked. "Kim, there's no way around that. He *has* to be informed."

"Then kiss it goodbye."

"I don't—"

"Look, Matt, think about it. Once the Council finds out we have this, they'll claim it. They'll probably make it a security issue. You won't have it long enough to get it out of the container."

For a long time he said nothing. She watched him stare at the artifact, and then look out at the sky. "You're right," he said. "Okay. Let's figure out who we can trust. We'll keep it down to an absolute minimum number of people. Rent a lab somewhere, away from the Institute."

"That's better."

"We can tell Phil."

"No."

"Kim, he's a son of a bitch, but he knows how to keep a secret. We can trust him."

"I don't care whether we can trust him or not. There's no reason he needs to know."

They argued back and forth. In the end Matt caved in when she simply refused to go along with the idea.

He sat staring out the window all the way back to the hotel, clinging to the *Valiant*, not speaking, his jaw set, his eyes by turns exultant and wintry. "Kim," he said, as they settled down onto the roof, "let me ask a question: Why are you so concerned about all this? The Council would recognize your part in the recovery; you'd become famous; you'd be wealthy before it was over. What more do you want?"

"I want to be part of the team that looks at it," she said. "I want to be there when things happen." She hesitated.

"—And?"

"I want to find out about Emily. How it happened that she was killed and dumped overboard. And who did it—"

The afternoon out on the lake had stimulated both their appetites. "The Blue Fin?" she suggested. It was a restaurant down on the mall, specializing in west coast cuisine.

"What do we do with *this*?" asked Matt.

"It's starting already, isn't it?" she said. "We'd better take it with us."

They were early for dinner and the restaurant was almost empty. They found a table in a corner, and set the carrying case down on a chair against the wall. Kim asked for a *shonji*, which had a rum and strawberry base. Matt, who rarely drank, stepped out of character and ordered a Tyrolean Pistol. And they both went for the catch of the day.

Matt had a strong voice. It was a rich basso profundo, and when he got excited people could hear him at a considerable distance. So he made a conscious effort to speak low. "What do *you* think?" he asked. "What'll the Council do about all this?"

"I don't know," she said. "But I think the celestials are psychos. So Woodbridge is right to be worried. After we've been able to get the information we want out of it—" she glanced at the container, "—we'll turn it over to him."

"How are you going to explain it?"

"We won't have to. We hand him the ship, and we give the public whatever advanced technology goes with it." Their drinks came and they toasted each other. "I don't think there'll be much anybody can do. He'll be annoyed that he wasn't brought in. But he'll know why, and it won't matter by then anyhow."

That night, in her hotel room, she connected with Shep and had him bring up Solly.

"You're playing with fire, Kim."

"I know."

"I have no faith whatsoever in any of your experts to keep this quiet."

"Solly, I don't know what else to do. I've thought about talking to Woodbridge—"

"No. Your first instincts about Woodbridge are correct. You give it to him, you'll never see it again."

"So where do I go from here?"

"There's no way to plan until you know what really happened out there."

"You're talking about the logs again."

"Right."

"I still don't know where they are, Solly."

"Who would? Somebody must know."

"Yeah." She looked into his eyes. "I can only think of one person who might."

To Matt's dismay, Kim reclaimed the *Valiant* when they returned to Seabright. She allowed him to hold it while they were on the train, and to ride shotgun with it when, on arrival, she took it to Capital University. There, she imposed on friends to get some private lab time, and took a complete set of virtuals, inside and out. Then she used a public phone to rent a United Distribution delivery box in Marathon under Kay Braddock's name. "Not sure who'll be collecting my mail," she told the clerk, and asked for an ID number. She then inserted the microship into a plastic container with plenty of padding and shipped it off to her delivery box.

In the morning she reported for work and received an assignment to write a series of articles for Paragon Media on Institute activities. Matt was in and out of her office all day. Was the *Valiant* okay? He kept looking over his shoulder and referring portentously to the vessel as the *bric-a-brac*. Where was it? Was someone watching it? What was she planning to do next?

It was fine, she assured him, neatly stashed where nobody would find it. *Ever.* That might have been a whopper, but it seemed to have the desired effect, both soothing and disturbing him. Suppose something happens to you, he argued. What then?

She shrugged. I'll be careful.

Matt had names, people they should consider bringing in. She took the list and promised to get back to him.

As to what she was planning, Kim was going to break the law once again. She sighed at the prospect, thinking how she'd come a long way from the very proper and respectable young woman who'd spoken to the gathered guests on the occasion of the first nova. Would he like to help?

"No. I will not. And I think you should forget it. Whatever it is." He looked disapprovingly at her. "Don't tell me anything," he said. "I don't want to know."

That afternoon she went into an electronics shop at the Seabright Place Mall. "I need a universal tap," she told the autoclerk. The universal tap was standard equipment for Veronica King.

"I'm sorry, ma'am," it responded. *"But we don't carry anything like that."*

"Do you have any idea where I can get one?"

"Not really. They're illegal. Available only to law enforcement agencies."

She tried a law enforcement supply shop, which carried uniforms of various designs, a wide variety of nonlethal weapons, and all kinds of communications equipment. Here she found a microtransmitter, known in the field as a *tag*. She talked casually with the clerk about universal taps. He confirmed that they could not be routinely purchased. "There's a form," he explained, showing her one. It was required for equipment normally unavailable to ordinary citizens, like surveillance gear.

The Institute funded an electronics laboratory at Hastings College, about forty kilometers up-country from Seabright. The Hastings affiliate was run by Chad Beamer, whom Kim knew quite well, and who liked her.

"It could cost me my job," Beamer said, after she'd told him what she wanted.

"I'll never tell," she replied.

He squinted at her. Beamer had a reputation as a heart throb, apparently well-earned. But he was also a good technician. "What's it for?"

"I don't want to lie to you, Chad," she said. Chad was smaller than the general run of males of his generation. His parents had opted for longevity rather than altitude. He would get an extra few decades.

"Okay. Are you chasing a guy?"

"That's as good an explanation as any."

He nodded. "Give me a couple of days."

■　　■　　■

Matt wasn't happy with the way she was proceeding. He asked her to stay, closed off his office, and directed that they not be disturbed. "This is taking *forever*," he said. "When are you going to give me access to it?"

"When I can, Matt," she said smoothly. "When we've got the lab up and running."

"That'll take another few weeks, Kim."

She held her ground. He gave up and let her go after she'd assured him that she'd provided for the possibility that something might happen to her. And she had: She'd written down a complete set of directions on how to recover the *Valiant*, folded it into an envelope, and given it to one of the Sea Knights, with instructions to see that it was turned over to Matt if necessary.

Her own determination to ensure that important information not be lost convinced her she was right about Markis Kane: He'd have wanted to preserve the logs against history. Somewhere there had to be a trail. Even if he were the monster the news services now accused him of being, he might well have wanted to save the record of his exploits for publication after he was safely clear of the law.

And the trail almost certainly led through his sole child, Tora.

Kim went home early, mixed herself a drink, and directed Shepard to bring up a simulacrum of Sheyel.

"I don't have much data on him," the AI protested.

"Do the best you can. And update him."

She listened to the electronic murmur which was Shepard's method of informing her he didn't feel equipped to perform a given assignment, and then Sheyel's image appeared before her. He was seated in his dragon chair, eyes half open, presented in an appropriately melancholy mood.

"Good afternoon, Kim," he said. *"It's good to see you again."*

"And you, Sheyel. I was sorry to lose you. I wish things had turned out differently."

"As do I. It seems I was foolishly determined."

They gazed at one another.

"It shouldn't have been vindictive," he said. *"It was there too many years without harming anyone."*

"You expected the appearance of the *Valiant* to get a reaction. I guess that's what happened."

"I wish I could change things. At least, Kim, I'm glad you're safe." He rearranged one of the cushions. *"Where is it now?"*

"It's gone. At considerable cost." She pulled her legs up onto the sofa and wrapped her arms around them. "Sheyel, I wanted you to know that I haven't walked away from this. I think I have a pretty good idea of what happened. I think Yoshi was killed by the same thing that killed you."

"Yes. That makes sense. Do you know how it might have happened?"

"Not yet. But I hope to find out within another couple of days."

"Good. When you have the rest of it, I'd be pleased if you came back. And talked to me."

"Yes," she said. "Of course."

Tora Kane lived in an isolated cottage situated in an oak grove about ten kilometers northwest of Seabright. Kim rode out on several consecutive days and strolled through the area early in the morning, recording when Tora left for the site, nine-fifteen, and when she returned, usually at around six-thirty. She noted that Tora owned a flyer, but not a dog. As far as she could determine, the archeologist lived alone.

She found a toolshed behind the house, which would provide a ladder when she needed it. That was a piece of good fortune: she'd expected to have to climb a tree.

The walks had been hard enough on her: despite modern medicine, she was not yet fully healed, and she knew her doctors would have complained angrily had they known what she was doing.

At home, she worked with Shepard to create a virtual lawyer who would be credible and persuasive. She settled on Aquilla Selby, the famed criminal attorney of the previous century. Selby had not believed in capital punishment, and had specialized in defending the indefensible, rescuing a long line of murderers and sadists from the extreme penalty, and in some cases even springing them loose on an unsuspecting public.

Selby had allowed his years to show, had very carefully orchestrated the aging process to acquire silver hair and a wrinkled brow, gaining the visible appearance of maturity that counts for so much in the courtroom, while simultaneously maintaining the medical state of a healthy thirty-year-old.

Kim touched him up a little bit, changed the color of his eyes from blue to brown, cut his hair to agree with current fashion, got rid of his beard, took a few pounds out of his midsection. She tightened his face somewhat, opting for trim cheeks and a narrow nose.

"What do you think?" she asked Shep, when the finished product stood before her.

"*He looks good,*" the AI said. "*He'd get* my *attention.*"

The image completed, she went to work on the voice, eliminating its distinctive Terminal City accent, the mellifluous tonality that, to a seventh-century ear, sounded cloying. She added some gravel and adjusted the pacing. When she was finished, he sounded like a modern native of Greenway's Ruby Archipelago.

Next she looked at her equipment.

Included in the package with the microtransmitter was a receiver and a flex antenna for long-distance reception. She rented a flyer and mounted the antenna on it, then went to bed and slept peacefully.

In the morning she heard from Chad. "It's ready," he told her.

She flew out that afternoon and picked up the tap.

"Remember," he cautioned, after showing her how it worked, "if you get into trouble, I don't know anything about it."

She promised they wouldn't be able to beat it out of her.

That evening she flew to within a kilometer of Tora's home, landed, and walked the rest of the distance. The lights were on when she arrived, and she saw movement inside the cottage. Tora had a guest. Several guests, in fact. Three flyers were parked on or just off the pad.

But she knew that the sleek orange-and-black Kondor belonged to the archeologist. She watched for a few minutes to be sure no one was outside, then circled around to the pad and taped the microtransmitter to the top of a tread, where it disappeared into the well. When she was satisfied, she retreated into the woods and turned on her receiver. The signal came through loud and clear.

27

No treasure should be thought secure against thieves so long as any one person knows where it lies.

—*The Notebooks of Colin Colin*, 2440 C.E.

Kim was up early next day. She had a light breakfast, and then changed her appearance to that of a trim young male, including a mustache, which she thought made her look quite dashing. Then she took her rented aircraft out to Tora Kane's neighborhood, timing her flight to be overhead when the archeologist came out the door. She had a cup in one hand and a leather case under her other arm when she got into her flyer and lifted off.

Kim monitored her flight until she was down at the dig site. Then she descended nearby in a glade, avoiding Kane's landing pad because she didn't want to take a chance of leaving a record of the aircraft with the house AI. There were only a few other dwellings in the area, but none within visual range. No one seemed to be abroad.

There was no way to be certain that she wouldn't be recorded by a security system. If that happened, Tora would get a picture of a young man, and the plan would be blown, but *she* at least would escape detection.

She went behind the villa, got the ladder out of the shed, and used it to climb to the roof. She now removed her universal tap from a jacket pocket and secured it to a cornice. It was painted the same dull brown, so it would be almost invisible to anyone arriving in a flyer.

Satisfied, she climbed down, put the ladder back, and left.

She returned home to work on Aquilla Selby's lines, but had hardly gotten started when Matt called to ask whether she was okay, by which he presumably meant had she been arrested yet? He also reported that he'd found a lab they could use to examine the *Valiant*, but that it would be a couple of weeks before they could get access to it.

He asked again whether she would not relent and give him access to the "bric-a-brac." He was so mysterious that she knew anyone listening would understand he was trying to talk in code.

"Best to leave things as they are," she told him.

"I don't understand why you don't trust me," he said.

And she said the usual things, it wasn't that she didn't trust *him*, but these things have a way of getting out, and they needed to concentrate on security, and so on.

He gave up, and informed her he'd pared the list of potential researchers to six.

"Three at most," she insisted, knowing even that was too many.

They agreed that no feelers would go out until the lab was available.

After he'd disconnected she sat for a while studying the Kane print, *Storm Warning*. It was an ominous landscape, ruined towers in the distance, oncoming thunderheads.

She ran through the Selby script several times before she was satisfied. Then she downloaded it into a compupak, had dinner, and went for a long walk in the twilight. The tides on Greenway did not share the rhythmic aspect they would have had under a single satellite. These were up and down all the time, pulled constantly in different directions by Helios and the four moons.

They were at extreme low tide, the ocean far out, more beach exposed than would usually be visible in a month's time. She strolled along the water's edge, letting the waves wash over her feet, watching the stars appear. They looked far away and she wondered again how anything capable of mastering those immense distances could behave so irrationally. Yet there had been the war with Pacifica.

Such things could happen apparently. The people who devised physical theory and constructed jump engines were not the same people who made political decisions, or who allowed themselves to be swept up by the current media craze, or to be ruled by centuries-old traditions that might once have served to hold nations together but had now become counterproductive.

Don't assume that a species is intelligent because it produces intelligent individuals. Brandywine's Corollary.

Maybe in the end she'd be remembered for some such principle rather than the discovery of the *Valiant*. She smiled and decided she'd be willing to settle for that.

The next morning she flew over to Bayside Park where she could use a private commbooth, ensuring that even if things went wrong no one would be able to track her down.

The booth was located in a mall along a gravel walkway off the ocean. It was still early in the season, and there were few people abroad: a few university students between classes, some locals taking their constitutionals. No tourists yet. The morning was bright and cloudless, and the air still cool, with a crisp wind coming inshore.

She tied in the Selby program and punched in Tora's number.

The link chimed at the other end.

A couple of kids with balloons chased one another through the mall. She watched the long lines of breakers moving toward the beach.

"Hello?" Tora's voice, audio only.

"Dr. Kane?" It was Kim who spoke, but Tora would be hearing the voice she'd constructed for Selby. "My name is Gabriel Martin. I was your father's lawyer some years ago."

Kim got a picture. Tora was wearing a light blue shirt and baggy blue slacks. Working clothes. She looked puzzled. "What can I do for you, Mr. Martin?"

Kim sent Selby's image and the construct lawyer, she knew, now materialized in Tora's projection area. He was a tall, aristocratic figure. "Doctor, let me say first that Markis was a close friend, as well as a client. I owe him a considerable obligation. I won't go into that at the moment; the details don't really matter.

"Unfortunately, I can no longer do anything for *him*, God rest his soul. But I *am* in a position to pass along some information that *you* might find useful."

God rest his soul. That had sounded pretty good when she inserted it. Real lawyer talk to clients. But it sounded so artificial now that she bit her lip and waited to see whether Tora would recognize the charade. She didn't.

"I appreciate the thought, Mr. Martin. And what information would that be?"

To Tora, the lawyer stood beside an expanse of desktop, covered with disks, pens, and a fat notebook. His wall showed a series of beribboned certificates, plaques, and a picture of Martin shaking hands with the premier himself. "I don't know exactly how to put this, Doctor, because it's only rumor, but I have it on quite reliable sources."

Tora waited for him to come to the point.

Kim stretched the moment out by having Martin advise her that the information he was about to pass on was confidential, and that if she repeated it he would have no choice but to deny everything and to withdraw from any further participation in the proceedings.

"Yes," she said, her impatience starting to show. "Quite so. So what is this about?"

"I understand the government has acquired the *Hunter* logs. The *real* ones."

Tora paled and then recovered herself. "I don't know anything about it," she said. "What real logs? I understood the logs were filed in the Archives years ago."

"Dr. Kane." Kim allowed herself to sound simultaneously sympathetic and well informed. "I understand your reluctance to discuss this. We are after all talking about violations of law, are we not? Violations to which you have been party."

"I beg your pardon." Her tone got cold. She had to be wondering just how much her caller knew, and probably more to the point, how much the government had.

"It's quite all right," Kim continued, in Martin's persona. "This information came to me because your father had friends at the highest levels. There are those who don't want to see more damage done to his reputation, nor any harm come to his daughter, nor see his estate embroiled in extensive litigation, as could be the case if certain charges could be shown to have validity. Or even if sufficient doubt could be raised concerning his role in the Mount Hope incident, and possibly in the deaths of Yoshi Amara and Emily Brandywine. I know you were your father's sole heir. And you should be aware that whatever monies or tangible goods you received out of the estate could be attached in any adverse judgment."

She looked cornered. Kim also squirmed under a sudden assault of conscience. But she told herself there was no other way. The woman could have avoided all this by cooperating. "Even at this late date?" asked Tora. "Isn't there a statute of limitations?"

"I'm afraid not. In a case of this type, in which lives have been lost and deliberate falsifications made to cover up responsibility—" He shook his head sadly. Kim had no idea whether that was true, but it didn't matter. Tora was buying it for the moment, and that was all that counted.

"How reliable is your information, Mr. Martin?"

Okay: time to close out. Kim had accomplished what she wanted to do. "It's correct, Dr. Kane."

Tora studied the lawyer's image. "If I need your help, will you be available?"

"Certainly," he said. "I'd be happy to do what I can for you."

"Thank you." Her voice was unsteady.

"I hope I've been of assistance. Good day, Doctor." And Kim disconnected.

She left the booth but used her commlink to call home and tie in with her monitoring system. The tag on the flyer would alert her if Tora went anywhere, just as the tap on the roof would listen in on any calls.

She wandered through the mall. Only a couple of the shops had opened. One carried sporting gear and she was looking at swimsuits when her alert sounded.

"Yes, Shep?" she said into her link.

"She's calling the Mighty Third. The museum. Do you wish to listen?"

"Please."

She heard the far-away ringing. Then an automated voice answered. *"Good morning. Mighty Third Memorial Museum."*

"May I speak with Mikel Alaam, please?"

"Who may I say is calling?"

"Tora Kane."

"One moment. I'll see if he's in."

While she waited, Kim recalled Markis's tenure as head of The Scarlet Sleeve. And Veronica King.

Hide in Plain Sight.

The Purloined Letter.

An observer would have seen a smile appear at the corners of her lips. *I'll be damned,* she told herself.

"Hello, Tora. Nice to hear from you. How are you doing?" Kim recognized Mikel's polite tenor.

"Pretty good, thanks, Mikel." She paused. "It's been a while."

"Yes, it has." He was embarrassed, Kim thought. This was probably the first time he'd spoken with her since her father's display came down. "What can I do for you?"

"I was wondering if you were planning on being in the museum later this morning."

"Yes. I'll be here. I have a conference at ten-thirty. Are you coming over?"

"Yes. I thought I'd drop by if it's convenient."

"Tora, I'm sorry about the problem."

"I understand, Mikel. It's not your fault." Her tone suggested otherwise. "When will you be free?"

"The meeting won't last more than an hour. After that I'm at your disposal." Kim detected a reluctance in his voice. He thinks she's coming to plead her father's case.

"Can we manage lunch?" It seemed as much a directive as an invitation.

"Yes. I'd like that. Very much."

There was some small talk, it'll be good to see you again, I've been meaning to call but we've been so busy. Then they agreed how much they were looking forward to seeing each other again and broke the connection.

Good. What to do next?

Hide in Plain Sight.

She'd hoped to follow Tora Kane to the *Hunter* logs. The risk was that she would destroy the records immediately upon recovery. Kim had hoped she would prove to be too much of a scientist to do that, but one could never be certain. In any case, she'd gotten lucky. She didn't even need to follow the tag, as she'd expected to do. Instead, Kim had been given an opportunity to get there first. To arrange things so that Gabriel Martin's dark warning looked valid.

But time was short.

She called Shepard.

"What can I do for you, Kim?"

"Shep, I want you to bring up a piece of correspondence from the Mighty Third. Duplicate their stationery and give me a letter from them agreeing to see one Jay Braddock today about the Pacifica War assignment. The letter should assure Braddock the run of the place."

"What's the Pacifica War assignment, Kim?"

"Don't worry about it. It doesn't exist."

"You want me to sign it too?"

"Lift Mikel Alaam's signature. He's the director."

"Kim, that's forgery."

"I don't know any other way to put his name on the document."

Shep's electronics were making funny noises. *"You know,"* he said, *"you've become a professional bandit."*

"Can't be helped."

"Where are you going now?"

"Clothes," she said. "I need a change of clothes."

Kim arrived at the museum at ten-forty, again dressed in male attire and sporting her mustache. She wore a tight undergarment to contain her breasts and a loose-fitting embroidered blouse to hide what she couldn't suppress. Her hair was now bright red. Her flesh tones had been slightly altered, and she wore dark lenses. Mikel himself, she was certain, would not recognize her. She also had two data disks, carefully labeled, in her pocket.

She flashed a congenial smile at a young woman in the administrative offices, altered her voice as best she could, and asked confidently for the director. "My name's Jay Braddock," she said. "I'm a researcher with Professor Teasdale." Teasdale was *the* prizewinning historian of the Pacifica War era.

"I'm sorry, Mr. Braddock—" said the young woman.

"*Dr.* Braddock—" Kim corrected gently.

"*Dr.* Braddock, but he's in conference at the moment." Her name tag identified her as Wilma LaJanne. Kim decided she was a graduate student.

"This is unfortunate," Kim persisted.

Wilma checked her computer. "His schedule isn't free until midafternoon."

"That can't be right," Kim said. With considerable dignity she produced the letter Shep had prepared for her. "I have an appointment. At ten forty-five."

Wilma looked at the letter, frowned, and moved her lower lip back and forth. "I don't know what to tell you, Dr. Braddock. I'll inform him when he comes out that you're here. There's not much more I can do."

"When do you expect the meeting to be over?"

"About eleven-thirty, sir. But it's really hard to say."

"That won't do at all," Kim said. "Not at all. I'm on a deadline, you understand. Professor Teasdale is not going to be happy." She contrived to look pained and then glanced hopefully at Wilma, inviting her to volunteer. When she didn't, Kim folded her arms and smiled at the young woman. "I wonder if you might be able to help. I don't really need much."

"I'd like to," she said doubtfully. "But I've only been at the museum for a couple of weeks."

Kim retrieved her letter, folded it, and slipped it into a pocket. "You know who Professor Teasdale is, right?" A nod. "You may also know she's working on a definitive history of the Pacifica War."

"Yes," she said, taking a stab, "I had heard."

"The museum had until recently a display on the *376* and the battle off Armagon. Back in the east wing."

"Yes. We took it down just a week or so ago. After the truth came out about Markis Kane."

Kim let her dismay show. "That was a terrible business, wasn't it?"

Wilma showed by the way she set her jaw that she was embarrassed the museum had ever raised an exhibit to honor such a man.

"Anyway," Kim continued, "the exhibit has some factual data which would be very helpful to us. I wonder if you could show me where the material is now? And arrange for me to have access to it for a bit?"

She looked around for someone to consult. Or pass the problem to. Fortunately there was no one. "I'm not sure I can do that, sir."

Kim tried a desperate smile. "I promise I won't disturb anything. It would be a great help, and I only need a few minutes."

Wilma was trying to decide whether the request had a potential for getting her into trouble.

"Professor Teasdale is a close friend of Mikel's," Kim added helpfully.

The woman's lips curved into a smile. Kim suspected she was somewhat taken with Jay Braddock. Amusing notion.

"Of course," said Wilma. "Let me see if I can find a key."

She went into one of the offices and Kim heard voices. Moments later a dark-complexioned man with ice blue eyes peered out the door at her, frowned, and withdrew without showing any further sign that she existed. Wilma came back with a remote.

"That was Dr. Turnbull," she said, without further comment, as though Turnbull were known far and wide.

She led the way to a cargo lift, and they descended into the bowels of the building. Wilma stood nervously off to one side until the lift stopped and the doors opened. Lights came on and Kim saw that they were in a storage area divided into cages. Wilma had to look around a bit, but she finally figured out where she wanted to go. "This way," she said, walking toward the back. More lights came on. Wilma pointed the remote, locks clicked, and the doors of two cages opened. "This is the stuff from the *376* display."

The command chair, the parts from the missile launcher, the assorted other sacred artifacts from the battle of Armagon, were already covered with dust. Someone had stacked containers nearby, but no packing had been done yet.

"What exactly were you looking for, Dr. Braddock?"

Kim wanted her to leave but Wilma stayed close by. Which meant she had orders to make sure the visitor didn't make off with anything. Okay, that was reasonable. "Details of command and control functions during the engagement," she said.

Kim put a hand in her pocket to assure herself the two replacement disks were still there. She'd labeled them in the manner of the two disks that had been on display: 376 VISUAL LOG, JUNE 17, 531 and 376 SYSTEMS DATA, JUNE 17, 531. It was one of the most celebrated dates in Greenway's checkered history.

There was material here that had not been in the original exhibition, mostly parts from the interior of the *376* and other ships involved at Armagon: lockers and chairs, a replica of a captain's quarters, an array of mugs carrying the insignia of the various vessels, uniforms, copies of letters sent by the Council to the families of those killed in action.

Kim mentally waved it all aside and concentrated on finding the logs.

"Can I help in any way, Dr. Braddock?" asked Wilma.

"Call me Jay," Kim said. She realized she had *not* been mistaken about her effect on the woman, who smiled at her invitingly. She knew the museum aide would not know where anything was: she'd had trouble just finding the cage. Best was to avoid calling her attention to the disks. "No," she said. "That's quite okay. I believe I can find everything."

Wilma backed off a bit and Kim saw a package wrapped in plastic with a sticker marked LOGS. It was the right shape, and it was on top of a worktable that was identified as having once been in the *376* tactical display center. Kim rummaged among other materials until Wilma looked away, and then she picked up the package and peeled off the plastic.

Two disks.

VISUAL LOG and SYSTEMS DATA, JUNE 17, 531.

At the same moment she heard the whine of the lift. Coming down.

Wilma looked toward the sound and Kim dropped the disks into her pocket and brought out the substitutes.

The lift stopped and doors opened.

There were voices.

Mikel. And a woman.

Tora.

"Oh," said Wilma, gratified. "That's Dr. Alaam now."

The meeting must have broken up early. "He knows I'm here?"

"I left a message."

Kim pretended to examine the substitute disks, then quickly rewrapped them and put the package back on the worktable.

Mikel and Tora were at the gate, both looking surprised. "What's going on?" asked Mikel, glancing from Wilma to Kim. "Is this Braddock?"

"Yes," said Wilma.

"I assumed you were waiting upstairs." He looked carefully at Kim, and her heart stopped while she waited for recognition to come. "Do I know *you*?" he asked.

"We've met once or twice," she said, speaking in a low register. "Professor Teasdale is still working on her history of the period, and I've been gathering materials."

"Yes," he said. "I recall. Well, good to see you again, Braddock. We're happy to cooperate, of course. I'd suggest in future though that you let us know in advance that you're coming."

"They did," said Wilma. "He has a letter from us." Diplomatically, and fortunately for Kim, she did not say, "from *you*."

"Oh." Mikel was pondering the comment when Tora Kane assumed center stage. "I wonder if we can get on with it."

"Yes," said Mikel. "Of course."

Kim smiled politely. "Well," she said, "I think I have everything I need."

"Already?" asked Wilma. "That was quick."

"We only wanted a couple of verifications." She nodded to Tora, who was standing with her arms folded, pretending to be interested in a navigational console. Kim could barely suppress a grin: they were waiting for her to leave so they could pocket the disks.

No. More likely, Mikel knew nothing. Tora was playing the same game Kim had. She wondered what kind of story she'd told the director. Or whether she had simply bought him off without explanation. In either case, nothing would happen while she and Wilma were in the neighborhood.

Kim made her farewells and, accompanied by the aide, slipped into the elevator. Wilma was clearly inviting Jay to make a move. When he didn't, she looked briefly disappointed and got off at the main floor. Kim rode up to the roof.

Tora's Kondor was parked in a bay off the taxi pad. Kim wandered over to it, removed the microtransmitter, climbed into a cab, and rose into the sunlight in high good humor.

She inserted the visual log and instructed Shep to run it.

The wall over the sofa changed texture, the flatscreen appeared, and she was looking at the *Hunter* pilot's room. A technician was working and his shoulder patch was visible: ST. JOHNS MAINTENANCE.

The date, translated to Greenway time, was February 12, 573.

Specialists came and went, calibrating sensors, checking subspace communications, and performing a myriad other tasks.

The sequence was identical with her recollection of the version she had taken from the Archives. She fast-forwarded. The technicians raced through their tasks, then left, and the picture blinked. The timer leaped ahead more than two hours and Kane appeared.

She switched back to normal play. Kane turned and looked into the imager, directly out of the screen at Kim. His jaw was set, his mouth a thin line. He ran through a checklist, got out of his chair, and disappeared. The imager shut off. Sixteen minutes later, ship time, it blinked on again.

"Hunter *ready to depart,*" he told St. Johns control.

"Hunter, *you are clear to go.*"

Kane warned his passengers they were thirty seconds from departure, and his harness locked in place.

Kim watched it all again: The launch of the *Hunter*, Kane's warning to Kile during the early minutes of the flight that the vessel would need a general overhaul when it got back, the jump to hyperspace. She watched the passengers come forward one by one and she listened to the now-familiar conversations. She hastened through the periods when Kane was alone in the pilot's room.

The *Hunter* team talked about what they hoped to find in the Golden Pitcher. The Dream.

Nothing else mattered.

Tripley's recurrent assertions, *"We're going to do it this time, Markis; I know it,"* took on special poignancy.

She saw again Kane's infatuation with Emily. And hers with him.

She watched moodily, not expecting the record to deviate from the one she remembered until *Hunter* arrived off Alnitak. And probably even then it would not happen until just before they encountered the celestial. She was wrong.

It was almost three A.M. on day six when Kane, wearing a robe, appeared in the pilot's room with a cup of coffee. He sat down, checked his instruments, looked at the time, and activated his harness. *"Okay, everybody, buckle in."*

Voices broke in over the intercom.

Yoshi: *"Would somebody please tell me what's going on?"*

Emily: *"We have a surprise for you."*

Yoshi: *"In the middle of the night?"*

Tripley: *"Yes. It's worth it."*

Yoshi: *"So what is it? Markis, what are we doing?"*

Kim froze the picture, sat back in her chair, and stared at Kane's image in the glow of his instruments. In the doctored version, this hadn't happened.

No surprises for Yoshi.

And she knew now why Walt Gaerhard, the Interstellar technician, had been reluctant to talk about the jump engine repairs to which he'd signed his name.

There had been no repairs.

There'd been no damage.

28

We value Truth, not because we are principled, but because we are
curious. We like to believe we will not tolerate manipulation of the facts.
But strict knowledge of what has occurred often inflicts more damage
than benefit. Mystery and mythology are safer avenues of pursuit precisely because they are open to manipulation. Truth, ladies and gentlemen, is overrated.

> —E. K. WHITLAW: Summary in the
> Impeachment Trial of Mason Singh, 2087 C.E.

THE *HUNTER* LOGS: FEBRUARY 17–19, 573

"It's the most beautiful thing I've ever seen." It was Yoshi's voice. But
only Kane was visible, relaxed in his chair. He was looking off to his right,
gazing out beyond the view of the imager. Kim, recalling the design of
the *Hunter*, knew he was looking through large double windows. The
overhead screen depicted the Alnitak region, the vast roiling clouds, the
dark mass of the Horsehead, the brilliant nebulosity NGC2024, the giant
star itself, and the sweeping rings of the Jovian world.

"We thought you'd not want to miss it." Emily this time. "There's nothing quite like it anywhere we've been."

She came into the picture now and sat down in the left-hand chair. "I
think," she said, "we should have dinner tonight out on one of the terraces."

"Precisely what we had in mind." That was Tripley. Kim judged from
the body language of Emily and Kane that their colleagues were not
physically present in the pilot's room. "In fact, we've made it a tradition
to do that whenever we've been out here."

Something on the control board caught Kane's eye. He made adjustments, looked at his screens, and frowned. "*Well,* that's *interesting.*"

"*What is it, Markis?*" asked Tripley's voice.

"*I don't know. We're getting a return—*"

"*What kind of return?*"

"*Metal. Moving almost perpendicular to the plane of the system.*"

Emily leaned forward to get a better look at the screen. "*Is that significant? I wouldn't think a chunk of iron's that much out of the ordinary.*"

"*This one appears to have some definition.*" After a pause: "*But don't get excited. I'm sure it's nothing.*"

Nevertheless, Emily's face took on an aura of hope.

"*Markis.*" Tripley again.

"*It's on your monitor now, Kile. We're still too far away to make anything of it.*"

"*You think it might be an artificial object?*"

"*I think it's a chunk of iron.*" He pressed a key on the control panel. "*So everybody knows,*" he said, "*the Foundation requires us in any unusual circumstance to record everything that happens throughout the ship until we resolve the situation. Save for private quarters, of course. We will go to full recording mode in one minute. So get your clothes on back there, kiddies.*"

"*Can we get a picture of the thing?*" asked Yoshi.

"*It's still too far away.*"

"*How far is that?*"

"*Seven hundred thousand kay. It's in orbit, about to drift behind the planet. We'll lose it in a few minutes.*"

"*Not altogether, I hope,*" said Emily.

"*No chance,*" said Kane. They watched it drop down the sky, disappearing finally behind the rim of the big planet.

"*Kile, I assume we want to take a closer look?*"

Tripley laughed. "*Sure. Why not, as long as we're here?*"

"*How long before we see it again?*" asked Yoshi.

"*Don't know. We didn't get enough to plot an orbit.*"

"*Just stay with it,*" said Tripley.

"*All right.*" Kane gave directions to the AI. "*If we're going to pursue we should get rolling. Everybody belt down.*" *Hunter* rotated, realigned itself, and the mains fired.

They'd been running for almost three quarters of an hour when the object reappeared. Kane tried unsuccessfully to acquire an image. "*It's still too far,*" he said.

"Markis." It was the AI. *"The object is in a long irregular orbit. It'll decay quickly. Within about six weeks, in fact."*

"When will we catch up with it?" asked Tripley.

Kane put the question to the AI.

"Late tomorrow morning," came the answer.

Two lamps burned dimly in the pilot's room.

Rings and moons dominated the windows. At 2:17 A.M., the AI woke Kane. *"We have definition, Markis."*

The object was *smooth*, not the rugged piece of rock and iron one would have expected. It was shaped somewhat like a turtle-shell.

Kane studied it for almost ten minutes, enhanced it, tapped his fingers on the console, nodded to himself. Eventually he opened the intercom. *"Friends,"* he said quietly, *"we have an anomaly."*

They padded one by one into the pilot's room, in bare feet, all wearing robes. All cautiously excited. Emily looked at the overhead, the others turned to the windows, into which Kane had placed the image. *"It's an enhancement,"* he explained. *"But I think this is close to what's really out there."*

They stared quietly. Yoshi stood near Tripley and they seemed to draw together. Emily's face shone.

"It's not very big," Kane said.

"How big is that?"

"A little more than a half meter long, maybe two-thirds as wide."

Kim could almost feel the room deflate.

"It looks like a toy," said Yoshi. *"Something somebody just tossed overboard."*

It was tumbling, turning slowly end over end.

Tripley stood near a desk lamp. He turned it off so they could see better. *"Just for argument's sake,"* he said, *"is there any possibility of a local life-form?"*

Emily shook her head. *"Alnitak puts out too much UV."*

"But we don't really know that it couldn't happen," Tripley said.

"Almost anything's possible," said Emily. *"But let's not get ahead of ourselves here."*

Antennas and sensor pods were becoming visible. Kane tapped the window. *"It has a Klayson ring."*

It might have taken a minute for the implication to set in. A Klayson ring indicated jump capability.

"Aside from the size," said Emily, *"anybody ever seen this kind of design before?"*

Kane shook his head. *"I've run a search. It doesn't match up with anything."*

"It's a probe," said Emily. *"Probably left by the survey unit when it was here."*

"Can't be," said Kane.

"Why not?"

"The Klayson ring."

"Some probes have Klayson rings," insisted Emily.

"Not this size. It's too small. We wouldn't know how to pack a jump system into a package like this. Unless there's been a major advance in the last few months."

"Are you suggesting," said Yoshi, *"it's a celestial artifact?"* She barely breathed the conclusion.

Kane got up, went over to the window, and studied the object. *"I don't want to get everybody excited, but I don't think we, or anybody we know, left this here."*

They looked at one another. Tentative smiles appeared. Emily pressed her hand to her lips. Tripley glanced around the room as if he feared someone would have a more straightforward explanation. Yoshi stood unmoving in front of the windows, beside Kane.

"Don't be discouraged by its size," said Kane. *"It might still be possible to talk to it. There might be an AI of one sort or another on board."*

"Let me ask a question," said Tripley. *"Does intelligent life* have *to be big?"*

Emily nodded. *"Theoretically, yes. Got to have big brains."*

"Theoretically. But is that really true?"

No one knew.

Kane looked up from his console. He seemed to be alone in the pilot's room. *"Kile,"* he said to the commlink.

Tripley and the others showed up literally within seconds.

"We're getting power leakage," he told them. *"It's not dead."*

"Magnificent!" Tripley jabbed his right fist in the air and turned toward the women. *"Ladies,"* he said, *"I do believe we've done it!"*

They embraced all around. Emily kissed Kane's cheek while he pretended to be annoyed, and Yoshi threw her arms around him.

"*From this point,*" said Tripley, "*we will proceed on the assumption that they're alive over there.*"

When they overtook the turtle-shell they were looking down on the rings from a point somewhere over the north pole. Kane closed to within forty meters of the object. He'd arranged the approach so that Alnitak was behind the *Hunter,* to prevent its blinding the imagers.

Everybody was in the mission control center, save Kane, who stayed in the pilot's room. Tripley sat down at a comm console, looked at his colleagues, and signaled to Kane, whose virtual image occupied a chair. Kane nodded and Tripley put his index finger on the transmission key. Kane had pointed out that the AI could handle all the transmissions, but the moment was a bit too historic for that.

"Okay," said Kane. "When you're ready—"

Tripley pressed the key once. Then twice. He looked up at his colleagues and beamed. "*Maybe,*" he said, "*the first communication—*"

He tapped it again, *three* times.

"*—between humans and their starborn siblings—*"

Four.

"*—has just been sent.*"

They looked at one another expectantly. In the windows, the turtle-shell tumbled slowly across a moonscape.

"*It's dark over there,*" said Kane.

Emily shook her head. "*It's too small. It's a pity. But I'll settle for the artifact.*"

"*You give up too easily,*" said Yoshi. "*Try again, Kile.*"

Tripley resent. One, two, three, four.

The room glowed with the colors of the rings.

"*I think Emily's right,*" said Tripley. "*If anybody were there, they'd certainly want to respond.*"

They tapped out the signal a third time. Then Yoshi sat down at the key and continued patiently to send.

"*Something to consider,*" said Kane, studying the image. He pointed at an object mounted in the nose of the turtle-shell. It looked like a bracket or fork. "*It might have an attack capability.*"

"*Why would they attack?*" asked Emily.

"*You're poking a strange animal. What I'm saying is that it* could *happen. It might be a good idea to think about it.*"

"*They're not going to shoot at us,*" said Tripley. "*Why would they bother? They don't even know us.*"

Kane's voice was unemotional. "*Think about our relative sizes. We're what, several hundred times as big as they are. If there's really something alive over there, I'd expect them to be nervous. If our situations were reversed, I sure as hell would be.*"

"*So what are you suggesting?*" asked Emily.

"*That we be prepared to back off on short notice. Which means if I say we're leaving, I'll want everyone to belt down quickly, and to do it without argument. I doubt that the occasion will arise, but I won't want to get into a discussion if it does.*"

"*Okay,*" Emily said, without bothering to conceal her amusement. "*If they shoot, we run. I don't think anybody's going to argue with that.*"

"*So what's next?*" asked Yoshi. "*They don't seem to have their radio turned on. What else can we do?*"

"*Blink the running lights,*" said Emily.

Tripley nodded. "*Okay.*"

Kane turned them off and then on again. Waited a few seconds. Turned them off. Turned them on.

They kept it up for a while. After a few minutes Tripley asked whether anyone else had an idea.

"*Yes,*" said Yoshi. "*Why don't we back away so they don't think we're pushy? Let them make a move, if they're inclined. They* have *to be as curious as we are.*"

They agreed it was worth trying, and Kane withdrew to a range of five kilometers and assumed a parallel orbit.

They spent the next few hours in a long, generally pointless and often circular discussion. The turtle-shell seemed unlikely to be a warship under any circumstances because the Alnitak region was a no-man's-land, a place that could not conceivably be of strategic value. It was also probably not a trader or commercial vessel for the same reason. And that left only survey and research. *If* the vessel was not completely automated, and if it *was* in fact a vessel, then it should be staffed by scientists. But if that were so, why hadn't they responded?

Tripley suggested they try the radio again. They changed the transmission to one-three-five-seven and put it on automatic. It ran for two hours before they gave up and shut it down.

"*We need to start talking,*" said Emily, "*about what we do when they don't answer.*"

"That's easy," said Kane.

Everyone looked at him, surprised. Kane customarily avoided making policy suggestions that concerned the mission, as opposed to technical matters or the operation of the ship. *"We take a lot of pictures and go home."*

"No," said Tripley. *"It's out of the question."*

"Even if there were no other considerations," Yoshi said, *"they seem to be adrift and in a decaying orbit. If there's anybody in there, and we leave them, they'll die."*

"If we go back with nothing more than pictures," said Tripley, *"the scientific community would excoriate us."*

"I can think of three possible reasons why they aren't responding," said Kane. *"One, it is automated. Two, they're all dead. Three, they're playing possum. Floating out here in a decaying orbit suggests they're damaged. They can't run and they probably can't put up a fight. They're looking at a vessel of monumental dimensions, probably by far the biggest they've ever seen. So they're hoping we'll go away. Or—"*

"Or—?"

"That help will arrive."

"You think they've been sending out a distress call?"

"Sure. If they can."

"Do we have any way of intercepting it?"

"We don't know enough about their equipment. If it's hypercomm, which it probably would be, we'd have to be astronomically lucky to pick it up."

Emily suggested they try the radio again.

"Why would it be any more likely to work this time?" asked Tripley.

"They've had time to see we mean no harm. They may feel more willing to take a chance now."

Kane directed the AI to begin sending, counting to four.

"I never considered the possibility," said Tripley, *"that anything like this could happen. We always assumed that, in the event of contact with celestials, they'd be just like us, curious, anxious to communicate, amicable."*

A new tone sounded in the speaker.

A blip.

And then a pair of blips.

And then three.

"Coming from the turtle," said Kane.

Four.

And *five.*

Tripley banged a big hand down on the console.

They continued counting through to *eight.*

Joy reigned. They pumped fists, embraced, shook hands. And there were a few tears.

"My God, they're really there," said Tripley.

"Are we getting this?" Emily asked Kane. *"For the log?"*

The captain looked directly at the imager. *"Yes,"* he said. *"They'll be watching this in classrooms a thousand years from now."*

Tripley broke out four glasses and a bottle of wine.

And they got another blip.

Then a pair.

"They're counting again," said Tripley.

Three. Five.

Eight.

They looked at one another, waiting.

"Eight," said Tripley. *"What comes after eight? They're waiting for an answer."*

Emily shrugged. *"Thirteen,"* she said.

"How do you figure?"

"Each number is the total of the two preceding."

"That's good enough for me," said Tripley. He switched the transmitter to manual and tapped out the response.

The signals came again: One, two, three, five, seven.

"Primes," said Emily.

Tripley grinned, enjoying the game immensely. *"Eleven,"* he said.

Emily stood near the window, looking out at the tiny craft. *"I think it's time for a visual."*

Tripley agreed. *"Good. But what do we show them?"*

"What are they most curious about?"

"Us," said Yoshi.

"Yes." Tripley was beaming. *"Let's have someone say hello. One of the women—"*

"Why one of the women?" asked Emily. *"I think everybody should get on the circuit. Let them see what we've got."*

"Okay. Let's do it this way, though. Emily, you've been looking for these people a long time. You go first."

Emily looked genuinely moved. *"Sure,"* she said. *"I can live with that. All right."* She was already jotting down notes.

Kane was obviously vastly pleased. *"Their language skills might not be a good fit."*

"This is not for them. It's for those kids a thousand years from now."

"—Who are also listening to this setup," Yoshi reminded her.

"It's all right. They'll understand."

Emily sat down and signaled she was ready. Tripley adjusted her image and hit Transmit. *"You're on,"* he told her. She looked directly into the imager and smiled her brightest smile. *"We know you can't understand any of this,"* she said, *"but we want to say hello to you anyhow. Greetings from Greenway. Can we assist you in any way?"*

The others followed. Tripley spoke with warmth of his hopes that this chance encounter would produce long-term benefits for both races. Yoshi wished a good fortune to *"our interstellar friends,"* and expressed her hope that this marked the beginning of a new era for everyone.

Finally it was Kane's turn. He didn't look as if he expected to be called on in this endeavor, but when Yoshi identified him as their captain and reported he had something to say, he rose to the occasion. *"We're happy to meet you. If we can be of assistance, please let us know."*

With that, he switched off.

"Well," said Tripley, *"how'd we do?"*

"I thought you guys were outstanding," said Kane.

"Any sign of a response?" asked Emily.

"Not yet."

Kane sank back into his seat. Tripley asked whether it was likely the turtle-shell would have compatible equipment to receive a visual image. Kane assured him it would.

They waited. The minutes dragged by. And a white lamp blinked on. *"Incoming,"* said Kane.

It resembled a butterfly.

In her living room, Kim, expecting to see a misty *thing,* leaned forward surprised. Her pulse began to race.

The butterfly looked at them out of cool, golden eyes. They were not compound, but were rather quite mammalian. It had a thorax and mandibles and multiple sets of limbs, apparently six altogether, but it was difficult to be certain. Spotted red-gold wings moved slowly.

It wore a surprisingly mundane green blouse. The lower half of the body was not visible.

There was no physiognomy capable of supporting, in human terms, an expression. From somewhere, it was impossible to be certain where, a sound was emanating, a singsong rhythm, almost a chant, interrupted by rapid sets of clicks.

The image was being picked up on monitors in both mission control and the pilot's room, and was also being displayed in the windows.

The creature was supported on a framework, presumably a chair-equivalent. A few gauges were visible on a bulkhead, and the pilot's room, if that's what it was, appeared to be normal size. Curious illusion that: anyone receiving the transmission would make some egregiously false assumptions. The butterfly appeared to be of the same general dimensions as a human.

It raised its upper left limb in a gesture that must have been acknowl-edgment. It maintained that position for one minute, seventeen seconds. Then the screen went blank.

"*What happened?*" asked Tripley.

Kane shook its head. "*Apparently end of transmission,*" he said. "*I guess they're not much for small talk.*"

"*Can we get a picture of the main hatch from outside?*" Emily asked Kane. "*Our main hatch?*"

"*Negative. We don't have anything that can acquire the angle. Why?*"

"*How about the cargo door?*"

"*We can do that.*"

"*What do you have in mind?*" asked Tripley.

"*I think we ought to send them an invitation.*" She explained her idea but Tripley, after he'd heard her out, looked uncertain.

"*You think it's wise?*"

"*What's to lose? If Markis is right and the ship's damaged, it might get us all off on exactly the right note.*"

"*All right,*" he said. "*Let's try it.*"

Kane pointed one of the port imagers at the cargo hatch, opened the air lock and turned its lights on. Emily straightened her blouse and checked her hair. When she was ready, he went to a split screen, putting her on one side and the open door on the other.

"*Hello again. Would you like to come on board?*"

The image of the miniature ship was back in the windows. It floated serenely against the star-clouds.

Emily waited. And tried again.

And a third time.

"*I think I'm insulted,*" she said finally.

▪ ▪ ▪

"What's the matter with them?" Two hours had passed and Tripley could not begin to conceal his frustration. *"You think they saw the open door as a threat?"*

"Don't know. We're looking at butterflies, for God's sake. You think they've had any experience with spiders?"

"So what do we do now?" asked Emily.

"The open door should be a universal," Tripley persisted. *"All it really implies is that they're welcome. Why don't we try it again?"*

"Let Yoshi wave at them," said Emily. *"Maybe she'll have better luck."*

Yoshi took her place in front of the imager, smiled sweetly, looked as unthreatening as she could presumably manage, and made friendly overtures.

There was still no response.

"I just thought of something," she said. *"They probably don't realize how big we are. As individuals, I mean. They'd expect there are thousands of us here."*

"You're right," said Emily.

"Meaning—?"

"A physical meeting might not be a good idea. At least for now."

"Transmission coming in," said Kane. *"Audio only."* He put it on the speaker.

They were back to blips.

One.

Two. Three.

And fourteen.

"Fourteen?" demanded Tripley.

"It's not a series," said Yoshi.

Emily took a long deep breath. *"I agree. But what are they trying to tell us?"*

The sequence repeated. One. Two. Three.

Fourteen.

And repeated again.

"They're telling us to go away," said Emily. *"Fourteen doesn't fit the series. They want to break off."*

"So what do we do now?" asked Tripley.

"Go home," suggested Kane. *"Take the hint and leave. I don't think you can do anything here except cause damage."*

"We can't do that, Markis," said Tripley. *"It's crazy."*

Emily looked tired. *"What do you suggest, Kile?"*

"Markis, do you still think they're adrift?"

"Yes. There's no question about it."

"Then we can't just leave." He was in an agony of indecision. *"We don't know how far they are from home. And we don't know whether they've got help coming."* He looked at Emily. *"Would you want to leave them here, have them get sucked into that—"* he indicated the gas giant, *"—and live with it for the rest of your life?"*

"Why don't we wait to see whether any one comes to rescue them?" suggested Yoshi. *"If nobody shows up within a reasonable time, then we could try to take them on board."*

"What's a reasonable time?" asked Tripley. *"For all we know, they're running out of life support while we debate. God knows how long they've been here."*

"But they're telling us," said Emily, *"to go away."*

Yoshi frowned. *"I'm not so sure. Maybe the message is a distress call. You break off the sequence, that means there's something wrong. Maybe they think we should recognize that. Just like we think they should recognize the open door."*

Tripley was out of patience. *"Look,"* he said, *"what's the worst that could happen if we pick them up? We go back to Greenway—"*

"—St. Johns is closer."

"—Greenway. We're going to need help. We'll have a team waiting for us when we get there. Do whatever needs to be done for the poor bastards. Then we give them the keys to the city and send them on their way."

"If it works," said Yoshi, *"it'd be a great way to begin relations."*

"Then we're agreed. Markis, you have any reservations?"

"I'd keep hands off. But it's your call, Kile. I'll go along with whatever you decide."

"Let's do it."

"How?" asked Yoshi.

Tripley took a deep breath. *"What you said. The thing doesn't seem to have much maneuverability. Let's just take them on board."*

Emily and Tripley suited up, went below, and depressurized the cargo bay.

"When I tell you to," Kane instructed them, *"open the door. But not before. I don't want you getting a direct dose of local radiation. We'll keep the star on the far side of the ship. But it still won't be safe so we want to handle this with despatch. Once the door's open, you shouldn't have to do*

anything. I'll bring the turtle-shell on board. But if there's a reaction and we have to maneuver, make sure you hold on to something. As soon as it's inside, close up. Okay?"

"Okay, Markis," said Tripley.

Thrusters along the starboard hull fired and the *Hunter* moved side-wise toward the target.

Carrying their helmets, they went into the air lock and sat down on the bench. The screen embedded in the outer door performed all the functions of a window. Kim's angle however did not reveal what they were able to see. *"So far there's no response,"* said Kane.

He took almost an hour to negotiate the distance. When he was sat-isfied, he signaled and Tripley opened the inner air-lock door. And then the outer.

"Still nothing," said Kane. *"It's about two minutes away."*

They moved out of the lock, giving Kane room to operate.

"We're about to cut gravity. Stay clear of the object. If it does anything unexpected, let it go. Somebody dies, it's a lot of paperwork, and in this sit-uation it wouldn't take much."

"You all right?" Emily asked her partner.

"I'm fine," said Tripley.

"Okay." Kane's voice was a monotone. *"We're about to shut gravity down. Don't make any sudden moves."*

The celestial appeared outside the open air lock.

"Stay clear," warned Kane. *"The turtle-shell will come through the door without help. When it's safely inside, close up. And then give it lots of room."*

The *Hunter*'s outside lights swept across the turtle-shell. Kim noticed what she had not observed before: The geometry suggested the hyper-bolic vehicle that had attached itself to the *Hammersmith*.

"Don't worry," said Emily. *"We'll be fine."*

"I'm sure you will. But keep your distance until we're sure it's safe. When we've done that, we'll have to figure out how to secure for the trip home."

"Maybe," said Yoshi, who was watching from the corridor, *"we should have talked this out a bit more."*

The turtle-shell was just outside the air lock. Kane was apparently moving the *Hunter* gradually toward it. Tripley stood watching. He was too close. Maybe mesmerized, but his face was obscured by the helmet. Emily took him by the arm and pulled him gently out of the way.

It entered the lock. Passed through and drifted into the hold. Into the lights.

"Hey," said Kane, *"we're getting a visual."*

Tripley threw a startled glance at one of the monitors. The picture of the spacecraft blinked off and was replaced by the butterfly. Its antennae were weaving and the singsong cadence had gone up an octave.

"I think it's frightened," said Emily.

"Maybe." Tripley looked from the screen to the microship. *"They'll be grateful soon enough."*

Tripley started toward the air lock, intending to close it. But the ship *moved*. It rotated a few degrees around its own axis, pointed its prow at the open sky beyond the air-lock door, and started forward. It was a kind of lurch, as though the directing force had less than total control.

"Stay clear," warned Kane. *"It wants out."*

Emily tried to pull Tripley back. *"They're terrified,"* she said. *"They've just discovered how big we are. Don't make any threatening moves."* And then, incredibly, she walked in front of the ship and held up her hands. *"It's all right,"* she told them. *"We only want to help."*

Several things happened at once. Tripley punched a button and the air lock started to close. Kane shouted a warning to Emily that they couldn't hear her and to get out of the way. The butterfly image vanished from the screen.

Foolishly, Emily held her ground, blocking the vessel's route back through the door, which was closing fast. *"Please,"* she said. *"Give us a chance."*

Twin beams of red light lanced from the fork on the ship's prow. They struck her squarely in the abdomen and propelled her into the air lock and sent her tumbling out the door. Tripley screamed and made a grab for her but he succeeded only in changing her course and very nearly going out himself. He stared after her retreating form, turned, and charged the turtle-shell. Kane ordered Tripley to stop. But it was too late. The mission director seized the microship and his momentum carried both of them across the chamber. They crashed into a wall and Tripley bounced away in the zero gravity, still holding tight to the celestial.

The outer door closed.

"Going to one gee," Kane said.

Tripley and the microship fell to the floor.

Emily, picked up by one of the screens, continued drifting away, trailing red bubbles.

"Monitoring zero—" Kane's voice broke. He needed a moment to regain control and finish: *"—Zero pulse."*

■ ▪ ▪

Yoshi was adamant. *"I say we turn them loose. Turn them loose, get away from here, and forget it ever happened."*

"They killed Emily," said Tripley. *"How can we just let them go?"*

"They were scared. They wanted out."

"There was no need."

Kane broke in: *"Nobody has more reason than I do to want the little bastards dead."* He stopped and his jaw worked. *"But this is a special case. Yoshi's right. Point them toward the hydrogen—"* he meant the gas giant, *"—and let them go."*

Tripley shook his head. *"That means she'd have died for nothing. What do we tell people when we get home? We found some celestials, but they didn't want to talk a whole lot. Don't know how the ship works, we didn't get a chance to ask. Don't know where they're from. Otherwise ask us anything. By the way, we lost Emily."*

"What do you want to do?" asked Kane.

"I say we take them with us. We're committed. For God's sake, Markis, we've paid the price. We owe it to her."

"If we'd used our heads—"

"It's late for recriminations. You want me to take the blame? Okay, it's my fault."

"That doesn't bring her back, Kile."

"I know. It was stupid. We took a chance. But we've got to make it count for something. How could we possibly walk away from this now?"

"Kile?" Yoshi's voice, strained. *"I don't think anybody'll thank us for this."*

"What do you mean? How can you say that? This is it. It's the Holy Grail."

"People will be happy to have the discovery, but we'll be a laughing-stock."

Tripley shook his head desperately. *"You wanted to bring them on board as much as I did."*

"Think about it," said Yoshi. *"We don't know what kind of hypercomm messages they've been sending out. Look out for the giants with their open doors. Shoot on sight. What do you think people are going to say to the pictures of you charging the ship and banging it against a wall?"*

"Markis, is that really on the log?"

"Yes, I'm afraid so, Kile."

"*My God. But the bastards are killers.*"

"*Only because they were being hijacked,*" insisted Yoshi. "*That's the way they saw it. And the way the media will play it. Look, I'm not trying to blame anybody. But we need to think about this. Reputations, careers, everything's going to go. We'll even show up in the history books as dummies of the first order. They'll be laughing at us for centuries.*"

They were in mission control. Emily's body had been retrieved and placed in her bunk. The celestial was centered on their screens, lying pinned by gravity to the cargo deck. "*We can't just throw this away,*" Tripley pleaded.

No one answered.

29

*The high-minded man must care more for
the truth than what people think.*

—ARISTOTLE, 340 B.C.E.

Kim reran the sequence in the cargo hold. She froze the picture at the moment of impact, when the bolt struck Emily, and she magnified it and focused on her sister's face plate. She could make out her expression, which betrayed more surprise than agony.

She died quickly, and that was some consolation. But there had been a few seconds after the attack, when the lights were going out, when Kim could almost read her thoughts: *I have it in my hands, a ship built by another civilization, and I'll never know who they are—*

The design of her colleagues now took on a kind of Greek inevitability. They would take the turtle-shell back to Greenway and find out what they could about it and its occupants. But first they had to negate the vehicle's capacity to do damage.

They accomplished the latter by determining that the weapon used against Emily was the "fork" mounted on the prow. They used a bar to break it off and then secured the vehicle in a stowage locker.

They next engaged in a heated debate before taking the eventually unanimous, if reluctant, decision to conceal the outcome of the mission. "*Until,*" in Tripley's words, "*the time is right to reveal what we've found. If that ever happens.*" Kane was most opposed to the plan, perhaps because he did not like deceit, but also and most certainly because it required him to falsify the ship's records. But he eventually succumbed to the argument that if they reported events as they had occurred, their careers would be ruined and their reputations destroyed. They would be remembered for their folly as long as the species endured.

So they would take the microship back to Greenway and examine it themselves. And in the meantime they hoped that maybe one of them would think of a way out of the frightful dilemma into which they had sunk.

The strategy required that Emily be left behind, since there was no way to explain her death. It was Tripley who devised the plan that they would "return" her to Terminal City, book a hotel reservation for her, use her ID to create the illusion that she'd gotten into a cab, and let the authorities figure out why she never arrived.

Having laid out their course, their last action before leaving orbit was to consign Emily to the void.

All this was on the record, as if Kane wanted to make it available to some future— What? Historian? Judge?

The logs ended immediately after the burial service. The screen went blank and the power blinked off.

Kim sat in the lengthening shadows listening to the ocean.

"Kim, you have a call from Canon Woodbridge."

"Put him on, Shep."

Actually, she got an assistant, a young male with a somber, self-important manner. "Dr. Brandywine?"

"Yes? This is she." If he gave his name she missed it.

"Dr. Woodbridge wishes you to come to Salonika tomorrow. He asked me to express his regrets that he couldn't call you himself, but he's extremely busy."

"Why?" she asked.

"He's always quite busy, Doctor."

"I mean, why does he want me in the capital?"

"I believe it's an award ceremony of some sort. He's quite anxious that you be here."

"You can't tell me what it's about?"

"I'm sorry. I don't have details. But transportation's been arranged. You'll be picked up at nine tomorrow morning. I hope that's not inconvenient."

Ten minutes later, Shep reported another call. *"Tora Kane."*

Kim sighed. She was on the sofa, trying unsuccessfully to read the latest issue of *Cosmic*, and she was not in the mood for more hostility. Nevertheless she straightened herself and told Shepard to make the connection.

"Brandywine," said Tora. The woman *was* difficult.

"Hello," said Kim.

The archeologist was standing beside an antique vase. "Would I be correct in concluding," she said, "that it was you I saw at the Mighty Third yesterday?"

"I don't think so," Kim said.

"Please don't waste my time. I'm not stupid."

Kim shrugged.

"I warned him it was a bad place to leave them," she said.

Was she talking about her father? Or Mikel? "What exactly," asked Kim, "do you want?"

"I have an instruction to carry out." She looked at Kim the way one might look at a beetle.

"An instruction? From whom?"

"From Markis."

"Oh?"

"First I need to be sure I have the right person. Did you, or did you not, steal something from the museum yesterday?"

"Just a moment." Kim cut the sound. "Shep," she said, "are we being recorded at the other end?"

He needed a moment to run a sweep. *"No,"* he said.

"If she starts to record," Kim said, "cut us off immediately."

"I'll do that, Kim."

"Give me the sound again."

Tora gazed at her from under half-lowered lids. "I hope you feel safe enough now to tell me the truth."

"I have the logs," said Kim.

"There's something else you should see."

"What?"

"Come tomorrow evening. At seven."

"You can't tell me what it is?"

She blinked off.

A government flyer touched down on Kim's pad at precisely nine A.M. She got in, showed her ID to the dex, and the vehicle lifted off and headed northwest through a sky heavy with rainstorms.

She was exhausted. The images from the *Hunter*'s cargo bay had given her no rest. She kept seeing Emily's eyes, and Tripley's mad dash to seize the *Valiant*.

What should she do now?

It seemed simple enough: release the news. It would be a huge story, and while the *Hunter* crew wouldn't emerge covered with glory, at least some of the suspicions of foul play would dissipate. But she couldn't do that without also divulging that a contact had been made. And that would violate the understanding she had with Woodbridge.

If people found out, there'd be no holding them back. Everybody with access to a ship would be headed for Alnitak. Where they'd encounter what? A species made hostile by the apparent hijacking of one of their ships?

The flyer dropped onto a rooftop pad at the National Security Center. By then rain was falling heavily. The vehicle taxied into one of the shelters and Kim found a young female escort waiting for her.

She was taken down several floors and shown into a small office. Moments later a door opened and Woodbridge appeared. He shook her hand, asked whether everything was going well at the Institute. Before she had a chance to answer, an assistant looked in and told him they were ready. "Good," Woodbridge said. Showing no interest whatsoever in conditions at the Institute, he led the way across a corridor into a conference room where roughly twenty people were milling about. It was a festive occasion. Cheeses, pastry, and wine had been laid out. Woodbridge began introducing her to the room's occupants—all seemed to have titles, Director This and Commissioner That—when a side door opened and everyone fell silent. The few who were not already on their feet rose.

Kim couldn't see who was coming in, but she heard voices just outside in the corridor and then the commotion was in the room and she saw that it was Talbott Edward, one of the members of the Council. He strode to the front, while people made way on both sides, and took his position behind a lectern. He waited for everyone to find a seat.

"Ladies and gentlemen," he said. "It's good to see you all again. I don't get up here often enough." Edward was tall, extraordinarily thin, immaculately groomed. He wore bracelets on both wrists, and his gaze had the quality of reflecting from his aides and guests, as if he didn't quite see anyone around him.

"Today I have an especially gratifying task to perform." He looked out over his audience, picked out Kim, and seemed to recognize her. *Did* recognize her, probably, she decided, because he was searching out the young woman seated beside Woodbridge. "Dr. Brandywine, would you come up here, please? And Canon, you too."

He welcomed her with a hearty handshake, his glance meanwhile returned upward. He smiled at Woodbridge, and proceeded to go on for several minutes about the advances of science and technology and how important it was that the Republic remain at the forefront of scientific research.

"Periodically, we at the Progress Directorate like to take time to honor the people who lead the charge." He seemed to think that was an especially telling phrase, because he delivered it again. "—Who lead the charge into the future. Today we want to express our appreciation to Dr. Kimberly Brandywine, for special contributions in the field of cosmology." Woodbridge produced a small white box and held it out to him.

Edward took the box, opened it, and extracted a silver medal with a red ribbon, which he held so the audience could see. "The Brays Stilwell Award for Special Achievement," he said. His hand moved in a graceful arc ending at her lapel, to which he affixed the medal. "Congratulations." He shook her hand, and shook Woodbridge's hand.

Kim had never heard of the Brays Stilwell. She said thanks, felt a rush of gratitude, and smiled at Woodbridge and at the Councilor.

Edward told her he knew she would continue her fine work. Then he shook a few more hands, glanced at the time, and disappeared.

The people in the audience approached her to look at the award and wish her well. "It's nice," she told Woodbridge. "Thank you."

"It's really quite a high honor," he said. "The highest we can give. But nobody'll ever really know why you got it. Except you, me, the councilman, and a few staff people."

She wasn't sure herself why she'd gotten it.

He put his hands on her shoulders, as if he were sending her off to battle. "Now, can I talk you into having lunch with me?"

It had just begun to get dark when Kim arrived at Tora Kane's home. Tora was standing at the pad, sipping a drink, when the taxi touched down and Kim stepped out. "Good evening, Brandywine," she said.

Kim nodded and looked at the cab. "Should I have it wait?"

"It wouldn't hurt."

It was a pleasant evening toward the end of April, just after sunset. The air was filled with the scent of the woods. A pair of squirrels stopped chasing each other around the bole of an ancient oak to watch the two women.

They climbed onto the porch and Tora invited Kim to sit down. She picked out a rickety wooden chair; Tora took the swing. There was a pitcher and an extra glass on a side table. "Blue riggers," said her hostess. "Would you like one?"

"Thank you," Kim said, determined to avoid returning the woman's surliness.

Tora filled a glass and held it out for her. "How did you find out where they were?"

"The logs?" Kim shrugged. "It seemed like a place that would have appealed to him."

"Hidden in a museum? On public display? Oh yes, he liked that."

The blue rigger was quite good.

Kim met her eyes. "You knew all along, didn't you? You knew what happened on the *Hunter*."

"Yes," she said. "I knew."

"You've seen the logs?"

"No." She put her drink down. Rocked back and forth. Stared into the growing dusk. "No. I had no wish to see the gory details. But I knew what happened. He was tortured by it."

"What about Mount Hope? What's the rest of the story?"

She opened a drawer on the side table and took out a disk. "He knew that somebody would eventually do what you have done, somebody would get at least part of the truth. If it hadn't been you, it would have been somebody else." A lamp burned inside the window. "My instructions were that, if the logs were found, this statement should be made available to the authorities. That's not you, but it seems that you're the logical person to receive it nonetheless."

Kim took it. "Do you want to watch it?"

"I've seen it."

Kim slipped it into a jacket pocket. "You should be aware that I haven't decided yet whether I'll make any of this public."

She shrugged. "Make it public and be damned."

Kim got up and turned to go.

Tora stayed on the swing. "*You* should be aware," she said, "that what you have is a copy. No part of the *Hunter* story is to be made public unless all of it is. If you don't see to it, *I* will."

When she got home, Kim put it on the flat screen.

The first image was the *Valiant*. A timer in the lower right hand corner gave the date April 3, 573, 6:48 P.M. The Mount Hope explosion, she recalled, had occurred on that same date at a little after seven o'clock in the evening.

The *Valiant* was on a table. It was bathed in light, and she could see part of a device that looked like a sensor suspended overhead. She couldn't make out anything else, but the table looked like the one she'd seen in Tripley's basement lab.

An arm came into the picture, adjusted the sensor. And she heard Kile's voice: *"How's that, Yosh?"* The arm was in a white sleeve. It withdrew, and Kim could see nothing except the microship and the tabletop.

"That's good. That'll do it."

And Kile again: *"Markis, we're ready to start."*

"Be right down."

The timer continued to run.

"Ready?" asked Tripley.

Yoshi again: *"All set."* Then her voice going higher: *"Hey, Kile, what's that?"*

Kim saw nothing.

"Not sure." The arm came back, went behind the ship on the port side, and blocked the imager's view. *"Hey, we've got an open hatch!"*

The table and the ship *rippled.*

Mist rose from a dozen places on the *Valiant*, as if the spacecraft were venting.

The arm jerked away.

And now the voices became confused.

"What is that?"

"They're not dead."

"My God, Kile, stay away from it."

"Get upstairs!"

The lighting changed abruptly, as if a curtain had passed in front of a lamp. And something that looked like an oversized dragonfly appeared from behind the ship and glided out of the picture.

Kile screamed for Yoshi to look out, and then Kim heard more shouts, but nothing from Yoshi. Someone heavy—Tripley, it must have been—ran across the floor and pounded up the staircase. There were more cries, some now coming from Kane, and she heard a sickening crunch, the sound of flesh impacting and bones breaking.

Yoshi.

Now the heavy steps came back downstairs. Kim understood that Yoshi had fallen or been pushed off the stairway, that Tripley was trying to do something for her, and then he was swearing he would kill the bastards—those were his words—and he hurried back up the stairs and out of the laboratory.

The *Valiant* remained untouched on the table until the record stopped.

A new image appeared: Markis Kane in a black, loose-fitting shirt. The date advanced to August 11, 575. More than two years later.

Lines had appeared in his face, and for several seconds he merely stared out of the screen. Kim thought he appeared unsure of himself. Not at all the Kane she'd come to know.

"I have no way of knowing," he said, "who will hear this account of the *Hunter*, and of the destruction of Severin Village. We are all culpable, everyone who was on the mission. For the sake of the others, and perhaps for my own reputation, I would have preferred these events continue as they have, one unremarked, the other unexplained. But I must assume that the listener knows enough that the rest should be made clear.

"Let me admit at the outset that the primary responsibility for the disaster that overtook Severin Village on April 3, 573, is mine. I consented against my better judgment to the seizure of the celestial vessel. I suggested and executed the tactic for bringing it aboard ship, an act which resulted directly in the death of Emily Brandywine. I further failed to dissuade Kile Tripley in his intention to bring the vessel to Greenway, even though I knew there was a potential for precisely the kind of disaster that occurred. That I have not stepped forward and acknowledged these facts has been dishonorable. I hope, before the truth emerges, as it surely must, I will be safely dead, beyond the grip of public opprobrium, or of any but divine justice.

"There was no indication of life aboard the celestial at any time after we had taken it onboard. We assumed that Kile's attack on the vessel had killed whatever had been inside. We had mixed emotions about that. It was not the way one wants first contact to occur. But they had, after all, taken Emily's life.

"Kile's intention was to keep the discovery secret for a time, and to bring in a few discreet researchers. He planned to use one of several laboratories available to the Foundation, for the purpose of dissecting the artifact and retrieving its secrets. But the problem was that the laboratories were all located in heavily populated areas.

"We did not know how the vessel was powered. But we thought it wise to assume it used the only fuel we knew of that made entry into transdimensional space possible: antimatter. That presented us with a unique problem. If they did indeed use antimatter, there was always the possibility of a breach in the containment system. Should that happen, should its power reach so low a level that it could not maintain the magnetic bottle, the vessel would explode, and take us and a sizable portion of the neighborhood with it. Consequently we needed a lab in a remote location.

"I should add parenthetically that we felt we had time, since every test we had run indicated that power was flowing through the ship, and that maintenance systems did seem to be stable. Of course, as the event showed, much of this was guesswork.

"To reduce the danger, Kile decided that the Foundation would sponsor a lab on Shimmer, where an accident could harm no one except volunteer technicians. A hypercomm message was sent before we left Alnitak, directing that work be started immediately. Nevertheless, it would be several months before the facility could be ready.

"In my own defense, I should point out that I argued throughout that the artifact be left in orbit around one of the Jovians in the helian system, where there could be no danger to anyone. But it was too much to ask of Kile, who was anxious to get to a place where they would have the capability to inspect the find. At the very least, he maintained, the bodies of the crew had to be examined as quickly as possible.

"Kile elected to take it to his summer home in Severin. It was a compromise choice, with less potential for disaster than there would have been in, say, Terminal City or Marathon. At the time, it seemed not unreasonable.

"I believed the chances for a catastrophe were slight, though what evidence I based that on I cannot now conceive. We thought, given a few days, we could determine the nature of the fuel and the state of any containment system. Unfortunately, we were not given a few days.

"We had no difficulty getting the artifact past the customs people. Yoshi walked it through, describing it as a toy for a nephew. She gave it a modest value, and was told it fell within her exemption.

"We took the artifact to Kile's home, where it turned out that the equipment he had available for analysis was considerably less than he'd implied. We had to go out looking for almost everything we needed. The result was that we wasted the little time we had. For example, we needed a full day simply to locate a Vanover sensor, which would allow us to look into the interior.

"I'm not altogether certain of some specifics regarding the events of April 3, because I was upstairs when I first realized there was a problem. Kile and Yoshi were down in the lab and they started screaming. I ran for the stairs and saw Yoshi coming up. She was scared out of her wits.

"Then I saw that an *entity* very much like a living cloud had apparently emerged from the ship. It immediately attacked Yoshi. When Kile and I went to her rescue, it released her, and she fell off the staircase, struck her head, and must have been dead when Kile reached her. Meanwhile, the entity came after me. It delivered an electrical shock, which left me temporarily stunned. As I went down, I thought I saw a small vehicle, a tiny lander if you will, glide past me in the creature's wake. It was hard to be certain, because I was a bit shaken up. Furthermore I'd sliced an arm as I fell and had got blood in my eyes. In any event, *something* blew a hole in a window, and the cloud and the lander, if that's indeed what it was, disappeared into the night.

"At about the same time Kile must have seen he could do nothing for Yoshi. He stormed upstairs, and asked me where the intruders had gone.

"I pointed to the window, and without another word he raced after them. I tried to dissuade him, and hurried outside just in time to see him lifting off the pad. I called after him not to go, but he persisted.

"I raised him on his commlink. He told me he was tracking the celestials, that he had them on his screen, and that he intended to make sure of them this time. Then he told me he would call me when it was over, and he signed off. I made repeated efforts to contact him after that, but he didn't respond.

"I went back to see if I could do anything for Yoshi. But she was dead. A few minutes later, I heard the blast that blew the side out of Mount Hope. The house shook and the lights dimmed and went out. When I went outside, debris was still raining down on the town.

"Fires burned everywhere. There were screams in the wreckage.

"And God help me I knew it had been the fuel cells, that the celestials had somehow transferred them to the lander, and that Kile and I were responsible.

"I did what I could to help. Emergency teams from Eagle Point and elsewhere came in quickly. I tried again to raise Kile, but I never heard from him again.

"At the time I believed people would know who had done it. How could they not know? We were just back, the explosion had been triggered by antimatter, Kile was almost certainly dead in the blast. We had another crew member missing, and a third dead in the village. Clearly we had been up to something.

"Nevertheless I could not face public humiliation, and I did what I could to keep these events from coming to the attention of the authorities. It seemed to me two things needed to be accomplished.

"The first was to dispose of Yoshi's body, so that it would not be found at the scene of the disaster and, when she was identified, raise even more questions. I wrapped it in plastic, weighted it, and put her in the river, above the dam, in the deepest part.

"Second, I had to remove the starship. I'd decided to bury it in the mountains, and then try to ride out the storm of suspicion which I knew would rise, and which indeed *did* rise, after the event. But when I got back to Kile's villa, to my horror his mother had arrived and taken charge of things. I had no immediate opportunity to retrieve the microship, so I left it, hoping that no one would recognize it for what it was. Several days later, when I visited her, she was talking about sending it to her grandson.

"The thing that attacked Yoshi is still loose in the mountains. People come back with stories, and it has become something of a local celebrity, although fortunately very few take it seriously. And they are written off as lunatics.

"I have felt some sympathy for the creature, lost and alone in a strange world. I do not believe it meant to injure Yoshi, but only wished to clear the way for the escape vehicle. I've even gone looking for it on occasion. If it's there, and if it recognizes me, it stays away.

"The lost crew of the microship, in spite of everything, has my respect. They killed two, and possibly three, of our people. Yet they must have known an explosion was imminent, and they took the fuel with them anyway. Did they do it for some incomprehensible reason? Or did they recognize they were in a populated area and sacrificed themselves in an effort to save creatures for whom they should have had no concern and no sympathy?"

The three great stars in Orion rose out of the sea at about nine o'clock. Kim sat on her deck, watching them. Next door, they were celebrating a birthday with loud music and rockets. When the noise subsided and the lights eventually went out, she was still there.

30

One assumes the kindness of a friend;
But the kindness of a stranger,
Ah, that is of a different order of magnitude—

—SHEYEL TOLLIVER, *Notebooks*, 573

"**A**nd *you* thought Tripley's grandmother put the body in the river." Matt's eyes contained a rare twinkle.

"I couldn't imagine who else might have done it. I never even thought of Kane."

"Do you think Tora knows?"

"She knows." They were on the sundeck at Kim's home. It was a trifle cool but the day was pleasant and the sound of the surf soothing.

"I wonder what the customs people will say when they find out somebody smuggled a starship past them." His eyes closed. "So what are you going to do now? You can't really sit on something like this."

"What do you suggest?"

"Turn it over to Woodbridge."

"Then what?"

"Then nothing. We're out of it at that point."

"Matt—"

"Look, Kim, I understand how you feel. The reputations of Kane and Tripley are hanging out there. People think they're killers. But they're the ones who mismanaged everything. You have an agreement with Woodbridge and he's absolutely right. We're just going to have to swallow this as best we can."

She stared out to sea. "Matt, we aren't talking reputations anymore. Or politics. Think about what happened out there. At Alnitak."

"They blundered."

"Yes, they did. They encountered a vehicle from another civilization, and they *hijacked* it."

"I know."

"One of the most important events in human history. We need to find a way to set things right."

"Are we talking about the *celestials*?"

"Yeah. That's exactly what I'm talking about."

"Kim, how in heaven can we do that? It's *done*. *Fini*. Too late."

"Maybe not. We could try mounting another mission. Go back to Alnitak and try again to talk to them."

"*That's* good. Wasn't it you the other day who was calling them murderous sons of bitches? Who wanted to kill them all? Wasn't it you who stirred up Woodbridge? Warned him that we shouldn't let anybody *near* the little bastards? I think that's quoted correctly."

"Matt—"

"—Who encouraged him to cancel Beacon? Which project, by the way, the director was proud of? And which your colleagues had been working on for *years*?"

"Matt, I was wrong. Think about what happened. The crew of the *Valiant* sacrificed themselves to save members of a species that had kidnapped and marooned them. Why do you think they did that?"

"I don't know. Maybe they weren't very bright."

"I think they're worth getting to know."

A couple of joggers were passing. They waved, and Kim and Flexner waved back. "Flip-flop," he said. "Are these things dangerous or not?"

"Of course they're dangerous. But think how the *Hunter* incident must have looked to them. Look, we know that the *Valiant* had a hyperspace capability. That would also mean they'd have hypercomm. If they were in trouble, as apparently they were, they'd already sent out a call for help. What would they have done when the *Hunter* arrived? Another message, right? 'My God, you ought to see this huge son of a bitch that just showed up.'"

"Okay."

"And what do they say next?"

"'They're trying to grab us.'"

"Exactly. The transmission probably gets cut off in the middle. That's why Solly and I found an unfriendly welcome when we arrived in the neighborhood. Ask yourself how *we'*d react if a giant ship grabbed one of ours. No wonder they wanted to know our address." She listened to him breathe and wondered why he was so fearful. Why was there no one like Solly in the upper levels of the organization?

Flexner shook his head. "It's too late to repair the damage now. I mean, how can you do it? It looks as if it's a shoot-first situation out there. And we can't even talk to them."

"Sure we can."

"Oh yeah. Two-four-six-eight. That's good."

"Matt, we've got to talk with something other than language. Something they'll understand."

He got up, walked to the end of the deck, and looked out at the sea. "What would you suggest?"

"The *Valiant.* I think we go back and do a gesture."

"Meaning—?"

"Return the *Valiant.* Tell them we're sorry and leave it to them to figure out what the words mean. The important thing is the gesture. So we stand out there, give them a clear shot at us, show them we trust them, and return their ship."

"Sounds like a formula for getting killed."

"Maybe," she said. "But people who'll sacrifice themselves for strangers—" A couple of kids playing tag ran giggling through the yard and past the Institute flyer. Kim watched them for a minute.

"Let me think it over," said Flexner. "We can make a judgment on that more easily after we've had a good look at the thing. After we have a better idea what their technology looks like." He gazed at her uncertainly. "What's wrong?" he asked.

"I don't think we can risk doing the lab work, Matt."

His face hardened. "Why not?"

"Because it'll get out. I don't believe we're capable of keeping the secret. Once it's out, we'll lose the ship and that'll be the end."

"We can keep it quiet," he insisted. "I've been careful about the people we're bringing in." He sounded frightened.

"No. We're only going to have one chance to do this right."

"Kim, it really doesn't matter what you and I think. Woodbridge would never allow it."

"I agree. So we don't tell him."

"No." He shook his head. "We can't do this."

Come on, Matt, show some guts for once. "Then you can forget about the *Valiant.* It'll stay where it is."

"Kim, I wish you'd be reasonable."

She pressed her advantage: "We'll have to move on this before word gets out that we *have* a celestial. We'll have to plan the rendezvous in such a way that nothing would be at risk except the ship and crew. Strip the data banks so there's no way to trace them back here, even in a worst-case scenario. Give everybody poison, if you want."

"Kim, you're putting me in a terrible position."

"I know." She looked at him. "Make it happen, Matt."

"Phil will never allow it."

"Don't tell him, either."

"*What?* How can I not tell *Phil*?"

"Matt, this time *you* have to make the call."

He got up, took out his remote, and started the flyer. "I'll let you know," he said.

She watched the aircraft lift into the sky, retrieved the Kane disk, relabeled it ACCOUNTING, and left it on the coffee table. In plain sight. Then she sat quietly for a few minutes watching the tide come in. "Shep, give me Solly."

"I disapprove, Kim. Your state of mind precludes—"

"Shep—"

She heard the electronic whine. It took longer than usual this time. But Solly appeared, wearing diving gear. He frowned, said something uncomplimentary about Shepard, removed his fins and converter, sat down on a virtual bench, and looked at Kim. *"Hi, babe,"* he said.

"Hello, Solly." Her strength ebbed out of her. "I wish we could do it again."

"Do what?" he asked.

"Dive," she said. "Dive deep."

He nodded.

She listened to the sea. "I miss you, Solly."

"I know. You'll just have to give it time. There'll be others."

"Please don't—"

"Sorry." And after a moment: *"I shouldn't stay."*

"That's Shepard talking."

"No. It's me." He gazed for a long moment into her eyes. The room seemed very quiet. *"I have a suggestion."*

"Okay?"

"I don't want you to take offense."

She knew what was coming. "I won't, Solly."

"It would be best if you let me be. For a while anyhow, until you've got things back together."

She stared at him. His image got blurry. "Solly, I can't stand it, not having you here."

"I know."

"You don't. You never went through anything like this."

"Kim, you were the best part of my life. And I wouldn't trade the voyage to Alnitak for anything. The price was worth it."

He grew indistinct and faded gradually, very unlike Shep's usual exit technique. When he was gone she got up, started for the bedroom, but paused at the foot of the stairs. "Shep?"

"Yes, Kim?"

"How did *you* know what happened on the *Hammersmith?*"

The AI didn't answer.

Two days later Matt called to tell her they were moving ahead with the Alnitak mission and that he was optimistic. She asked whether there was anything she could do.

"Just stay out of trouble," he said.

It was midafternoon. She'd just gotten home after completing a luncheon speaking engagement at the Seabright Literary Society. A heavy rain was pounding the island. At this time of year storms came in every day at a quarter to three. They moved as punctually as the trains. She was sprawled on the divan, listening to the weather, thinking about the *Valiant,* when Shep broke in. *"Kim,"* he said, *"Tora Kane would like to speak with you. She says it's urgent."*

Kim looked around the room. It was not very tidy. "Put her through, Shep. Audio." And after the click: "Hello, Tora. What can I do for you?"

"Kim, I'm at home. Can you come over? There's something I want to show you."

"Sure. What's it about?"

"Not on an open circuit. I'll tell you when you get here. Please hurry."

So they were on a first-name basis now. Puzzled, Kim sent for a taxi. Ten minutes later she was in the air, headed north. Rain beat down on the aircraft and the wind gave her a rough ride. But the storm subsided as she came in sight of Tora's villa. The flyer descended onto the pad and Kim got out, instructing the vehicle to wait. She splashed through puddles and climbed onto the porch.

"Can I help you?" asked the house AI.

"Dr. Kane asked me to come by."

"I'm sorry. Dr Kane is not at home."

"That can't be right. Are you sure?"

"She is not here. But I will be happy to relay a message to her, if you wish."

Kim stared at the front door. The house stared back.

She used her commlink to find Kane's number and then put through a call. It chimed twice.

"Kane."

"Tora, this is Kim Brandywine."

"Hello, Brandywine. What can I do for you?"

"I'm at your place. You asked me to come over."

"You're where?"

"At your place."

"My place? I don't know anything about it. Who'd you talk to?"

"Forget it," she said. She switched to Shep's circuit, but he didn't answer.

Not good. She strode quickly to the taxi and ordered it back home.

Two hours later she walked into Matt's office. He looked up from his desk, surprised to see her, startled at her appearance. "You okay?" he asked.

She closed the door behind her and sat down. "Somebody's been at Shep."

"Uh-oh. What did they get?"

"I think we can assume everything."

"The Kane disk?"

"That too."

He looked around the office as if suddenly wondering whether it was secure. "Why? Who would do it?"

"I can only think of one person."

"Woodbridge?"

"Yep."

"So what's *everything*? Do they know what we talked about this morning?"

"There's no way to be sure. Shep didn't have any of it, but it's possible somebody was listening."

Matt nodded slowly. "So what did they get that they didn't already have?"

"The *Valiant*."

"They know where it *is*?"

"They know it exists."

"That's not so good." He inhaled. Exhaled. Looked uncertain. "I was going to call you."

"About—?"

"I've spoken with Dr. Agostino."

"I thought we agreed we wouldn't bring him in."

"Come on, Kim. Be reasonable. He understands the situation and he's willing to set up a contact team."

"*He's* probably why I got raided."

"I don't believe it. When'd it happen?"

"Around three."

"I talked to him less than an hour ago." It was almost five o'clock.

"All right," she said. "Look, they'll be coming after the *Valiant*. We need to get moving."

"The plan was to leave next week. We thought *that* was pushing it."

"Not good enough. We need to be on our way tomorrow."

"That's not practical."

"Forget practical. We'd be better off clearing out tonight. Tell everybody we go tomorrow. Anybody who can't be there, leave without."

"You'll need supplies, Kim. This kind of thing can't be managed overnight."

"This one has to be. Do it overnight or forget it."

"I'll do what I can," he said. "We'll be using the *McCollum*. It's in port and ready to go. All we need is the people."

"Then get them started. Have we got a pilot?"

"Ali Kassem. Do you know him?"

"Met him once or twice." Solly had spoken well of him. That was good enough.

Matt called her at home late that evening. "We got a late request," he said. "Can you talk to the Terminal City Business Association tomorrow?"

It was the signal. They would leave tomorrow night.

She complained that it was short notice, and he apologized, said he'd originally planned to handle it himself, but something had come up, and he'd appreciate it.

"Okay," she said. "But you owe me."

And she went to bed happy.

31

Nothing in this hand, nothing in my sleeve—
> —Standard routine for magicians, nineteenth
> and twentieth centuries, C.E.

Kim slept soundly through the night and was up at six, ate a good breakfast, and finished packing. She put her wet suit and a metal sensor in a carrying case, instructed Shep to inform callers during the balance of the day that she was on assignment in Marathon and after that to say simply that she was on vacation and would be unavailable for the foreseeable future.

Shortly after nine she arrived at the train station and directed the loader to ship her bags through to Terminal City, and signed in. By 9:40 she was on her way to Marathon.

Marathon was a garden town, populated predominantly by people who were satisfied to live off the basic allotment, and to devote their lives to the pursuit of leisure and the arts. It had more theaters per square meter than any other place in the world, more game rooms, more libraries, more swimming pools, and probably more sex.

According to legend, its name commemorated the ultimate one-night stand when Annie Muldoon, a personage at the edge of history, took on the town's entire adult male population, said to have numbered an even one hundred, and to have exhausted them all in a single night. There was a statue of Annie, with a bunch of bananas thrown over one shoulder, in the city hall courtyard. Kim saw it from the train window as she pulled into town.

She got off, ate lunch, and rented a horse, which she rode through woods still wet from an early morning rain, past waterfalls and wallball courts, to the UDI office. United Distribution was located on the upper floor of a small log building. The lower level featured a communications shop and a liquor store. She went up a flight of stairs, followed the signs into a service area, and presented her ID number to the dex.

The system produced her package, laying it on the counter so she could see the label she'd addressed from Eagle Point. *"Is this correct?"* it asked.

"Yes," she said.

"Press here, please." It wanted her thumb print on the delivery receipt. She complied, carried the package downstairs, and hefted it onto the horse. A man sleeping on the front deck woke up, looked at her, and said hello. Kim returned the greeting, climbed into the saddle and started back toward the station.

She rode slowly. It was a lovely spring day, but she was preoccupied with her surroundings, prepared to bolt at the first sign of danger. The forest made her vulnerable, and it occurred to her belatedly that selecting a horse over a cab might not have been a good idea.

But no one appeared, and she arrived safely at the stable. She returned the animal and walked across to the station, where she sat down on a bench to await the train to Terminal City.

There were only a few others on the platform: a couple of families with children, several people dressed in ski clothes apparently headed for the mountains, and two persons who appeared to be traveling on business.

The Terminal City train came in from the east along a slow curve riding just above thick woods. It was silent at low speeds, and the view was blocked off by the station roof, so there was no advance warning that it was coming. It simply appeared on the bend, glided in, and settled into its well. A few passengers got off; the people who'd been waiting on the platform boarded. Kim, carrying the UDI parcel, joined them.

The train was more than half empty. She found a compartment where she could be alone, closed the glass door, and settled into a seat. They moved forward out of the station, gathered speed, slowed again to maneuver through a couple of ridges west of Marathon, and then climbed to the treetops and began accelerating.

Rivers and lakes flowed past. There would be no towns before Little Marseille, 150 kilometers away. That was not because there *were* no towns in the region, but because the velocity of the train required that it be kept away from inhabited areas. One rarely saw a human being from inside a maglev car traveling at full gait. Anyone who appeared tended to be down flat and holding on.

Kim undid the wrapping on the UDI parcel, opened one end, peeked in, and caught her breath. There was a scaled-down starship inside, but it was *not* the *Valiant*. She looked again at the label: it was the one she had addressed from Eagle Point.

Her heart began to hammer. She took it out of the package. The vehicle was the *376*.

Woodbridge had a sense of humor.

She heard movement in the aisle, the compartment door opened, and a blond man in a charcoal jacket came in, glanced at her, and sat down opposite. She recognized him as one of the people who'd boarded with her at Marathon.

She closed the container. The nearby countryside was a blur; a distant range of hills passed majestically.

"Anything wrong, Dr. Brandywine?" the man asked.

She did not look at him. "You know there is," she said.

He was silent a few moments. Then he showed her an ID. She missed his name but saw the words NATIONAL BUREAU OF COMPLIANCE circling a shield. "I wonder if I can ask you to come with me," he said.

"Where?"

"Please." He rose and opened the door for her.

She stepped past him.

"To your right, Doctor," he said.

She preceded him down the passageway, passed into the next car, and, at his instruction, stopped outside a closed compartment. Curtains had been drawn over the windows. The blond man knocked. The door opened and he stepped aside.

Kim looked in and saw Canon Woodbridge. And the *Valiant*. It was on the seat beside him, a cloth thrown over it. But she knew the shape.

"Please come in, Kim," he said, motioning her to sit down. "I'm sorry we're meeting this way. I know this has been hard on you." The door closed softly behind her.

"Hello, Canon." She managed a smile. "I didn't expect to see you here."

"No. I'd think not." He glanced down at the *Valiant*. "Tell me," he said, "is this *really* a starship?"

She tried to look puzzled. It was difficult under his penetrating gaze. "I'm not sure what you mean."

"Kim." He sounded disappointed. She could trust him to do the right thing, his demeanor told her. Everything will be fine. Have no concern. "This will go much better if we're honest with each other." He drew the cloth aside. "Is this the ship from Orion?"

"That appears to be it," she said, in a tone that conceded defeat.

"Incredible." He touched it gently, as if fearing it might disintegrate. "It's so *small.*"

She folded her arms and sat back, staring across at the seat opposite.

"I'm disappointed that you had so valuable an artifact in your possession and failed to inform me."

"I'd have preferred to inform no one."

"Yes," he said. "Apparently. I thought I could trust you."

"I knew you'd take it from me."

"Kim." The train had begun to sway and he put a restraining hand on the artifact. "I don't think I understand your motives in this matter. I mean, this goes far beyond what's good for you or me. What did you plan to do with this?"

"It's of considerable value." She dropped her eyes. Guilty as charged, you son of a bitch. "I was going to keep it."

He studied her. "Hold it for ransom?" he asked at last.

"Just keep it."

"You continue to surprise me, Kim. You seem to be making a career of stealing starships." He replaced the cloth. "You're really quite a little bandit, aren't you?"

"It *is* mine, you know," she said. "By right of discovery."

"Oh, we both know better than that. Technically, I would think it belongs to the Tripley heirs. And I can assure you we'll return it to them when we're finished examining it."

"There won't be much left by then, I suspect."

"Probably not." He sighed. "But it's unavoidable. Who knows what sort of technology is embodied in this? I understand the younger Tripley had it in his office all these years and never knew what it was."

"Ben? Yes, that's so."

"Hard to believe." Something in the countryside caught his eye, and he turned to look. Kim followed his gaze to a distant bridge across a river. Two kids sat on it with fishing poles. "The simple pleasures, eh, Kim?"

She didn't respond.

"Well," he said, "nevertheless, you won't come away empty-handed.

By no means. We'll be making a public announcement shortly, and I'll see that you're suitably recognized."

"Another medal," she said.

"Yes. The Premier's Medal is in order this time, I would think. That's quite an honor. It would of course depend on your cooperation."

"Thanks," she said.

"It carries with it a considerable stipend. And you'll be able to name your price for speaking engagements."

"Eventually," she said, "we're going to encounter these creatures. How are you going to deal with that?"

"To be honest, Kim, I hope we've seen the last of the celestials. I don't like them, they're lost out there somewhere, and we should have no real trouble staying out of their way. Traffic is extremely rare in the Alnitak area. In fact, we've done a study. How many ships do you think have been out there during the last century, other than the survey and several visits by Kile Tripley? And your own, of course?"

"I've no idea."

"The answer is *zero*. Nobody. So we probably don't have a problem unless we invite one."

"You're simply going to ignore the fact there's another civilization in the region? This whole thing is just going to *disappear*?"

"Kim, I'm surprised at your change of heart. A few days ago you would have been happy to send the fleet after them."

"You know why I changed my mind."

"The Kane statement."

"It tells me we can *deal* with these creatures, Canon."

"Oh, I'm sure we can. After an initial period of instability. Risk. Uncertainty. Who knows what sort of effect interaction with a strange culture might bring? We live quite well; there are no problems. The status quo is rather nice, don't you think? Everybody lives a good life. It seems to me we've nothing to gain and perhaps everything to lose by pursuing this."

"I don't think that's exactly the spirit that brought us out from Earth."

"Kim, be realistic. Have you given any thought to what contact might mean? Even assuming these creatures are not malevolent, although I'd have to say that remains open to question, think about the potential for mischief. It's quite likely your celestials are far ahead of us technologically. What happens when cultures of unequal capabilities encounter each other? What happened to the South Sea Islanders? The Aztecs? Or, if you prefer, reverse the coin. If *we* have superiority, *they* will be damaged. And that principle seems to be operative regardless of the intentions of the superior society."

"We can take precautions against that."

"Can we? I doubt it."

"Canon, this is a chance to get a whole new perspective from an intelligent species. The potential for new knowledge is unlimited. But even that's not the point. They're like us in some very significant ways. We know that now—"

"We don't really know anything, Kim. Look, I'm not saying you're not right. I'm saying, *we don't know*. Why take the risk?"

"We've an obligation," she said, "at the very least, to say hello. We're the part of the universe that *thinks*. How can we fail to act simply because we want to eliminate risk? You're talking about the status quo. Is that really what we're about?"

"That's all a trifle abstract for me." Woodbridge sighed. "This would be so much easier if you were a bit more practical, Kim. Nevertheless, maybe history, in its very long view, will demonstrate that you're right and I'm wrong. Or maybe not. For the moment at least, life is quite pleasant in the Nine Worlds, and this thing in Orion is a very large *unknown*. We are therefore going to try to keep it at a safe distance."

"You understand," she said, "this breaks our agreement. I no longer feel bound to remain silent."

He shrugged. *"This,"* the microship, "changes the equation. I'm sure the government will be making an announcement within the next few days."

The train slowed to navigate a long curving defile.

"You're going to make it public?" she asked. "Why?"

"Oh, there's no way to keep this sort of thing quiet. Once we begin bringing people in to look at it, the story will get out quickly. We're not nearly as good at keeping secrets as people like to think."

"So missions will be going out to Alnitak after all—"

"They'll be going to Zeta Tauri. That's where the celestial incident will have occurred. It'll be leaked, and we'll deny it, of course. So everyone will believe it. And the missions should be quite safe there."

"Unless I tell them differently."

"This is what I referred to when I suggested we would want your cooperation. If you persist in going your own way, Kim, we'll simply write you out of the scenario altogether. We have an alternate narrative set up. It does not include *you*, so there is no reason anyone would believe you." He pressed his palms together. "I don't want you to think I'm threatening you. I'm simply trying to spell out the realities. Please understand that I take no pleasure in any of this, but it's essential that we avoid future contact with these things. You, of all people, should be able to see the wisdom of that position."

He rapped on the door. Two women came in, carrying a container. They bundled the *Valiant* into it and asked Woodbridge whether he needed anything. He did not, and they left, taking the microship with them.

"If you can see your way to cooperate, Kim, I'll try to arrange to have you present when we dissect it."

Her time was up. He rose and opened the door for her. "You're a talented woman," he said. "If you're interested, I think the conciliar staff would have a place for you."

Kim went back to her seat, collapsed into it, and stared desultorily out at the passing countryside. Gradually the forest changed to marsh. They slowed to negotiate a curve back toward the west and Kim saw the sky-hook.

The train leaped ahead again, passed beneath a series of ridges, and raced out across a lake. The shock wave struck the water like a ship's prow. At the water's edge, a crocodile watched them pass.

They slowed again, settled to earth, and emerged through a patch of cypress into a wide stretch of parkland. A few kids turned away from a ball game to wave. People on benches looked up and then went back to reading or talking.

The train joined the main east–west line at Morgantown Bay and ran the short gauntlet of cliffs, sea, and islands into Terminal City. It passed slowly through the downtown area, glided into the terminal building, and settled to a stop. The doors opened.

Kim walked dejectedly out onto the platform. There was no sign of Woodbridge or his people. She picked up her bags, held out the one with the wet suit and the metal sensor, and tagged the rest for Sky Harbor. *To be held till called for.*

No one seemed to be watching her. She checked the timetables, noted that she had fifty-five minutes before the next departure for Eagle Point.

The train she'd just left was filling up. A bell sounded, doors closed, and it rose on its magnetics and pulled slowly out of the station. It would be heading back east.

She went to the terminal roof, hailed a cab, and told it to take her to the Beachfront Hotel. It rose into clear air, swung onto a southeastern tangent, and moved swiftly across the city.

At the Beachfront, she took an elevator down to the lobby. A cluster of shops ringed the area. She wandered into one, bought a comb, went out to the registration desk and reserved a room. Then she got back on the elevator, rode up past her floor, and went instead to the roof. Two cabs were just landing. She took one and instructed it to proceed to the train terminal.

There was still no indication of surveillance. Good. They had what they wanted, she hoped, and would not further concern themselves with her. She arrived at her destination, strolled over to an ADP, inserted her ID, and got a ticket to Eagle Point. Then she found a bench and watched a holocast talk show.

Ten minutes later her train arrived. She boarded, sat down, and lazily started browsing through the library. The doors closed and they left the station on schedule. The train cruised above the parks and residences on Terminal City's north side. It crossed the VanderMeer Bridge to the mainland, and began to accelerate. The trees thinned out and they moved over rolling fields.

The quiet motion rocked her to sleep. She dreamed of the shroud but somehow knew it was a dream and forced herself awake. The car was full of sunlight and skis and the laughter of children. Everybody seemed to be on vacation.

A drink table approached, and Kim helped herself to a frozen pineapple.

It was late afternoon when they glided into Eagle Point. She got off, walked over to the tourist information booth, and consulted the commercial registry. Finding what she wanted, she went up onto the skywalk and minutes later entered The Home Shop. She bought some white ribbon, and had it cut into six strips, each about twenty centimeters long.

Next she proceeded to the Rent-All Emporium sporting goods outlet, down at the next arch. There she picked out a collapsible boat, a converter and a jetpack, and several tethers designed for mountain climbing. They delivered everything to Wing Transport, where she rented a flyer. An hour and a quarter after she'd arrived, she was flying south over countryside that had grown painfully familiar. She picked up the Severin River, and followed it through the canyons and over the dam to Lake Remorse.

The lake was bright and still in the afternoon sun. No boat moved across its surface. It was almost, she thought, as if this area were disconnected from Greenway, and had become part of whatever strange world from which the shroud had come.

She took the metal sensor out of her carrying case and tied it into the flyer's search system. That done, she skimmed the shoreline once, perhaps to ensure that she was alone, perhaps to be in a position to flee if anything rose out of the trees to come after her. She shuddered at the memory and made an effort to put it out of her mind.

At Cabry's Beach, someone had put up a memorial for Sheyel, Ben Tripley, and the three guards.

She hovered over the place, tempted to go down and pay her respects. But time was short. She promised herself she would come back.

Kim turned north onto the same course she'd followed when fleeing the shroud, and retraced her flight across the lake. She homed in on the clutch of dead trees, measured angles between them and the town and the face of the mountain. She had been about sixty meters offshore when she pitched the *Valiant* into the lake.

Right there!

She descended to within a few meters of the surface and moved slowly across the face of the water, watching the sensor. It lit up a couple of times, but the position wasn't quite right. Too far east. Too far out.

Eventually she got the hit she was looking for. She marked the spot with a float, found a landing place, and took the flyer down. When she'd come back to Remorse with Matt, she'd not felt much, just a kind of numbness. But today she was alone again, and the area oppressed her, weighed on her spirits.

She tried to concentrate on Solly, to imagine him alongside her, telling her not to worry. Nothing here to be afraid of.

She hauled the boat out of the aircraft, pulled the tag, and watched it inflate. A hawk appeared high overhead and began circling. She was glad for its company.

She tied her tethers together, making two lines, one approximately twenty and the other forty meters long, and laid them in the boat. She added her strips of ribbon, and picked up two rocks, one white and one gray. These she also put in the boat.

When everything seemed ready she got back into the flyer and changed into her wet suit. She strapped on the jets and the converter, then disconnected the sensor and put it in her utility bag.

She launched the boat with a sense of bravura and rode out to the marker. Depth registered at twelve meters. Deeper than she'd hoped. But by no means out of reach. She initiated the sensor search. *That* way, closer to shore.

Kim moved to the indicated spot, tied the shorter line around the gray rock and dropped it over the side to serve as her anchor.

It would have been easier to work with a partner in the boat, as she had with Solly above the dam. Now she had to forego the advantage of an observer with a tracking screen. She attached the sensor to her lamp, strapped the lamp to her wrist, and slipped over the side.

The lake was cool and clear, but dark in its depths. She arrowed down until she touched bottom. Then she turned slowly 360 degrees, watching the sensor, waiting for the blinker to brighten. When it didn't, she tried moving out, swimming in a circle, and immediately got her directions confused. The easy way was not going to work.

She went back up to the boat and thought about it. A flyer passed, moving south. She watched it until it was gone.

It was getting late. The afternoon was beginning to change color.

She paid out her second line and tied the ribbon to it in five-meter increments. When she was finished she looped it over one shoulder, put the white rock in her utility bag, went back over the side, and descended to the anchor.

She connected the line with the ribbons to the anchor line, measured out five meters and marked the outermost limit with the white rock.

Something hard-shelled, a turtle probably, bumped into her and scurried away. A good sign.

Holding on to the first ribbon to prevent moving beyond the perimeter, she searched the area immediately around the anchor, out to five meters. When she got back to the white rock, she switched her attention to the area *outside* the perimeter, and completed a second circle. Then she moved the rock to ten meters and repeated the process.

She found the *Valiant* on the next circuit, lying upside down in a tangle of vegetation. She removed it gently, clasped it to her breast, congratulated herself, and rose slowly to the surface.

32

I love to sail forbidden seas—

—HERMAN MELVILLE, *Moby Dick*, 1851 C.E.

Matt met her at the boarding tube. She was carrying the *Valiant* in a Gene Teddy box, which was adorned with a picture of the popular children's character. "Is that it?" he asked.

"That's it." She was surprised to see him there. But he looked like a man being led to execution. "Something wrong?"

"No. Why do you ask?"

"No reason. It was good of you to come see us off."

"'See you off'? I'm going."

It had never occurred to her that Matt would put himself at risk. "Good," she said. "We can use all the help we can get. When are we leaving?"

"Two more people are on the way up. As soon as they get here, in about an hour—"

"Sooner the better," she said. "I suggest we plan on leaving as soon as they're in the door."

He took the box and they started up the tube. "Something happen?"

She told him about Woodbridge. He listened with a deepening frown. "Do we have cover for this mission?" she asked.

"It's listed as a return to Taratuba. Nothing unusual. But he knew you were coming to Terminal City."

"I make a lot of trips out here. Nothing unusual about that. And I've booked a room at the Beachfront Hotel. We should have a few hours." It was essential to be away before Woodbridge found out he had nothing more than an ornament and began looking for her. If there was a problem with the Patrol this time, she wouldn't have Solly in the pilot's room.

"All right," he said. "We'll try to get going as quickly as we can. But I don't want to leave anybody behind. These people dropped everything for this—"

"They don't know why, do they?"

"They've only been told they won't be sorry."

"I hope that's true."

If the *Hammersmith* had resembled a cheap hotel, the *McCollum* suggested a run-down office building with temporary quarters for people who'd got stranded during a blizzard. It was gray, dark, and oppressive. Usually, when Kim wanted to suggest how desperately the Institute needed contributions, she showed pictures of the *Mac.*

The ship itself was a box with rounded edges. The rooms were spartan, intended for dual occupancy, with sufficient space to house twenty-four passengers. Its facilities weren't all that bad: the rec area was decent, it had an updated mission center, a good briefing room, and the pilots thought it was the most dependable vehicle in the Institute's modest fleet. That probably wasn't saying a great deal.

The utility deck was located on the top floor. And an 8.6-meter telescope was mounted on the roof.

"We picked up a robot bouncer," Matt said.

"A *what?*"

"An automated system we can send outside to get rid of anything that attaches itself to the hull."

Several of the team members were gathered in the passenger cabin. There was a mathematician, a biologist, a linguist, and several others. Matt introduced everyone. Kim knew a few. They shook hands and everybody started asking questions. What's it about? Where are we going?

They'd come on faith. Trusted Agostino, God help them.

She explained that she needed some time in her quarters. There were two more coming, and they should be along any moment. When they got here, she'd come back and tell them what all the mystery was about.

Then she excused herself and retreated to her room, asking Matt to let her know as soon as everyone was on board. Ten minutes later there was a knock at her door. She opened it and found herself looking into the smiling features of Ali Kassem, the ship's captain.

"Kim," he said. "What's going on?"

"Hello, Ali." She made way, and closed the door behind him. "Nice to see you again."

"You too. What's all the secrecy?"

"How much do you know?"

"Only that we're not going to Taratuba."

"Sit down, Ali," she said. "Are they giving you hazardous duty pay?"

"Should they?"

"Yes."

"You're serious."

"Very."

"All right. So fill me in."

She encapsulated everything into a three-minute narrative, omitting Woodbridge's effort to seize the *Valiant*. When she finished he looked shaken. "Are you still willing to go?" she asked.

"What do you do if I decide it is not for me?"

"I'll be in some difficulty."

The rest of the team arrived in good order. Other than Kim, Matt, and Ali, there were eight persons on board. They gathered in the briefing room, where Matt explained he had wanted to invite others, and in fact *had* invited others. Some had wanted specifics, others said they couldn't come on such short notice. Eight, he said, was inadequate to the task, but it would have to do. Then he turned the meeting over to Kim.

"We have only a few minutes before departure," she said. "So I'll try not to waste anyone's time." She stepped up onto a raised section of floor. "We've made contact," she said.

The room went dead silent. Nobody moved.

"With celestials. It's true. It happened. In fact, there've been *two* events."

Now she had them. They blurted out questions but Kim waved them aside. She described the *Hunter* and *Hammersmith* discoveries, and told them what had really occurred at the Culbertson Tunnel. She told them that the Council was determined to maintain secrecy for the time being, and that was why no one had been able to explain anything in advance. She showed them the *Valiant* but would not allow them to inspect it. "You can do all that later," she said. "What you need to know now is that we hope to reestablish communication, that we hope to compensate for the mistakes made twenty-seven years ago, and that we know almost nothing about what we face. We're pretty sure they are now hostile, and we can assume they will not hesitate to destroy the *McCollum*. We'll be out there alone. Consequently you might want to reconsider whether you want to come." She turned to Ali. "Anyone who wishes to leave has an opportunity now to do so. Once we get underway, you're committed."

"*How* dangerous?" asked their anthropologist, Maurie Penn.

"You know as much as I do now. I'd say *substantially*."

"Count me in," said the mathematician. "A chance to *talk* to another species? Hell, yes."

There was no real debate. For one thing, they were out of time. For another, the prize was simply too bright. Those who might ordinarily have been reluctant to put their lives in jeopardy for any reason, like the AI specialist Gil Chase, were overwhelmed by the possibilities of the situation. They would all stay. Certainly, they were saying, what else would you expect?

The formal meeting broke up. The seats swung back to acceleration positions, and Ali made for the pilot's room.

Maurie Penn sat down beside her. "This is not the way I'd have wanted to do this," he said. "A mission like this. There should have been some preparation."

"Conditions don't permit it," she said.

Ali's voice alerted them that departure was imminent. The cabin lights dimmed.

The seats in the briefing room had individual monitors that could be keyed into any of the visual inputs from the external imagers. She switched over to a view of Greenway and looked down at Equatoria. The northern snows had given way and the entire continent was now green. The Mandan archipelago trailed off to the west, over the rim of the world.

The skyhook, long and arcing as if a heavy wind were blowing against it, dropped down and down into the cloud banks where it faded from sight.

Kim felt a slight push.

"Underway," said Ali.

Forty-some minutes later, without a word from the Patrol, they slipped into hyperspace and Kim breathed more easily.

■　■　■

The *Valiant* came under immediate scrutiny. After the initial wave of euphoria, some members concluded that Kim had dragged them along on a frivolous—and deranged—mission. But Flexner's reputation held the day. Matt was solid, down-to-earth, not one to be swept off his feet. There might therefore be something to the story.

Eventually, after everyone had had a chance to look at the microship, she cautioned them against attempting to take it apart, and secured it inside a glass case in one of the unused rooms on the top floor. Reluctantly, she activated an alarm system.

"Not a good idea," Matt told her, "to signal that you don't trust your people."

She knew that. She apologized to them but explained that she knew they were scientists and that the temptation might be overwhelming. "We need it intact," she said. And then she explained the real purpose of the mission. "We're going to give it back to them."

Eyes widened and people started to argue. Tesla Duchard, the biologist, looked as if she were going into shock.

But Kim defended her view, and to his credit, Matt supported her. "The *Hunter* mission did a lot of damage," he said. "If we can rectify that, and establish a constructive relationship, we'll come away with far more than a busted ship."

There was some grumbling, but in the end they bought it.

Sandra Leasing, who designed and built star drives, concluded that the *Valiant* used a transdimensional entry system that was in no way different from their own. "Probably," she said, "there *is* no other way to manage things."

"The real question for me," said Mona Vasquez, a psychologist, "is the missing propulsion tubes. How does it travel in normal space?"

"Only one way *I* can think of," said Terri Taranaka, a physicist, "if you're not throwing something out the rear, you have to throw something out the *front*, something to *pull* you along."

"And what would that be?" asked Maurie.

"A gravity field. You create a gravity field along the intended course, just as we create one in here. And you *fall* forward into it."

"Do *we* have that kind of capability?" asked Tesla.

"We do," said Matt. "But we couldn't generate a strong enough field to make it practical. In time, though, it'd be a good way to go. If only because you wouldn't have to take along a load of reaction mass."

Kim ran the *Hunter* logs for the team and enjoyed hearing them gasp when the celestial pilot appeared. *"Cho-cho-san,"* said Terri. "Butterfly."

They discussed the *Hunter*'s reaction to its unexpected find and began considering what might await them, and how best to respond.

She decided also that it would be necessary to tell them about Woodbridge's effort to seize the *Valiant*. When they reemerged into real-space in the vicinity of Alnitak, they'd undoubtedly receive an official message demanding return of the artifact. And she had to inoculate them against that. Especially, she had to win Ali over.

But she waited for the right time. They passed the midway point of the journey on a Thursday, and marked the event by throwing a party. This group turned out to be big on parties, and Kim liked that. The atmosphere in the ship remained festive and there was a lot of talk about being at the intersection of epochs. That was Gil's terminology. Gil was aloof and formal, and quickly earned a reputation for being cooler than the AIs he created and serviced. Kim had known him for years, and he seemed to her to be a particularly selfish man, dedicated exclusively to advancing his own priorities. But it happened, on this occasion, that his priorities were in sync with hers.

Toward the end of the party, Paul McKeep commented that it was a good thing the Institute had kept the existence of the ship quiet. "The government's too conservative," he said. "They'd never have allowed us away from the dock." Paul was their mathematician.

Kim threw a sidelong glance at Ali to make sure he was listening. Then she raised her voice slightly: "There's something you folks ought to know."

"Something *else*?" laughed Mona.

"Yes," she said. "We didn't quite succeed in keeping a lid on the *Valiant*. Woodbridge found out about it and tried to take it from me."

"How'd you manage to keep it out of his hands?" asked Ali.

"I gave him a duplicate."

That brought a round of laughter.

But Ali never cracked a smile. "You know what that means," he said.

"Yes." Kim looked directly into his dark eyes. "When we make the jump, we'll find a recall waiting for us."

He frowned, turned, and left the room. The others fell silent. Kim looked at Matt, intending to follow him, and make sure he would resist pressure from home.

But Matt shook his head. *No*, he was saying. *This is not the time.*

■　■　■

There was an echo to the voyage. Kim could not repress memories of the flight with Solly. The distances tended to collapse, as if she were on a train running through dark but familiar countryside, and the landmarks were all abstract, temporal, racing by. Places she'd been before. Here we were playing chess and Solly kept winning so I got annoyed. And *there* was where we finally beat Veronica King to the solution, in the case of "The Haunted Balcony."

She knew when they arrived at the place where Kim's image, as Clea, had performed the torchlight dance.

Stupid. Somewhere she had been incredibly stupid and had let it all slip through her fingers.

They spent most of their time devising their contact strategy. They intended to begin broadcasting as soon as they arrived, to ensure they couldn't be missed. A new kind of Beacon Project, Kim thought.

They debated endlessly how best to establish a syntax and vocabulary. "We don't want to play more number games," Gil Chase reminded them.

They knew the two technologies had a common system for exchanging audio and visual signals. "We can use pictures in the beginning," Eric Climer said. He was a linguist. "But it would have been helpful," he complained to Kim, "if I had known in advance what this was about. I could have brought the proper software."

They formulated lists of questions to ask once a common language had been devised. *How far back can you trace your history?* To even begin to phrase that question they'd have to work out a joint system for measuring time.

Where are you from?

"No," said Maurie, "don't ask that. It sounds too much like intelligence-gathering."

"What do we do," asked Sandra, "if they put that kind of question to us?"

"Considering what's already happened," said Paul, "we'd better avoid giving them any information of that nature."

Kim nodded. "I agree." She didn't want to be responsible for the arrival of an invasion fleet if they encountered a worst-case scenario.

"But if they get the idea we don't trust them," said Matt, "how can we expect them to trust us?"

"We can't," said Mona. "But we don't need a great deal of mutual trust. At least not in the beginning. They'll certainly understand our reluctance to divulge that kind of information. I think our best approach to this is to be honest."

"So what other questions," asked Terri, "do we want answered?"

"*Is there anyone else?*" said Ali. "*Have they found anybody else out there?*"

"*Your ships seem to have armaments. Why?*"

"*What's your explanation for order in the universe? For the existence of the universe itself? Why isn't there nothing?*"

"*Have you been able to establish the existence of alternate universes? If so, have you been able to learn anything about them?*"

"*Do you believe life has a spiritual dimension?*"

"How are you going to define 'spiritual'?" asked Mona. No one had any idea.

"*What do you do with your leisure time?*"

"Do we really care about that?" asked Terri. "Why would we want to know whether they play bridge?"

Maurie, who'd proposed the question, shook his head in dismay. "What people do with their leisure tells us a great deal about the nature of a society, what its values really are, for example, as opposed to what its members *say* its values are."

"What if they ask *us* that question?" said Mona. "Are we going to admit that ninety-nine percent of our population sit around indulging in electronic fantasies?"

"Best not do that," said Gil. "If these *things* are hostile, that would only invite attack."

"So we lie," said Matt.

"Sure." Gil looked frustrated. "We don't want to create problems down the line. Maybe we *should* be thinking more about what they're going to ask us than vice-versa. Because they may think the same way we do. So what do we say when they ask questions designed, for example, to test our technological knowledge?"

"I don't think we need to worry too much about that," said Paul. "All they have to do is shoot at us and see how quickly it takes us to leave town."

Nobody seriously believed there'd be a biological presence at Alnitak, but everyone was convinced the *Mac* would find an automated outpost of some sort, a scanner watching for one of the giant ships to reappear. There was no way humans would not have established one, and nobody could imagine an intelligent species simply abandoning interest in a place in which *two* encounters had occurred in recent decades. Although it occurred to Kim that Woodbridge would have forced just such an abandonment had he been able. What did that say about human governments?

They agreed, by a vote of seven to three, that any effort by the celestials to attach an object to the hull would be deemed hostile, and the contact attempt would be terminated at that point. Ali explained to Kim later that he didn't care much about the outcome of that particular vote since the safety of the ship was *his* responsibility, and she should not doubt for a minute that he'd require anybody's authorization to clear out if he didn't like any aspect of the behavior of their prospective clients.

If an object actually arrived despite their best efforts, and secured itself to the *Mac*, they would send the robot out to break it loose. To ensure it didn't circle back, the robot would burn it with a few thousand volts before tossing it aside. No hatch would be opened at any time after the operation commenced. The robot was dispensable and would be left behind.

If nothing appeared to either challenge or welcome them, they would broadcast a greeting and wait things out. The *Mac* carried enough supplies for a ten-week stay in the region. If there were no developments during that time, they'd leave an automated scanner and broadcasting station of their own and return home.

As could be expected, a few shipboard romances developed. Paul and Terri paired off; Eric created a bit of tension by running dalliances with both Mona and Tesla. Matt, who was married, either refused to take advantage of Sandra Leasing's obvious interest; or he did it with sufficient discretion that Kim saw no evidence of it.

Ali remained professionally courteous to everyone, but he maintained a discreet distance from the women. During the course of a wandering discussion one night in the rec room, he commented casually that emotional attachments between captains and passengers were not conducive to good order.

Kim was well below everybody else's age, and she knew her companions perceived her as little more than a child. It was just as well; she was still too close to Solly to think about any kind of relationship. And considering the cramped conditions on board the *Mac*, everything became public within a few hours anyhow.

During the final days prior to arrival at Alnitak, tension began to build.

The renowned twenty-fourth century psychologist Edmund Trimble had argued that extended life spans were detrimental to human progress. For one thing, he said, life tended for most people to consist of a series of missed opportunities. Consequently, after seventy or eighty years, people became not only inflexible, but increasingly cynical. As it had turned out, Trimble's fears were exaggerated but not altogether groundless. The average age for the members of the contact team, not counting Kim or Ali (who was only 41) was 126. The general conviction, based on all these years of experience, was that something would go wrong. What they expected to go wrong was that no one would be waiting at Alnitak: that the opportunity had been missed and that all they would have to show in the end would be the *Valiant*, the *Hunter* logs, and maybe another *intruder* chasing them around.

On the last night before arrival, they celebrated Kim's thirty-sixth birthday. They broke out a few bottles and toasted her. Gil provided a cake, they put up ribbon, and enjoyed a celebration whose level of festivity, it seemed to her, far exceeded the significance of the event.

33

Ships that pass in the night, and speak each other in passing,
Only a signal shown and a distant voice in the darkness,
So on the ocean of life, we pass and speak one another,
Only a look and a voice, then darkness again and a silence.
— LONGFELLOW, *Tales of a Wayside Inn*, 1863 C.E.

Kim was sitting with Ali in the pilot's room when they made the jump back into realspace, into the Alnitak region. She heard the *ooooh*s and *aaaah*s downstairs as everyone got a look at the view.

The captain's manner throughout the flight had been detached, unemotional, under control. The sort of perspective you'd want in an emergency. She was consequently pleased to see him catch his breath when the great illuminated star-clouds appeared in the windows. He turned the lamp down and got up from his chair.

"It's why the *Hunter* stopped here, Ali."

"The hand of the Almighty," he said. "Still at work."

Kim had grown familiar with the instruments on the *Hammersmith*, and she'd made it her business to acquaint herself with those of the *Mac*. Especially with the long-range sensors, which were set to sound off at the first indication of an object moving contrary to orbital requirements. Her eyes went to them now, looking for telltales but finding none.

Ali stood for several minutes in the crystalline light, and then directed the AI to adjust course for the gas giant. He turned toward Kim. "Good luck," he said.

"I hope so."

She summoned the team to the mission center, where they briefly reviewed the plan. Matt asked whether there'd been an incoming transmission yet.

Yet. Now that they were here it *did* seem inevitable. "No," she said. "We haven't heard anything."

They began broadcasting a visual program. It consisted of a portion of the numerical interchange between the *Hunter* and the *Valiant*, and the recorded Mona Vasquez, in her most inviting manner: *"Hello. We are happy to have the opportunity to greet you and to say hello."*

They'd deliberately repeated the "hello" in an effort to imply its use. "It would be," Maurie said in his somewhat pretentious manner, "an appropriate beginning."

"We hope," Mona continued, *"to establish a long and fruitful collaboration for both of us. We look forward to exchanging ideas and information with you at the earliest opportunity."*

Mona added that she and her friends were a long way from home, and that they had made the voyage specifically in the desire to meet the entities who had been seen in the area of Alnitak a long time ago. She emphasized the star's name. Its spelling and its picture appeared beside her.

She got some mocking applause when the broadcast finished. There was a sixty-second delay and it started again.

No one expected an immediate response, but Kim remained hopeful at the beginning. Although after the first few hours, when it became apparent that contact would not come quickly, she grumbled inwardly, fought off discouragement, and went to lunch.

The team members drifted idly through the ship, anxiously awaiting whatever might happen. Most congregated around windows, and Kim found Mona in one such location holding forth to Terri and Maurie.

"What happens here," she was saying, "is that you get a better sense of the sky's *depth.* It's not like Greenway or Earth, where all you see at night are stars and moons, and it could all be just a shell with holes poked in it. Here you look out and you see those clouds and you know they go on forever. It would *have* to have a radically different impact on a developing civilization."

"If there were one," said Maurie.

"That's right," said Terri. "And there isn't. You wouldn't get any local life-forms out here. Too much UV."

"It wouldn't have to be orbiting Alnitak," said Mona. "It could be parked up there anywhere. Just give it a little distance, and it loses the radiation and keeps the view."

They were seated in a circle. Kim sank into a chair.

"I wonder," Maurie said, "what kinds of societies would have developed if Earth had had skies like this?"

"Religious fanatics," said Kim.

Terri chuckled. "They got that anyhow."

Mona shook her head. "I'm not sure you'd get religious zealotry under these kinds of conditions. I think it would be easier to see the mechanical aspects of the environment, which aren't so obvious at home."

"*Kim.*" Ali's voice, from the pilot's room. "*Message for you.*"

"On my way," she said.

When she got there, the heading was onscreen:

To: GR 717 *Karen McCollum*
From: SOA
Subject: Artifact
Personal for Dr. Brandywine

SOA was the Secretariat for Off-World Affairs. "Run the text, Ali."

"You can read it in your quarters if you like, Kim." He looked worried. "Is this their reaction to your dealings with Woodbridge?"

"Probably." She smiled. "It's too late for them to do much now. Run it."

Dr. Brandywine:
If you have the object with you, be aware that failure to deliver it immediately into official hands will result in prosecution. No further warning will be sent.
Talbott Edward

Edward was Woodbridge's boss. The man who'd given her the Brays Stilwell Award.

"How does he expect us to do *that*?" asked Ali. "He knows where we are."

"C.Y.A."

"I'm not so sure." His dark eyes were hidden in the half light.

"What else?"

"I think we'll be having company." He swung around to face her. "Do you really intend to give the microship back to its owners? Its *original* owners?"

"Yes."

"How?"

"Easy. Once we find them."

"Tell me how."

"Just lean out the door and hand it to them."

"Isn't that dangerous? These are the same creatures who tried to kill you in the Severin Valley."

"I think that was an anomaly. I think the thing that got stranded became deranged."

"I hope they're not *all* deranged."

"They *have* to be rational, Ali. Or they wouldn't be out here."

She heard a sound deep in his throat. "Maybe," he said. "But that sounds like an epitaph to me."

They settled into a routine during the first few days, working on individual projects, watching the sensor screens. Maurie and Terri never tired of standing by the windows and looking out at the view. To Kim it seemed as if the emptiness looked back. Gradually the assumptions that had held sway throughout the flight—that contact was virtually inevitable, that the celestials would be waiting anxiously for the appearance of another giant ship—came to seem first unduly optimistic, then doubtful, and finally hopelessly naive. They began to speculate that the opportunity had been lost. Fumbled away by the clumsiness of the first expedition. Kim even overheard some comments that suggested she and Solly might have done better if they'd thought things out a bit.

The current situation, the silence that roared at them from the empty sky, was perceived as somehow *her* fault. If she had gone to *them* in January with what she knew instead of coming out here alone, they might have salvaged everything.

She saw it in their eyes, heard it in their voices. And as the days dragged on, and the gas giant came to fill their windows, their attitude toward the *Valiant* changed. If it had once been a unique artifact, a *link* with another civilization, it now became simply an oddity thrown up by the retreating tides of history, a symbol of human incompetence.

"At least," said Paul, "we know now we're not alone."

"Maybe it's just as well if we don't find them," said Maurie.

The remark brought frowns from everyone.

"Why would you say that?" asked Gil.

"How old would you guess their civilization is?"

Matt let his impatience show. "We've no way of knowing," he said.

"They could easily be a million. *Six* million. What's a civilization that's been around that long going to look like? Do we really *want* to talk to them?"

"Why not?"

Maurie took a deep breath. "What could we possibly have to say to them that they'd be interested in?"

Kim was playing chess with Mona when Ali buzzed her. "Please come up for a minute."

She left the game and climbed the stairs to the top floor. When she walked into the pilot's room, he was wearing a strange expression. "We're being scanned," he said.

"By whom?"

He shrugged. "No idea."

"Where are they?"

"Don't know that either. We can't track it back. But *somebody's* keeping an eye on us."

"You think the fleet has arrived?"

"Maybe. But I doubt it's any of *our* people. If it is, they're pretty good. The scopes don't show anything out there."

The screens were blank. "So what are we saying? That we've found what we came for?"

"I'm only saying that the technology behind the scan is of a very high order."

"Marvelous," she said, clapping him on the back. "What can they learn about us?"

Ali propped his jaw in his palm. "Which way we're headed, of course. What kind of engines we have. Maybe they're able to do an analysis of light leakage. Hard to know what their limits might be. If it's really celestial. This is where it would have been helpful to have dissected the microship."

Kim ignored the implication. "Is there a chance they can see into the ship?"

"I don't think anything we have, or anything anybody could devise, could penetrate *this* kind of hull. *Mac*'s hull. It's designed to survive in high-energy environments. We could take her in pretty close to Alnitak, if we wanted, without frying the help. So *no*, they wouldn't very likely be able to do *that*. But they're probably able to get a sense of our electronic capabilities, of armaments or lack thereof, of engine architecture, that sort of thing."

"Thanks," she said. "Anything else?"

He shrugged. "Listen, don't get so carried away with this that you forget they have a tendency to bite. Okay?"

She returned to the mission center, called everybody in, and passed the news. *Somebody's watching us.* The reaction was mixed, a sense of exhilaration combined with a dash of disquiet. Paul recommended they begin broadcasting the second-phase package. The others agreed and Kim passed the instruction to Ali. A minute later he reported that transmission was underway.

The second-phase package contained a vocabulary list with pictures and pronunciations of 166 objects that the team hoped would be common to the experience of both species. They included words like "star," "planet," "cloud," "river," "ship," "rain," "forest," "lamp." Eric, who claimed to have gone to acting school and in any case had exquisite diction, had provided the voice.

They'd also included linking verbs with examples of their usage, a few personal pronouns, and the interrogatives *who, what, where, when,* and *why*. Eric maintained that the explanations of the latter, which were elaborated by pictures of sample cases, probably would not be understood, but the terms would be so helpful that it seemed worth the effort.

The package was transmitted realtime rather than compacted, on the theory that celestial technology might not be compatible. It was fifty-six minutes long, and would be repeated every hour.

Ali called down early during the first broadcast with the news that the scan had stopped. Its total duration had been roughly seventeen and a half minutes.

Kim thought it would also be a good idea to accompany the transmission with an image of the *Valiant*. While the package was running, she looked again at the various views which she'd loaded into the transmitter: the microship seen head-on; the microship from above, bathed in the light of Alnitak; the microship in silhouette against a blue planet; a dozen others. Best, she sensed, would be to send a single image.

She chose finally the *Valiant* in full sunlight, seen from the port side and slightly below. It was majestic, a lovely vehicle traveling bright skies. It exuded optimism and power, and she hoped it would strike the celestials with the same kind of emotional force *she* felt when she looked at it.

"That should get a response," said Matt, who'd come up unnoticed behind her. "It just demonstrates once again that you need to have PR people along when you do a first contact."

Kim grinned at the thought. Flexner's Theorem. But it was true.

She was trying to put herself into the heads of the celestials. They *had* to be motivated, at least in part, by a desire to know what had happened to their ship, which had disappeared so many years ago. Here then were those who knew about the missing vessel, prepared apparently to talk about it. How could they resist that?

When Ali told her she was clear to transmit, she invited Matt to punch the button.

"Yes," he said. "By all means." And he sent the sunlit *Valiant* into the void.

"We'll hear from them within the next few hours," she predicted.

They went back to the mission center where the entire team was gathered to await what most earnestly believed would be the historic response. "You don't want to be in the washroom just now," Tesla told Kim.

Shortly after the first transmission had been completed, Ali informed them they'd been scanned again. "Only for a few seconds," he said.

They waited, not talking much, watching the screens for incoming visuals, keeping track of the broadcast status of their own package.

Not long after it had run a second time, Ali reported another scan.

And more than an hour later, still another. "Every sixty-three minutes, looks like," he said.

The afternoon wore on. Eventually Tesla wandered off to the washroom.

They had dinner at six. It was quieter than usual and they exhorted one another on the need for patience. Ali, who usually ate in the pilot's room, dined with them.

The scans continued through the evening, always separated by sixty-three minutes and seventeen seconds. "We're probably going to have to wait while whatever's out there communicates with its home base," said

Matt. "If they have nothing better than hypercomm, that could take a while."

That possibility cheered no one. But Kim thought that the present situation was a distinct improvement over the response she and Solly had encountered.

She gave up at eleven-thirty and went to bed, read for an hour from a collection of political essays, and finally dropped off to sleep. She woke again around three, wandered out into the corridor and made for the washroom. Downstairs she could hear voices in the mission center, Sandra and Eric, and somebody else she couldn't make out.

Sandra was laughing.

A few minutes later she was just returning to her compartment when Ali's voice crackled over the comm. "Kim, I hate to wake you—"

"Go ahead, Ali. I'm here."

"We haven't had a response. But there's something else you should see. Can you come over for a minute?"

She threw on a robe and crossed the hall to the pilot's room.

Ali sat in front of one of the auxiliary screens. As she entered, he turned toward her. "The fleet's arrived," he said.

She didn't know what she'd been expecting. But that brought a stab of disappointment. "*Our* fleet?"

"Yes, indeed. A banshee and a pair of escorts."

"Coming this way?"

He nodded.

"How much time do we have?"

"Before they get here? About eight hours."

"That's not so good," said Kim.

"They appeared on the scopes a few minutes ago."

"But they couldn't have been the source of the scans?"

"Negative. No way."

Well, she thought, at least *somebody's* coming to talk to us.

34

Silence is deep as Eternity.
　　　　　　—THOMAS CARLYLE, *Sir Walter Scott*, 1838 C.E.

By morning nothing had changed. "To tell you the truth," Ali said, "being watched by something I can't see is uncomfortable. I'm glad the banshee's here. Makes me feel a lot safer."

Kim drank her coffee without replying. By now everyone on board knew that the fleet had arrived. Some admitted feeling the way Ali did. But they all knew it spelled the end of the mission.

The scan warning blinked on, burned steadily for *three* seconds, and went off. They were always three-second flashes now, still coming on their precise schedule. "You think the banshee's getting the same treatment?" she asked.

"Probably."

"I wonder what *they* make of it."

"I'm sure they're not happy. They're probably keeping everybody close to battle stations."

"Incoming from the fleet," said the AI.

Ali glanced at Kim. "Maybe they'll tell us. Okay, Mac, let's hear it."

"Audio only. Relaying."

Kim sank back in her cushions.

"*McCollum*, this is the commanding officer of the RE *Dauntless*." The voice rumbled with authority. "You're directed to leave this area immediately."

She looked at Ali. "They don't have any authority out here, do they?"

Ali made a face. "Technically, no," he said.

"So tell him to go harass somebody else. He's interfering with a civilian enterprise. Here, *I'll* tell him—"

She reached for a headset but Ali held up a hand. "I'm sorry, Kim. I have to cooperate. It would be my license."

"But you said—"

"I said *technically* they have no authority. But we're Greenway registry. They have lawyers."

"Everybody's worried about his job," she grumbled.

"Well, what do you expect?" he demanded, frustrated. "We've had almost a week out here. What's happening that's worth making major sacrifices for?" He switched on the speaker. "Captain, we'll start preparations for departure immediately."

"Not just yet, Captain Kassem," said the *Dauntless*. "Do you have a Dr. Kimberly Brandywine on board?"

Ali looked sidewise at her.

"Go to visual," said Kim.

The warship's commander was tall, blond, with wide-set blue eyes and a neatly trimmed mustache. There was no evidence of flexibility in his rock-hard features. This was not a man with whom she would want to negotiate. "Go ahead, Captain. This is Dr. Brandywine."

"Doctor, I'm informed you're in possession of a piece of government property. Is it with you now?"

She looked toward Ali.

He shook his head. No use lying. They'd only board and search. "It is," she said.

"Very good. Please use care with it. We'll be drawing alongside shortly. I'll expect you to have it ready for me."

He signed off.

"It probably doesn't matter anyhow," Ali said. "You can't give the *Valiant* back to the owners if they don't even want to say hello." He looked subdued.

"Are we still sending out the vocabulary package?"

"Every sixty minutes."

Everything was coming apart. The *Valiant* would go into a government laboratory somewhere, search efforts for the civilization which produced it would be misdirected, and Kim would not hear about butterflies and shrouds again during the course of her lifetime. The world would never learn of the sacrifice made by the celestials at Mount Hope. And when we do finally meet, at whatever remote date that might be, it will be as potential antagonists. "Every hour," she said. "That seems stupid, doesn't it? Under the circumstances? I mean, we're not getting any results."

"We don't seem to be."

"Shut it down, Ali. We've still got some time. Let's try something else." She brought up the *Valiant* package, the *Valiant* running beneath crescent moons, the *Valiant* hovering in the sky over the nightside of a world illuminated by vast pools of light, the *Valiant* fleeing before an exploding nova. Kim had done her work well, and the ship looked by turns regal and exotic and elegant. The only thing it lacked was a clean red-orange flame from a pair of thrusters. "Send these," she said. "Send them all."

Ali passed the instructions to the AI. *"Canceling second-phase package,"* it said. *"Proceeding with* Valiant *transmission."*

They watched the console. Lights blinked, and the visuals went out.

There was a terrace on the second level with an aft view. Nobody was using it, and Kim strolled onto it and stood in the starlight looking at the sky. The banshee and its escorts were back there somewhere, less than two hours away.

"It was a good try, Kim." The voice startled her. It was Matt's, and she read concern in his face. "You can't blame yourself."

"I don't," she said.

His tone changed. Grew optimistic. "You've confirmed a major discovery. We know they're here. And we have an artifact. That's not a bad piece of work."

"We also know," she said, "that if we ever *are* able to talk to celestials, what their first question's going to be."

"Well, we'll just have to explain as best we can."

"Killed the crew and took the ship. Good luck to us, Matt."

"Kim—"

"Let it go."

He settled into a chair. "They're scared, Kim. You really can't blame Woodbridge. He's just taking your advice."

The great star-clouds glowed in the night.

"Don't put this on me," she said. "I'm tired of that game. He has as much information as I do. He knows what happened at Mount Hope. He knows what the *Valiant* crew did."

"But he has more responsibility than you do. If *you're* wrong, well, maybe we lose a ship. A few lives. If *he* gets it wrong, there could be a catastrophe. God knows what it could bring down on our heads. We haven't really done a study to determine what contact would mean. Despite Beacon, despite all the missions, we never really thought through the potential consequences." The chair creaked as he shifted his weight. "Let it go. In the long run, we'll be better off."

"You really believe that, Matt?"

From the adjoining corridor she heard the bleep that accompanied the scan marker. The *whatever* was looking at them again. Making sure they hadn't changed course. She wondered what they made of the warships. The presence of the fleet, if it provided comfort to Ali and some of her colleagues, was as likely as not to scare off anything in the neighborhood.

"You know," she said, "if we don't get it right this time, we may not get another chance."

"We do what we can."

Kim looked out at the stars, at Matt, sitting now with his eyes closed, absorbing pain, doing what he'd always done, trying to make the best of things. *In the long run, we'll be better off.* He'd left the door open, and she could see down the passageway, which ultimately led back to the Institute. "I don't understand," she said, "why they haven't responded. I'd think they'd want to talk about the *Valiant,* if nothing else."

He shrugged. "Who's to say? Maybe they think we're looking to grab another one if it shows itself. Or maybe just transmitting pictures doesn't convey the message."

"What would?"

"I don't know. What's the message?"

"Hello," she said. *"We're sorry."*

"Then maybe they need to be informed we have the *Valiant* with us. They don't really know that—"

"Yeah." She thought about it. "You might be right, Matt. All we've done so far is send—"

"—A lot of images. Maybe we need to show them the ship."

She opened a channel to the captain. "Ali, when's the next scan due?"

"We just had one."

"It's still running at sixty-three minute intervals?"

"That is correct."

"How much time have we left before the good captain arrives?"

"Hour and a half, give or take."

"There's still time," she said.

"Time for what?" asked Matt and Ali simultaneously.

"To go outside. Ali, can you arrange things so that when the next probe comes, we're in the shadow of the planet? We'll need whatever shelter we can get from the sun."

Matt didn't like it, but he could not withstand her determination. "I go with you, though," he said.

"You ever been outside one of these things?"

"Have *you*?"

At the other end of the corridor, a staircase ascended to an air lock. Kim and Matt took the *Valiant* from its display case. They set it on the floor and Kim wrapped it carefully in plastic.

Ali, speaking from the pilot's room, tried to dissuade her. Neither of you has any EVA experience, he argued. It's dangerous. It's pointless. I'd prefer you not do it.

Kim thanked him for his concern. "Have to try," she said. "It's all we have." They carried the microship up the stairs into the air lock, selected a pair of p-suits and dressed.

Ali came to make sure they had everything right. He lectured her some more, but ended by telling her he'd do the same thing if he were in her place. "Might as well," he said. "We aren't going to get to come out here again."

Then he retreated onto the landing and Kim began depressurizing the lock.

"It's good timing, if nothing else," he told her, speaking now through the suit radio. "Next scan is due in eight minutes. What do you expect to happen out there anyhow?"

"We hope," she said, "to shake hands with a celestial."

The air lock's outer door opened. Kim and Matt stepped through. It was like going onto a rooftop at night.

This upper section of hull was flat and rectangular, bordered by a waist-high handrail. They were still within the ship's artificial gravity field.

Kim put the *Valiant* down, walked to the edge of the roof and looked over the side. It was dizzying. She felt as if she stood atop an infinitely high building whose foundation was lost in the void. The gas giant, with its system of rings and moons, lay off to her left, shielding her from the sun. "What happens if I fall off?" she asked Ali.

"Nothing," he said. "You won't fall. But you *would* float away. So it's probably a good idea not to go too close to the edge."

Matt stayed in the center of the roof with the *Valiant*.

"One minute to the next scan," said Ali.

Kim walked over and put a hand on Matt's shoulder. He looked lost. "You want to help?"

"Sure."

"Okay." She removed the plastic from the microship. Following her lead, he took hold of one side of the vessel, she the other, and they lifted. "All the way," she said. They raised it shoulder high and then got it over their heads.

Ali counted down the seconds. "Okay, folks. We have a light. We are being scanned."

She imagined she could *feel* the tingle of the probe passing through the three floors of the *Mac*, passing through her, locking on the *Valiant*.

"This is *not* going to be productive," said Matt. "It feels like a religious ceremony."

"It *is* a religious ceremony." She juggled it, tried to lift it higher, and almost lost it.

"Careful," said Matt.

"Still scanning," said Ali. "It's going long this time."

Kim, remembering the scan had been running at three seconds' duration, began counting. "I think we got their attention," she said.

"I hope so."

She got to nineteen.

"Marker's out," said Ali. "That's it."

They lowered the *Valiant* and laid it back on the roof.

"Kim." Ali's voice again.

"Yes?"

"It went *twenty-six seconds*."

Matt looked around, maybe to see whether lights had materialized among the stars. But the skies showed no change. "Might as well go back inside," he said. "Nothing more we can do out here."

Kim struggled to sit down beside the *Valiant*. The suit was exceedingly awkward. "I'm going to stay out for a while," she said.

"Kim—"

"I'm okay. I'm just not ready to quit yet." The air-lock door stood open. Light spilled out onto the roof. "Once we go back in, it's over."

He came and stood close to her.

She looked out into eternity, past the great ringed globe, past the scattered diamonds of individual stars, past the rivers of light. And she thought of Emily, dead at the moment of triumph.

Ali's voice: "We have movement."

Terri Taranaka was watching the screens in the mission center. "Kim," she said, "we're getting something!"

Kim struggled to her feet. "Not the *Dauntless*?"

"Negative," said Ali, sounding excited. "The *Dauntless* is still in our rear."

"Which way? Where?"

"Bearing zero six zero," said Ali. "Up about thirty degrees."

She had to look back to the air lock to reorient herself to the front of the ship. Up here it was hard to tell.

"It just *appeared*," he continued. "I don't know where it came from."

Even though it lay behind the planet, Alnitak's glare was still harsh. Matt held a gloved hand over his visor and peered in the indicated direction. "Don't see anything, Kim," he said.

Neither did she.

"We're getting an anomalous reading," said Ali. "Configuration keeps shifting. I don't think it's a ship."

"What else could it be?" Sandra's voice.

Kim's pulse began to pick up. "Not shape-changing?" she asked.

"*Dauntless* is on the circuit, Kim. I think they're getting a little excited over there."

"How far is it? The thing with the shifting configuration?"

"About eight kilometers. And closing. I can't understand how it could have gotten so close without our picking it up earlier."

"Kim." Eric's voice. "We're getting a visual."

"Text message," said Paul. And then he let out a shriek. "It's from *them*."

And Maurie: "You *sure*? That's English."

Kim heard applause, but it quickly died away.

Eric again: "I don't know what they're talking about."

"Uh-oh," said Mona.

"What does it say?" demanded Kim.

"It says, *Where are they?*"

"Where are *who*?" asked Matt.

A chill felt its way up Kim's spine. "I think," she said, "they want to know what happened to the crew of the *Valiant*."

"Kim." Ali's voice. "That thing out there *does* look like a cloud. It's coherent. Moving with purpose."

"I hear you."

"I think it's another shroud. You better get inside."

"Matt," she said. "You go. Close the air lock and do not open it unless I tell you to."

"Not a good idea," said Terri.

"Kim, I want you both inside. And hurry it up. It's only a couple of minutes away."

Matt went quickly to the air lock and stood in the patch of light, waiting for her. She looked down at the *Valiant* and out off the starboard side, about a third of the way up the sky. And saw *nothing*.

"Come on, Kim," Matt said. "We can't do anything out here except get ourselves killed."

"Kim." It was Maurie. "I think you're right. They want to know about the crew. What do we tell them?"

Crunch time. "Tell them they're dead. We're sorry, but they were killed. Accidentally."

"We do not have 'dead' or 'killed' in the vocabulary. Or 'accident.'"

Ali again, his voice a command: "Kim, get inside. We're out of time."

"Matt—"

Matt shook his head *no* and pushed the door shut. Then he turned and came back across the roof.

"That was dumb," she said.

"I won't leave you out here alone."

She was trying to recall the vocabulary. They had lots of words like stone and grass, tree and leaf, water and earth, light and dark. They had cloud and sun, starship and engine. They even had colors. How to convey death?

"Tell them 'Their engines are stopped. They have gone dark.'"

"You sure?"

"Yes, I'm sure, Maurie."

"Okay. Doing it now."

"We need a way to express regret. Anybody have any ideas?"

Mona said: "'We wish it had not been.'"

"We have," said Gil, "no word for 'wish.' Or for syntactical complexities."

Kim had not taken her eyes off the patch of sky from which the shroud was approaching.

The debate over how to address the celestials descended into a frustrated silence. "Defective vocabulary," said Terri.

"We did what we could," replied Eric. "You have to get the fundamentals down before you can do philosophy."

The sky rippled. Several stars disappeared.

"It's here," Kim said.

"Kim." Ali sounded angry. "Why are you still out there?"

"Eric." Sandra was speaking. "Try 'The leaves on our trees fall to the ground.'"

"Yes," said Kim. "That's good."

"We should have brought a writer," said Paul.

She could see the cloud approaching, could see stars through its veils.

"How about, 'Our plants become dry'?"

"Yes. Good. Send it too. Can't have too much regret at a time like this."

Kim and Matt stood side by side, not moving. The shroud looked very much like the creature from Severin, except that this one seemed to be smaller. "Same basic model," she told Matt.

But no eyes this time.

Nevertheless she knew it could see her. Or was aware of her in some manner that did not involve visuals.

"'Our life is now dark,'" she told Maurie while she resisted an urge to back away. Matt, to her surprise and his credit, stayed with her.

"We don't have any way of expressing time, Kim. No word for 'now.'"

"Send it without the 'now,' Maurie." Heart pounding, she picked up the *Valiant*.

The shroud opened, blossomed, as had the one at the lakefront before engulfing its victims.

She held out the microship.

"Don't make any sudden moves," said Ali.

Kim could barely move at all. Her suit felt claustrophobic.

"We're getting a reply," said Tesla.

And Eric: "It says: 'We are you.'"

"Makes no sense."

"What are they trying to say?"

"'We're of one mind,'" suggested Matt, his voice shaking. "Maybe they understand what we're trying to do."

"You really think so?" asked Tesla.

Kim sincerely *hoped* so.

Ali's voice: "You guys okay out there?"

She felt a tug at the *Valiant*. She let go, watched it begin to fall, but slowly, still in gravity's grip. The mist swirled across its polished hull, embraced it, and the shroud gathered it in.

Kim, heart pounding, heard applause.

And then she and Matt were alone on the roof.

35

During the first few hours, we struggled at the "I am a little red pencil box stage." But gradually we got past basic syntax. Furthermore, Eric picked up some of their language, which we were able to reproduce on a synthesizer, and we actually started to talk to one another.
—MAURIE PENN, *Notebooks*, xxvii, 611

Kim had little opportunity to celebrate her victory. Within an hour of watching the *Valiant* float off into the darkness, off the scanners and scopes of the *Mac* and the fleet vessels, she was arrested by the captain of the *Dauntless*, charged with willful misuse of government property and, against the indignant protests of everyone involved, taken on board the banshee to be returned to Greenway.

That wasn't the problem. At least not the major one. Matt used every argument he could think of to persuade the force commander to rescind his order that the *McCollum* depart immediately. Ali contrived to scramble a key navigational system, and thereby gained twelve hours during which the contact team worked frantically to establish a constructive relationship with the celestials.

Kim was treated well enough. Her movements were restricted, but her quarters were a step up from *Mac*'s accommodations. The crew were polite, if not especially convivial. They had been told, she suspected, that she was a major violator, so they maintained a respectful distance. The captain declined to interview her or to see her, explaining through an intermediary that he had no wish to be called into court to testify as to what she had said or not said about her activities.

The small task force of which the *Dauntless* was part did not leave until the *Mac* was safely on its way home. Then it too slipped into hyperspace and started the long flight back to Greenway.

Kim did little other than read, work out, and sleep. She twice forwarded requests to the captain, explaining that the scientific project of the age, perhaps of all time, was now going forward, and asking whether the *Dauntless* could perhaps pop out of hyperspace for an hour to allow her to file a report to her superiors.

"Quite redundant," the captain replied politely through his representative. He'd be pleased to comply with her request, but he had already forwarded a report. As had the *McCollum*. He had a copy of the latter presented to her. It contained the electrifying news that the celestials had agreed to a future meeting, to be conducted during the five-hundredth revolution of the gas giant. Several months away.

So it happened that during the second week of August, the *Dauntless* jumped back into realspace and Kim arrived at Sky Harbor once again expecting to be arrested. And again she was surprised: She was greeted by the Premier himself while a band played, an audience cheered, and the media recorded everything for posterity.

I've told you, and I've told you, Matt had said, smiling at dockside, *never underestimate the power of public relations.* It was too big a story, the news too good. There was no way a politician could ignore it. If the celestials turned out later to be dangerous, well, with luck that would happen during somebody else's watch.

On the way down in the lift, she watched a special report called "Meeting at Alnitak." Agostino was prominently featured as the person who'd stayed on top of the Mount Hope puzzle when everybody else had given up, and who'd ultimately put the pieces together. Kim was barely mentioned.

The news had electrified the world. Kim learned later that the Council initially made an effort to keep everything quiet, but it simply had not been possible.

Preparations for the next meeting were already well underway. She received a message from Agostino congratulating her on a job well done and promising her that, if she were not incarcerated, she would be welcome to go.

Analysis of the scans she'd made of the *Valiant* indicated that Terri had been right, that the vessel had moved through realspace by manipulation of gravity. The method was much more efficient than anything available to the Nine Worlds, but unfortunately, without the original vessel, it would be impossible to determine how the system worked.

There was some irritation about that, especially when the celestials, after subsequent meetings, showed a lack of enthusiasm for explaining their technologies. At about this time Kim's role became more wisely known, and she briefly became the target of reconstructive journalism. Someone even wrote a book exposing her as a traitor.

The design of the *Valiant* also revealed the need for the presence of something like the shroud: those parts that would require periodic maintenance or adjustment seemed to be in areas that could not be reached without major disassembly. These *were* accessible through a series of ducts, except that the ducts were far too narrow to accommodate even the minuscule crew. The approximate size of the individual crew members turned out to be roughly five centimeters, top to bottom, or wingtip to wingtip, however one chose to measure.

Information was still scarce regarding the nature of the shrouds. And in fact there was, early on, considerable debate as to which of the two races was in charge. The shrouds are now believed to be artificial life-forms, biological AIs, designed for a wide range of purposes. The creatures piloted, maintained, and, if necessary, defended the starships.

Kim received invitations to appear on various HV shows, to write her memoirs, and even to run for office. *Midnight Lace* invited her to pose against the memorial at Cabry's Beach.

The rendezvous mission went well. Kim went along, permanent stations were established by both races at Alnitak, and the first so-called face-to-face conversation was attempted. Eric Climer represented humanity and became a worldwide celebrity largely because of a picture showing him with a butterfly on his shoulder.

Afterward, when she got home, she received a call from Canon Woodbridge. It was their first conversation since he'd attempted to seize the *Valiant.*

"You've done well," he told her. It was a late evening in early fall, sixteen months after the flight of the *McCollum.* It had rained much of the day and the sky was devoid of stars.

"It's kind of you to say so, Canon."

He was seated at a table, his piercing eyes illuminated by a small lamp which cast its glow into her living room. "You took a gamble, for all of us, but it appears you were right."

"You sound sorry it turned out that way."

"No. I'm glad we're not being threatened." He leaned toward her and laid a finger alongside his jaw. "Kim, I don't want you to misunderstand what I have to say. I'm grateful this Orion species is benign. *Apparently* benign. The fact is we really don't know yet what the long-range effects will be on the way we live. I've always had a great deal of respect for you. So I don't say this lightly, but I want you to know that what you did was the most arrogant and irresponsible act I've seen in my lifetime."

Eventually, Mike Plymouth showed up. Guardian of the Archives.

He was waiting for her one wintry afternoon when she came out of the Institute. It had by then been almost three years since the break-in.

"Mike," she said. Embarrassed. Flustered.

He smiled. "Hi, Kay."

"My name's Kim."

He nodded. "I know. You went to a lot of trouble to get my DNA."

She detected no rancor in his voice. "I'm sorry." They stood looking at each other. "We needed a sample. How'd you find me?"

"It wasn't hard. You're one of the most famous people in the Republic."

"Well," she stumbled, "I apologize. I—"

"I know," he said. "No need. It's all right."

Snowbanks were piled high around them and another storm was on the way. "I'm glad you came. I'd have contacted you, but I was embarrassed."

"I understand." He looked hesitant. "I was wondering. We still have an outstanding dinner engagement. I'd be pleased—"

She hesitated, started to explain that she had a commitment that evening, wondered why she was begging off, and decided what the hell. "Of course, Mike," she said. "I'd love to."

They went to the Ocean View and ordered a couple of glasses of white wine to dawdle over in the candlelight. It was still early, the restaurant was almost empty, and soft music was being piped in.

They talked about her voyages to Orion and when she tried to change the subject, to ask him how things were going at the Archives, he laughed and brushed it aside. "Same as always," he said. "Nothing exciting since the big break-in."

He asked how she'd felt when that first message had come through, *Where are they?*, and what had run through her mind when the shroud approached while she stood atop the *McCollum*, and what it had been like being in the same room with one of the *Cho-Choi*, as the celestials were now known. Terri's name for them had stuck.

In sequence, she said, exhilarated, terrified, and the last event had never happened. "Only Eric got to share space with one. They're so small, and there are so many complications that the physical meetings are difficult to bring off. It was intended to be purely symbolic. We and they will probably never spend much time hanging out together."

He asked why their ships were armed.

"That's a misunderstanding," Kim said. "The device that killed Emily isn't a weapon. It's used to project a gravity field in front of the vessel. It rearranges space. Or matter and energy, if they happen to get in the way."

There was also a widely held view that the new species wasn't as bright as humans. Their civilization was, after all, almost thirty thousand years older than ours, and yet their technology did not seem greatly advanced.

"Cyclic development," Kim explained. Dark ages. Up and down. "It looks as if we can't rely on automatic progress. We've had a couple of dark ages ourselves. The big one, after Rome, and a smaller one, here. The road doesn't always move forward." She looked at him in the candlelight. "These periodic downturns may not be simply aberrations. And that knowledge alone might be worth the price we paid."

"So what are you going to do now?" he asked.

What indeed? She had offers from facilities throughout the Nine Worlds, positions that would allow her to unload the fund-raising job and become a serious astrophysicist. "Pick and choose," she said. "Do what I've always wanted to do."

He reached across the table and took her hand. "I never forgot you," he said.

She smiled. "I can see that."

"Will you be leaving the area?"

"Probably."

"Anything I can do to persuade you to stay?"

She moved closer to him and touched his cheek. "We do always seem to be moving in opposite directions, don't we, Mike?"

Later, he rode out with her to the island, and she invited him in. It had begun to snow.

"No," he said. "I'll pass for now. I'd rather have you owing me an invitation. That way I can be sure I'll see you again."

Epilogue

JANUARY 18, 623

*T*he stone was set in a corner of Cabry's Beach, not particularly notice-able unless one was looking for it. The engraving read, simply, IN MEMORY OF . . . , and listed five names: Sheyel Tolliver, Benton Tripley, Amy Bricker, and two others. The remaining security guards.

Kim probably owed her life to Amy and her comrades.

During the more than two decades that had passed since that terrible night on the beach, life had come back to Severin. The village had been rebuilt, boats had reappeared on the lake, and a train station had been erected. Even the refreshment stand was back, and during the summer a new raft floated just offshore. It was off-season now, early December, but the place was nevertheless not as dark as she remembered. The village lights filtered through the trees, and the new city hall tower was visible if she was willing to stand at the water's edge.

Overhead, lights moved through the sky.

Some of them would be carrying dignitaries from throughout the Nine Worlds to greet their first nonhuman visitors. Well—maybe not quite the first.

Tomorrow, they would arrive in Severin, guests and hosts. Speeches would be made, bands would play, and a second memorial would be dedi-cated: To the crew of the *Valiant*, who gave their lives for a people they never knew.

The term "crew" was probably meant to include the shroud, and she didn't care much for that part of the idea. But she had no way of knowing what that abandoned creature had been through, so she was willing to for-get. Nevertheless, she remained conscious of the stone behind her.

The Cho-Choi don't name their vessels, and the designator doesn't translate well, so everyone agreed that the name humans had given the microship was appropriate to the occasion. Several vessels of the Valiant class had already arrived at Sky Harbor in commemoration of the event.

Their home world was located three hundred light-years the other side of the Golden Chalice. Human ships had visited their worlds last year and had returned with tales of wondrous sights.

The Cho-Choi, like humans, had thought themselves alone. And also like humans, they seemed delighted to find they had company in a universe thought to be windswept and full of echoes.

Kim looked out across the lake. Homes were going up on the far side too.

Her taxi had set down almost exactly where she'd landed with Solly on that January night just after the turn of the century.

She scanned the tree line. There was where we went into the forest. And Tripley's villa had lain in that direction, a few points south of west. It was gone now, had been taken down years ago.

"It all turned out pretty well." She spoke the words almost aloud, as if she were not quite alone.

Solly would have been amused to discover she was still a fund-raiser. Kim was older now, and had faced the reality that she simply didn't have the abstract or mathematical skills required of a first rate astrophysicist. She could have gotten along, but instead she'd gone back to the work she discovered she enjoyed, that she was good at: talking to people and persuading them to donate to a good cause. It wasn't very glamorous, but it did feel significant. She was still contributing, supporting the general effort with the one real talent she seemed to have.

The good cause now was Stellar Survey. Money was pouring in, ships were being built and launched, and the human race seemed to be on the move again. Curious ruins had been found in the Triangle, two thousand light-years out, on the far side of the sky from Orion. And the new Chang Telescope might have sighted evidence of a Type II civilization in Andromeda.

Last week, the Solomon Hobbs reported evidence of ancient stellar engineering from Lyra Omega.

There are other mysteries. The Cho-Choi insist that their distant ancestors once had a tunnel into an alternate universe. But the engineering techniques have been lost.

To Kim's satisfaction, Emily and her colleagues have their place in history, largely because no lasting damage was done by the Hunter. Now they are only remembered as having initiated contact.

But the species may have learned something. Survey's exploration teams, who are carrying on the search for whoever else might be out there, are extensively trained in how to respond to a contact. Similar training is now required of anyone seeking to purchase or pilot a deep-space vessel.

She gazed around the beach. It seemed smaller than she remembered.

Her link sounded. It was Flexner, who'd gone over to Survey with her. "Yes, Matt?"

"Kim, where are you?" He sounded annoyed.

She sighed. "I'm on my way."

"Good. We need to know exactly what you're going to say tomorrow so we can set everything up for the interpreters. And that has to be done tonight."

She would be speaking, not in her own right, but as Emily's sister. "I'll be there in ten minutes," she said.

"Good. And Kim?"

"Yes?"

"That means we have to stick to the script, right?"

"Right," she said. "Absolutely." She took a final look around, and climbed into the taxi. "Severin," she told it. "Lakeside Hotel."

It lifted off. Cabry's Beach dropped away and she glided among the stars.